GET THE FIRST BOOK IN THIS
SERIES FOR FREE!

Sign up for the no-spam newsletter and get *BREACH*.

Details can be found at the end of
***DUEL OF DEATH*.**

DUEL OF DEATH

BRONWYN LEROUX

CHAPTER ONE

Jaden didn't think he'd survive. The crushing weight of Bree's death was nothing compared to the agony of Kayla's disappearance. As he dismounted from Han, his legs buckled so severely, he had to catch himself before tumbling to the ground. When Han landed seconds later, his worried frown told Jaden his stumble hadn't gone unnoticed.

"I'll be alright. It's dark. The ground's uneven."

The frown didn't leave Han's face. It only deepened as they neared Taz. Jaden was appalled to see her hooked up to an IV. Atu had healed her wounds, but her movements were feeble as her head turned to see who approached.

Spotting them, Taz smiled weakly. "Come to visit the wounded warrior?"

Despite her infirmity, Taz still sounded imperious. Jaden grinned. "Who says we're here to see you?"

Taz twittered. "And here I thought we meant something to you."

Jaden would've been mortified if he hadn't caught the tiny twinkle in her eyes. "Well, now that you mention it . . ."

Han pushed past, almost knocking Jaden over. "How do you feel?"

Taz tilted her head so she could look Han in the eye. "Healer says I will make a full recovery provided I get my rest."

1

Jaden cocked his head. *There it is again. That undercurrent between Han and Taz. Is it deference in Han's voice when he addresses Taz? Loyalty? Love?*

Han purred. "We should leave then so you can sleep."

He nudged Jaden, and Jaden scowled. While Jaden hadn't figured out what was going on between their gliders, he still had questions. And Jaden wasn't about to let Han bully him away from Taz before he had answers.

Fortunately, Taz had the same mindset. "Not before you tell me about Kayla. Have you found her?"

Han bristled when he realized Jaden wouldn't leave and, worse, planned on entertaining Taz's questions.

Jaden patted Han's shoulder. He understood Han didn't want Taz upset. But keeping the truth from her would only make her more agitated. Sparing Han a reassuring glance, Jaden sank down and stroked the soft fur along Taz's neck.

"We need your help to find Kayla. And no, that doesn't mean you flying around. It means you giving us some direction, so we know where to look." Taz moved as though to rise, but Jaden kept her down. "Leave us to find her. You know we love her just as much as you do. We need you to heal so that when we find her, you're strong enough to help retrieve her if need be."

Taz huffed. "Very well. I can see I won't get past you two ogres."

Jaden allowed a smile to touch his face, but he'd heard the weariness in Taz's voice. On cue, her eyes closed. "Taz?" Her eyes fluttered open again, but they were glazed. "Can you tell us what happened?"

Taz moved a little, trying to rouse herself. "Kayla was asking questions. I couldn't answer them." Her voice faltered, and her eyes drooped.

"Taz?"

"Jaden, leave her be. She needs her rest," Han urged.

"And what happens when she wakes again and we haven't found Kayla? Do you think she'll rest then?"

Han growled, his displeasure evident, but his voice was resigned. "Go ahead."

Softly, Jaden tapped Taz's shoulder. She stirred. Her eyes opened again. "Kayla. Did you find her yet?"

"We need your help. You said Kayla was asking questions. You saw her before you were hurt?"

Taz moaned, moving her head side to side. "No, no, not then." She swallowed. "Water?"

Jaden jumped when a hand reached past him with a cup. Turning, he found Atu. "When did you get here?"

"I've been here a while already. I wanted to check on Taz." Atu leaned past Jaden and dribbled water into Taz's mouth.

Slurping, Taz worked her tongue around the water so she could swallow it. "Hmm, thank you, Healer."

Atu nodded. "I'll leave the water here. Can you reach it?" Taz's tongue slipped out sideways and into the cup. "Good. You need to keep drinking. Now, can you tell us more about Kayla?"

Taz's eyes sharpened. Then, as though she knew she didn't have much time, the words flooded out. "Before we left on our second mission, while Jaden and Pallaton were speaking, Kayla had questions. Because I suspected a traitor, I said I would answer her questions later, never expecting the traitor would be Tarise. I thought the traitor was one of our own." Taz stopped and took several deep breaths.

Jaden frowned. Taz hadn't been there when Tarise had confessed. "How did you know it was Tarise?"

"Healer told me."

Jaden needed to clarify something else. "One of your own? You mean a glider?"

Taz nodded once, but her eyes were losing focus again. "Find Kayla." Then her eyes rolled back, and she passed out.

Jaden leaned forward, but Atu stopped him. "Don't wake her again. She needs to sleep. As do you."

Even as he glared at Atu, the healer's words slapped him with reality. Feeling his exhaustion down to his bones, Jaden sprawled next to Taz. He allowed himself one second to savor his relief before glancing at Han. "Did any of what Taz said make sense to you?"

Han was just as perplexed. "She mentioned concerns about some members of the Legion. But she said nothing about that conversation with Kayla."

Weary as he was, Jaden's interest piqued. "What concerned her about them?"

Han's pause made Jaden wonder what it was his glider wasn't saying. "The Legion has been hidden in your world for a long time. And some of its members still cling to the old ways."

"The old ways?" Jaden was losing patience. "Stop playing games and give me straight answers! I have enough questions Zareh won't answer. Don't you start too!"

Han lifted a shoulder. "Let's just say there was a hierarchy in our society at the time the Legion left our world. Some still believe in that hierarchy. And if the usurper planted them in that hierarchy before they left our world, they would still be loyal to him."

At Jaden's scowl, Han explained further. "Think of your world a few centuries ago. There were kings and queens and their courts. Our world was like that once, where royalty ruled. And like your human courts, ours had their own intrigues. Plenty of spies reported to the nobles of that time."

"And let me guess—Slurpy was one of those nobles?"

Han looked startled. "How did you know?"

Jaden shrugged. "Considering the time that's passed, Slurpy probably hadn't yet acted on any of his baser impulses. Or been banished for doing so. Ergo, he was someone of importance, someone high enough in the court to think the power belonged to him." Jaden thought a moment. "So, because he was a noble back then, he probably had spies who reported to him?" Han nodded. "And you think he selected some of those spies for the Legion?"

Han snorted. "More likely the usurper inserted them than selected them. I wouldn't put it past him to have had a few of the original team murdered so he could replace them with his own people."

"Then discounting Taz's convictions concerning traitors in the Legion would be imprudent. Going forward, we should compartmentalize the information we dispense. But that's an issue for another day. The question now is how do we find Kayla?"

Han's face grew serious. "I'm not sure."

Jaden was drained to his soul. How had things turned against them so fast? He should've listened to that voice in his head that told him to go with Kayla when she left. Was that really only a few hours ago? It seemed an eternity since Kayla had zoomed away in his family's 'pod. Then Zareh's arrival. And the resulting battle of their lives. Losing Bree.

Sobs rose in Jaden's chest. *Sweet Bree! How can she be gone?*

As much to escape his grief as to feel like he was doing something to find Kayla, Jaden swept to his feet. Black spots formed in front of his eyes. His head hurt. Then the ground rushed up to meet him. Then . . .

How did I fall asleep with Kayla's life at stake? Jaden jerked up but lay back as vertigo washed over him. Bile filled his mouth. He swallowed the bitter substance back down.

"Easy, bro." Atu's voice was distant.

Jaden tried to speak, but the words wouldn't form. *And what's that irritating thing in my arm?*

Atu answered his unspoken question. "You passed out."

Jaden felt his frown. *What an odd sensation.*

Atu must've realized he didn't understand. "You were trying to do too much too soon after losing so much blood in the battle. It was your body's way of making you pay attention."

Jaden's brain struggled to escape the quicksand encasing it. The more he tried to think, the further the muck dragged him down. *I lost blood?*

Slowly, ever so slowly, his memories came back. The battle. The injury to his leg. Bree. And Kayla. Kayla had been taken! He and Han had gone to see Taz to find out what they could about Kayla's disappearance.

"Have we found Kayla yet?" His voice was croaky. The words sandpapered his soul.

Atu's expression answered before his words. "I'm sorry. She's still missing." When Jaden made to rise again, Atu pushed him back down.

"How long?" Irritated when Atu didn't understand the question,

Jaden said, "How long have I been out?"

Atu's face cleared. "About eight hours."

"Eight *hours*?" Jaden tried rising again.

This time Atu's hand was firmer. "Bro, do I need to get Markov in here to tie you down?" Something in Atu's tone had Jaden sinking back into the pillow. "You couldn't have done anything, anyway. Taz hasn't woken up again yet, and even if she had, you and Han would've been bumbling around in the dark."

Oh, yes. Now he remembered. When they had gone to see Taz, right after the battle, night had just fallen. Like the shot of light that had fired through the mountains at that last second before the sun disappeared, the memory of the words on the leather strip lashed him. *Living with hope.* He would have to hold those words close. He was too near the edge to not have something to cling to. And without Kayla, those words were his lifeline.

Jaden finally scanned his surroundings, noting he was in his own room. *How did I get here? Never mind. It doesn't matter.*

He smiled with a grim twist. When Atu smiled back tentatively, Jaden said, "No, I'm not trying to trick you. I just realized I'm useless to Kayla if I don't get my strength back." A trace of uncertainty still lingered in Atu's eyes, and Jaden held up a hand like he was making a promise. "I swear, I won't go anywhere until you say it's okay for me to move again. What would be the point of trying to rescue Kayla only to pass out and get caught myself? That would be the last nail in all our coffins."

Atu's smile finally reached his eyes. "Fair enough. I'll let Markov know he's off the hook."

"Any chance you have a potion that will bolster my blood production and restore my energy?" Atu's glare returned. Jaden lifted his palms up in the air. "Okay, okay, just thought I'd ask. If you can't do that, can I get some food?"

Atu chuckled. "That's better. If you keep the food down and your vitals look good in another four hours, I might let you out of bed. Until then," he reached for a pitcher of water next to Jaden's bed, "drink!"

CHAPTER TWO

Pain. It racked Jaden's body. Every inch of his body hurt. Especially his head. Miniature hammers turned the tender parts of his brain to pulp. Wincing, Jaden raised a hand. The plastic tube snaking from his arm and off his bed snagged his attention.

Jaden frowned. He remembered Atu telling him to drink. After that, nothing. A glance at his PAL told him he'd slept most of the day. It was late afternoon. Those few thoughts began the deluge.

Memories screamed back with disturbing clarity. His emotions tumbled after, a mess of grief, anger and despair. How could he not have protected Kayla? It was the one thing he had sworn to do. Losing her to a simple thing like letting her travel alone was inexcusable. And Tarise! The traitor! If he ever saw her again, she'd better have someone protecting her. He wanted to put his hands around her neck and squeeze until the life left her. As it had Bree.

Sobs racked him then, making his head hurt even more. How was he such a loser? Why had he gotten his friends involved? Why hadn't he just lied to them? At least they would've been safe. But his moral compass hadn't allowed him to. And look at the mess they were in now. Jaden sniffed. He needed a tissue.

When he found the only thing on the table beside his bed was the empty water pitcher, he bellowed with rage, yanked the tube out of his arm, and stumbled to his feet. The world spun. He felt sick. Jaden gave it a second, sitting on the edge of the bed.

Slowly, the world righted itself. The nausea subsided. Cautiously, Jaden rose, keeping one hand on the edge of the bed just in case. Although his legs were shaky, they held, and the world stayed on its axis. Placing one foot in front of the other, he headed for the bathroom.

"Just where do you think you're going?" Markov's voice was clipped. His powerful shoulder slipped under Jaden's arm.

"I needed a tissue."

Without a word, Markov led him back to the bed and helped him onto it. "I'll get you some. And more water. Then I'll fetch Atu so he can put that line back in."

Grabbing the pitcher, Markov disappeared into the bathroom. He returned bearing a full pitcher and a box of tissues. "Here you go." He gave Jaden the box, then topped up a glass with water. When Jaden finished blowing his nose, Markov passed him the water.

Jaden took it and drank. "Thanks."

Markov eyed him. "Were you having a pity party without me?"

Jaden wasn't sure whether to punch him or laugh. The smile won out. "Yeah. Things suddenly just got to me."

"Grief will do that. As will exhaustion. Both require more rest before you can resume saving the world again."

"It's not the world I'm worried about."

"Kayla?"

Jaden nodded. "I need to find her. I need to know . . . need to find out if —" Jaden trailed off, unable to say the words.

Markov was grim. "If she's still alive. Yeah, I hear you."

Jaden's resolve crumbled again. "I don't know if I can do this without her. No, I know I can't. And if —"

Markov cut him off. "She's not dead. I've been thinking about this. That monster took your parents so he could get to you. Don't you think he knows he could use Kayla the same way? Possibly to greater effect?"

Jaden reeled as if slapped in the face. He'd been so focused on Kayla's welfare that he hadn't considered why she was snatched. Not only for Tarise's benefit. *Duh! I can be dense sometimes! I knew this. I just didn't allow myself to think past the tiny box of Kayla's disappearance.* Anger replaced fear. Jaden snarled. "Is Tarise here?"

Markov took one look at his face. "If she was, I wouldn't let her near you."

"Why not? She's responsible. She should pay! If Tarise hadn't betrayed us, Bree would still be alive. Kayla wouldn't be missing. Tarise is the rat who sank the ship. I want to chop off her head!"

"Jaden, calm down."

"I will not! Where is she? You bring her to me this instant, or I'm getting out of this bed and finding her—with or without your help!"

Realizing there was no way to calm Jaden when he was like this, Markov took a different tack. "She's gone. We don't know where she is. We think the usurper might've taken her too. And even if Tarise was here, she wouldn't be able to help."

"Explain!" Jaden managed through gritted teeth.

"After you and Han left without saying goodbye last night, we asked Tarise to tell us about the usurper. She was so upset about Bree she just blabbed everything. Said she'd met the usurper in a cave, but that was only a meeting place—not where we could find him. She began telling us about their meeting, but before she could say more, she grabbed her hand and began screaming again." Markov shook his head as though he still couldn't believe what he'd witnessed. "I've never seen anything like it. Her hand blistered like she was holding it in a fire. She was in so much pain she couldn't talk. She wailed at us to leave her alone, that it was the only way the punishment would stop. Then she ran off, and we let her go."

"You let her go?" Jaden yelled.

Markov backed up a step. "Bro, she knew nothing. She wouldn't have been able to help us even if she did. Did you not hear the part about her hand?"

Jaden blinked. Then a twisted grin marred his face. "Now that's what I'm talking about!"

Markov shook his head, bewildered. "Dude, I don't know if I even know you anymore. Come on, this isn't like you. What would Kayla say if she was here?"

That stopped Jaden cold.

Pouncing on the pause, Markov said, "Are we going to stoop to the Usurper's level? Are we going to lose our humanity? Or are we going to rise above this adversity? Let's give Tarise a second chance. Let's try understand where she was coming from and grant her some grace."

Jaden's shoulders drooped. Markov was right. Maybe not about Tarise. But about rising above this disaster. If he didn't pull himself together, they would not finish this mission. *And then what was the point of all of this suffering? Slurpy's already won if we do nothing except sit around and mope.*

"What now?" Wary, Markov studied Jaden.

"It's time for us to win. To find that last artifact. End this once and for all. If we do, all of you will be safe."

Markov looked incredulous. "Bro, whose decision do you think it was for us to get involved?"

"No, don't lay that on yourselves. I roped you into this. I told you what was going on in the realm you couldn't see. I crossed timelines and set those monsters free."

Markov put a hand on Jaden's shoulder. "Who do you think asked to know? And whose decision was it to attend your meeting so we could find out what was happening? Don't you think we deserved the truth? The right to decide our own fates? Don't be such a jerk."

Jaden gaped, then started laughing. He shook his head. "Well, when you put it like that . . ."

Markov smiled for the first time since entering the room. "Now that we're *finally* on the same page, how about we make some plans?"

CHAPTER THREE

Jaden inhaled deeply, savoring the crisp, clear air. He was leaning against the doorway on their rooftop landing deck. It had been two days since Markov's visit. Only fifteen minutes ago, Atu had pronounced him well enough to get out of bed.

Jaden had stumbled up to the roof, disconcerted by how weak he was. Steadying himself against the doorjamb, he closed his eyes and raised his face to the sun. Rustling overhead had him opening his eyes. Han was hovering.

"Han! It's great to see you!"

"You're back on your feet." Han's relief was tangible. Then he scowled. "You really need bigger houses."

"Why?"

"It wasn't fun being the only one who couldn't get in to see you while you were recovering."

Jaden chuckled. "Sorry about that. I'll see if my folks are up for putting in bigger windows. That way, you can at least hover outside and talk to me through them."

"That won't help," Han grumbled.

"Why not?"

"Do you think I can squeeze between the walls of your house and the next?"

Jaden hid the smile this time. "Ah, friend, I have missed you! How's Taz?"

Han's face clouded. "Not as good as you, but getting there. Want to go see her?"

"Absolutely!"

Jaden wasn't sure if he'd manage the aerial mount, but whatever magic allowed it didn't seem impeded by his lack of strength. In minutes, they reached the open space Atu had set up for recovering gliders. Pallaton was circling Taz protectively. Jaden grinned. "Greetings, Pallaton!"

"Gatekeeper! It is good to see you back with us again."

"I see you've been busy," Jaden said, nodding his head toward several of the Legion patrolling the recovery area.

"It seemed wise to take precautions," Pallaton rumbled. "We didn't want any Gaptors attacking those wounded in the battle."

"I'm grateful you weren't one of them. I'm sorry for those you lost."

Pallaton dipped his head before darting away.

Han angled them down, and seconds later they were on the ground. Jaden approached Taz, shocked by how frail she looked. Had he looked so awful? He glared at Han. "She *is* getting better, right?"

Han's face was solemn. "Yes, but she lost a lot more blood than you did."

Reaching Taz, Jaden sat down next to her, as much as to give his legs a rest as to be close enough to talk. "Hello, friend."

Taz's eyes opened, and she attempted a smile when she saw Jaden, but Jaden noticed how much effort it took. "Jaden. I'm relieved to see you up and about again."

"I'm looking forward to being able to say the same about you. I'm guessing you aren't resting because you're worried about Kayla?"

Taz grimaced. "I'm trying not to worry, but every time I fall asleep, all I can see is her in some dire situation! Much as I try, I can't get to her, so I wake up again. It's like a recurring nightmare where the scenery changes but the situation remains the same."

"Yeah, like those dreams where you're doing something fun, and then next minute you're falling out of a plane, down a waterfall, off a cliff. The only way to escape death is to wake up. But you know, someone told me how to get rid of those kinds of dreams."

Taz perked up. "Really? How?"

"You force yourself to stay in the dream—to reach the end of that fall. Or in your case, reprehensible as the thought is, to not be able to get to Kayla as she meets whatever fate awaits her."

"Does that really work?" Taz sounded suspicious.

"It did for me. In fact, after I pulled off not waking up, it was the weirdest thing. The nightmare stopped, and there was this blank section. Then I dreamed about something else. The best part is that I've never had one of those types of dreams since."

Taz frowned. "How do you force yourself to stay asleep?"

Jaden shrugged. "I think in some part of your brain you know you're dreaming. You know what you're seeing isn't real. This allowed me to order myself to stay asleep until I hit the bottom. Not sure how it works for bat brains though." Jaden smiled when Taz's face soured.

"How many times have I told you we aren't bats?"

"Ah, but you look like bats," Jaden chuckled. "So —" Han's wing clipped him on the ear, cutting him off. "Ow!"

"You deserved that," Han sniffed.

Jaden laughed. "I did indeed. Now, let's ask Taz what we came to ask so she can get her rest."

Taz tried to sit up, but, catching Han's stern gaze, she sank back again. "I have little to tell you. I lost my link with Kayla, so Han and I went to your house to investigate. When she wasn't there, I took off for her home."

"Alone?"

"Yes, there was no reason to think anything would happen to me. Flawed reasoning, I know, but hindsight is always twenty-twenty. They ambushed me on my way to Kayla's home. Didn't see the brutes who took me out. I'm not sure how many, but more than two."

"I'm sorry." Taz waved his apology away. "Did you see the 'pod Kayla was going home in?"

"No, I'm sorry, I didn't." Taz grimaced and rolled her head to one side.

"What's wrong?" Jaden leaped to his feet, alarmed. He regretted the sudden movement when spots danced before his eyes. They vanished as quickly as they had appeared.

"Every time I try think too hard, my head . . ." Taz wilted where she lay.

"Atu! Atu!" Jaden yelled, not even sure if he was there. Reaching down, he touched Taz's neck. He couldn't feel anything through the thick fur. *What am I thinking? I'm not a medic. How would I even know where to find her pulse?*

Just as he really began to panic, Atu came running. Slamming to a stop next to them, he panted, "What?"

Words weren't necessary, though. Atu took one look at Taz and closed his eyes. That golden glow Jaden had seen only once before streamed from his hands and bathed Taz. Taz's eyes flicked open briefly; then she was out again.

Atu leaned back with a tired sigh. "What were you doing?"

"Just speaking to her, I promise! Is she okay?"

"Yes, she's breathing again. And she will be okay *if* she gets her rest. Leave her to do that!"

Jaden nodded vigorously, stopping the motion when the spots came back. "Yes, we will."

Atu raised a weary hand to his head. "I think I'll take a nap right here next to her."

For the first time since Atu's appearance, Jaden studied him. He had black bags under his eyes, and his skin was pale beneath his tan. "Don't you want to sleep at the house? You look like you need the rest."

Atu shook his head. "No, if Taz has another episode, I need to be right here."

"I'll get Markov or one of the others to bring you a sleeping shell." Jaden thought about what else he could do. "And some food."

"Thanks." Atu lay down next to Taz. Almost instantly, he began snoring.

"So much for the sleeping shell," Jaden muttered.

"Taz will keep him warm enough," Han observed. "What do we do now?"

CHAPTER FOUR

Jaden's legs wobbled. He sank down next to Taz and Atu again, panting as he waved off Han's concern. "I just need a moment."

Silently cursing the blood loss he'd suffered in the battle, Jaden wished the near-constant weakness would vanish. He slumped onto his back, allowing himself a minute's respite.

What's the point of trying to find out where Kayla disappeared to or how it happened? She's gone. There's no way I can reach her in that other dimension, which is surely where Slurpy's taken her. He wouldn't have risked leaving her here in this world. That's where he whisked my and Atu's parents off to. No, Slurpy wouldn't have wasted time getting Kayla across the breach.

Can I cross it if another one of those mysterious rings opens again? No, the last time I was near it, it zapped me full of some weird energy and left me unconscious. And I didn't go through the breach. I closed it.

A ragged sigh escaped. Suddenly sick to his stomach, Jaden leaned forward, putting his head between his knees. He dragged in several deep breaths. When the nausea passed, he lifted his head, then lay back down again. He closed his eyes. Desolation. He knew how it looked. He'd never known he could experience it.

Yet that tiny speck of hope persisted. Kayla might not be in Slurpy's realm yet. And as long as that small chance remained, he had to find the 'pod.

"Jaden?"

Han's worried voice reminded him he wasn't alone. "I don't know what to do. This isn't a problem I thought I would ever have. But whoever would've guessed I'd have to know how to cross the breach? Or know how to fight mutants from other worlds? Or do any of the other unbelievable things I've had to do since all this began?"

Han was silent for so long Jaden wondered whether he would respond. But he did. And it wasn't what Jaden thought it would be.

"If we're trying to find Kayla, shouldn't we use the arcachoa?"

"You have nothing to say about the mission? About how it's my destiny? Or how I'm doing okay?"

"You don't need that. You need Kayla."

The insight struck Jaden dumb. It was true. If he had Kayla, he wouldn't be doubting himself. He wouldn't be wallowing in self-pity. Instead, he would move onto the next step. Reaching over, he touched the only part of Han he could reach—his leg. "Thanks, buddy."

Han eyed the hand on his leg. "If you're done feeling me up, how about we try the arcachoa?"

Jaden laughed. "Yeah, because I've always wanted to touch your leg! It's pretty scaly. You might want to consider using some lotion." Han lifted a wing and Jaden rolled away. "No, you're not clipping me on the ear again!"

Han looked pleased with himself. "In that case, time to get to your feet. We have work to do."

Han launched himself into the air and Jaden watched as he gained altitude, then curved around to head back to where Jaden waited. Stumbling to his feet, Jaden wondered for the second time about his ability to aerial connect. He was weaker now than he'd been on the roof. But he needn't have worried. As he landed on Han's back and moved to his familiar position, he was thankful for small mercies.

"Let's head for my home. That's the last place we know Kayla was before she disappeared."

They flew the familiar route, coming up on Jaden's house in seconds. Jaden retrieved his medallion from his wrist pouch.

"Ready?" he asked Han.

Han nodded, and Jaden inserted the medallion in Han's arcachoa, the perfect medallion-shaped space between Han's ears. Time dilated as light blazed before settling into the glowing circle that would take them through the time tunnel. As it sucked him and Han in, Jaden forced himself to relax. Sound became as dead as the surrounding air. Light swirled in untamed wild arcs across their path, making him nauseous as usual. Then the light closed in on itself, encompassing them before the tunnel spat them out.

Jaden gulped down air, taking stock of where they'd ended up. "We're in the right time and place."

Grimly, they watched the replay of Kayla's departure. Jaden heard himself offering to go with her. Kayla declined. She settled into the 'pod and then zoomed away.

Without a word, Han followed. Jaden flinched when a Gaptor darted in front of them. His DD was in his hand before he remembered this had already all happened before. He couldn't help Kayla from here. Desperate, he leaned forward on Han's back, silently urging Kayla to pay attention.

But as Han drew level with the 'pod transporting her, Jaden could see her eyes were closed. She reclined in her seat, oblivious to the danger lurking outside. In fact, all around. Three other Gaptors had joined the first, and they now ringed the 'pod.

Jaden couldn't stop the cry of rage as they attacked. Tearing into it with claws and teeth, they ripped the engine off. The tiny craft wobbled, then flipped sideways before spiraling downward.

"Kayla, get out of there!" Jaden knew Kayla couldn't hear him, but he had stopped breathing. If the 'pod crashed in the state it was in, Kayla likely wouldn't survive. Helpless, Jaden watched as Kayla scrambled around the cockpit. *What are you doing? Why aren't you using the escape hatch?*

In slow motion, Jaden watched the 'pod spin through the air. Kayla pushed on the escape hatch, then turned, and her hands flew over the controls. Then back to the hatch again. He understood. The attack had somehow disabled the hatch. Kayla couldn't get out.

He let out a guttural cry, wrenched from his very soul. Jaden didn't know if he could watch Kayla die. But a small part of his brain told him she had to have somehow survived, or they would've found her by now. Partly hiding his face behind his hands, he stared as Kayla snapped back into the pilot's seat. She put on her safety harness, then assumed the brace position for the inevitable crash.

Just before the 'pod hit, the Gaptors swooped down and flipped the 'pod right way up with their wings. For a second, Jaden thought they would latch onto the craft, pick it up, and cart it away. But the dumb beasts had waited too long. The 'pod was too close to the ground and they couldn't get under it.

The 'pod smacked down, the sound horrendous: a sickening thud followed by screeching metal as the 'pod skidded along the ground before cracking into a tree. Literally cracking. The 'pod split open like a pea pod, spilling Kayla onto the ground.

Blood. So much blood. It was everywhere. Covering the interior of the 'pod. Smeared along the ground where Kayla was dumped out. Over the back of her head. The back of her head!

Jaden leaned over Han's side and retched. He couldn't take any more. He wanted to die. *Why can't they attack me? Do they always have to attack those I love?*

"Jaden, she's moving. Look!"

Had Han really said that? Convinced he was hallucinating, Jaden half-heartedly looked at Kayla. His heart skipped a beat. She *was* moving! "Han, get down there! We have to help her."

"We can't."

Han's voice was soft and carried all the pain Jaden felt. He was about to yell at Han when he remembered where they were. The sobs broke loose.

His body heaving, Jaden watched as Kayla tried to draw her DD. As she tried to defend herself. As the monsters swept the DD aside and snatched her up in their hideous talons. His heart broke hearing her cries of agony as they subjected her injuries to this brutal treatment.

Jaden closed his eyes. He couldn't watch anymore, couldn't take this. His energy gone, he slumped onto Han's neck. Abruptly, the air rippled.

"No!" Han cried.

Jaden sat up to find the cause of Han's distress. Light shimmered. Then he and Han were sucked back into the time tunnel, the silence their only companion as it shunted them back to their own time.

As soon as they exited, Jaden shouted, "What happened?"

"They opened a breach and took Kayla through it."

"What? How did they do that?"

"I don't know. I can only guess the usurper has worked out how to open the breach at precise locations. It's the only explanation."

"But why are we back in our own time?"

Han gazed back at him, his concern evident. "Jaden, if she went through the breach, every artifact she had went with her when that gate closed. With no artifact to keep us there, the arcachoa couldn't continue operating."

Jaden scrubbed a hand over his face. He had to get with the program. If he couldn't keep it together, he would be incapable of completing the mission. It was the only sure way of getting Kayla back. Realizing Han was still casting anxious glances his way, Jaden rubbed the fur along Han's neck.

"I'll be okay, buddy."

"I don't know whether to believe you."

Jaden put effort into a smile. "Let me rephrase. I *will* be okay as long as we keep moving."

Han brightened. "And where are we moving to?"

"We need to gather the crew. Let them know what happened to Kayla. Make some plans." Jaden thought a moment. "Let's meet in the mountains where Sven set the ambush for the Gaptors."

Han's eyebrows shot up. "So far away? Why do you want to meet there?"

"First, we know we already have one traitor. If Taz's suspicions are correct and we have more, identifying others might be easier if the gliders aren't all crowded together. This is the second reason for going there—the gliders can be part of the meeting without being squished together. Finally, that place is so isolated, we'll know if anyone is there that shouldn't be there, meaning we can minimize prying ears overhearing what they shouldn't."

"You want us to be part of the meeting?"

"I think it's important we get your input. The gliders have been battling the Gaptors and the usurper far longer than we have. Your insights will be invaluable."

Han grinned. "At least we're good for something."

This time Jaden didn't have to force a smile. "You know you're the best weapon we have." He actually laughed when Han puffed out his chest. "Okay, okay, before that goes to your head, let's finish planning this meeting." When Han opened his mouth, Jaden guessed what he was about to ask. "Yes, all the gliders plus my childhood friends and both my parents and Kayla's. Tough as it will be for them to hear it, they all need to know what happened to Kayla. Then we need to agree on a course of action. If we're going to get Kayla back safely, the only way I can think to do that is to get to whatever Slurpy doesn't want us to reach before he does."

"Jaden, are you not feeling quite yourself again?"

"What do you mean?"

Han hesitated. "Well, you sounded okay until that last sentence. Then you made no sense at all."

Jaden groaned. He was having a tough time trying to remember what he had said and what he hadn't. He probably hadn't explained that part to Han. "I'm fine. I'm just losing track of what I've said aloud and what I've been thinking. Does it help you understand that last sentence if I tell you I think Slurpy is just as much in the dark as we are about how we finish this mission?"

Han thought a moment. "What you're saying is it's a race between him and us to reach the final objective? And if we beat him to it, we can win and get Kayla back before he can harm her?"

"Exactly."

A slow, toothy smile spread across Han's face. "What are we waiting for?"

CHAPTER FIVE

Blackness so thick she could touch it, darker than sin. Kayla groaned. Her head felt like it had been split in half. Her throat was parched. Every muscle, tendon, and nerve screamed in agony.

Kayla lifted a hand to touch her head . . . she couldn't move! Apprehensive, she tried again, confirming she could *not* lift her hand. Not even a finger! Panic churned like an ocean wave about to dump her. *Where am I? Why can't I think? What happened?*

Kayla clawed through the muck clogging her brain. She tried again. *What's the last thing I remember?* Jaden. Saying goodbye on his rooftop. Getting into the 'pod to take her home. Closing her eyes because she was so tired. And then . . . Bam!

Kayla's eyes widened as she remembered the collision. Then confusion fogged her brain once more. The 'pod couldn't have crashed into anything. Its sensors prevented collisions. A horrifying thought struck her. What if she had collided with something not of this world? Had a Gaptor attacked her 'pod?

Fighting her rising terror, Kayla dissected the problem. A Gaptor attack was the only thing that made sense. As distressing as the idea was, she had to play this scenario out. Gaptors had attacked her transport. So how had she survived? If the 'pod crash hadn't killed her, why hadn't the Gaptors?

She groaned as a fresh wave of pain punched every nerve ending. The wrecked 'pod would explain her injuries. She tried moving her finger again. No luck. Had the crash paralyzed her? Squashing her hysteria, she focused on reaching a conclusion.

So Gaptors took out my transport. My 'pod crashed. Somehow, I survived the wreck. And being killed by the Gaptors. What happened after that? Where was she? And why couldn't she see anything?

For an appalling moment, she thought she might be blind. But after closing her eyes for a second before opening them again, she realized two things. First, she could open and close her eyes. Second, there was a difference in the level of light when her eyes were open or shut. Definitely not blind.

Irritated by getting sidetracked, she rallied her wayward thoughts. Her brain finally began functioning again. The only reason she wouldn't remember what had happened was if she'd blacked out after the accident. While coming to that realization was comforting, the blacking out part wasn't encouraging. Either she had cracked her head hard enough to black out, or her injuries had been severe enough to render her unconscious. Each had their own ramifications.

Consciousness had returned in this dark place, along with the possibility she was paralyzed. Paralyzed! How would she finish the mission? But other things could paralyze. Like Gaptor EMPs. Unfortunately, being unable to move meant she couldn't check for either her medallion or ring.

Frustrated tears leaked out. Maybe this place wasn't as detestable as she thought. But if someone rescued her after the wreck, wouldn't she be in a hospital, a place with lights and movement and friendly faces? Her spirits plummeted. She'd just confirmed her suspicions.

The Gaptors had certainly taken her. Reinforcing this conclusion was the memory of Clara's dream. Clara told them she and Ty had woken up in an unknown place, unable to move or speak. How dark it had been, a blackness so thick Clara felt like she could touch it.

Abruptly, Kayla gasped for air. She was suffocating. Was the air here that dense, or was it realizing Gaptors had taken her? The same way they'd taken Jaden's parents. And Atu's parents. If that were true, was she in the Gaptors' world now? Was she beyond Jaden's reach? The sobs only aggravated her injuries, but she couldn't hold them back. Would she see him again? Or any of the others she loved and cared for?

The sobs morphed into hiccups as she struggled to breathe. This couldn't be happening. Hadn't Zareh warned them of the dangers of traveling in a transport? But Jaden's home was such a short distance from her own. How could they have known the Gaptors would strike so precisely? Weren't they supposed to be stupid beasts?

No, this reeked of a far more intelligent mind. Just like that, her tears dried up, and anger fired her veins, ramping up the pain. But she didn't care. The usurper's fingerprints were all over this. She was in his domain. And he wanted her for something.

Slight scratching sounds interrupted her thoughts. Kayla tried turning her head, to no avail. She wanted to beat the air and scream and thrash about and punch something, all at the same time. She had never known helplessness like this before. Having to lie here and take whatever came was intolerable. *Useless limbs!*

Hot, fetid breath swamped the air above her. Kayla gagged, the odor repulsive in the extreme, then gagged again. Her continued dry heaving told her she'd had nothing to eat or drink in a while. Perhaps another reason her brain was being so uncooperative.

Another whiff of that disgusting smell. Then something cold and hard pressed against her face. Kayla cringed inside, unable to retreat from whatever it was. Sweat prickled her forehead, the tiny drops fusing into beads before they trickled down the side of her head. A drop rolled into her ear. She didn't need the unpleasant sensation to remind her how helpless she was.

When the hard object only pressed more sharply against her cheekbone, Kayla would've cried out if possible. Liquid splashed onto her face. Surprised, Kayla's mouth opened involuntarily. Before she could modulate the action, she was gulping the liquid, thirsty beyond reason. Water! Blessed water. Greedily, she swallowed a mouthful, then another, the actions uncontrollable. Water went down the wrong way. She choked.

I'm drowning! Frantic, Kayla coughed and spluttered, trying to rid her lungs of the water. *Is this thing trying to drown me or give me a drink of water?* Its stench hovered nearby. It hadn't left. When her lungs finally wheezed clear, she sucked down air.

The hard object pressed against her cheek again. Kayla pursed her lips, keeping her mouth closed. If she drank too much too quickly, she'd have other issues to deal with. Water sloshed over her face, but she kept her mouth closed, praying the water wouldn't go up her nose.

Just when she thought she couldn't take it a second longer, the container disappeared. The loss of pressure and sudden relief to be free of potentially drowning only made her other injuries scream for attention. A drum beat a painful rhythm through her head. Every part of her hurt and ached with an intensity that made her consider a potential infection. Since she couldn't move her limbs, it was impossible to gauge the extent or condition of her injuries.

Without warning, the world overhead lurched. Kayla's heart slammed into her throat before she registered this wasn't something to fear. She was moving. Or rather, whatever she was lying on was moving. Like she was on a gurney. Maybe it *was* a gurney, and they would take care of her injuries. Perhaps she couldn't move because her injuries prevented it.

Kayla wanted to smack herself in the face. *Who am I kidding? More likely they're rolling me to my death. Think, Kayla, think!* She calmed her racing mind enough to process events. It's what Jaden would've done. *I miss him! And . . . no, I can't think about him. I have to find a way out of this.*

Kayla began with what she *did* know. She couldn't move because the Gaptors had loosed their EMP on her. No, that couldn't be right. Her medallion protected her. Or had she lost her medallion? Worse, had she also lost her relic stone? Only a combination of those factors would allow the Gaptors' EMPs to affect her this way. The medallions insulated their holders from the Gaptors' EMP, and the relic stones released those held captive by its numbing effects.

Desperate, she tried feeling for the ring on her finger—and her finger *moved*.

She was so shocked, the sharp intake of air happened before Kayla could hide it. Her bed stopped moving. That stink as the thing came near her face again, as though it could see her in this inky blackness. She dared not move. The thing—was it a Gaptor?— hovered over her for what seemed an eternity. Then the bed began rolling again.

Hiding her relief, Kayla tried moving her finger again. When not one, but two fingers moved, she kept the grin off her face. Repeating the action, she found what she had been searching for. Her ring was still on her finger, which only confused her more. If that was true, the Gaptors' EMP wasn't numbing her. Kayla bit down on her scream. Maybe the crash really *did* paralyze her.

No, no, no! If that's true, I wouldn't be able to move my fingers. What's wrong with me? Why are my thoughts so scattered? Kayla suddenly noticed the light. Scanning for the source, her eyes whipped side to side. Then it was there, shining in her eyes, so bright she squeezed her eyes shut against it.

As the image faded against the backs of her eyelids, she realized what it had been: the bright round disc of an operating theater's light. *They really are planning to cut me into pieces. Tiny, little, itty, bitty pieces they'll send to Jaden one at a time to prolong his agony.* Kayla knew she was spiraling into delirium, but she couldn't stop herself.

Every terrible thing she had ever imagined seemed to converge in her mind. Then she heard the voice, and her mind froze. It was the most beautiful voice she had ever heard. And it petrified her. Chills pierced her very soul. Maybe that's why her thoughts were so dark, so lost. Without a doubt, *he* was here. Kayla's blood curdled in her veins. She was going to die. There was no escaping the fact.

A murmured reply. *What are they saying?* Kayla struggled to hear over the blood roaring through her ears, her adrenaline spike only exacerbating the problem. More words.

"You can repair her?"

Repair her? What am I? A broken toy?

"Yes, my lord. But it will be a few days before she's fully functional again."

Fully functional? So I am paralyzed? Functional for what? What does he have planned for me? Her finger brushed against her ring, and she was suddenly desperate to hide it. *What if* he *takes it while I'm unconscious? Or takes my medallion?* In the background, the blips and beeps monitoring Kayla chorused a little faster.

"My lord, please, she's getting nervous. It will hinder her recovery."

"Your antiquated techniques are unnecessary. I'll tend to her serious injuries. We don't have time to wait for her to heal. You can mop up the rest."

"Yes, my lord. May I please put her under before we continue discussing her situation?"

Hell no, you can't! You keep me awake so I can hear every evil plan you have for me. Kayla saw the mask descending. Didn't they know they shouldn't give patients water right before surgery? She wanted to scream, to tell them to stop. But the mask planted itself over her nose. *It would be . . . only . . .*

CHAPTER SIX

As they flew to the valley, the scene of their last battle, Jaden used his PAL to request his friends' and family's presence at the meeting. He sent an additional request to Markov, asking him to contact the other riders. Then he pinged Atu, requesting that he summon Pallaton with his reed so the Legion could attend as well.

That done, Jaden absorbed the scenery passing below. It was a relaxing exercise, and by the time they reached the clifftop meeting place, it had soothed his soul. Dismounting, he ambled over to a boulder and sat down. Sitting, it turned out, was a bad idea.

With nothing to do, Jaden's mind went to Kayla and fixated on all that blood. Especially the blood on the back of her head. Was Kayla still alive? How serious were her injuries? Would Slurpy provide medical attention? Worse, how was Jaden going to answer these questions when someone invariably asked them?

Unable to tolerate thoughts of Kayla's fate for a second longer, Jaden bounced up and began pacing. He took several steps before realizing standing hadn't made him dizzy. Finally, he was free of the debilitating effects of his blood loss.

Probably a result of all the rest Atu had forced on him. And the food Han had made him eat. Lowering his stress levels by concentrating on the scenery probably hadn't hurt either. Jaden would make resting and eating a priority. He needed all his strength for what lay ahead.

In the distance, Jaden saw the first gliders approaching. *Excellent!* They could soon get on with things.

The gliders slid in one at a time, dropping their riders before arcing away to circle further afield. The new arrivals exchanged greetings. Several people commented how pleased they were to see Jaden up and about again.

Jaden smiled and chatted with those he knew and those he didn't. Assessing numbers, Jaden noticed Stovan's absence and felt a twinge of disappointment. A quick conversation with Markov confirmed Stovan had opted to stay home. Did Stovan blame him for Bree's death?

Jaden searched for another face. His own soured at the thought of Tarise. She had better stay away.

When everyone had arrived, with Tarise notably absent, Jaden whistled. They turned and looked at him expectantly. *Here we go again.*

"Thanks for meeting me. The battle we shared here was tough for all of us." Jaden glanced around, noticing Kayla's parents were holding one another. "I know this is an unconventional place for a meeting, but I thought it would be best to gather where our gliders can also be part of the conversation."

"Any news about Kayla yet?" Vicken asked, impatient for an update on his daughter.

Jaden's blue eyes turned the color of cold steel. "Yes," he answered quietly. As though him lowering his voice cast a spell over the others, the silence that settled seemed unnaturally loud. Taking a deep breath, Jaden shared what he'd learned.

"You don't know if she's still alive then?" Sadie's voice quavered.

"I'm sorry. I don't. However, I think it's unlikely the usurper would take Kayla just to . . . get rid of her. He needs her for leverage against me."

Jaden studied the Melmiques, waiting for the anger he expected. Anger that he had gotten their daughter involved in this. Anger that he was the reason she was missing. Anger that he hadn't protected their daughter.

He saw only resolve. Vicken squared his shoulders. "In that case, what are we doing to get her back?"

"Pallaton," Jaden called to the massive leader of the Legion. Pallaton drifted closer. "Do you have any idea how we might cross the breach?"

Pallaton shook his head. "If I knew how to do that, don't you think I would've already taken my Legion after the Interpreter?"

Jaden blinked, *Of course!* Without Kayla, they had zero chance of interpreting the next clue. He had thought if they beat Slurpy to the prize, they would get Kayla back unharmed. Only if they didn't get her back before this ended, they wouldn't have the faintest hope of succeeding.

"May I ask a question?" Markov's voice cut across Jaden's thoughts. "Sure."

"Do you think the Gaptors we killed in the battle were the bulk of the usurper's army?"

Pallaton rumbled, his face thoughtful. "Why do you ask?"

Markov scratched his chin. "I'm thinking if Slurpy," he shot Jaden a grin as he referred to the usurper using the derogatory name Jaden had assigned him, "wants world domination, he'll need a much larger force."

Pallaton shrugged. "Your observation has merit. Unfortunately, the usurper went underground millennia ago, so we don't know the size of his army or where they might be."

Markov nodded. "The real question, then, is where are they? With centuries in hiding to create those monsters, he certainly hasn't run out!"

Jaden debated telling Markov that Zareh had been working on something to find the Gaptor nests in the other world. But even if Zareh found a solution—a big "if"—how did they know the technology or method he used *there* would work here? No, now was not the time nor place to share. Jaden didn't want to give false hope.

Aren addressed the issue Markov had raised. "You said it. I don't think he has run out. He's just stashed them somewhere."

Markov's face was grim. "Then we need to find them!"

"We do," Jaden agreed. "But how? Does anyone have any ideas?" He glanced at the circling gliders, hoping one of them might have an answer, but silence and dejected nods met his gaze. "Alright," Jaden sighed. "Another thing we need to figure out. Without knowing whether there *are* more Gaptors gathered in our world and where they are, we can't eliminate them before Slurpy sends reinforcements. In the meantime, I propose you all head back to Sven's to finish your training."

"We don't need more training. We need to take those suckers down!" a voice shot back.

Jaden couldn't locate the source. But the emotion rippling through the assembled humans was unmistakable. They wanted payback. He, Stovan, and their friends hadn't been the only people to lose loved ones.

"I agree." Jaden hesitated. *Should I say this? If so, how do I say it to cause the least pain?* "However, I think if we train a little more, we might fare better in our next encounter."

Silence. Jaden was wondering if he'd have to say more when Markov stepped in.

"You're right. It would behoove us to train as much as possible before our next battle."

There were a few murmurs, but then heads began nodding in agreement. Jaden pounced on the positive energy. "If you train at Sven's, his unique defense system will keep you safe. Here, you have no such protection."

The nods and affirmations were more energetic now. Jaden's tension eased.

Until Vicken shouted, "That doesn't help us get Kayla back."

Jaden raised both hands to quell the renewed murmurs. "Going to

Sven's is only the first step. With you there, you'll be safe until we need to call on you for Kayla's rescue."

Vicken nodded, but Jaden sensed he had something else he wanted to say. When Jaden waited, Vicken angled his head sideways and lifted his chin. Jaden interpreted that to mean, "Later."

"Any more questions?"

"How long will we stay at Sven's?" Markov asked.

"Only until we find Kayla. Or the remaining Gaptors. Or a battle comes to our doorstep."

Markov's face was grim. "And you promise to call on us when you need us?"

"I do."

Accepting this, Markov exchanged their complicated handshake and said his farewells. Then he and Jaden's other friends headed for the cliff edge, their gliders already prepared for the pickup. When the remaining riders drifted away, indicating acceptance of his plan, Jaden hurried over to Sven and pulled the enormous man aside.

"Two things before you go: first, if Tarise ever shows her face again, do you have somewhere to confine her until all this is over?"

Sven gave Jaden a hard stare. "You really want to go down that path? It's not good, no, not good!"

"I understand, but we can't trust her. I won't lose anyone else to this quest because she's gone running off to tattle on us again."

"But she's your friend! Why would you want to put her in a cage?"

Jaden's jaw clenched so tightly, squeezing the words out was difficult. "I think she only regrets what she did because of what happened to Bree. She doesn't care about Kayla. And if Slurpy tells her he'll do something to Kayla if Tarise helps him, don't you think she'll jump at the chance?"

Sven's shock was enough for Jaden to know his bitterness was showing. Attempting to relax the muscles in his jaw, Jaden said, "Slurpy won't hesitate to use that pain point he has on Tarise's hand if she refuses to do his bidding. Therefore, wouldn't it be better to keep her in a place where she can't do anything even if she wanted to?"

Slowly, Sven shook his head. "I still disagree this is the path we should choose. However, I will consider what I can do to ensure secure . . . accommodations for Tarise if she ever returns."

"Thank you."

Sven muttered a few unintelligible words, making Jaden shift uncomfortably. Maybe he shouldn't have asked Sven to create a prison, considering Sven knew first-hand what it was like to be a prisoner. Jaden sighed. It was too late for retractions.

"You said there were two things?" Sven grumbled.

Jaden couldn't blame him for not wanting to hear the other part. If the first topic was so awful, Sven was probably dreading what Jaden might say next. Perhaps this option would cheer him up again.

"Do you think you can work on something that will duplicate the effect of the medallions in keeping the riders safe from Gaptor EMPs?"

Sven's face changed from apprehensive to thoughtful. "A tall order, given we probably don't have a lot of time, no? It took far longer than expected to create even a fraction of the effect of your relic stones."

Jaden clapped a hand on his back. "But you did it. I have faith this is another obstacle you can conquer. Perhaps start with those amazing incapacitating cannons you have at the entrance to the valley leading to your home."

Sven's face was hilarious. His eyes opened so wide, Jaden thought his eyes would pop out. Then he began patting down his body as he searched for something to write with. Then, realizing he hadn't said a word, his face split into a huge smile.

"You may be onto something there. If I can adjust the frequency and use—"

Jaden interrupted. "Before you go on telling me things I probably won't understand, how about you get on your glider? The others are waiting."

That was, except for Vicken, who had snuck up on them.

Sven turned, and, noticing the waiting crowd, he chuckled. "It seems they are."

Sven was about to move away when Vicken put out a hand to stall him. "I might not be joining you." Sven remained where he was, waiting for an explanation. "Jaden, with all due respect, I think I am more than qualified at doing what everyone else is still learning at Sven's. Let me stay with you, and we can work on finding Kayla together."

Jaden had been expecting this. "While that's true, with your knowledge, couldn't you speed up everyone else's training?"

Vicken shook his head. "The smart suits this genius created take care of that. Sadie will go with the others so she can learn, but we've spoken and agreed that I should stay with you."

Jaden's brows knit together. "The problem is that if we're attacked by a Gaptor's EMP while you're flying with me, you'll be defenseless. I wouldn't be able to live with myself if something happened to you and I had to tell Kayla."

"He won't be defenseless," Sven boomed.

Jaden cringed from the sound. "Why?"

"Because he'll have this." Sven held up his medallion before pressing it into Vicken's hands. "You keep this safe for me, yes? And while you do, you find for your daughter for me. She's the only one who can keep this one in line, no?"

Vicken's eyes glittered. "Are you sure?"

Sven nodded, and Vicken closed his fingers around the medallion. "In that case, thank you. I will take good care of it. You look after yourself and my wife."

"I will keep your Sadie safe," Sven promised, lumbering away. "Now, my workshop calls. I have things to design."

He leaped off the edge of the cliff, and anything else he might have said was lost. A second later, a glider almost as large as Pallaton rose from below the cliff edge and curved away, Sven astride his broad back.

Sven circled an impatient arm in the air and roared. "Let's go!"

Jaden watched them leave. "I'd hate to be his glider."

Vicken chuckled "Bad enough having to lift the guy, but it must be a hundred times worse when you've had to catch him first!"

35

Jaden laughed. Surprised, he stopped. It was the first time he had really felt alive again since they had taken Kayla.

Vicken studied him. "It's because you have a plan. I always feel better when I take action."

Jaden acknowledged the truth of Vicken's statement with a nod. "Let's get on with it then."

CHAPTER SEVEN

Jaden watched Taz stumble to her feet, the vivid green grass under her thick and lush from the recent rains. Even the air had been washed clean. Crisp, untainted by pollution, sweetened with pine. This field, set aside for Taz to begin her strength training, was spacious, secluded, and on the outer edges of Atu's healing center.

Jaden didn't like that the healing center was so close to where their last clash with the Gaptors had taken place. But Atu hadn't had the luxury of being picky about location during a battle. He had needed somewhere close enough to ferry the injured there with minimal delays before they received the care they needed.

On the plus side, the location was defensible. The healing center sat on the side of a mountain, high enough to offer a clear vantage of anyone approaching and with evergreens running right up to its edges. Not only did the trees provide shelter against an aerial attack, they also insulated the field from the icy winds that ran up the mountainside.

Jaden turned from his study of the area and concentrated on Taz's efforts. Atu had waited days before declaring Taz's condition stable enough for them to bring her here. Since then, she had spent her time resting. Now, she took a few tottering steps, then steadied herself.

Han quivered next to him, making Jaden aware of the supreme effort it took for Han not to assist Taz.

"She'll be okay. She needs to do this on her own," Jaden soothed.

"Fine for you to say."

There it is again. That undertone. Wanting to root out the cause this time, Jaden tried for nonchalance. "So you have feelings for her?"

Han didn't take his eyes off Taz. "Of course I have feelings for her. We grew up together, trained together, and learned side by side. We've known each other all our lives."

"You're not answering the question." When Han finally looked at him, Jaden raised his eyebrows. "Well?"

"It's not like that. It can't be," Han mumbled.

"Why not?" Han said nothing, just refocused his attention on Taz. Time for the real question. "Does it have something to do with that glider calling her '*The* Tazanna?'"

Han sucked in air so loudly it was impossible not to hear. "Who said that?"

Han's anger didn't mean he hadn't answered the question. On the contrary, Han had confirmed Jaden's suspicions. "You're just annoyed because you want to keep her secret."

But Han loomed over him, all menace. Jaden took a step back. For the first time since he'd met Han, Jaden was a little scared. Han looked capable of anything—most notably, murder.

"Han, buddy, no need to get upset!"

Han backed off and shook out his wings. Then he glanced around, making sure no one else could hear. "Jaden, it's important that I know who said that."

"Why?"

Han pressed his lips together. After a moment, he said, "Why is not important. Who, is."

Jaden mulled his response. Now that Han had confirmed his suspicions, the pieces snapped into place. "Okay, don't bite my head off for saying this, but," Jaden leaned close to Han and whispered, "Taz is royalty, right?"

The murderous glint returned to Han's eyes. "What makes you think that?"

"Calm down. There was more than one clue. Your deference. The way Pallaton treats her. Taz herself—her imperious tones and how she thinks everyone will do her bidding."

"She does not!"

Jaden grinned. "Yeah, had to throw that last one in there to check you were still listening."

"Jaden, you need to tell me who called her that name."

"Because you think they're the traitor?"

Han looked taken aback. "You have got to stop doing that!"

"Tell me, if so many of them know she's royalty, why is it a problem for one of them to call her 'The Tazanna?'"

"Because only those who were in the court at the time they sent the Legion to your world would know that reference."

"And you think because they were in the court, they're one of Slurpy's spies?"

"Yes."

Jaden sighed. "Sorry, buddy, I don't know who said that. I just remembered someone did."

Han slumped. Then he straightened. "I know how we can find out."

"How?"

Han's only answer was a toothy grin and a cryptic, "We need to find Pallaton."

With a quick farewell and words of encouragement to Taz, Jaden and Han went searching for Pallaton. They found him patrolling the area around Jaden's home.

"Greetings, Gatekeeper, Ohanzee," Pallaton rumbled when he saw them.

Jaden hadn't thought of Han's real name in so long that hearing it again was strange. But that wasn't what bothered him. "Why do you insist on calling me 'Gatekeeper?'"

Pallaton frowned. "I thought it fitting to refer to you by your proper name."

"Whatever," Jaden said, tossing a hand in the air. He didn't want to get off track. He nudged Han's neck to remind him.

"Greetings, Pallaton," Han said before launching into what they wanted.

When he finished, Pallaton nodded. "I can make that happen. Where shall we meet?"

Han looked back at Jaden. "Do you have any suggestions?"

Jaden thought a moment, then realized he knew the perfect spot. He gave Pallaton directions.

"Excellent." Pallaton beamed. "I couldn't have chosen a better place. Shall we say an hour from now?"

Han blinked. "You can have them here that soon?"

"I believe I can."

When Pallaton offered no further explanation, Han nodded. "An hour it is then."

"Now what?" Jaden asked as Pallaton took off. Too focused on how Han would ferret out the mole, Jaden didn't care how Pallaton would get the Legion here from Sven's home in only an hour.

"We go to Kayla's home."

"We're asking Vicken to help?" Jaden had stopped calling him Mr. Melmique a few days ago when Vicken had told him in no uncertain terms they were long past formalities. A shiver ran through him. No doubt a man with his background knew ways of getting answers from people (or gliders) who didn't care to part with them.

"It would be beneficial to have his skills should we need them."

Jaden frowned. Han was implying Vicken *wasn't* the solution. So why were they going to the Melmiques? Then he grinned. "Han, you sly devil! I know how we'll do this."

Han's chest vibrated under Jaden as he laughed. "It's the best secret weapon we have."

As they approached the Melmiques' home, Jaden saw Vicken's glider hovering near the rooftop landing site. Calling a quick hello to the glider, Jaden dismounted and headed indoors. He wasn't even halfway down the stairs when Vicken appeared, weapon at his side.

"I see you're prepared." Jaden pointed at the gun.

Vicken lifted his shirt to show his DD sheathed there. "Always."

Jaden grinned. "Ready for some action, then?"

The way the man's eyes lit up was scary. No, it was more than that. It was his whole bearing. Like he went into combat mode—or something. Looking more closely, Jaden saw his weight had shifted onto the balls of his feet. His grip on his gun had tightened. And his eyes, while still, were somehow scanning the area. The man was just plain sinister.

"Are we going?"

Vicken's question caught Jaden off-guard. He'd been so intent on studying Kayla's father he'd forgotten Vicken was probably waiting for him to lead the way.

"Yes, our gliders are waiting upstairs. Before we go, is Iri here?"

Vicken sent a quizzical glance before nodding and leading the way to Iri's room. "Just so you know, she hasn't really spoken much since she lost Tinks."

"I don't blame her. I was there when it happened, and I'm still rattled by it."

Vicken stopped and pointed at an open doorway. Jaden passed him and then paused outside the room a moment, just observing. Iri lay curled up on the bed, her back to the door, her head tucked under an arm. If Jaden hadn't seen the slight rise and fall of her shoulders to indicate she was breathing, he might've rushed in to check whether she was still alive. She was so still.

Abruptly, Iri sat up. Jaden jumped. She smiled when she noticed, but sorrow lingered in her features.

"Hey, Iri, how are you doing?" Jaden walked into the room.

She moved over to make space as he took a seat on the bed next to her. Tucking her legs up into the circle of her arms, she shrugged. "I've been better." Iri studied him with that gaze that made Jaden feel like he was under a microscope. "What's up?"

"You guessed I need something?"

Iri rolled her eyes. "Even without my senses, it wasn't difficult to see you came here with a purpose."

Uncomfortable at being such an open book for her, Jaden decided on a direct approach. "First, let me say how sorry I am for your loss."

Jaden almost wimped out when Iri's eyes filled with tears. He put a hand on her arm. Then, when the tears rolled down her cheeks, he pulled her into a hug. He held her there, rubbing her back, hoping the contact provided some comfort.

It was some time before Iri pulled back, a smile on her tear-streaked face. "What would Kayla say?"

Jaden smiled. "She would've asked why it took me so long to do that."

Iri's face sobered. "Yes, she would've, wouldn't she? Still no word on her—or from her?"

"No, but that's not why I'm here."

Something in his scent or his coloring must've given him away. "You're here because you need my help?"

"Yes. Do you feel up to it?"

Iri was already off the bed. "Anything is better than sitting here replaying what happened."

Jaden rose slowly. That was undoubtedly true. "You'll need something warm. We're heading for the mountains." Iri faltered, and Jaden rushed to reassure her. "Not that place. Somewhere else."

Without a word, Iri grabbed her coat and then looked at him expectantly. "Spit it out!" Iri demanded when he said nothing.

Again, she had read his uncertainty. "Do you think you'll be okay with flying with Han and I? Or . . . did you want your own glider?" Iri's silence made him bumble on. "I wasn't sure what you'd be up to handling, so if—"

Iri cut him off. "I'll fly with you and Han. Give me a minute to change into my smart suit."

Jaden nodded and left the room.

Seconds later, Iri opened her door. "Let's go."

She strode down the hallway, leaving Jaden watching her retreating figure. How he wished Kayla was here. She would know what to say and how best to comfort Iri. But she wasn't, and that was the tragedy. Jaden's tenuous hold on his self-control slithered through his fingers; his mind racing down all the paths Kayla's fate could've taken. A hand on his arm brought his thoughts to a screeching halt and jerked him back to reality.

"It's no use wondering what happened," Vicken said. "Focus on moving forward. Figure out what the next step is and take it. Trust that enough steps will lead us to her."

Jaden swallowed the lump in his throat. What Vicken said was true. *Am I the only one who can't read other people today?*

Shaking his head, Jaden said, "You're right. Let's deal with this issue and get it squared away. Then we go on from there."

Vicken clapped him on the back. "Good man. Let's go."

Jaden was of half a mind to ask Vicken how he didn't let the worry cripple him. Kayla *was* his daughter. Surely he must feel something? Covertly studying Vicken's face as they moved back toward the stairs, all Jaden found was an impassive front.

"I've learned not to let things show if I don't want my enemies finding my weaknesses. You would be wise to do the same," Vicken said, not looking at him.

Shivers coursed through Jaden again. *How did Vicken know?* Then Jaden sighed. *How did I think I would get away with watching Vicken without him being aware?*

They reached the roof to find Iri had already connected with Han. When Han spotted Jaden, he swooped down, and seconds later Jaden was scooting into place behind Iri. Then Vicken and his glider joined them, and they set out for the familiar valley in the Shadow Mountains.

CHAPTER EIGHT

Kayla woke, the grogginess of a deep sleep persisting. It took several seconds for her to place where she was, then to recall what happened just before she'd gone under. When she remembered her ring, she inhaled sharply. Relief surged as her fingers rubbed against the familiar stone. *Yes, it's still there.*

She'd never heard of any hospital allowing you to keep your jewelry on for a surgery. Or giving its patients water before a procedure. That thought still rankled. Then the painful truth punched her like an iron fist in the gut. She groaned.

This *wasn't* her world. It was Slurpy's. To survive, she would have to learn how to play in it. For her first "lesson" she would map the layout of this place. *No use planning an escape if you don't know where you're going.*

That first step decided, Kayla took the next. Ever so slowly, she tried sitting up. Disappointment countered her initial delight when dizziness forced her back down. *Okay, not ready to be vertical yet.*

Deciding she could still evaluate her injuries, she inched her hands over her body. Starting with her head, she found bandages. *No surprise. Head injury confirmed—check. Probable cause of excruciating headache and dizziness—check.*

Her fingers worked down her neck and stopped. She hadn't thought about it earlier, but there was no doubt now. Her medallion was missing. It was a bitter blow, enough to make her want to cry, and she wasn't one giving to crying about things. Kayla tried consoling herself with the possibility she'd lost her medallion in the crash. That someone hadn't taken it from her while she lay unconscious and defenseless. She could get lost in a sea of misery if she allowed it. Best not to dwell on things she couldn't change, even if the loss devastated her.

Forcing herself onward, her hands continued their assessment, probing her shoulders and arms and upper body. *Bandages around my left forearm. Tenderness along my ribs.* She couldn't quite reach her legs. *If I can just roll onto my side . . .* Kayla almost passed out from the pain lancing her leg. Her eyes watered, and she panted as she tried breathing past the agony.

She had most likely broken her left leg. She leaned back against her pillow. All her serious injuries were on her left side, either caused by the impact with the Gaptor or from the 'pod hitting the ground. *It doesn't really matter which. I won't be running off anytime soon.*

Kayla closed her eyes. Weariness swamped her. *If I can lie here for a few minutes and think, perhaps I might come up with a better plan.*

She didn't mean to fall asleep, but when she woke sometime later, she was glad she had. For the first time since she'd arrived, her mind was clear. Her body didn't ache so violently. And could that empty feeling possibly be hunger?

"Hello?" Kayla's voice was croaky and barely above a whisper. She tried again. "Hello?"

No reply. She wished there was light. *Don't my caregivers know humans need sunshine? That sunshine facilitates healing?* About to call out again, she froze when there was a sound at the far end of the . . . room? *Is that a key turning in a lock?* Something ticked across the floor. *A Gaptor's claws?* The odor assaulting her nose provided the answer. *Ugh!* A clang made her jump as metal bashed on metal. Then the skittering retreated. *Definitely claws on the floor. But what was it doing here?*

Tentatively, Kayla reached out to where the banging had sounded.

Drifting, her fingers found something. Running them along the cold, unyielding bars that formed the frame, she created a mental picture. It was a metal stand. *Do I even want to know what that thing put on the table?*

Images of torture tools lined up on a tray paraded across her mind. She grimaced. Even though Clara's dreams had hinted he was a monster, Slurpy hadn't resorted to torturing them. *Let's hope he's not about to start now.*

Taking a breath, Kayla dared to allow her fingers over the rim of the tray on the stand. A curved edge. Then . . . Kayla yanked her hand back. *Ow! That was hot! Food?* Kayla sniffed. Discerning anything over the still pungent stench that clung to the air courtesy of the beast that had delivered the tray was difficult.

"It's food."

Kayla knew that voice. "Tarise?"

The last time Kayla had seen her, Tarise had been racing away in her 'pod, furious because she thought Kayla stole Jaden. But here she was. Had they attacked Tarise's 'pod right before they attacked hers? It was possible, considering Kayla had left within minutes of Tarise. "Are you a prisoner too?"

"Just eat the food."

The way Tarise said that sounded odd. With emphasis on the word *just*. Did that mean she didn't want to talk to Kayla? Or something else? Kayla opted for a friendly approach. "Are you hurt?"

No reply. Options chased through Kayla's mind. *If they took Tarise's 'pod down the same way as mine, maybe her injuries make it difficult to talk? Or the Gaptors zapped her with their EMPs? Without a relic stone, she can't counter the numbing effects. If that's true, though, she wouldn't be able to speak at all. Then again, her strained voice might be because the effects were wearing off. Hadn't Jaden's parents said this was the reason for them being subjected to repeated EMP blasts?*

"How long have we been here?" Silence. Kayla debated broaching the elephant in the room, but decided against it. Discussing Jaden would only alienate Tarise further, meaning there would be no chance of answers. Not that she was getting answers, anyway. "Tarise?"

There was an audible click. *A door closing? Was the monster waiting by the door, listening to us all this time?* Kayla waited a few more moments, holding her breath. The silence was literally deafening. Nothing at all.

Kayla wasn't sure how, but she knew she was alone again. *Does that mean Tarise is free to walk around here? That she isn't a prisoner? How can that be?*

Her stomach growled. Kayla reached for the plate. *I'll think better on a full stomach.*

Kayla took her time, chewing her food before swallowing. The food was bland but palatable. Obviously no internal surgery or they wouldn't give her solids. Feeling around the rim of the plate, she found a glass. Lifting it, she sniffed at the contents. No discernible odor. Cautiously, she took a sip. Water. Gulping down a few mouthfuls, she set the glass down before eating more food.

Whether it was having food in her stomach or the after-effects of surgery, she wasn't sure, but Kayla suddenly felt tired beyond reason. She flopped back onto her pillow. *I needed surgery to repair my leg? The break must've been bad.* Reaching down, she brushed light fingers over the bandages that swathed her upper leg. There was still a fair amount of pain. Not as much as she expected, though.

She yawned. *Wow, I'm exhausted. Yes, that's what I was thinking. Am I tired from the surgery or because my stomach's full?* Another yawn swallowed her face. Kayla was too tired to work it out now. She would sleep. And when she woke, she would plan more.

Hours later, when she finally resurfaced, she almost wished she hadn't slept. Her brain was sluggish again. Thinking was an effort. Her body ached like she had forgotten to take her pain meds. And she was . . . *going to be sick!* Kayla lurched sideways, getting her head off the bed before her stomach contents spewed out.

The retching didn't stop until long after her stomach was empty. *Perhaps it wasn't such a great idea to eat solids after anesthesia.* She wiped her mouth, then debated what to do with the goo coating her hand. *I don't want to dirty my sheets. Who knows how long it would be before they gave me clean linens? If they even will.*

47

But there weren't exactly other options. Grimacing, she plucked at the sheet until she had one of the far corners in her clean hand. Then she wiped her hands and face before flinging the sheet back to the far corner it had come from.

The semi-violent motion had her head pounding again. More dry heaving over the edge of the bed followed. When it finally ceased, she sagged back against the pillows, exhausted. The sickly smell of puke stuck in her nose, not making her feel any better. She wished she had some water or a warm washcloth.

This time, she didn't hear the door open. *Perhaps because a door didn't open? Has Tarise been here with me this whole time?*

Tarise coughed. "Ugh, it smells disgusting in here."

One answer at last. Tarise couldn't have been here, or she would've heard Kayla vomiting and no doubt said something snarky sooner. If she wasn't in the room, was she free to enter Kayla's room? Or had someone forced her in? Without light, it was impossible to know.

"Any chance of getting a light in here?"

Tarise grunted. "If that's what you want, my suggestion would be to *not* ask for it. They have a habit of turning what you want against you."

That tone again. Like Tarise was speaking in code. Or was Kayla so desperate for answers she was making things up? Maybe she should try another line of questioning. "Do you know if any of the others are here?"

A distinct pause. Kayla probably wouldn't have noticed at any other time. Except now, with her senses on high alert, the pause had Kayla thinking of agents in interrogation rooms with hidden comms in their ears. Was Tarise being fed questions and/or answers?

"I don't know."

The reply was flat, lacking that odd tone. Maybe a true answer? Another test then. "Are you free to walk around?"

A dry laugh. "How do you know I'm walking?" There was only bitterness in her tone this time.

"Did they do something to you?"

"Isn't someone always doing something to someone else?"

Not an answer. Why is Tarise being so vague? Kayla's mind went back to the hidden comm theory. If Tarise was being fed questions and answers, it meant someone was watching them. Their conversations were being monitored. Perhaps this was what Tarise had been trying to warn her about while not saying the words.

Kayla remained quiet as she thought of how best to deal with this. It prompted Tarise to speak first.

"Afraid?"

Yes, petrified, but I'm not telling you that. Silence had benefited her a moment ago. Kayla would allow it time to work again. What felt like about five minutes later, Tarise relented.

"If you won't speak, I'm leaving."

This time, Kayla heard the click. But it wasn't the sound she had been listening for. Her ears had been searching for different sounds, and she had heard them, soft, yet unmistakable. The squeak of rubber on tile. The whisper of hands pushing wheels. Tarise was in a wheelchair. *Ziggety, what have they done to her?*

CHAPTER NINE

Jaden hadn't wanted to meet near the valley where the battle had taken place. Not only did it hold too many raw memories, but they'd also just used it when last meeting with the Legion. Who knew how much scouting a traitor might've done in the area in case of an ambush? They couldn't pick a place the traitor might be familiar with. It had to be somewhere new.

This spot was perfect. Jaden scanned the familiar landscape. Here, all those months ago, he had first seen the Gaptors. The place he and his family and friends had traversed since childhood. An area Jaden had hiked too many times to count.

He surveyed the area from high above, as Han circled. Sapphire Pool marked the very end of the trail. Most of the blue ice covering the lake during winter had melted, elevating the lake's water levels and giving the cerulean water a clear, crystalline quality that begged dipping a hand in and savoring its perfection.

Despite the elevated water levels, plenty of boulders still surrounded the pool with bare patches of coarse sand between. Jagged cliffs enclosed the lake, with the cliff at the far end crowned by its ever-present glacier. The glacier, blazing white in the sunlight, drew attention to countless sparkling drops oozing out and tracing thin silver streams down to the lake far below.

Jaden studied the surrounding cliffs. They were the perfect natural barrier. There was only one way to reach the lake. Only one way in, meaning only one way out. An ideal place to corral the Legion while they found the mole.

When they did, escape would be impossible. Or at least, Jaden hoped so. Technically, gliders could escape by flying, so there *was* a second way out. Jaden had to trust Han and Pallaton had that covered.

As the Legion milled around the natural opening, like espresso swirling through milky coffee, Jaden studied them. They filled the space until it was their own. Had they made the valleys near Sven's home theirs too?

Another question came back to haunt Jaden. "How do you think Pallaton got the gliders here from Sven's in such a short time?"

Han shrugged. "I wondered that myself. The only answer that makes any sense is that Zareh had a hand in it."

Zareh! If anyone could pull off the impossible, it was him. That meant Pallaton had a way of contacting him. Something the Legion's leader hadn't shared with Jaden. It also meant Zareh knew they were trying to find a traitor. Scowling, Jaden seethed at being kept in the dark. Again.

Han sensed Jaden's anger. "Don't let it bother you. If you think you don't have all the answers, neither do I."

"There has to be a better way to do this than stumbling around in the dark all the time, stubbing our toes!"

"Agreed, but I also understand compartmentalizing the information minimizes the chances of the usurper beating us to the prize."

Jaden couldn't refute that. Addressing Iri, seated in front of him, he said, "Are you ready?"

Iri nodded.

"Then let's land and finish this," Jaden told Han.

"I think we'll stay up here and keep watch from the air," Vicken said, reminding Jaden he and his glider were there.

Jaden nodded. No sense telling the man it was a solid plan. Vicken was probably already ten steps ahead of them now that he knew what they hoped to accomplish.

Once Han dropped Iri and Jaden, they waited near the entrance to the enchanting lake and observed as gliders landed after yet another unheard and unseen command from Pallaton.

"It's beautiful up here," Iri said, breaking the silence she'd held since they'd left.

Her tone hinted at something else. Focusing on her, Jaden found Iri fidgeting. Instantly, he understood. *Finally! Something I divined!*

He took Iri's hand in his own, pulling her around so he could look into her eyes. "Don't worry. They don't have to know how you do what you do. And if I'm right, the thought of a traitor will incense the other gliders so much that they'll focus on the villain and ignore you."

Iri attempted a smile. "Thanks."

"Besides, what you do is awesome. How could anyone not want to know you?"

"You'd be surprised," Iri muttered.

Ugh, I blew it again. Jaden, when will you learn to say less?

Iri grinned. "I appreciate you trying to make me feel better though."

"And I suppose that's meant to make *me* feel better?"

"That depends. Does it?"

Chuckling, Jaden shook his head. Han landed and hopped over, assuming a protective stance behind them. He ruffled his wings, settling them. But when he did it a second time and then a third within seconds, Jaden turned.

"What's wrong?"

"I had a thought."

"What?"

"Can Iri do this?"

It was Iri's turn to look at him. "Do what?"

Han grimaced. "I just assumed your skills would work equally well on gliders as they do on humans. I never thought to test that theory before we brought you here."

Shrugging, Iri said, "There's only one way to find out. What's your name?"

Han blinked, surprise keeping him mute.

"Humor me," Iri said. "Just answer the questions."

Obligingly, Han replied, "Ohanzee."

"Is your voyager's name Jaden?"

"Yes."

"Have you always lived in this world?"

"No."

"Do you love Taz?"

Han's face was priceless. Jaden guffawed. Han glared at him and then Iri. "What kind of question is that?"

Iri giggled. "Never mind. Yes, my abilities work on gliders."

"You know what you're looking for?"

"Anything that will show us the traitor."

"It's time then," Han said, dipping his head toward Pallaton.

It surprised Jaden when he heard the low whistle this time. The assembled gliders quieted and looked at Pallaton expectantly. It turned into curiosity when Pallaton took to the skies above, intensifying when Han, not Pallaton, addressed them.

"Thank you for coming. You have all served the Legion faithfully since they sent here you so many centuries ago. Your long years of service are both respected and appreciated. That is why, it is with regret, that I must tell you we have a traitor in our midst."

Iri's hand shot out. "That one and that one!"

Jaden was still wrapping his mind around the fact there were two when Han surged upward. Han darted toward the first culprit, and Pallaton and Vicken's glider somehow knew to go for the other.

Pandemonium broke loose. The traitors took to the air. Gliders near them chittered and squeaked, chasing the fleeing renegades. The air throbbed with beating wings and harsh cries.

Jaden's arm went up, shielding himself from the wings threatening to slap him down. Ducking, he grabbed Iri and pulled her toward him. In one fluid motion, he pushed her down so she was on the ground, then crouched over her.

An unearthly scream made Jaden's head turn involuntarily. His heart leaped into his mouth. The traitor closest to them was being ripped apart by the gliders swarming him. Appalled, Jaden watched a wing turn to shreds. The traitor fell sideways, then tumbled downward. The attacking gliders streamed after him.

A shrill whistle rent the air. All motion ceased, like someone had pushed the pause button in the middle of the action scene. *What is going on?*

"Kill them, do not. Need them we do."

Jaden would know that convoluted way of speaking anywhere. *Zareh!* "What are you doing here?"

Zareh turned blazing eyes on Jaden. "No time for your nonsense, have I. Take with me, the traitors I will. But not before you a piece of my mind, I give. Grateful, you cannot be? Always, so enraged you are. And endless questions ask, you must!"

Jaden had never seen Zareh angry before. But instead of making him back down, it only fueled the fires simmering within. "Have you ever considered why I might be angry? Did you give me a choice in all this? Or Kayla? Or any of the others you dragged into your little war? No, you thought you knew best and just decided for us, people's personal opinions be damned."

Zareh bared his teeth, each sharp little point accentuated by the sunshine. "True, that is not! Only put you on the path you were destined for, did I."

But Jaden wasn't listening. He had a few things to say, and he would say them. "Why do you always have to be so cryptic? Would it kill you to give us the answers we need? Did it ever occur to you that the information you're withholding might allow us to finish the mission sooner? Without all the cloak and dagger stuff? Or that if you'd bothered to give us enough warning before the last battle, Kayla would be safe. Bree would still be with us. And we would know what in the hell we should do! We wouldn't be floundering around in the dark!"

Before Jaden had time to react, Zareh bounced into the air and hovered inches from Jaden's face, his sharp little beak snapping a hair's breadth from Jaden's nose. At this range, Zareh's eyes took up his whole face. More frightening, his eyes were glowing. The fire burning in those dark, glittering coals blistered Jaden's face, the heat crinkling the skin on his cheek.

Jaden scrambled back, a hand gingerly touching his seared cheek. Zareh's features were feral. *Maybe confronting Zareh this way wasn't one of my finer decisions. Where's Kayla when I need her? She's always my voice of reason.*

Attempting to pacify the little beast, Jaden raised both hands in a gesture of resignation. "Calm down! You'd be asking the same questions if you were in my position."

Zareh growled, a guttural sound that made Jaden want to take another step back. "Dare to presume, you should not. Your prime question already answered, Han has. Debate it no more, I shall." Turning his back on Jaden, Zareh faced the assembled gliders. He flicked a hand toward the traitors subdued on the ground. "How fare they?"

Jaden had never felt more dismissed in his entire life. It was as if Zareh had wiped him from existence. Only then did Jaden notice the two captives—make that one captive. The glider that had lost a wing had succumbed to his injuries. The other members of the Legion looked ready to butcher the sole survivor. But with another flick of his hand, Zareh took to the air, followed by a group of gliders leading the hapless prisoner. In an instant, they disappeared.

The air whooshed out of Jaden. It was worse than being sucker-punched. He sank down, defeated. Zareh had come and gone, taking the traitor with him. Jaden had no more answers now than when they'd arrived.

As he dragged in deep, calming breaths, his brain began functioning again. Had Zareh just said Han had answered his question? If so, was Zareh invisible? It was the only way he could've known what Han had said. But then Jaden remembered the first time he'd met Zareh at the very beginning of their mission.

Jaden and Kayla had just survived their first Gaptor attack. They hadn't known their encounters with otherworldly beings weren't yet over. Still in shock, they made their way up to Kayla's room. And Zareh had been waiting for them.

Considering all the interactions they'd had with Zareh since, he had provided the most information then. Jaden's face soured. He couldn't believe he'd thought Zareh was being stingy back then.

Zareh had told them he was from another world. When Jaden asked how he had known what he and Kayla had been up to, Zareh said he could see them from his world. He had likened the situation to looking in a mirror: to seeing what was happening, but not being able to communicate across the barrier.

But he'd also said the reason it took so long to reach them and render aid was because he needed time to cross between worlds. If that was true, Zareh had lied, either then or now. Either he could travel between worlds instantaneously, or there was no mirror and he could do the impossible and make himself invisible. Both meant he'd waited to help them.

Jaden growled. *When is any of this ever going to make any sense?*

Deciding he didn't want to lose himself in the sea of endless questions, he searched for Han and found him whirling about with the other gliders over the lake.

A hand touched his shoulder. "Was that Zareh?"

Jaden remembered he wasn't alone. Iri looked at him, worry written all over her face. But her question was the catalyst he needed to bring himself back.

"You didn't meet Zareh when he came to warn us about the battle?"

"No, I went to the bathroom, and when I returned, he'd already left. Markov told me about his visit. So was that him?"

"Yes. As aggravating as ever."

When Iri just hummed, Jaden asked, "What does 'hmm' mean?"

"He was here before."

Jaden's face scrunched up. *Can you all please stop talking in riddles?* He tried for patience, which would've pleased Kayla. "What do you mean?"

"I mean he was already here when we arrived. I didn't understand what the colors meant. They were there, but I couldn't attach them to anything." Iri frowned. "This is the first time that ever happened."

"When you say you couldn't attach the color to anything, do you mean you could see a color but not a person?"

Iri nodded. "He was here the whole time, watching us but somehow invisible."

Well, that answers my question. But he had to be sure. "Did his color or scent change to show he was lying when he said . . ." Jaden trailed off. Now that he thought about it, Zareh hadn't actually said he wasn't there the whole time. Jaden ran his hands through his hair and growled for the second time that day. "Never mind. It's time to go home. Ready?"

"Before we go, one last question." Jaden nodded. "Is Zareh a celestial being?" She giggled when Jaden gaped. "I only ask because his colors are so vibrant. And they have an afterglow. I've never seen that on anyone else."

Jaden shrugged. "Your guess is as good as mine. You saw how few answers he gave. He says nothing he doesn't mean to. Which doesn't make our task any easier."

"I suppose not. Maybe we should plan what we really want to ask him. And then next time he appears, you ask the questions, and I'll study his reactions. We might get more answers that way."

Jaden grinned. "I knew I liked you."

Beaming, Iri said, "Then we just need to decide what we want to ask."

CHAPTER TEN

Two days later, Jaden, Iri, Atu, and their gliders gathered on the field of Atu's healing center. It was early afternoon, and the air was balmy. Jaden lifted his chin and let the sun play over his face, soaking in the delicious heat. The moment spoiled when he thought about Kayla's whereabouts. Was she warm? Was she being taking care of? Or had they just left her to . . .

"I'm ready." Taz beamed as she joined them.

Jaden turned questioning eyes on Atu. "What's the prognosis, Doc?"

"Let's wait until after her test flight to establish that, shall we?" With a nod to Taz, Atu said, "Show us what you can do. Remember, nothing too strenuous at first!"

Taz lifted effortlessly into the air and then made a slow arc away from them. Han was examining her every move.

"Everything look okay?"

"Tazanna looks strong," was Han's only comment before he took to the air.

Aren joined him, and they raced to join Taz. Mostly, their gliders remained where their voyagers could monitor Taz's progress, only dipping further afield now and then.

"Have they increased their speed?" Jaden asked a moment later.

"They have," Atu confirmed.

When the gliders completed their circuits, they made their way back, with Han and Aren landing ahead of Taz. The waiting group applauded as she dropped next to them, executing a perfect landing.

"I believe I'm ready to begin our training sessions again," Taz purred, basking in their positive affirmations.

Jaden gave Atu a playful shove. "Really? You had to heal her this quickly so she's back to fighting form? You know what that means for us, right?"

Everyone laughed. Even Taz.

"It's nice to hear you in better spirits," Taz said, so only Jaden could hear.

Her tone made it clear he wasn't the only one missing Kayla. Jaden stood on his toes so he could reach Taz's neck. He massaged the soft fur along the ridge there. "We'll find her."

Taz's eyes were bright gazing back at him. "I know you will."

"How come I don't get massages like she does?" Han complained.

Jaden laughed and turned from Taz to bestow the same affections on Han.

"Okay, enough with all the mushy stuff." Han's eyes were still a little glazed. "Now that Tazanna is healthy again, what are our plans?"

"Use the device engineered we have to find the Gaptors, you do."

They all jumped. Jaden was surprised their gliders hadn't noticed Zareh sneaking up on them. Jaden's eyes snapped to Iri. She grimaced, understanding his disappointment. They hadn't expected Zareh to return so soon. They had prepared no questions. Jaden groaned. Hadn't he said once before that the only thing he could expect on this mission was the unexpected? As such, shouldn't he have planned for Zareh's unforseen return?

"Would you care to tell us more, Honored One?"

Honored One? Jaden wanted to laugh out loud. *How can Taz call him that?* Sobering, he remembered Taz had known Zareh—or at least known about him—far longer than Jaden had. *Should I be more deferen-*

tial? Does this little imp have the power to set my path? That thought made him laugh out loud, although it was a bitter sound.

When everyone turned and stared, Jaden waved a hand. "Sorry, carry on."

How can I think he can't *direct my path when that's exactly what he did setting me on this mission?* The thought made Jaden sick. He felt Iri watching him and spared her a quick but ineffectual smile. She frowned but said nothing. Jaden's skin suddenly tingled in warning.

Whirling, he caught Zareh giving him a death stare. The weight of it hit Jaden front and center. It was a fierce reminder that Zareh might be small, but his power was not. Jaden could all but feel himself shrinking under that gaze.

Satisfied he had made his point, Zareh averted his gaze and answered Taz. "The traitor, captured by you, useful proved. Give us the last key, he did. Functional our machine, it rendered."

Taz frowned. "Machine, Honored One?"

Jaden didn't understand what Zareh was talking about either.

Zareh gave an impatient wave of his short arms. "Tell you about the unique frequency the Gaptors bodies emit, I did. Remember that, you do?" Taz nodded, and he continued. "Working on a device, that frequency to pinpoint, we have been. But to test it, a live Gaptor we needed. Served that purpose, the traitor did."

Jaden understood. "Your machine finds the Gaptor nests!"

"It does. Waiting for you at your home, the device is. Use it to eradicate the nests here, you must.

Yeah, yeah, but what about the most important thing? Jaden couldn't help himself. "Did you ask that traitor where Kayla is?"

Zareh pinned him with another stare. "Patience, young one. Eager to recover Kayla, I know you are. Do that we shall, enough time being given."

A speeding train rushed through Jaden's head. He wanted it to slow down, but it careened onward. Not bothering to order his thoughts, he spat them out as quickly as he could. "You do know that if we don't find Kayla, we can't complete this mission?" When Zareh only continued staring, Jaden tossed his hands up. "It's not only me that needs her. Can't you see that?"

Zareh chittered. "Important, Kayla is. Find her, we shall. But more important, it is now those nests to destroy. Possible Kayla thre may be, it is. On her whereabouts, no word have I, so no certainty there be that in our world she is. Just as easily here, she could be."

"And it's equally possible the usurper is here in our world!" Jaden spat. Zareh bared his teeth, and it reminded Jaden why he should be careful of upsetting him. "Can you be a little more proactive in trying to find her? Please?"

Zareh sighed theatrically and rolled his eyes. "Do that, I will. Possible it is that help with such a task, you can."

Jaden perked up. "How?"

"When these nests you find, search for a communication system, you should."

"Communication system?" Jaden repeated. He felt like an idiot.

"That which makes the clicking sound you and Kayla heard."

"Oh, right."

"If such a system you find while destroying the nests you are, secure it you must."

"Why? Don't you already have a way to intercept their communications? Isn't that how you knew they were gathering to attack us?"

"A process have we, but perfect, it is not. Considerable delay in the data being interpreted, there is. If an actual communication system of theirs we had, almost instantaneously on the communications we could act."

Something crystallized for Jaden. This was why Zareh hadn't warned them about that terrible impending battle earlier. This had caused the delay between the communication and Zareh coming to alert them. "That's why your warning was so close to the attack?"

Jaden almost didn't believe his eyes when Zareh nodded. *An actual answer!*

"Why the device we need, this is. Destroy it, do not. Steal it, you should. And no trace leave that took it you did."

"Sure, piece of cake," Jaden muttered, wondering how they would accomplish that. "Anything else?" He wanted to add, "Your high and mightiness," but an image of those sharp little teeth flashed across his mind and stilled his tongue.

"Suffice, that will. More details to Tazanna, provide I will." A flighty series of clicks and twitters between Zareh and Taz followed.

Jaden frowned. Did Zareh think there was another traitor? What other "details" was he giving Taz? Why wouldn't Zareh share it with them too? Rage surged through him once more, flushing his face. He clenched and unclenched his fists as he waited out the twittering.

When it ceased, he opened his mouth, but between one blink and the next, Zareh vanished. Cursing under his breath and ready to smash his fist into something, Jaden stomped away. Atu and Iri trailed after him.

"Why are you so angry?"

Iri's question only intensified the need to hit something. But Kayla wouldn't have approved. Jaden breathed and counted to ten before replying. "Why does Zareh never give us the information? Right there, instead of telling us, he passed the information along to Taz. Why?"

Iri shrugged. "Perhaps it was easier to explain to Taz since neither of them are from this world. Maybe their communication system is faster than ours. Maybe their history means he can share a lot of information without having to explain things."

Jaden's mouth opened and closed. *Huh, I didn't think of that.* "Be that as it may, do you think he's trying to hide something from us?"

It was Iri's turn to pause. "It's possible. But I sensed nothing deceitful in him right then."

"Being who he is, do you think he can hide those things from you?"

"I guess. But if that's true, why didn't he hide himself at the lake when we were trying to find the traitor?"

Another good question. The world was conspiring against him today. Time to give this up. "How about we get out of here?"

If the sudden change in topic threw Iri or Atu, neither showed it. Instead, they traipsed after Jaden back the way they'd come. They found their gliders waiting where they'd left them.

"Time to head home?" Han asked.

"Yes, please." The gliders took to the air. While they waited for their gliders to swing back around, Jaden noticed Atu combing through his ever-present pouch. "Something wrong?"

"No, I was just checking my supplies."

"All good?"

"No, I need to hunt down some herbs to replenish a few items. Aren and I will be home later."

"Stay safe," Jaden said as Iri leaped for Han and he followed.

The trip home was uneventful. Han dropped Jaden and Iri, then wasted no time on goodbyes as he streaked away with Taz. Han's joy at being reunited with a healthy Taz was palpable.

As Jaden and Iri watched them leave, he asked, "So, Han *does* love Taz?"

"Now what sort of friend would I be if I betrayed a trust?" Iri said with an impish grin.

Chuckling, Jaden led her indoors, relieved she seemed to have regained some of her levity. "Time we found that device Zareh mentioned."

But search as they did, they came up empty.

"He said it would be here, right?" Jaden asked.

"He did." Iri frowned. "I see now why you get upset with him. It would've been helpful if he'd told us *where* in your home it would be waiting."

Jaden grinned. "I'm glad you're coming around to my side of things. You see what he does? He gives you information, and you think you understand only to find you have no clue when it's time for action."

"I say we call it quits. Perhaps he told Taz where we can find it. We'll have to wait until we see them again."

"I agree. Let's find some food!"

With a chuckle, Iri followed him to the kitchen.

CHAPTER ELEVEN

Kayla felt like they had abandoned her. She hadn't had contact with anyone in days, not even Tarise. Not that she minded not hearing or smelling the Gaptor entering and leaving her room, delivering her food and water while she slept.

Two thoughts struck her. First, her head had stopped pounding. Second, she was sleeping all the time. Worry resurfaced at the second thought.

An infection in her leg would explain all the sleeping and the continued mental fuzziness. It would also explain the pain that still flared whenever she tried to put weight on her leg, enough to make her want to pass out.

But while the pain hadn't receded one iota, it also wasn't spreading. Shouldn't she feel the effects in other areas if her leg was infected? She would have a fever. But she didn't.

Kayla was still working through the problem when someone spoke. "Enough time on your own?"

Again, she hadn't heard Tarise enter. "How long have you been sitting there?"

A bitter laugh. "So you worked it out, did you?"

"Tarise, what did they do to you?"

"Nothing I care to repeat. But I can tell you I haven't seen Jaden or any of the others while they've been carting me around."

No tone. A flat statement. Except for the last three words, tinged with . . . regret? Anger? Resignation?

Tarise sighed. "Are you still not speaking to me?"

Kayla realized she hadn't responded. "Thank you for telling me the others aren't here. I guess it's just the two of us then. When did you get here?"

"About the same time as you."

Vague. "Not before?"

"Why would I get here before you?"

"Because you left Jaden's house before I did. Meaning they would've taken your 'pod out first. Ergo, you could've arrived here before me."

Tarise snorted. "You didn't leave that long after me. Why would they bring us here separately?"

To mask her sharp intake of breath, Kayla pretended to clear her throat. *Does Tarise know she slipped up? Should I press her on the point? Or pretend I didn't notice and continue this charade even though Tarise is potentially playing me? Either of her own accord or because she's being coerced?*

Kayla went with playing dumb. "I suppose it makes sense they brought us here together. Probably why you haven't seen Jaden and the others. I expect they stayed at the house long after we left, and none of them were stupid enough to leave on their own."

Silence. It only fed Kayla's suspicions.

"How's the food?"

The radical change in topic was a clear sign Tarise didn't intend further discussing either her abduction or their friends, which only added to the picture Kayla was painting. While their last conversation had aroused Kayla's suspicions, today's discussion was doing nothing except confirm them. Considering that, she should answer the question. No use letting Tarise guess Kayla didn't trust her. "Palatable."

"At least it's better than the water. You'd think they'd give us something else to drink now and then."

There it was. That weird tone again. And Kayla finally understood.

The water! Tarise is trying to warn me about the water. Kayla's mind raced. The EMPs couldn't affect her because her ring countered the numbing effects. Therefore, her captors had to find another way to incapacitate her so she couldn't escape. What better way than drugging the water?

Testing her conclusion, Kayla said, "Yeah, you'd think they'd vary our beverage options as much as our food."

"I'm glad you agree."

That flat tone again. *It must mean she's telling the truth*, Kayla decided. *But why would Tarise help if she's playing me?* The only feasible answer was that Kayla still didn't have the whole picture. She would have to work on that. "How about staying for dinner?"

Tarise laughed, the sound mirthless. "Inviting me on a date?"

Kayla wasn't sure how to react. One minute Tarise was warning her; the next she was displaying her contempt. *Maybe that's part of the show? To stop those who are monitoring our interactions from guessing Tarise is trying to help me?*

Kayla's headache worsened. The mental gymnastics weren't helping. "No, I guess we'll never be friends. Why don't you disappear down whatever hole you crawled out of?"

Kayla's tone was cooler than she'd meant it to be. But if Tarise was playing a part, Kayla could do no less. She had to make those listening dismiss any notions of collusion.

"Ah, there's the Kayla we all know and love. That's my cue to go. Enjoy your meal."

Slight emphasis on the word *meal*. Tarise was definitely telling her not to drink the water. It also confirmed that Tarise wasn't holding her less-than-polite comment against her. "Bye then," Kayla replied, but the click indicated Tarise had left. It didn't matter. As long as whoever was listening had heard Kayla supposedly didn't care, that was the important thing.

Minutes later, there was the familiar scrape of claws on the floor. Kayla quickly sucked in air and held her breath. She didn't want to smell the Gaptor. The stench always made her feel sick. Dumping the food tray, the beast lumbered out again.

Kayla released her held breath. Still, with her next intake of air, the creature's lingering stink made her wish she had held on a little longer. She waited until the nausea passed and for some time after that before she reached for the tray.

If she wasn't already sure someone was listening to her conversations, she knew now. Instead of water, the plastic mug held juice. Probably still laced with whatever they'd been using to drug her.

But she needed fluids. For a moment, Kayla regretted her comment about the water. It provided better hydration than juice. Deciding she would leave the juice until after she'd eaten, she finished what was on the tray. Only when she reached for the juice did she figure it out.

They *had* been listening. This time, they had drugged the food. Her eyes were already drooping. Maybe if she could get in a few mouthfuls of juice, she might dilute the . . .

Kayla had never seen such a strange sight. She blinked, trying to make sense of it. A tree shimmered with iridescent drops. They plopped off every branch, steaming and hissing where they hit the ground, as though a huge temperature differential caused the reaction.

Bending down, Kayla touched the ground. It was neither hot nor cold. It must be the water. She took a step toward the tree, thirsty beyond reason. Then she saw the pits forming where the water hit. Not a temperature difference, and it wasn't water—it was some kind of acid, burning into the ground.

Kayla gaped as the pits became pockets. Then holes. All the while, the tree continued spitting its poisonous beads. The holes became craters. Without warning, the earth beneath her gave way. Kayla was falling. She screamed, trying to latch onto something, anything, to break her fall.

Her hand hit something. A root. She grabbed at it. But the root felt wrong. Then it writhed and moved under her hand. She shrieked, the fangs of a snake suddenly in her face. Kayla let go. The snake couldn't save her and getting bitten wasn't on her to-do list.

Abruptly, Kayla hit something, and her leg felt like it had snapped in two. The wail of pain sounded wrong.

She woke, her throat hoarse from screaming. Sobbing, Kayla

clutched at her leg. That part had been real. Had she been thrashing about in her bed, aggravating the injury?

"Why the commotion?"

Tarise's voice was cold, uncaring. It took Kayla more than a moment to compose herself. "Sorry, bad dream."

Barely a beat passed before Tarise said, "It must've been something you ate. Go back to sleep."

And there it was. The slight emphasis on the word *ate*, confirming what Kayla realized right before she passed out. They had drugged the food. Except they hadn't designed the drug and the food to work together, causing the nightmare instead of a deep, dreamless sleep.

"Maybe I'll stick to water from now on." Kayla hoped Tarise understood.

"Do what you must." Tarise's reply was blasé. "I'll do what I can to convince them not to give you that meal again as it obviously doesn't agree with you." That almost sounded compassionate until Tarise added, "I can't have you interrupting my beauty sleep."

She delivered the last sentence with spite. Both a warning and . . . what? Irritation? Either way, another slip. For someone who was a genius, Tarise wasn't acting like it.

Her leg shot out another burst of agony. Kayla groaned and gingerly touched her leg. "Is there any way you could get them to come and look at my leg? It's killing me. I think it's infected."

Silence. Then a hand touched her forehead. Kayla got such a fright she jerked back. How had Tarise become so good at sneaking around? The voice whispering in her ear was even worse. A slithering hiss of sound and air as the words rushed past her ear, almost too soft to hear.

"It's an implant in your leg meant to keep you from moving."

Then Tarise leaned back, her voice loud and infused with boredom. "You don't have a fever. There's no infection. You'll live. I'm going back to bed. Try not to wake me again."

A moment later the door clicked, and Kayla was alone again. Her brain buzzed. So much information in such a short time. She almost couldn't focus on a single thing. Forcing herself to calm down, she began mentally checking off the list in no particular order. First, Tarise had been walking! She hadn't been in a wheelchair. So either the wheelchair had been a ploy, or Tarise's injuries had healed enough to allow her to walk again. Second, Tarise had needed an excuse to get close to her to pass along that gem about the implant. That was third —and holy cow! What a third!

Kayla would never have dreamed she had an implant in her leg. All this time, she thought she had broken it. She analyzed her condition clinically, like she should've done earlier considering her medical training. *Yes, it all makes perfect sense. I should've seen this before.*

Itching to test how far she could move her leg before the implant spiked her with pain, she resisted. If someone was listening to their conversations, who was to say they weren't watching as well? If they noticed Kayla testing her leg, it would broadcast Tarise had provided the information and be the end of any chance of escape.

Although that raised the fourth point, something she had wondered countless times before. Why was Tarise helping her? Tarise hated her for "taking Jaden away." Kayla had seen her rage on that rooftop before she left. There was no way someone got over that level of jealousy or resentment in mere days.

It meant only one thing: Tarise needed Kayla as much as Kayla needed her. Without the other, neither would escape. That was why Tarise had warned her about the drugged water. And drugged food. She couldn't have Kayla semi-lucid when they made a run for it.

And that brought Kayla to her final point: She could, most definitely, *not* trust Tarise. It wasn't only the sudden feigned friendship. The so-called "help" Tarise was giving with her warnings. It was also the inconsistencies in her narrative. How had Tarise known the time lapse between the Gaptors taking her and then taking Kayla? How could Tarise "convince them" not to drug the food again? Then there was the sudden absence of the wheelchair. Possibly because Kayla's screams had made Tarise too rushed to remember the wheelchair?

Kayla froze as a horrifying possibility occurred to her. Was Tarise in charge here? Had Tarise somehow orchestrated all of this? As farfetched as that sounded, Kayla couldn't ignore the option. Tarise was playing her own game. And if Kayla didn't figure out what it was, she was in for a world of trouble.

CHAPTER TWELVE

Waking the next morning after a night spent tossing and turning, Jaden was more than irritable. They had no clue to Kayla's location. They still had to find Zareh's device. Then they had to destroy the Gaptor nests *and* locate and liberate a potential communication unit, all without alerting their enemy! What about his original mission? Wasn't that more important?

Grunting as he rolled out of bed, Jaden stumbled to the bathroom. Feeling better after a piping hot shower blasted him, he bounded down the stairs. Reaching the kitchen, he found his mother standing there, a mug of coffee in her hand while she stared into space.

"Mom?"

Clara blinked. "Morning." A smile crossed her face. "Want some breakfast?"

"If you're offering . . . "

Clara's smile only widened as she turned and began taking things out of the refrigerator.

"What were you thinking about?"

"Hmm?" Clara gazed at him absently. Then, as if his words had registered, she said, "I'm glad to be home again."

Should I say it?

"And before you go giving me your puppy dog eyes," Clara said with an eye roll, "I'm fine. I think the little 'interlude' we had with the usurper put a few things into perspective. No, I don't think I'll ever stop being terrified you and Kayla and the others have to deal with all this. That said, I have to believe if Zareh chose you, it's because he believes you can do it. For him to have faith in someone is a powerful thing."

Jaden just sat there. He didn't know what to say. How had Zareh of all people been able to assuage his mother's concerns? He supposed seeing the little rascal pull people across worlds might have been a factor. Should he have been grateful to Zareh for this? Perhaps.

"Well, there's not much more I can say after a speech like that. Except to promise I'll be as careful as possible."

His mother put down the eggs and hugged him. "I know you will. And I believe you can do this."

Jaden suddenly found it hard to swallow past the lump in his throat. Clearing it, he said, "A man's got to do what a man's got to do. But he can't do it on an empty stomach. How about I cut some grape-fruit to get the party started?"

By the time breakfast was ready, his father, Atu, and Iri had joined them. Iri was a surprise addition, having opted to stay over rather than going back to the Melmiques the previous evening. It was a lively breakfast, and as Jaden sat back, replete after his meal, he soaked it all in. All too soon, his father was leaving for work, taking his mother with as she had mentioned running some errands.

With the kitchen suddenly empty, Jaden felt like half of him was missing until Iri covered his hand with her own.

"We're still here. And now that your parents have left, perhaps we can discuss what's next?"

Jaden smiled. "Thanks. And as for your suggestion, I can't say what we do next. We're supposed to find the device and destroy the Gaptor nests, but I am thinking we need the gliders for both."

"In that case, shall we go to the roof and see if they're there?"

Jaden stood. "As soon as we've cleaned the kitchen."

They had just finished wiping down the counters when Jaden

heard the door to the roof opening. How could his mother be home already? He was nearing the stairs when a voice called down.

"Jaden? It's Vicken."

Surprised, Jaden met him as he reached the last step. "Hello. What are you doing here?"

"Viho brought me on Taz's orders." Vicken nodded to Iri and Atu.

Jaden had to think for a moment. Then he remembered Viho was Vicken's glider. "Why?"

"She said Zareh told her my talents would be helpful for whatever you have to do next."

There was no doubt about that. Was that the only thing Zareh had told Taz? "I presume the gliders are all up there?"

"They are. They said to hurry."

Jaden snorted. "Of course she did."

Vicken grinned. "Yeah, it's only ever her that gives the orders."

Chuckling, Jaden turned to Iri and Atu. "Let's grab our packs and go meet the lady before she loses it."

Minutes later they had their suits on, were toting their packs and heading up the stairs.

Vicken muttered something.

"What was that?" Jaden asked.

"Viho was a little sparse on intel when he fetched me. And Taz had no time to chat when I arrived, just shooed me inside for you three. Can you enlighten me? I'm feeling a little like the errand boy today."

Jaden laughed. "How do you feel about scouting Gaptor nests, then destroying them, while hoping to find a mysterious communication device that we must somehow acquire without leaving a trace we took it?"

"Bring it on!"

Jaden was still grinning when they exited onto the roof. "Wow! You didn't tell me *everyone* was here." It was quite the gathering. Not only were Han, Taz, and Aren there with Viho, but Pallaton and several members of the Legion floated nearby "Are we expecting trouble?"

"Zareh thought it prudent to travel in numbers," Taz replied.

"Uh-huh," was all Jaden said as he again wondered what else Taz knew but wasn't telling them. "We're ready to go except for one thing. Did Zareh tell you where we can find the device?" Jaden did a double take. Taz was smirking.

"You didn't find it?" Her voice was saccharine.

"If we had, we'd already be on our way instead of jawing here." That wiped the smirk off her face.

"He said to look under your bed."

Jaden gaped. "Under my bed? What kind of hiding place is that?"

Iri turned smiling eyes on him. "You didn't think to check there first?"

Scowling, Jaden said, "I didn't think he'd put it in such an obvious place. I mean, if you're hiding something there, why bother?"

Iri and Atu doubled over with laughter.

"Stop! It's not funny!"

"Your face sure is," Atu noted between sniggers.

Jaden stomped away and barged through the stairway door. He grumbled all the way to his room where he knelt next to his bed. At first, he saw nothing. It was dark, so he tapped his PAL and turned on his flashlight. Even then, he still had to hunt to find it.

Tucked under the top end of the bed was a chess pawn. Shorter than his little finger, it lay on its side as if abandoned there. If Jaden hadn't cleaned his room—was it really months ago?—he would never have found it with all the other things cluttering up the space. Now, the pawn was the only item, something anyone searching for a "device" could easily have overlooked. Considering the shape and size, perhaps this wasn't such a lousy hiding place.

Jaden closed his fingers around the object, then almost dropped it. *Ow! Hot! Well, it is a machine of sorts.* Although the tiny components that made it functional were an engineering miracle. Scooting back upstairs, Jaden burst through the door.

Iri looked at him expectantly. "Well?"

Jaden decided he would have some fun. "Does it look like I have it?"

Iri studied him further, and Jaden remembered who he was

dealing with. But she gave a little smile and turned away, saying nothing.

It was Atu's turn. "You didn't find it?"

Taz drifted closer. "I don't understand. Zareh said it would be there."

Pulling a random item from one of his pockets, Jaden looked at it. "Maybe this is it?"

"A piece of string?"

Atu looked so perplexed, Jaden wanted to laugh. "I suppose it could be. Or how about this?" He pulled another item from his pocket.

Atu's face soured. "Really? A marble?"

"Well, these are all things that live under my bed."

Taz huffed as she drew back. "You *did* find it. You're just teasing us."

"Well, if the string and marble aren't working for you, how about this?" Jaden withdrew the pawn.

"That's it?" Iri drew near and took it from him. "Wow, it's warm."

"Yeah, so you can all quit teasing me about not looking under my bed. Even if I had, I wouldn't have thought that was the 'device' Zareh mentioned. Does it look like a device to you?"

Atu laughed and slapped him on the back. "Chill! Yes, I agree. We wouldn't have found it either. How did you know this was what you were looking for?"

"It was the only thing under my bed."

When Atu raised shocked eyebrows, Jaden gave him a pained expression. "Really? I'm not *that* messy."

"I'm not saying anything." When Jaden looked like he might add something, Atu said, "Except I'm glad you found the device. Let's be on our way."

Jaden did his second double take of the day. "Where is Atu and what have you done with him?"

Giggling, Iri said, "Yes, we don't know this take-charge person."

Atu only grinned. "Shall we?"

"We shall. It's high time we were on our way." Clearly, their antics were wearing on Taz.

Seconds later, they were all airborne, Iri choosing to fly with Aren and Atu this time. Jaden glanced at Taz as Han pulled up next to her. "You're up. Time to tell us how to operate this device."

They flew well beyond the bounds of Daxsos before Taz told him Zareh developed the device so that only the gliders could interpret the frequencies. After his initial irritation, Jaden supposed it made sense. They *had* developed it in the glider's world for them to use. Obviously, it would work for them and not humans. The upside was, for once, the decisions were up to someone other than him.

Enjoying this revelation, Jaden obeyed as Taz instructed him to twist the top of the pawn off the base to activate the device. This executed, the gliders circled, concentrating on the signal. Jaden frowned, observing confusion on multiple faces.

"What's wrong?"

"I expected several signals. Instead, there is only one very strong signal coming from the north," Taz replied.

At her words, several of the nearby gliders nodded agreement.

"Could that just be the closest one?"

"Possibly, but unlikely. Zareh told me that once they had the device working in our world, it was like dots popping up all over the map. They could discern all the locations simultaneously, no matter how distant."

Jaden thought a moment. "Then we concentrate our forces on that spot. Once we've cleared it, we run the device again and see if we can find others. Is this location anywhere near Sven's?"

Taz eyed him. "How did you know?"

Jaden laughed. "I didn't. I was only asking because I thought it might be wise to head for Sven's and pick up some reinforcements before we hit that nest. Any objections?"

CHAPTER THIRTEEN

Every time they traveled to Sven's, the journey felt shorter. Perhaps it was. The voyagers had smart suits and aerolators now, so the gliders could fly at optimal speeds. In addition, Taz wasn't insisting they practice routines en route. Instead, they were flying directly to Sven's with no detours or distractions.

Jaden glanced at Iri, flying with Taz. Rather than have Taz flying solo while Iri doubled up with someone else, pairing them up had been practical. Still, Taz had balked at flying with anyone other than Kayla. And Iri had looked like a kid who'd just had her bike's training wheels ripped off. Both sides voiced vehement objections before finally giving in. Now they flew as a temporary team, both still looking uneasy with the arrangement.

Jaden could relate. He couldn't imagine doing this without Han. Trying to get to the next stage without Kayla was rough enough.

Jaden realized they were descending. The entrance to Sven's home was within sight. However, before they even landed, Jaden heard a familiar voice in his ear.

"Jaden! What are you doing here?"

"Markov? Are you watching the cameras?"

His friend chuckled. "Sven's got us all on rotations. Just your luck I was on duty when you arrived."

"Really? You think the others might've zapped me with those cannons if they saw it was me coming to join you?" Although he tried, Jaden couldn't keep the bitterness from his voice.

"Dude! Why would you say something like that?"

"You know why."

"Seriously, get past yourself! When are you going to accept everyone who took part in that battle did so of their own accord? And they were fully prepared to accept whatever the consequences were?"

"Does Stovan see it that way?"

"He's coming around," Markov admitted. "For obvious reasons, it's taken him a little longer than the rest of us."

Silence loomed large between them.

"We're coming up on the wall," Han informed Jaden.

"Got to go," Jaden told Markov. "We'll see you at Sven's in a few minutes."

Han and the other gliders made short work of negotiating the cliffs walling off Sven's home. Before Jaden was ready, Han was descending again so Jaden could dismount. He did so, his apprehension growing with each passing second. *How am I going to face Stovan after what happened to Bree?*

He hadn't seen Stovan since the battle. Of all his childhood friends, Stovan had been the one person who hadn't come to visit him during his convalescence.

"Jaden! Markov told me you and the others were on your way!"

Jaden's grin was a spontaneous reaction to the man who was larger than life and had a heart to match. Despite living the life of a recluse, Sven was the most congenial, hospitable person Jaden had ever met. Jaden barely managed a reply before Sven's hug engulfed him.

Somehow, it was exactly what he'd needed. When Sven released him, Jaden's confidence had returned. "Thanks."

Sven didn't bother hiding his surprise. "For what?"

"For being you and always being so accepting."

The older man eyed him. "You still haven't forgiven yourself, no?"

Without waiting for a reply, he forged on. "That will be a problem if you don't resolve it—and soon." Jaden gave him a skeptical glance. "I know of what I speak. You would do well to listen to me. Regrets have their place. But in the middle of a mission, they only serve as a distraction. Your focus should be on finishing the task. Make sure it's there before you leave my home, no?"

Jaden plastered a smile on his face and clapped Sven on the back. "You're a good man."

Abruptly, Sven looked annoyed. "Don't blow me off. Promise me you'll do this?"

Sighing, Jaden said, "Sven, I promise I'll do my best. But this isn't a switch you can turn on or off."

"But the longer you avoid facing the truth, the more difficult you make it for yourself."

"And what truth should I face, Sven?" Jaden knew his tone was snarky, but he couldn't help it. His own temper was rising. "Bree's dead!"

At that exact moment, Stovan stepped out the house. Jaden groaned inwardly. *Do I have the worst timing or what?*

Jaden was bewildered when Stovan didn't break stride. His aim for Jaden was unerring. Jaden wanted to back away, only that wouldn't help. If Stovan decked him, he deserved it. Stovan reached him, and Jaden stiffened. But Stovan pulled him into a rough hug. Of all the ways they could've reconnected, Jaden hadn't envisioned this.

"Don't blame yourself. It wasn't your fault," Stovan mumbled.

Jaden's arms tightened around his friend. "I'm so sorry. If I had known—"

"How could you have? And Bree wouldn't have wanted us to fight about it. If anything, it would've annoyed her that we weren't saying how amazing it was when she wielded her DD without cutting her glider's head off."

Jaden couldn't help the half-sob, half-laugh that escaped. He was also powerless to stop the tears that streamed down his cheeks. The laughter won out and, smiling through his tears, Jaden said, "Yes, I can almost hear her berating us for not giving her credit for what she accomplished."

Stovan gave a rueful smile. "Let's get inside. It's almost time for dinner, and I have to say, I think Bree would've been proud of our efforts."

Grateful he didn't have to speak and swallowing the lump in his throat, Jaden followed Stovan into the house. Surprised, Jaden stared at the long tables Sven had set up in what had once been the living room. Most of the riders already sat with their meals. A few stragglers were still dishing up their food.

When Sadie saw them, she rushed over. Her husband got her attention first, but Jaden wanted to tear up again when he was the next person she hugged. He wished his own parents were here. But they had remained at the house, their purpose twofold.

First, they'd promised Sadie and Vicken they would be there in case Kayla miraculously showed up. Second, they had to attend to their houseguests. Atu's parents had elected to take his place at his healing center while he came on this mission, so they'd needed a place to stay.

"How are you holding up?" Sadie asked, her face reflecting her concern.

"Better on some days than others," Jaden confessed. "How about you?"

"Much the same. Vicken told me what you're doing here. I hope we find Kayla at that base."

"You and me both." He kept his voice low, not wanting to explain his presence to the others just yet. He had to make sure all his friendships were intact before he made another withdrawal from the relationships.

By the next morning, Jaden knew he couldn't put things off any longer. Whispers were already rampant. Requesting that everyone join him at breakfast, Jaden wasn't disappointed when they all showed up—even those who should've been monitoring the security systems.

"Thanks for coming. I know you're all wondering what I'm doing here, so let me provide answers." Without preamble, he gave a brief rundown, avoiding questions about Zareh and skimping on details about how the comm system was discovered. They didn't need to know it had nearly cost him and Kayla their lives.

"Now that you know, the next step is scouting the nest and figuring out our best plan of attack. Anyone interested in joining Vicken and I on this mission?"

Iri, Atu, and Markov's hands went up immediately. Several others quickly followed, but he only noticed the most important ones. Stovan. Shianna. Sven. Relief washed over him in waves strong enough to make him want to wobble on his feet. It felt like he'd been holding his breath and was now suddenly able to breathe.

"Thank you. You don't know how much your support means to me," Jaden managed. "If you'll let Atu have your names, I'll choose a team by this afternoon. Understand ahead of time that I can't pick all of you. Our reconnaissance team will be small. Don't be disappointed or offended if you aren't selected."

Satisfied when he saw nods of acknowledgement, Jaden said, "Alrighty, it's time to eat!"

Chuckles rippled through the room. They shouted vigorous agreement. He smiled. Kayla would be proud of him. He tried suppressing the little stab his heart endured every time he thought of her, but it was impossible. She was always there, in his heart. And in the back of his mind lurked the worry, the fear, the uncertainty. Would he see her again?

"This is the next step."

Vicken's voice, quiet and intended for him alone, snatched him from that dark place. "It's just taking so long."

Vicken put a hand on his shoulder. "Believe me, I get it. But patience and due diligence will help more at this point than blindly rushing at the problem."

Jaden nodded. "Thanks. I appreciate you being here."

Laughing, Vicken said, "Where else would I be? She's my daughter!"

The words stayed with Jaden for the rest of the day. So much so, when it was time to choose a team, he gave both Sven and Vicken voices in the decisions. Sven had been with their newest riders the longest, and with his military background, Jaden trusted his judgment. With Vicken's skill set, he was the perfect person to work out their surveillance strategy. When Vicken gave Sven the specifics of his plan, they thinned the list to the final two candidates.

Ultimately, it didn't surprise Jaden when they selected Markov and Stovan to join him, Vicken, Iri, and Atu. It reassured Jaden knowing those coming with them were people he already knew and trusted. It would make communication and implementation infinitely simpler.

He caught Sven in his workshop that afternoon, asking the question that had been burning him since they'd arrived. Especially after he'd seen Stovan and felt guilty anew that this was the reason Bree hadn't been able to defend herself. If he wanted to protect the others from the same fate, they needed a solution. "Any luck yet in creating something to make our riders impervious to those EMPs?"

Sven's glum face answered before he spoke. "Without a Gaptor, we can't start on a solution. Those monsters have been absent from my valley, and we haven't found a single one when scouting the immediate area. It's like they've all disappeared. Your explanation about that nest might be the reason they're AWOL. Perhaps when you destroy the nest, you can capture a Gaptor for me, no?"

Jaden grinned. "I'll do my best, but I'm not making any promises."

Sven's laughter boomed around the room. "Good enough."

That evening, Vicken went over the plan with the team, making sure they all knew their roles. Earlier, Jaden and Vicken had agreed Vicken would take the lead. His surveillance experience made him the best man for the job. And they needed the best if they were to succeed.

By the time they finished their meeting, Vicken had detailed every eventuality to the last possible outcome. It only convinced Jaden he didn't want to know the extent of the man's other skills. He was truly scary.

Vicken leaned back and studied the group. "Questions?" When everyone shook their heads, he said, "Time to rest then. It will be an early start tomorrow."

Vicken wasn't kidding. They were up before dawn. It took them two days and most of the third to reach the well-hidden cave Sven's drone had ferreted out for them. It was an excellent waystation: secluded enough to rest before the night's mission and close enough that getting to the nest wouldn't take long.

When they had told the gliders about the mission, Han suggested a nighttime foray. Unlike the gliders, the Gaptors weren't nocturnal. Their twilight attacks, according to Han, were a "last-ditch effort to get as much killing into the day as possible" before they retired for the evening.

Jaden couldn't resist smiling, remembering the way Han spat the words out. Like the Gaptors were lazy cowards with no integrity. Considering they were aberrations cooked up in a lab rather than natural creations, did they even have personalities? Or were they just creatures of the habits drilled into them?

Han dropped even lower, and it reminded Jaden he would need to dismount. "See you inside."

"We won't be joining you. You forget, this is naturally the time we're awake. And who better to keep an eye out for unwanted guests than yours truly?"

Jaden chuckled. "I wouldn't want anyone else. But it's freezing out here."

"Have you also forgotten the temperatures in our world are so much more extreme than yours?"

Jaden had. "Okay, tough guy, you stay out here where it's nice and brisk. Give a holler if you see anything you don't like."

Han grunted acknowledgment, and Jaden dismounted. He watched Han arc away to allow the next glider to come in. As the other gliders swooped down to deposit their riders, Han began patrolling the area. Satisfied they were in good hands—or claws—Jaden made for the cave.

Vicken had already started a fire. Jaden hurried closer and raised his hands to its heat. "You're not worried about smoke attracting attention?"

Vicken shook his head. "No. Those breezes you felt when you

came in will blow any smoke along the side of this mountain. And they're blowing away from the Gaptors' nest."

"Anything else you'd like help with?" A superfluous question. Looking around, Jaden noticed Vicken had already arranged his supplies and equipment in some kind of order along the far wall.

"No, just get warm. You'll need your brain unfrozen so you can think once we get started."

The others dribbled into the cave right then and joined Jaden at the fire. Despite Atu's cold potion, they were all feeling the intense chill.

"My fingers are frozen," Iri complained, sidling up next to Jaden and putting her hands over the fire.

"I can't feel my ears," Markov said, rubbing them.

Stovan pushed a tissue against his reddened nose. "My nose won't stop running."

Without a word, Atu dug into his pouch and pulled out the cold potion. "You all need another application."

An hour later, the grumblings had turned to rumblings. Jaden couldn't take it. He had to ask.

"Did we bring any food?" When the others laughed, Jaden huffed. "Don't act like I'm the only one who's hungry. I can hear your stomachs growling from here."

Vicken plucked a bag from the pile along the wall and handed it to Jaden. "Sven said you would need this."

Curious, Jaden opened it. Inside was a veritable mountain of sandwiches. He grinned. "I think I'll be keeping these."

"No, you'll be taking one and passing them along," Markov said.

Jaden studied Markov a minute, then decided it wasn't worth the effort it would take to keep Markov at bay. "Okay." But he snagged two sandwiches instead of one before handing them over.

Markov only shook his head as he took his own sandwich and passed the bag to Iri. The bag did the rounds several times before it was empty. Stomachs full and bodies warm again, they crawled into their shells for some sleep, safe in the knowledge their gliders were watching over them.

CHAPTER FOURTEEN

Kayla finally drifted into a fitful sleep after her stunning conclusions. When she woke, she was still tired. And irritable. *How am I going to escape this place with an implant in my leg?*

She stiffened, realizing it was the perfect time for a little testing, soon enough after she woke that they might think she was still sleeping. If she moved her leg, they wouldn't find it suspicious. They'd think she was just trying to get more comfortable.

Anticipating the pain, Kayla gritted her teeth and then moved her leg sideways. Pleasantly surprised when there was no pain, she tried lifting it, just a tad. A twinge. Like whatever was in her leg didn't like the upward motion. She didn't have to roll onto her side. She already knew that was torturous.

So some kind of programmable motion sensor calibrated to cause pain if my leg moves like I want to stand. There's no way I can do the next test while pretending to sleep. Or is there? Kayla mimed stretching, like she was only now waking up. As subtly as she could, she slid down the bed, keeping the leg with the implant straight as she levered it over the edge.

Nothing. No pain. She bent the leg at the knee, like her leg had flopped over the edge, careful not to move her thigh as she did so. Still no spike of pain. Enough for now. Enough to confirm that as long as her thigh was horizontal, there was no pain. Any movement vertically or any attempt to put weight on the leg (as happened when she rolled onto her side) would trigger the sensor and shoot torment into her body.

Not that any of that helps. Unless . . . She felt for the metal stand. Finding it, she ran her hand down the main stem. There it was. A knob to adjust the height. If she made the stand the same height as the bed, she could lever her leg onto it and stabilize its horizontal position.

While that might allow me to move, I won't be fast. I must figure out how to hop along without jiggling that leg. Maybe if I tie the leg flat to the top of the stand with a sheet, I can minimize the jostling? Because, ziggety, if I have more than a few jolts of the pain that thing emits, I might pass out in the middle of my escape.

Elation coursed through Kayla at the thought of escape, but she didn't smile A prisoner would have no reason to smile unless they'd found a way to best their captors. There were still two things to figure out: how to get light in this room and how to get enough sustenance without being drugged.

Kayla was still considering the problems when the door clicked open. No clacking of claws. Tarise.

"I heard you weren't appreciating our hospitality."

Even the marrow in her bones froze. That mellifluous voice. Kayla was too terrified to speak.

"Come now, I make an observation and you have nothing to say?"

Kayla remained quiet. She remembered one of Tarise's warnings. *Don't ask for what you want, or they'll use it against you.* Well, she wouldn't ask for anything. In fact, she wouldn't *say* anything. Then she couldn't let anything slip.

There was a quiet chuckle. "I see. Well, it might interest you to know I've taken action against those who would've interfered with our relationship."

Panic. *What did he do to them? No, I'm making assumptions. Who are "they?" Is it Tarise? And what does he mean by "relationship?"*

"You don't have to worry about your food or water being tainted again."

Wait, what? You didn't order that? Never mind. One more thing off my list.

"I get no thanks?"

Kayla debated the wisdom of opening her mouth. Deciding in favor of living, she said. "Thank you."

"Ah, a little appreciation. That's what I like to hear."

He *really* didn't want to hear what she had to say about him. *Pompous, arrogant ass.* She grinned inwardly at the thought of him being a donkey. Then absurdly, anger welled within. *Who does he think he is to come into my world and try to take it away? Why can't he stay where he is?* Kayla quelled the rising fire. Rage would only make her say or do something rash.

"Was there something you wanted to say?"

Panic again. *Can he read my mind? No, if he could, I wouldn't still be breathing.*

Slurpy sighed. A loud, theatrical sound. "I suppose if you won't speak, then I'll do the talking. The fact is, I'm very interested in that birthmark of yours."

Kayla flinched.

This time the chuckle held true glee. "Oh, so you know it has meaning?"

No surprise he can see me even though it's blacker than his heart in this room. Steeling herself, Kayla focused on containing her reactions. No facial expressions. No internal monologues. Just a mute, unmoving, unemotional statue.

Slurpy tutted. "Since you seem disinclined to converse, perhaps a little insight into what lies ahead?" He sniggered. "I have to confess, I'm not being benevolent stopping those drugs. In fact, it's my little gift to you. I want you lucid enough to feel every slice of my scalpel on your skin."

Kayla shuddered. *He is going to torture me.*

Her involuntary action only added to the excitement in his voice. "I'll take that birthmark from you. Take that key and use it. And believe me, when I take it, you will feel every delicious fraction of an inch as I peel it off your skin so slowly, you'll want to rip it off yourself and give it to me."

The excitement had morphed into fury rippling through that melodious voice. It was almost as terrifying as what he planned to do.

Kayla's throat closed up. She struggled to breathe, to pull in enough oxygen past her rigid airways. Spots danced in front of her eyes. *Short, shallow breaths. Not good.* Kayla concentrated all her energy on breathing. *Slow, in and out. Deep breath in and out.*

The palm slapping her face was such a shock she lost her rhythm. Her hand touched her stinging cheek, her eyes darting in the usurper's direction. When she saw his eyes, she regretted it. Black, glittering coals, glowing red in the center, lit from within by a slow-burning fire. Unnatural. Hateful. Evil.

"You will *not* ignore me. You *will* answer me when I speak."

Kayla opened and closed her mouth, but she wasn't sure what to say. Her brain was fried. Had he asked a question? She thought he'd been telling her what he would do to her. Another shudder racked her body.

"Yes, that will suffice for now."

His voice held satisfaction. Pleasure, even. Verbal communication hadn't been necessary. He'd been after her fear. And now that he'd seen it, it was as if she had appeased some craving.

"See that you learn something from today, or the next time we meet, it will be more than a pat on the cheek."

When he stalked away, taking those burning eyes with him, Kayla went limp. Waves of fire, then ice, raked over her body as it tried to cope with the adrenaline racing through her. Neither fight nor flight had been an option. Her body struggled to remedy that.

It was at least an hour before her heartbeat finally slowed. But her breathing still came in sparse gasps. Every time she wrangled it back to normal, her mind slithered back to the encounter, and she lost her progress.

Huffing out a sigh, Kayla gave up on her breathing. If she continued hyperventilating, she would pass out and that would solve the problem. Not the way she wanted it solved, but it would do the job. Instead of fighting the ordeal, she allowed herself to dwell on it. Especially the part about her birthmark.

How does Slurpy know about my birthmark? Duh, he probably has spies everywhere. But the nagging doubt she had about Tarise wouldn't allow her to get past it. The more she thought about it, the more Kayla became convinced Tarise had told Slurpy. *The question now is did that traitor tell him before or after they captured me?*

An interesting question and one that merited further consideration. But Kayla set it aside as she focused on the real problem—her birthmark. True, it linked to the ancient language and translated as *key*. But did the usurper know the way they marked things in that language gave clues to the real meaning? That her birthmark represented a noun and not a verb?

She didn't think he did. Because if he knew, he would also know her birthmark itself wasn't the key, the physical item that would open the lock. It was intended as a sign, something to lead the way. Or did he know something about the ancient language she didn't?

Kayla attacked the problem more aggressively. If he knew something else, something she wasn't seeing, she had to work it out. Before he came back. Before he hacked her birthmark off.

Trying to put that thought away was like trying to stuff a genie back into the bottle. The fear clamped down again, raising her heartbeat and setting her breathing off-kilter, right when she'd distracted herself enough to normalize it. *I'm focusing on my breathing again. Not helping! Focus on the problem!*

Kayla's face scrunched up as she tried to recall every twinge of her birthmark. Before she'd received her books with the ancient language, her birthmark had never bothered her. Only when she took those books and arrayed them on her bed, ready to study them for the first time, had her birthmark itched unbearably.

Then it itched enough to propel her off her bed to her mirror, so she could find a reason for the itching. Unable to find any bites or other explanation, she had glared at the birthmark—then caught sight of the symbol adorning the cover of each book in the mirror's reflected image of her room.

Disbelieving of what she was seeing, she had turned and stared at the books, her eyes skittering between her arm and the books several times. Not only was the symbol the same shape as her birthmark, it was identical in size. At the exact moment she realized this, her birthmark stopped itching. Like it had fulfilled its purpose—drawn her attention to the books.

After that, she knew she had to learn the ancient language. She'd applied herself to the task, and her birthmark hadn't bothered her again for years. Not until a few months ago when this insanity started.

The more Kayla focused on the times her birthmark bothered her, the more things crystallized. It led to a startling revelation. Every time she was near something important to the mission—from finding her medallion to recognizing other seekers to finding artifacts—her birthmark had literally itched enough to make her want to scratch it off her arm.

But when she touched those leather strips . . . that was another reaction entirely. Her birthmark burned then, like someone had set it on fire. Kayla frowned. Could the burning simply be a more intense version of the itching? Perhaps indicating that while the rest of the things were important to the mission, the leather strips were important to *her*? Or *more* important to the mission?

"No more nightmares?"

Kayla jumped. She hadn't heard Tarise come in. Stuffing thoughts of her birthmark far from her mind, Kayla reminded herself she couldn't trust Tarise. No way would she say anything that could be overheard or passed along that might help the usurper. Kayla mentally squared her shoulders. She needed to get Tarise off-balance. Make Tarise spill things she shouldn't.

"You mean other than the walking nightmare that just paid me a visit?"

Tarise's hiss indicated she hadn't known the usurper had been there. "You mean 'him?'"

"I do. And he was eager to tell me how he planned to cut off my birthmark." Kayla had no clue how she sounded so calm. When Tarise said nothing, Kayla added, "Slowly and painfully."

A small sigh. Or a muffled sob? Kayla wasn't sure. She opened her mouth to spit out another barb, but the hand touching her own made her recoil.

"I'm sorry."

The whisper was so faint Kayla had to strain to hear the words. While Tarise sound genuine, the whisper also masked any intonation. *How convenient.* "For what?"

"I don't want him doing to you what he did to me."

Kayla wondered whether she wanted to know. "And what was that?"

"Just know you're not the only one who's a prisoner here."

With that, Tarise pressed something into her hand and stepped back. Kayla's fingers explored the object. Hiding her shock took extreme effort. *Is this what I think it is?*

"Don't say I didn't warn you." Tarise's voice was back to its usual volume—and without inflection except for the word *warn.*

Abruptly, all the games were too much. All the guessing. The scheming. More than anything, Kayla wished she could just speak plainly to Tarise—and that Tarise would reciprocate. However, even if Tarise's actions were sometimes oblique, they consistently highlighted the need for her secrecy. Tarise's warning had to mean she should be ready for escape. Because that's what the scalpel in her hands was—a means to an end.

CHAPTER FIFTEEN

Six hours later, Vicken roused them, and they were on their feet again, grabbing their assigned supplies. In minutes, they exited the cave, packs over their shoulders and kitted in their smart suits, their goggles' night vision making the world glow green.

Those weren't the only enhancements Sven had made. The lenses of the goggles would now tint almost black in the presence of extreme light. Between this and the new sound suppressors built into the masks' earmuffs, they would no longer be blind or deaf when destroying Gaptors.

Their gliders had obviously been waiting; Han dropped down almost the moment Jaden stepped outside. He aerial connected and then grinned when Han shot them skyward. "Anxious, buddy?"

"No, eager to get on with this."

The bloodlust in his voice surprised Jaden. "Easy. We're just there to scout. We won't be doing any killing tonight."

"More's the pity," Han grumbled.

Jaden only smiled as they waited for the others to join them. Then they flew to a spot near the top of a nearby mountain that had shielded them from the Gaptor nest on the other side. Reaching it, the gliders slid in, allowing their riders to disembark before sweeping back to circle nearby. Close enough to engage the enemy if needed, but far enough to avoid accidentally being spotted.

When the riders had all dismounted, Vicken said, "Ready?" At their nods, he led them toward the peak.

The snowshoes Sven provided made easy work of the untamed terrain. Despite this, Jaden was sweating in minutes. The air was also thin enough that he wasn't the only one taking advantage of his aerolator. By the time they reached the crest, his calves were burning. *And I thought I was in good shape! That little stint with blood loss must've taken more out of me than I realized.* Then he glanced over and caught Markov rubbing a weary hand over his face. *Okay, so it's not just me.*

Using the hand signals he had taught them, Vicken ordered them onto their bellies. The group shimmied up the last piece hiding them from the Gaptors on the other side, using the trees as cover against any Gaptors that might be overhead.

Sneaking a peak over the apex, Jaden glanced down, then gaped. The view was breathtaking. The sides of the mountain gleamed white as the snow threw its radiance back into the sky. The trees dotting the mountainside appeared as painted black outlines drizzled with gray where patches of snow had accumulated. At the base of the mountain, a frozen lake glittered black, unyielding as steel reflecting the moonless sky.

Clearly, the Gaptors didn't know the value of keeping the high ground. Then again, hadn't their gliders repeatedly told them the Gaptors were brainless brutes? Jaden's first sweep of the area was for Kayla. There was no sign of anything human down there. His heart sank.

What had he expected? Hadn't he known deep down she was in Zareh's world? Why had he even dared hope he might find her here? Because Zareh said she might be here. Because Zareh said he had no word on her whereabouts, hinting Slurpy could've returned her to this world. Jaden should've known better than to trust the little critter.

Swallowing his anger and bitterness, Jaden eyed the Gaptors resting in clumps close to the lake's edge. All except three were sleeping—if that's what the odd lumps signified. He squinted, trying to work out exactly what he was looking at.

The Gaptors were almost folded in on themselves. Their legs were tucked under them, their bodies curled over their legs, and their wings shuttered along their sides. Their long necks snaked around half their body so that their heads rested at the very top of the pile, allowing their razor-edged beaks to droop past the edge. *I suppose that's one way to sleep without slicing yourself to death.*

Markov nudged him, and Jaden realized they were moving again. Doing his part and nudging the person next to him—Iri—he scooted after the others as they slid through the trees toward the nest. They moved quickly, Vicken setting the pace. In his briefing, he told them the aim was to get down quickly and quietly. However, he warned them that care was essential.

"One slip, one sound, and they'll know we're there. The aim is to get in and get out, unseen and unheard."

His words echoed in Jaden's mind as he moved as stealthily as he could. When they finally reached the tree-strewn ledge hanging over the very edge of the lake, Jaden was puffing again. He hoped the Gaptors wouldn't hear. *Do they have super-hearing like the gliders?*

Apparently not. The lumps remained motionless. The only movement came from the three Gaptors patrolling the lake's circumference. Not that anyone could call it patrolling. They didn't keep to any pattern or convention Jaden knew of. Not only did they fail to space themselves to counter a threat, they didn't go anywhere near where the others slept. *Don't they think the trees hold any danger?*

In fact, they kept gathering at a spot directly under the ledge where Jaden and the others observed them. The first time they did, Jaden held his breath, thinking the Gaptors had sensed them. But the Gaptors muttered a short, unintelligible conversation before separating and tromping around the lake again.

Jaden felt a hand on his shoulder. Vicken pointed out a spot and then motioned for Jaden to activate the magnifiers in his goggles. Doing so, Jaden focused on the area.

The most obvious thing, the thing he should've noticed the first time around, was that the sleeping lumps were arranged in a near-perfect circle, as though clustered around something in the middle. Except there was no fire, only a pine tree. And . . . *What is that?*

Under the tree's spiny branches, red rays seeped from beneath a black shroud carelessly tossed over the object underneath. Jaden craned his neck, hoping for a better view. As if some greater being had heard him, a breeze lifted the shroud, revealing . . . something. Something not of this world. A glowing, pulsing patch of red goo. It had no fixed shape. Rather, the edges rippled, and the goo rearranged itself continuously, as though whatever this was, it was a living thing.

The breeze passed, and the cover flapped back down. But that glimpse was enough to confirm something was down there. Maybe this was the communication system Zareh was after. Turning his head, Jaden grinned at Vicken. The man's eyes glittered behind his goggles; his teeth glinted in a savage smile. A chill shivered through Jaden. Not for the first time, he was thankful Vicken was on their team.

About to slide back down the ledge, Vicken abruptly held up a fist to freeze them in place. Slowly, Jaden turned his head, in time to see the patrolling Gaptors converging on them again. They would have to wait before moving.

However, this time, the Gaptors didn't huddle. Jaden went still, getting one of those feelings of his. Iri, lying next to him, must've sensed it, because she slid a hand out to touch his and raised her eyebrows. Jaden shrugged. He had no clue whether this warning was a signal to pay attention or whether they should already be running.

Iri motioned to Atu. Then Atu's worried face, followed by Markov's and Stovan's turned his way as they caught the gist. On Jaden's other side, Vicken tensed, then moved as he reached for his DD. But Vicken wasn't watching him. His eyes were on the Gaptors below. Where Jaden's should be.

Jaden glanced down, aware the others were still studying him. As subtly as he could, he motioned they should pay attention to what was happening below. All heads turned, following his directive. What they saw made Jaden's limbs tense for flight.

Two of the Gaptors turned outward, flanking the third, who stood between them. All three sniffed at the air with their vicious beaks, their heads turning from side to side as though searching for something. Hardly daring to breathe, Jaden watched as the two on the outside spread their scraggly wings. The shield they formed around the third Gaptor wasn't effective for totally blocking the view of anyone on the ground. But it was definitely a waste of time preventing anyone above them from watching, which their group was.

The slight tink-tink-tink of something chipping at the ice broke the stillness of the night. Jaden stayed in place, despite curiosity driving him to lean further over the edge. *The view from here is just fine.* Moving in any way might alert the two sentry Gaptors to their presence. Not a thought he wanted to follow through to its conclusion.

Jaden bit back his impatience as the middle Gaptor continued chipping away at the ice. Admittedly, the sight of the black blood oozing from the edge of its talon was making him queasy. *Why doesn't the stupid thing use a tool?* When the ice suddenly gave way and the Gaptor nearly tumbled head first into the icy water below, Jaden wanted to clap a disbelieving hand to his face.

Recovering, the Gaptor lumbered back toward the edge of the lake. Reaching under the low branches of a spruce, he fumbled around the base of the tree for a moment, then stood, holding a rope that had been buried under the snow. Lifting the rope, he followed its course back to the hole in the ice. The hairs on Jaden's arms rose, and that familiar chill intensified, rippling down Jaden's spine. *This is it! This is what that feeling warned me about.*

Holding his breath, Jaden watched the Gaptor gently pull on the rope, using care so as not to allow his talons to slice through. Bit by bit, whatever the rope held under the ice was dragged to the surface. After what felt like forever, a plain metal chest slipped out of the hole.

Little grunts and garbled words passed between the Gaptors. The two sentries helped the middle one lift the chest onto the ice, then drag it to the side of the lake. There was some animated chattering and wing flapping before they settled down again. *What's that about?*

To Jaden's amazement, all three Gaptors fell down and began scratching around in the snow. Iri vibrated next to him. Her face was red with suppressed laughter. When she saw him looking at her, she slowly moved her hand, mimicking a key turning in a lock.

Jaden grinned. *They'd lost the key!* If he had ever doubted they lacked intelligence, this little adventure tonight proved it. Jaden turned his attention back to the Gaptors, who were still sifting through snow. His smile faded. As amusing as this was to watch, the longer they stayed here, the higher the chance of the Gaptors' finding them. But what *was* in the chest?

The muted shriek below drew his gaze. The monster who had made it was upright again, holding something in its talon. From the way the others stood and flapped their wings to shake the snow off, he assumed it was the key.

This time, the Gaptor holding the key didn't bother checking his surroundings. He had had enough of this farce. Bending over the chest, he snapped the key into the lock and tossed the lid open.

At first, Jaden thought snow was in the chest. The pearly luminescence that flowed out was lovely: soothing, white, and run through with hints of pinks, purples, blues, and grays. Jaden's aerolator mercifully stifled his grunt as he realized what was actually in the chest. Medallions! Hundreds and hundreds of them!

That's why the Gaptors aren't worried about the trees! Why they're focused on the lake. They aren't guarding the communication system. They're protecting this cache of medallions! Jaden wanted to run and jump and shout and dance like a lunatic, all at the same time. But he held his position. It was even more important now that they didn't give themselves away.

This was what they had been looking for, had hoped was still in their world, what they had prayed hadn't already been sent to Slurpy's world or destroyed. They had needed to find that "whole lot of medallions." And here they were.

If they could recover this cache, they could protect all those riders without medallions from the Gaptors' deadly EMPs. Sven would be off the hook. They would have a fully protected, fighting army. They would have a chance.

Another thought blindsided him. There weren't that many Gaptors down there. Maybe twenty or thirty. *How is this a nest?* His stomach lurched as he realized where their group was—on top of a ledge. Which probably had an overhang.

Fear clawed at his insides. He gingerly moved his arm and touched Vicken.

When Vicken's gaze met his, Jaden knew Vicken had reached the same conclusion. Gesturing Jaden should be quiet, Vicken pulled a small, square box from one of his seemingly infinite utility pockets. Opening it, he set the tiny screen in front of them, then slid the snake-like cable over the edge of the overhang. Using a tiny joystick, he manipulated the cable until its eye zoomed in on what lay under the ledge.

Jaden's spirits plummeted. The Gaptors had stacked themselves on top of one another, like carcasses thrown on a pile for incineration. But these Gaptors weren't dead. The mass seethed and moved like a single living organism. Here and there, glints announced open eyes or light bouncing off the steel plates on moving necks.

As silently as he had fed the cable out, Vicken retracted it, his mouth a thin line. A screech below drew Jaden's attention. The three Gaptors who'd been patrolling were tossing the chest back into the lake. Hisses followed as they hunched around the hole they'd made. *What now?*

When they stood and hobbled away, Jaden blinked. The place where the hole had been was completely iced over again, leaving no sign a hole had ever been there. Deciding it wasn't worth wasting time figuring out how they had done it, Jaden observed the guards once again beginning their quirky rounds of the lake. Seconds later, Vicken signaled they should move and their group eased back off the ledge, beginning the long climb back up the mountain.

CHAPTER SIXTEEN

Desperation lent speed to the wings of their gliders as they raced back to Sven's. They had debated using Atu's whistle to summon the Legion, but ultimately agreed attacking without a plan would be suicide. They'd have to risk hoping the precious chest wouldn't disappear.

To speed things up, they contacted Sven about their return as soon as it was safe to converse. Considering he'd been struggling with finding a solution for counteracting the Gaptors' EMPs, he was delighted to hear about the medallions. His next question was what he could do to minimize their turnaround time.

As a result, by the time Jaden and the others reached Sven's, it was bustling with activity. Han deposited Jaden, and this time, Jaden didn't wait for the others before rushing to find Sven. He hadn't taken five steps before he crashed into his parents. He blinked. "What are you doing here? Did Kayla come back?"

The smile dropped from his mother's face. "No, she didn't."

Jaden gaped at her. "Then why are you here?"

Guilt flooded him when he saw her disappointment. *She was expecting me to be happy to see them, and instead I'm harping on about Kayla, making it sound like I don't want them here. Idiot!*

Jaden tugged his mother into a hug. "I'm sorry. I am glad to see you. I just wasn't expecting it—and with all the other things going on I wasn't thinking. I'm such a klutz. Will you forgive me?"

His mother's arms tightened around him. "Yes."

Jaden gave her a quick squeeze before releasing her and hugging his dad. Somewhat present, Jaden thought to ask, "How did you get here?"

"When you left, Pallaton was considerate enough to leave some gliders so we could join you. He thought we might want the opportunity to choose whether we trained with the others—considering the first time there was a choice, we weren't around."

That was a polite way of saying they'd been Slurpy's prisoners. "Do you?"

Clara glanced at Ty. "We haven't decided yet. But we're leaning towards helping Taema and Sava. They could use a few more hands."

Jaden blinked a second time. "They're here too?"

Ty laughed. "Yes. The gliders they were caring for recovered and were eager to join their kin. There was no reason for Taema and Sava to stay in Daxsos and a means for them to join us."

"And see their son," Jaden pointed out.

"That too," his mother said, grinning.

His dad put a hand on his shoulder. "Now, what's this situation you were referring to? Where were you rushing off to?"

The urgency came hurtling back. "Oh, no! Got to go. Sorry! I don't know how much time we have. Find Markov. He'll explain. I have to find Sven."

With a quick squeeze to each of his parents' shoulders, Jaden dashed off. He found Sven in his workshop, arranging the items Jaden had asked him to assemble. Jaden almost smiled at the memory of Vicken's praise for his idea.

"If you ever looking for a job, come see me," Vicken had said. "You seem to have a knack for this."

While the compliment pleased Jaden, it also left him thinking if he didn't have that talent, then perhaps Zareh might not have chosen him. But that meant he might never have met Kayla, so perhaps it wasn't all bad.

Jaden ran an eye over the supplies. "Do we have enough?"

Sven beamed. "You think I haven't been preparing for this since our first meeting?"

"Sven, you're the most prepared person I know. Thank you for that. Without you and all you've done, we'd be in a lot of trouble."

"You do know I did this for myself too, no?"

Jaden grinned. "Say that all you want, but I remember what you said when we first met. That this house and everything in it was for when the Gaptors returned, whether or not that was in your lifetime. So don't think I believe you for a second."

Sven's laughter boomed, making Jaden laugh too. Right then, Markov strode in.

"Glad to hear you think this is a party."

"Dude, of all people, I thought you'd relish this kind of stuff!"

"Yeah, well, playing at war is one thing. Facing it in real life is quite another."

Jaden sobered. "I know. It's abhorrent, isn't it?"

Markov only nodded, then glanced at the workbench. "What do we have here?"

Jaden and Sven talked him through the supplies and Jaden's intentions for each.

"It sounds like a solid plan. What does Vicken think?"

"That I couldn't have come up with a better plan myself," Vicken replied, joining them.

Jaden's ears warmed at the genuine compliment. "Thanks," he muttered.

"How much longer?" Vicken asked.

Sven beamed. "Everything's ready. As soon as we load this equipment, we can leave." He glanced at Jaden. "Although you might explain the plan to everyone else? I only told them to prepare for a battle and nothing more. They have questions."

The loathsome burden of leadership bent Jaden's shoulders. He sighed. "Fine, let's deal with that so we can get back before the Gaptors pull up stakes. We don't want to lose that cache."

"Not to mention the comm system," Vicken added.

"That too." They left the room and headed for the "mess hall," as they had dubbed it.

Everyone was already there. It gratified Jaden to find them battle-ready: kitted in their smart suits and accessories, DDs strapped to their bodies, hair pinned back and faces set with determination. He searched out the one face he needed affirmation from more than the others. When Stovan gave him a grim nod, Jaden let go of the past.

He would never forget Bree. She was a primary reason for doing this, why they had to succeed. "Thank you for being willing to go to war with me again. It's difficult, knowing we've already lost loved ones. Even more so when we know there is still loss to come. If any of you have doubts about what we're doing, now would be the time to step down. There is no shame in this. We must all do what we need to. Whether it's joining in the fight or whether it's stepping back and cherishing those we love, it's a personal decision and one I cannot make for you."

Jaden waited a moment, but the determination on the assembled faces only hardened. "I won't say this next fight will be easy. No fight ever is. But we go into this battle with a few advantages we didn't have last time."

He detailed the plan. By the time they understood their roles and how things would work, they were eager to leave and stop wasting time. It was a soothing balm to his battered soul.

"Alright, let's do this, then! For those we have lost! Let's honor their sacrifice by seeing this through to the end. Let's make our world safe again. A place where a maniacal dictator will never have dominion!"

Cheers erupted, and then everyone was moving, rushing to the workshop to pick up the items they were to carry and then hurrying to waiting gliders. Jaden couldn't help marveling at the efficiency. Sven truly was a master at this.

As Jaden prepared for Han's descent, he realized it hadn't been more than two hours since they'd returned. Hopefully, they'd been swift enough so they could get back to the Gaptor nest and carry out their plan. Jaden prayed they wouldn't arrive to find the Gaptors—or the medallions—gone.

* * *

Jaden could literally feel anxiety biting at their heels as they bolted back to the nest. When it started snowing, trepidation whispered through him. The whisper became a murmur when the wind picked up. And it was a full-blown scream by the time they reached the back end of the mountain from which they would launch their attack.

Jaden had to shout to make himself heard over the roaring wind. "Han, can the gliders fly in this?"

Han looked back over his shoulder. "This is what we live for. Especially when there's a battle in the offering."

"Explain."

"We have smaller wingspans than the Gaptors, and not those spindly fingers they call wings. Who do you think gets the worst of it when there's wind?"

The glee in Han's voice had Jaden chuckling. "Alright. But you, Taz, and Pallaton need to keep things tight. I can't lose any of you. Make sure you quit if things get too hairy out there."

Han shot him a look that told Jaden his comment was insulting. Their gliders would not back down if their voyagers were in trouble. Sighing, Jaden rubbed his glider along the soft fur just behind his neck. "Have it your way. But please, be careful!"

"You too," was all Han said as he descended for Jaden's dismount.

Jaden flailed as the wind blew him off course from his intended drop point. He hit the ground. Thankfully, this was a nice, open area, or everyone would've been dodging trees as they landed. Wading though the snow, Jaden made his way to the others. They were arranging the supplies so they could carry everything and still defend themselves.

Jaden rearranged his own supplies, then glanced around. "Anyone missing?"

Visibility was deteriorating by the second, and Jaden could barely see past the first few lines of riders. When no one reported their accountability buddy missing, Jaden hoped they had everyone. "Let's go, then. Remember, be as quiet as you can. Tread carefully. We don't want any snow running down the mountain to alert them to our arrival."

With that, he began the short climb to the crest of the mountain. He blinked in surprise when Markov and Stovan flanked him, and Vicken hugged his side.

Markov must've sensed his surprise. "We can't have you going down. We need a commander."

Jaden didn't know what to say. While he appreciated the gesture, he didn't want them front and center in harm's way.

As if reading his mind, Stovan said, "We're fine where we are. Stop worrying about us. Make sure we get the win today with as few losses as possible."

Allowing a curt nod, Jaden focused on getting the team in place without detection. Not that this would be as impossible as he'd thought. The wind howling around them was both a blessing and a curse.

The decreased visibility from the windswept snow meant the Gaptors would have more trouble seeing them coming. It also meant that Jaden couldn't keep track of the team. He would have to trust the beacons Sven had given the riders would lead them to their assigned positions. And that none of them would walk into trouble they couldn't handle.

Fighting the wind, Jaden put one step in front of the other, one eye on his own beacon and the other on the surrounding woods. Musical tinkling snagged his attention. Icicles clung to the trees, clinking together as they embraced the wind in a death dance.

"Watch out for flying ice!" Jaden barely got the warning out before the first icy projectile launched itself and speared past his head. With a loud crack, a second icicle broke free. Jaden wasn't fast enough, and it nicked his ear as it sped past. He raised a hand to touch the spot, noticing a third icicle aiming for Markov. Pushing Markov to the ground, he saw an entire batch of icicles shoot themselves from a tree right in front of them.

"Down! On the ground!" Jaden yelled into his comm. Stealth be damned. He could barely hear his own voice over the wind. No way the Gaptors could hear either.

The deadly barrage sailed over his head, then disappeared in the swirling snow. He heard a few curses. "Everyone okay?"

"Just a few scrapes," someone answered.

"Keep low," Jaden ordered. "We don't have that much further to go before we would've been on our stomachs, anyway. And stay alert! Just because they can't come at you sideways, there's nothing to say they won't fall on top of you."

Although the likelihood of that happening with this wind is minimal. Nevertheless, he had needed to say it. With the wind lashing snow against their goggles and ice shards cleaving the air overhead, they crept forward. The group diverged to the various locations Sven had chosen for optimal placement according to his drone footage.

Jaden crawled onward with his honor guard. They were much closer to their position than he'd realized. Luckily, the Gaptors hadn't heard him shouting. He couldn't make another mistake like that.

Holding back a sigh, Jaden slipped into position and glanced at his watch. Despite the disruptions, they had made excellent time. He and the others waited until the appointed hour. With the wind and snow and poor visibility, would their plan work?

As if on cue, he heard faint twittering. Their gliders had arrived. Jaden strained to hear what the Gaptors were doing. He knew they were within thirty feet of where the outlying Gaptors had been sleeping when Sven captured the drone images. *If I can hear the gliders, surely the Gaptors can too? Are they gone? Are we too late?*

Sudden shrieks made Jaden jump. The shrill calls put his worries to rest. *The Gaptors are still here, alright. And pretty riled up about the gliders overhead if their raucous calls are anything to go by.* Jaden rolled onto his back to observe the sky. He didn't have to wait long.

Massive black shapes rose upward, their bulks displacing the snowflakes. Was it just a trick of his eyes, or were they also dimming the light the snow threw off? It was as if the very blackness of the evil they represented sucked away all light.

But there was no time to ponder the phenomenon. Jaden rose, a phantom in the swirling snow and raised the gun. Its grip resembled a remote control while its barrel flared to a wide mouth, a duplicate of the weapon Sven used on them the first time they had met. The weapon that brought their gliders down. The one Sven had modified to make the cannons now protecting his valley.

Jaden's timer vibrated against his arm. He prayed their gliders were out of range, sticking to the plan. Hitting the command on the remote, Jaden felt the pulse leave the weapon, then heard the slight popping as the pulse spread into the neighboring air. Sven had briefed them on using the ray gun, so Jaden knew to ensure he locked the remote in position before putting it down.

"Heads up," Jaden commanded. "They're about to come down."

No sooner had he said it than the first Gaptor hit the ground a few feet from him. Drawing his DD, Jaden charged the beast and sliced its head off. The Gaptor disintegrated with the usual spectacular show, but he didn't have to close his eyes or wish he could block his ears. Sven's light and sound blockers were amazing!

Without stopping. Jaden dived under a nearby tree, waiting for the next Gaptor to crash down. When it did, he didn't have to lift a finger. The boom rocking the ground and light flashing around the Gaptor confirmed it died on impact. Before Jaden could draw breath, Gaptors began raining down so thick and fast, keeping up with killing the incapacitated monsters was difficult.

Evading the icicles still firing from every direction and darting under trees between killing blows, Jaden was soon covered in the putrid gore that passed for Gaptor blood. The more time that passed without him spotting a single glider, the more relieved Jaden was. Their gliders had escaped the ray gun's initial blast and were staying clear of its radius. Which was life for them considering they had been so much higher than the Gaptors, and if the Gaptors were dying from the drop, their gliders would've too.

Jaden decapitated another Gaptor. He glanced up when light flashed far above. Distance and the roar of the wind whipping the snow into a blizzard around them diminished the thunderous sound of a Gaptor's demise.

It must've escaped the pulse, only to fly upward into the waiting gliders. More lights flashed and pops sounded through the snow swirling blue into the night sky. Han would be ecstatic about getting some action.

Jaden glanced to his left, hearing the thud of another Gaptor smashing to the ground. Knee-deep in carnage, he hurried over, his speed making him reckless. As he angled toward the neck, he didn't see the stinger swinging around. A dull thump behind him made him jump. He whirled and found Vicken standing over the dismembered stinger, his DD still glowing.

"Don't just stand there. Kill it! Its stinger would've spiked your head if I hadn't been here."

"Thanks for the save." Jaden didn't have time for more words or to soak in the fact that he'd almost died. Only time to admonish himself to be more careful. With a swing that began at his side and took his arm in a full circle, he chopped the Gaptor's head off.

CHAPTER SEVENTEEN

Jaden surveyed the slaughter. Eradicating the Gaptors had taken less than twenty minutes. They'd only lost one glider. Two riders had sustained serious cuts from flying ice. Other than that, the rest of the injuries were minor.

Jaden glanced at his arm, oozing blood through the bandage he'd tightened around it. It was a superficial gash, but it hurt more than the depth warranted. The graze on his ear still stung, and he could feel countless other scratches through the freezing holes in his smart suit where icicles had nicked him. All things considered, nothing drastic. Not as drastic as a stinger through the head.

Dismissing the disturbing thought, Jaden stomped toward the frozen lake where the others were gathered. They parted for him as he made his way to the front of the group.

"Care to do the honors?" Atu asked.

Sven had already cut a precise hole in the ice, as they had instructed him to while the rest of them were killing the downed Gaptors. There was no sign of him now. "Where's Sven?"

Atu chuckled. "Where do you think?"

Figuring that out didn't take a genius. "With that strange thing we saw when we scouted this place?"

"Yeah, where else? Now, how about getting those medallions out?"

"One more question. Where's Vicken?"

"He and Markov are setting charges to blow this place sky high. Now can we get the chest?"

Jaden grinned. It was very unlike Atu to either be so chatty or impatient. "Maybe we should find the key first," he teased.

Atu's face twisted into a snarl, then switched to a grin. "Okay, you've had your fun. If you don't start pulling on that rope, I will." So saying, he leaned down and picked it up.

Jaden watched, horrified, as Atu jerked and shuddered, then went stiff before crumpling into a heap. "Atu!" Jaden was at his side in an instant, feeling for a pulse. It was there, but erratic. *Where's Kayla when I need her? I don't know anyone else who's a medic. Maybe . . .*

Atu sat up so suddenly Jaden backed away. His friend coughed and then rubbed a hand over his chest. "Ow!"

Jaden leaned in again and studied Atu's face. "Are you okay? What happened?"

Still rubbing his chest, Atu glanced back at the rope. "It had some kind of charge. I think my suit took the brunt of it."

"You sure you're okay though?"

"Yeah," Atu said, holding out a hand. "Help me up."

Jaden did, noticing Atu was a little unsteady on his feet. A whiff of one of his potions took care of it.

"My suit's toast," Atu moaned.

Jaden could see tiny burn scars along parts of the suit where the suit's material had melted. He whistled. "Just as well you didn't pick that rope up without a suit on."

"Yeah, that wouldn't have been fun. Do you think I killed the charge or whatever was in the rope?"

"Let's find out." Jaden pulled out his knife and threw it at the rope. Nothing. No spark. No flash. No dancing knife. "Okay, trying something else," he muttered as he pulled up his compass on his PAL, then swiped it away again when he remembered it worked on satellites and not a magnetometer sensor. "Last way I know of." He bent his hand so that the back of his palm faced the rope.

"Jaden, don't!"

The hint of panic in Atu's voice was almost comical. "Trust me, this is the safest way to touch it. If there's a current, it'll contract my muscles and pull my hand away. Unlike you, where your hand was around the rope. When the current contracted your muscles, it closed your hand further and prolonged the contact."

With Atu still looking like he didn't trust the science, Jaden touched the rope. Nothing. He held it there for more than a minute in case the wretched thing worked with a pulse instead of a straight current. But whatever charge the rope had carried was gone.

"Alright, let's try that again." Jaden picked up the rope and pulled. All he did was give himself rope burn as the chest resisted and the rope slid through his fingers. "Care to give me a hand?"

Hesitantly. Atu grabbed the rope. Together, they pulled. With the same result.

"That chest is heavier than it looked," Atu puffed, looking at his hands. "We need a few more people."

They need more than a few, and it felt like a tug-of-war dragging the chest from the lake. For every two inches they gained, they lost one before finding their grip on the rope again. By the time the chest finally broke the surface, they were sweaty and irritable.

But the sight of it cast jubilation through the ranks, giving them the strength to hoist it free of the water. Once it was on the ice, it skated back toward them, but came to an abrupt stop when it hit the area where the ice and frozen ground met.

"One last pull to get it all the way onto the ground," Jaden called. "One, two, three!"

They all tugged—and ended up on their rear ends. Offering no resistance, the chest shot up the bank, into the air, and thunked down next to Jaden. Gingerly, he put a hand out before retracting it. He glanced around. "Iri?"

"I'm here," she said from somewhere behind him.

"Any reason you can see for me to not touch this chest?" Jaden didn't want to repeat Atu's mistake of touching before testing. And the way the chest had resisted coming out of the water was plain unnatural.

Iri moved closer and studied the chest from several angles. "Nothing I can see. Go ahead."

Despite this, Jaden used the back of his hand again. Nothing happened and Jaden sighed, relieved. He touched the handle where the rope met the box, intending to detach it. At the slightest nudge, the chest moved. Jaden blinked. "Iri?"

"Still nothing. I think it moved because you touched it."

Jaden poked at the chest with a finger. It slid along the ground as if it were no heavier than a feather. "How come we needed all these people to pull it out of the water, but now it moves like it has no weight?"

Iri shrugged. "I can't answer that. Is it important?"

"No, I suppose not."

"Let's be thankful it will be easy to get back to Sven's and move on," Atu commented. "I don't fancy sticking around. Something just feels wrong about this place."

Iri nodded. "Yes, it's as though those dead Gaptors tainted the air in this area."

It was all she needed to say to get Jaden moving. "Right, let's go. Everyone back to their gliders. Vicken? Sven?"

"Here," Vicken answered. "I've set the charges. As soon as we're clear, we can blow the place."

"Sven?" After a second, Jaden repeated it, more stridently. "Sven!"

"Yes, oh, sorry. I didn't register you were calling. Yes, I'm here."

"Have you figured out how to transport that thing?"

"I believe I've secured it for travel," Sven mumbled. "Or as near as I can be to being sure."

"We're out of time, so it will have to suffice. I don't want to be here if Slurpy sends more Gaptors through. We don't know if he can tell his beasties are dead, but there's no point in waiting around to find out."

"I'll meet you at the pick-up point," Sven replied before falling silent again.

"No more tinkering." When there was a problem to solve, Sven could get caught up in his head.

"No, I'm already on my way." Sven's heavy breathing confirming it.

"Mount up!" Jaden called, and the assembled riders filtered back to the pick-up point.

Minutes later, their group was circling the area. With everyone off the ground, it was time.

"Blow it," Jaden told Vicken.

"Let's put some space between us and the blast. The detonator's range allows for that."

At Jaden's nod, Han took the lead, and the rest of the gliders followed, rising to crest the mountain. They were almost at the very top when the explosion behind them rocked the air. A thunderous crash followed, and a large swathe of snow separated from the underlying pack.

The avalanche built in speed and size, rushing down the mountain and snapping trees like twigs. Seconds later, it spilled over the ruptured remains of the Gaptor nest and then onto the ice of the lake. It continued running all the way to the other side and piled up against the far mountain.

"Well, that went better than we thought it would!" Jaden crowed. "If Slurpy sends someone to investigate, they'll spend weeks digging through that snow to find anything. With luck, he'll think the avalanche took the camp out."

Vicken grinned. "You think that was luck?"

Jaden rolled his eyes. Clearly, Vicken's skills had delivered precisely what he'd planned. "Excellent execution."

Vicken laughed and then spurred his glider on. "Time to get back, open the chest, and figure out that comm system."

By the time they got back, though, everyone was exhausted. It had been almost thirty-four hours since Jaden had last slept. They had eschewed stops on the way home in favor of getting home sooner. Now, back in a secure location, all anyone could think about was sleep. Stashing the chest and device in a bunker Jaden hadn't known

Sven possessed, but that didn't surprise him to learn about, they all found the nearest the sleeping spots and crashed.

There was plenty of anticipation the next morning as Sven deposited the chest on the center table in the mess hall. When Jaden told him they couldn't recover a key, Sven had only laughed.

"You don't think I have something for that?"

Jaden was on the verge of telling him the chest might not be all it seemed based on their experiences, but he stopped himself. He would sound insane. If he'd known what would happen, he needn't have worried.

With a flourish, Sven produced a slim metal tube the size of his little finger. Directing its beam into the key slot of the chest, he pushed a button on the tube. Moments later, the lid snapped open. "You like my toy, no?"

But Jaden wasn't listening. He gawked at the chest. With the lid gaping wide, medallions were floating out, boosting themselves as though escaping a prison. His mouth fell open when the medallions hovered for a second before zooming in different directions all over the room. Small *oohs* and *aahs* escaped as each medallion stopped in front of an individual, making their way back to their generational owners.

Jaden didn't bother wondering how this was possible. He was beyond being surprised. "Take the medallion. The one floating in front of you is rightfully yours."

Everyone else was either too shocked by the magical distribution or as beyond questions as Jaden was because, without a word, the riders claimed their medallions.

Jaden grinned at Markov's awed expression. When Markov raised wide eyes, Jaden chuckled.

"I have my own medallion," Markov whispered.

"What are we supposed to do with them?" Vicken said, still turning his own medallion over in his hands as he inspected it.

"We needed the medallions to protect our riders from the Gaptors' EMP blasts. Now that we have them, we can end this," Jaden replied.

Even though he'd spoken quietly, the whole room went silent the moment he opened his mouth. They all stared back at him.

"You mean finish this for good?" Markov was the one who dared ask what they'd all been thinking.

"Yes. Problem is, I don't know how we do that." Jaden glanced into the chest. "Also, it seems we're missing people. This chest is still half full of medallions."

CHAPTER EIGHTEEN

Kayla had never been one to rely on others. With all the moving their family had done, she'd learned to be self-sufficient. It was easier to not have to disappoint someone else when they invariably moved on. Or be disappointed.

But this? Tarise is implying escape. Why offer me the opportunity to join her? Something's wrong with this picture. Tarise made no bones about wanting Jaden for herself. Except that plan backfired somehow. Tarise ended up here, as much a prisoner as me. But if she can escape back to Jaden and leave me here, well now, that would meet all her objectives, wouldn't it?

Kayla played along. Perhaps she might yet turn the tables on Tarise. "Yes, I'll heed your warning and be more civil the next time 'he' pays me a visit." That should be enough for whoever was listening to think Tarise had been warning her to be circumspect around the usurper.

Kayla blinked against the dark. How do they see in this infernal blackness? I need to get light in here. If I escape, I need my eyes accustomed to light. Otherwise, I'll be blind the moment I step outside. Assuming there is an outside. Or perhaps that's the point of all this darkness. To hinder escape.

As though Tarise approved, either of the words Kayla had spoken to sell the lie or of Kayla accepting her plan, her voice wasn't as cold when she spoke again. "I'll see you in two days."

So specific. That wasn't suspicious at all. Why doesn't Tarise just tell them when we're escaping? Aloud, Kayla said, "Why two days? Somewhere else you have to be?"

Tarise was silent for a fraction too long. Kayla paused. Her question had put Tarise off-balance. But why? Ugh, this is aggravating! I get an answer then don't know what it means!

"They said I couldn't see you tomorrow," Tarise blurted.

A weak excuse. Did Tarise really think Kayla would buy that? "Why not?"

This time, Tarise was snippy. "You think they tell me everything?"

It wouldn't surprise me if they did. If you're just playing both sides. Doing their bidding while planning your escape. Pretending you want me to escape with you because you need my help. Because you plan on double-crossing me as soon as you have what you want, perhaps using me as a scapegoat while you make a clean getaway. Kayla kept resentment from her voice but it was difficult. "I never said they did. I just hoped you might have an inkling why."

"Well, I don't. It seems this discussion is as pointless as our friendship. Maybe I won't see you in two days."

If there had been light, Kayla would've seen Tarise flounce out. But only the click of the door told Kayla she was alone again. Time to work on her own plans. First, she needed to figure out the layout of this place. Doing that would also tell her whether she needed to get her eyes adjusted to light. After that, she would reassess and make further plans accordingly.

Tarise's words suddenly echoed in her head. Why did they say Tarise can't see me tomorrow? Kayla went cold. Goosebumps peppered her skin. Is tomorrow the day Slurpy plans to cut into me? To slice off my birthmark?

The thought made Kayla sick. She focused on getting past her horror, debating whether this was even a plausible theory. Concluding it was only made her more skittish. Is there another reason to stop drugging me for an extended period? Slurpy isn't a fool. He'll only stop long enough so I can fully experience the pain he intends inflicting. So he can savor every second. Then . . . Kayla didn't want to think what would happen after he had taken what he wanted. After she had served her purpose.

Kayla sucked in a sudden sharp breath. It means only one thing. I have no choice. I have to escape today. I must wing it. That didn't mean she had to rush into it. Didn't mean she couldn't at least have some plan. Her brain ran through scenarios until it found an acceptable solution.

When she began screaming a few minutes later, it wasn't for show. She hadn't expected reopening the wound on her arm would hurt so much, but it was way worse than she'd imagined. She hadn't held back the hearty, full-blooded cry of agony. Blood dripped from the area at a steady clip now, enough to make a mess but not enough to weaken her.

Achieving her goal under the sheet's shielding privacy—where spying eyes couldn't see she had done this to herself—had taken some maneuvering. But she'd managed. After securing the scalpel Tarise had given her in the bandages around her leg, Kayla had used her fingers to find the spot on her arm where the skin glue formed a nodule. A sure sign of a novice bonding her skin.

Not allowing herself to think about what she was planning, Kayla had gripped the nodule firmly, then ripped upward. Pain shot white light through her. But she didn't stop. Enough of the nodule was attached to the rest of the glue to open a fair-sized section. When it tore free, Kayla sagged with relief. She only hoped the tear was clean. It would make repair faster.

Kayla continued wailing until the door banged open. Claws skittered across the floor. Then there were shrieks, so shrill she raised her hands to slam them over her ears. Before she could, the bed began rolling, and she had to grab at the sides.

Kayla didn't smile. This was only the first of a list of things which had to go her way to escape this nightmare. She clutched at her arm, pretending it was more interesting than her surroundings, but her eyes scanned the tunnel. Thankfully, the lighting was dim. Enough for her to see without blinding her.

She marked their path as they rolled across tunnels intersecting theirs, noting how many intersections passed before they finally made a right turn. Then another right turn. Five more openings. A left turn.

The commotion to her right almost made her lose track. She doubled over with a loud wail, and the bed stopped moving long enough for her to peek into the room.

The woman standing with her back to the doorway, hands on her hips, every line of her body telegraphing anger, was shouting. She was making enough noise that she either hadn't heard Kayla's wail or didn't care. Even though her back was to Kayla, her voice was unmistakable. Tarise!

"Where is he? I have to see him! She doesn't trust me."

Kayla's mind worked furiously. "He" has to be Slurpy. "She" is me. Why is Tarise in such a tizzy? Unless there's a clock on this?

An irritated female voice replied, "I already said I didn't know. I also told you to let me get the last of his creations through, and then I'd help you find him."

Only then did Kayla see what was causing most of the commotion. Countless Gaptors were stuffed together at the far end of the room, their wings and beaks clacking into each other. They fidgeted, each Gaptor trying to find a clear space for itself, the mass of claws scraping on the ground enough to generate a constant clatter.

That wasn't what drew her attention, though, or made her pulse spike. At the very back of the elongated, narrow room, an arch glowed, pulsing light through the room like a beating heart.

Before she could see more, the beast rolled her bed away. She'd ceased wailing when the bed stopped moving. The Gaptor, perhaps intending on checking on her, hadn't bothered. Perhaps he thought a stop was all she'd needed.

Whatever his reasoning, Kayla couldn't believe he'd stopped when he had. The Gaptors really lacked mental acuity. Because, if she wasn't mistaken, the room he had allowed her to glimpse contained the portal between worlds.

The revelation was so stunning she forgot to count the rooms and passages they passed. Only when the bed took such a radical right turn that she almost rolled out of it, did she remember she was supposed to keep track.

As if fate were intervening—or was it a darker force?—she heard clicking. Not just any clicking. A sound identical to the one she and Jaden heard all those months ago at the storage facility. The sound an old rotary telephone made if you left it off the hook for too long.

We were right! It's how Slurpy communicates with his minions! Then her bed was crashing around another corner, and she focused on the turns again. But there weren't any more. Seconds later, the only turn the bed made was into a room she remembered from before. The one with the bright overhead disc for a light.

Intentional or not, Kayla was thankful the light wasn't on. If it had been, it would've blinded her. Casting her eyes around in a quick scan, she wondered whether the light being off had been intentional after all—so she could see the strange instruments lined up on a tray and along the one wall.

Not medical instruments. Things with curly ends and spiky tips and long wands, reminding her of the tools they found in those dungeons where they retrieved the first artifact. Had he been in that place too? All those centuries ago?

The sudden loss of the Gaptor's revolting odor made her aware he'd left the room. He hadn't said a word. Just dumped her here and left. Kayla realized it was just her and the nurse in the room. The woman had her back to Kayla as she checked the tools lined up on that tray against a clipboard in her hands. But even from this angle Kayla recognized her as the woman who had been in the operating room with Slurpy that day.

Kayla croaked, loud enough to get the woman's attention. "Water!"

The woman whirled. Evidently, she hadn't heard Kayla being delivered. "You're only supposed to be here tomorrow." Then her eyes went wide at the sight of the blood. "What happened to your arm? I thought I fixed that!"

Dropping the clipboard, she dashed over and grabbed Kayla's arm.

Her proximity was what Kayla had hoped for. Not wasting the opportunity, Kayla whipped her free hand up, chopping it into the woman's throat. The woman's eyes bulged, and her hands went to her throat as she gasped for air.

Kayla's hands were both free now. In a fluid motion, too fast for the woman to react, Kayla grabbed the woman's head and slammed it down on the metal edge of her bed. Pain stabbed her leg. Kayla muffled her cry, angling her body so she was ready for another attack. But the woman collapsed onto the floor, unconscious. Now what?

CHAPTER NINETEEN

It was a miserable night. Despite his exhaustion, Jaden slept in fits and starts. Every time he woke, getting back to sleep again took forever. His brain whirred like a fan trying to cool an overheated CPU. How did they find the owners of the other medallions? Was Kayla still alive? How could he cross the breach? On and on the questions went until he finally dozed again. When dawn filtered past the drawn shades, Jaden gave up on sleep and went scrounging for food.

Passing the monitoring room where they kept tabs on not only the entrance to Sven's valley but communications in general, he heard excited chatter. He poked his head inside. "What's up?"

Atu turned serious eyes his way. "Come in. You've got to see this to believe it."

Mystified, Jaden ambled closer until he could see the screen Atu held out to him. He stared, not sure what he was looking at. Then it shifted, and he got a better view. Memories of the desert came roaring back. The unnaturally large rats with teeth almost as long as his hand. That hideous spider weaving webs of cabled steel. The snake with polished metallic scales.

Something else caught his attention. He was glad he hadn't eaten yet, or it would've ended up on the floor.

"My reaction too," Atu said, taking his screen back.

"Can you explain it?"

"No."

"When did this start?"

"I've gone back through the footage. As far as I can tell, it began when those Gaptors came through that gate. The day when it wasn't just us who could see the Gaptors and gliders. But the changes were so small, I think everyone missed them until they became what they are now."

Shocked, Jaden stared at Atu. "You think this is an ongoing process? That they'll keep changing?"

In answer, Atu turned to the bank of screens in front of him. He began throwing images onto the wall behind the monitors. "It's easiest to see the progression in domestic animals."

The screens showed several shots of the interior of a home. It looked familiar. "You hacked someone's security system?"

"I didn't have to. This is Shianna's home. She gave me the codes."

A hand shot up into the air from behind the backrest of a large chair. "Hey, Jaden."

Shianna had been so quiet, Jaden hadn't realized she was in the room. "Heya, back. What do you make of this?"

"It's incredible. I've never seen transformations like this. Usually, it takes generations, and then the changes are tiny adaptations to the environment. But these changes happen in the space of a few weeks. Watch!"

Although Jaden understood her fascination, it was disturbing she didn't see the bigger picture. "You do realize these . . . things could be dangerous?"

Swiveling in her chair, Shianna focused the full power of her emerald gaze on him. "I know. Just because I'm passionate about the subject doesn't make me blind to reality. Why do you think I'm here studying the phenomenon?"

Jaden stared at the screens. The first was an image of Shianna's cat, an adorable tabby with black and gray stripes and a black mark resembling an *M* on its forehead. On the second screen, Shianna had highlighted changes to the ears. They were longer and more tapered. The third screen showed her cat yawning, highlights emphasizing the pronounced canines.

On and on, until the final screen where a revolting hairless pink blob hissed at the camera. Its fangs extended beyond the mouth and dripped with saliva. The ears had hardened into things bristling with tiny, shiny spikes. The wickedly curved claws looked like they could shred Kevlar.

"Jaden?"

He registered Shianna was waiting for an answer but ignored the question. "Will she ever go back to being what she was?" He'd loved that cat.

Shianna's eyes shimmered with sorrow. "I don't know. That's why I'm here. There has to be a reason for this. There has to be something we can do to reverse whatever is happening."

Jaden slumped into a nearby chair. "And this isn't just limited to house cats?"

Shianna shook her head, replacing the images on the wall with others. Things that could've been birds. More that looked like they had been insects. He closed his eyes at what had to have been a dog once. "Are they all changing as quickly as your cat?"

"Some changes have been faster, others slower but more dramatic. The common denominator is whatever they might've used to protect themselves before is now more a weapon than a defense."

"Any reports of these things attacking people yet?"

Atu answered this time. "No. But looking at these things, it's only a matter of time."

Jaden was silent as he digested the information. The changes began when the gate had appeared. Would they stop if the gate appeared again or accelerate? Why were the animals in his world changing? He glanced at Shianna.

"We know when the changes started. What do you think triggered them?"

Shianna shrugged. "My best guess is the atmosphere of that other world affected the animals closest to it. Or they pumped something through from that world. Whatever was in that air was the catalyst for the mutations."

"But if that's true, wouldn't the changes only affect a negligible part of the animal population?"

"That's just it!" Shianna exclaimed, her eyes shining. "Logic says it should only have been birds affected at that altitude. So why are animals on the ground showing symptoms? After asking myself that question, I began charting the progress of the changes—or at least, how they looked based on the limited information I could gather. And do you know what I found?" She didn't wait for an answer. "It started in the area directly under that open gate! An almost perfect circle. Since then, the circle's been growing. Jaden, I think it contagious!"

Jaden's legs would've given way if he wasn't already seated. How were they going to fight this? "How fast is it spreading?"

"Slowly enough I think it's a direct contact disease."

"So you think the cats got it from eating infected birds?"

"Yes. Other animals could've contracted it the same way or from coming into contact with the excrement of infected animals."

"It's possible to contain it, then?"

Shianna rolled her eyes. "How are you going to contain birds?"

"How do we stop it?"

"I've been conversing with the CDC. They're sending a team."

Jaden scrubbed his hands over his face. Wasn't it enough to deal with the Gaptors? Now they had to cure the world too? And, oh yes, still find time to get that last artifact and somehow finish this mission? And how were they going to do any of it without Kayla? It was too much for one person.

Jaden felt Shianna's hand on his shoulder. "Chill, dude. I've got this part of the equation. You go find Kayla and finish this thing you started. With any luck, severing the link between our worlds might prevent the spread."

Jaden almost laughed at the ludicrous statement. It was a shot in the dark. But he would take it. That meant getting on with the mission. But they had no map—or none they knew of. Zareh had said the map was already in their possession. He'd said something else, but right now, Jaden couldn't recall what. He'd have to think. Maybe there had been a clue there.

"Thanks, I appreciate you taking the lead. I really don't have the bandwidth to deal with much more."

Shianna only gave his shoulder a quick, comforting rub. "Why do you think I'm doing this?"

Jaden couldn't resist. "Because it's in your wheelhouse. And you have to understand it."

She grinned. "You know me too well. Now, shoo! Get out of here. You have things to do and so do I."

Jaden laughed. "Atu, you heard the lady. You coming? We have answers to find—and plans to make!"

Jaden studied his mother. Her face was distant as she stared into the past. Or rather, into that memory of the dream she'd had. The vision of what would come to pass.

Or would it? They had changed things when he had given her his ring.

The question remained. Had she seen animals? Or had she simply been unable to recall that? Or not dreamed for long enough to see? *Ugh, enough questions!*

He focused on his mother again. Jaden knew it was a big ask. Every time she spoke of that place, she relived the agony. But he needed to know, and she was the only one who might provide answers.

When he had voiced concern to Atu about asking his mother, the healer had offered to create something to give his mother a temporary window into that memory without suffering the usual traumatic after-effects. Jaden had pounced on it. Going back there was already an ordeal for his mother. He didn't want her experiencing any more discomfort than necessary.

She'd been willing to oblige once Atu explained how the potion worked. Several minutes in now, his mother still hadn't said a word. Jaden glanced at Atu. Atu only shook his head, indicating Jaden should give his mother time. Jaden started when his mother suddenly began speaking, her words a little slurred.

"I loathe this place! It's beyond depressing. I can almost touch the horror shrouding it. All these people in this heinous situation. And they're all terrified." She was quiet for a moment. Then her breathing picked up, her voice higher than before. "They're running past me, screaming, trying to get away."

Jaden tried for a soothing voice. "Mom, I can't imagine how awful it is. Try to see past the people. Do you see any animals?"

His mother's eyes roamed, but she wasn't seeing the room they were in. She scanned that other place. The land of her visions. The place of nightmares come to life.

"I can only see people. And no, they're just people. They haven't grown horns or fangs. They're all so desperate!" Her voice hitched. Her eyes closed as though she wanted to escape the images.

Maybe Jaden needed to try a different tactic. "Mom, look at the ground. Don't look up at the people. Can you see any insects?"

Clara's head dropped. Her hand moved. "It's so cool. And soothing." Her fingers rippled like they were sifting through something.

Jaden raised an eyebrow at Atu. He shrugged. "Mom, what are you touching?"

Clara's eyes shifted as she focused on what she held. "I don't know. But it's soft and powdery. And it's so cool. The earth is so hot." She made as if to rise.

Jaden leaped up and cradled her in place. "Mom, you can't move there yet. I know it's nice and cool. But before you go there, find an insect or animal first." When his mother's face crumpled, Jaden's heart shriveled. He couldn't take much more of this. "Mom, could you stay a little longer? Maybe find an insect for me?"

His mother's head moved again as if she were looking. "It's all gone. They're all dead. There's nothing left. Except this." Her hand moved, and Jaden suspected she was touching the cool thing again. "It's the only lovely thing remaining." Abruptly, her fingers stopped moving.

"What's wrong?"

His mother frowned. "I don't know. There's a little piece of something hard here."

Jaden watched as her fingers sorted through whatever it was she saw. Then her eyes widened. "What are you doing here?"

"Mom, what is it?"

She appeared bewildered. "It's a piece of a medallion. I can make out the little ink pot and part of that pearly background." Then, her fingers were scrabbling again. "Oh, no! They're all gone! He burned them!"

"What's gone. Mom?" Jaden urged, but he thought he already knew.

His mother's face grew desperate as she seemed to pull little pieces of things out from the pile. "The medallions! They're all gone, turned to ash, except for these tiny pieces."

Her voice was rising. Jaden turned to Atu, but this time, his friend was already moving.

"Here, Mrs. Jameson, breathe this. It will help." He placed a small bunch of leaves under her nose.

Without hesitation, she inhaled. Her eyes snapped back, finding the real world once more. "Did I find the animals?"

Jaden glanced at Atu.

He rolled his eyes. "I told you your mom wouldn't remember anything."

Facing his mother again, Jaden said, "No, Mom, you couldn't find any. There weren't any left for you to find."

Clara pulled a face. "Sorry." Then she smiled at Atu. "Thanks for helping me get there without having to relive the experience—or remember doing it."

"Anytime."

Clara studied Jaden. "If you like, I can try again?"

"Thanks, Mom, but I don't think that'll be necessary. I don't think we'll find anything there no matter how many times you go back."

"Alright. I'm off to find something to eat. I'm ravenous!"

Jaden chuckled. "I thought that was my line!"

She giggled, that lovely sound tinkling out of her. "See you later."

Jaden watched her leave, then placed a hand on Atu's shoulder. "Thanks. I really appreciate what you did for her."

"Sure. If it was my mom, I wouldn't want her to experience any of that more than once or have to deal with the aftermath. So, what did you make of it?"

Jaden scratched his chin. "Well, she found something she didn't before. That proves the tonic worked. If that's true, and she didn't see any animals or insects, I'm thinking it's also true they weren't there to see. If she could remember the details of the ash, then figure out what it was, she would've found the animals had they been there."

"Hmm, my thoughts exactly. That means we still don't know if the changes we're seeing in the animals are part of that future or not."

"Pity. It would've been nice to have confirmation. But here's what I don't get. Of all the places she could've been sitting, why did she end up right next to the ash pile of medallions?"

"You're thinking there's more to that than coincidence?"

"Oh, didn't you know? I don't believe in coincidence anymore."

Atu chuckled. "Yeah, I hear you. Why do you think they were there?"

"The only working theory I have is that the image or memory highlighted the medallions' importance. Not that we didn't already know that. But perhaps also to hint that we should gather them; to be sure we collect *all* the medallions—what for, I don't know. The ash pile suggests Slurpy incinerated some or all of them. In which case, the memory is a warning that if Slurpy gets his hands on even some of them, we can't win."

"What's to say he hasn't already destroyed some?"

"Nothing. That's the problem. We could do all this and then still end up not having every single medallion. But we do have one thing going for us."

"And what's that?"

"If the medallions were all kept in that chest here in our world, chances are favorable Slurpy hasn't smuggled them across to his world yet. Maybe when Zareh was enchanting the medallions, he also added something to prevent from being taken from our world to theirs."

"A failsafe to prevent Slurpy from getting his hands on them?"

"Yes. Assuming that's true, there's still hope."

"And isn't that what the last clue was all about?" Atu mused.

"That brings us full circle. Time to find that next map."

CHAPTER TWENTY

Atu looked put out. "What about figuring out why we need *all* the medallions? Or what we need to do with them?"

Jaden shrugged. "That will have to wait. If those questions are like anything else on this quest, the answers will come when we need them. Until then, we use the medallions for the one thing we know they're good for - protecting the riders against the Gaptors' EMP's."

"I'll let it go for now. Although we should tell the others. You never know. Inspiration could hit, and one of them could come up with the solution."

"I agree. Now, about finding the map. Do you have—"

"Jaden! We need you in the control center."

Markov's interruption was so abrupt, registering first the words and then the urgency behind them took Jaden a moment.

Without a word, he raced after Markov back to the comm room, Atu following them. They burst into the control room. The commotion made Jaden want to roar for silence. He glanced at the screens. And froze.

Every screen showed chaos. People rioting in the streets. Smashing windows. Acting like lunatics. Attacking others who got in their way.

Grabbing what others were looting from stores and racing away before the looters could reclaim the goods.

"What is going on?"

The hubbub in the room was so loud, Jaden didn't think anyone had heard him. But Markov leaned closer.

"The Gaptors have figured out what power stations do. They've been blasting the sites with their EMPs. Power grids are going down all over, and not only on our continent."

Jaden swallowed. "They're attacking the entire world?"

Markov nodded, his face grim. Atu had gone pale.

Jaden stared at the screens, his mind churning. If the Gaptors were taking down the power, the time for Slurpy's assault must be close. Without power, the world would stop. People would return to a level of subsistence living. It would render the ordnances of this world impotent. It would lay waste to weapons with the ability to wreak complete devastation. What chance did they have against a force like this?

"How much of the power grid have they taken down so far?"

"They're only just getting started," Vicken replied.

Jaden wasn't surprised the man had snuck up on them. He nodded a greeting, which Vicken acknowledged before he continued speaking.

"The images you're seeing on these screens are from isolated cities. However, they're representative of the chaos that will follow in other cities when their power goes down. The more cities that go down, the more complex the problem becomes and the more the infrastructure that supports a city will erode. And when you tally the combined effect, the picture isn't pretty."

His silence left the rest to Jaden's imagination. "Not much hope then if we don't finish this mission. It seems the visions my mom had weren't so far off the mark."

Before he could say more, a hand tapped his shoulder. Someone thrust a headset into his hands. "For you."

Befuddled, Jaden put the headset on. "Hello?"

"Jaden, it's Shianna. Over here—at the far end of the room."

Jaden glanced that way and saw her standing on a chair and waving her arms in the air.

"Hurry over here. I have the CDC on the line, and I don't know how much longer we'll have a connection before the power outages cut us off."

Jaden plowed through the crowd, pushing and shoving his way through until he reached her. She grinned, gave him a quick hug, and got down to business as she faced the screen in front of her.

"Dr. Breegan, this is Jaden Jameson. Please tell him what you just told me."

In the screen's background, past Dr. Breegan, Jaden saw the part of town over which the gate had opened. The CDC hadn't wasted time getting here and setting up a field tent. He was about to introduce himself, but Dr. Breegan's first sentence told him the man knew who he was and where he fitted in.

"Jaden, I wish you had told us about these Gaptors when you first saw them. It's not only their beaks and claws that are dangerous. They're the reason for the changes we're seeing in these animals. Any time a drop of their blood touches something or they release their EMP, everything near them gets contaminated. Changes manifest within twenty-four hours."

Jaden squashed the helplessness that threatened to overwhelm him. "What about the rate of change? Any idea why some animals change faster than others?"

"The working theory right now is animals subjected to repeated exposure exhibit accelerated changes."

"But a single exposure is enough to start the change?"

"Yes."

"Since this appears to be an animal to animal transmission, will you work on an antidote?"

"Already in process, as is work on a vaccine. Just because we've seen no changes in humans doesn't mean they aren't happening at a microscopic level. I'll be sending some people to examine you and your team."

"Why?"

"Your exposure to these creatures is the most extensive. If anyone were to exhibit signs of infection, it would be you."

Really? I have to add this to everything else we're dealing with? When will it stop?

Atu tapped his shoulder. "May we speak alone for a moment?"

Jaden pulled the headset off, surprised to find Atu had a headset of his own. "What's up?" Jaden asked as he and Atu took a few steps away from the others.

"Dr. Breegan makes a valid point. While I can confirm we're not infected, that may not be true for any of the riders I haven't healed."

A million questions ran through Jaden's mind, but he asked the most pertinent. "How can you be sure?"

"If you ever trusted me, believe me on this. I'm sure. We're not infected. But it would be a good idea for that team to come out and examine the others."

Jaden was beyond trying to understand Atu's gift. The only way to get a direct answer was to ask a direct question. "Can't you heal the others, the same as us?"

Atu shook his head. "It doesn't work like that. Believe me, if I could, I would. But there's a real chance it may have infected some of these riders. He should send the team. I'll give him a list of names of those I haven't healed. Let him establish whether they're at risk. If not, we can cross that off the list of things to worry about. But if they do find changes that aren't yet visible to the naked eye, perhaps Dr. Breegan's team can compare our blood or tissue with the infected to come up with a cure."

"Alright, let's find a place they can test people other than here."

Atu's eyebrows shot up. "Why?"

"I just have a feeling that the fewer people who know about this place, the better."

"One of those feelings?"

"Yes."

"How about if we use the healing center in the mountains?"

Jaden thought a moment. "Yes, easily defended and far from our army. Can you arrange it? I'll ask Sven about setting up some of those cannons of his."

As though speaking about him conjured Sven from wherever he'd been hiding, Sven barreled into the room, his face red and his breathing labored. Spotting Jaden, he hurried over, ignoring the screens and their proclamations of impending doom.

"He took it!"

"Who took what?" Jaden asked.

"That little fuzzball! He bypassed my security, marched in, and waved his little arms—and poof! The device was gone! As was he."

It took Jaden a second. "Zareh came and took the comm device we recovered from the Gaptor nest?"

"Yes! What do you think I'm telling you?"

"Did he say anything?"

"No, not even a thank you! He just complained that I shouldn't be meddling with things I didn't understand and—poof!"

Sven's outrage was comical, as was the way he said, "Poof!" Jaden bit back his smile when he remembered how much Sven enjoyed understanding how things worked. "He's a frustrating little rascal, isn't he?"

Sven nodded. "And if I ever see him again, I'll tell him so."

The chuckle escaped. Jaden couldn't help it. Shaking his head, he said, "Now you understand how I feel about the aggravating runt. Let's talk about something more interesting. How do you feel about setting up some defenses around Atu's medical camp?"

Sven's eyes sparkled with interest. "Tell me more."

An hour later, Jaden gathered everyone. They met in the mess hall, sitting on the tables, chairs, and floor, too many for such a small area. Jaden waved a hand for silence. The hum died down.

"You've all seen what's happening out there. I'm sure you've also figured out that things will only get worse unless we rid ourselves of the Gaptors. But before we go charging off into battles again, there's something you should know."

In the briefest terms possible, Jaden outlined Clara's dream, then explained the significance of the ash pile. After that, he opened up the floor to suggestions regarding how the medallions could destroy the Gaptors.

"What would happen if we piled them together?" someone shouted.

"Nothing, they'd just be a pile of medallions," someone else quipped.

There was general laughter. The person who'd spoken first said, "How do we know it won't work?"

"Because nothing happened when they were all in that chest together," came a reply.

"But they weren't all in there, were they? The seekers' medallions were missing," someone else shouted.

It was the first time this had occurred to Jaden. More importantly, it meant something else. He raised his hand again to quell the conversations erupting all over the room. "That's a valid point. Even if we wanted to try something now, we can't. There's still at least one medallion missing. And if we need to have them all for this to work, we have to find Kayla before we can try anything."

Gloom cloaked the room.

"That doesn't mean I don't want you thinking about potential solutions. When Kayla's back, we'll need options." A few murmurs. "Until then, become proficient with your gliders, masters with your weapons, and innovative with your plays. There will be another battle. And this time, we'll smoke them."

Cheers. Grins. He'd done his work. Time to find Atu and Iri and figure out where the map was.

Grouped around a coffee table in the living room that evening, the three of them considered their options. Jaden debated mentioning what was on his mind.

"Tell us, Jaden." Iri's quiet command was as unnerving as her ability to read him.

He shifted in his chair. "I've been thinking about Kayla's birthmark."

Iri understood. "You mean its translation of 'key?'"

"Yeah. Do you think it's possible her birthmark *is* the map?"

Iri frowned. "Wouldn't the translation have been 'map' if that was the case?"

"You know how convoluted all these clues have been. What if Zareh designed it that way so that Slurpy wouldn't know she was a map?"

"Do you think that's why he took her?" Atu's voice was grim.

"I've tried not to think about that. But it's time I did. At first, I thought he took her so he could get to me. I mean, he tried taking our parents, and that didn't work. Perhaps he figured taking Kayla would be more effective."

"If that's true, then why hasn't he summoned you or offered to trade Kayla for you?" Iri countered.

"Yeah, I wondered about that too," Jaden said. "But what if that wasn't why he took her? What if he somehow knows or figured out she's the key?"

Iri's eyes flicked to Atu's, and Jaden noticed the silent exchange. "What?"

"Don't get mad at us for saying her name—" Atu began.

"Tarise!" Jaden hissed. "You think she told Slurpy what Kayla's birthmark meant?"

"I wouldn't put it past her," Atu said.

Jaden's face scrunched up.

Iri frowned. "What's bothering you now?"

Jaden put his head in his hands. When he spoke, his words were barely audible. "If Kayla is the key, doesn't that mean her chances of survival just dropped significantly?"

Their silence wasn't reassuring.

"We can't work with that theory. We have to believe she's still alive. I mean, if she wasn't, wouldn't all of this already be over? Wouldn't the Gaptors be in control?" Atu's voice was harsh with conviction.

"His argument has merit," Iri said, as if to further convince Jaden.

Jaden sighed. "I don't have a choice, do I? I have to believe she's still alive. I have to believe we'll get her back." Jaden scrubbed his face. "Setting that aside—if Kayla isn't the map or the key to it, then where is the map?"

Atu frowned. "How would we know? No, why should we know?"

"Do you remember what Zareh said when we told him we didn't have the map? When he came to warn us about the battle?"

Atu gave it some thought. "I only remember him telling us the battle was coming." He glanced at Iri. "You?"

"No. I didn't even see him. He appeared and vanished in the time it took me to use the bathroom."

"In that case, let me help you. He said we didn't get a map because it was already in our possession. He said something else, but for the life of me, I can't remember what."

Iri shrugged. "Let's rule out the options, then. What have we gained since this started?"

Jaden began counting them off on his fingers. "Our medallions. The relic stones. My grandmother's key. The toy chest—no way, you think it's on the toy chest?"

"Unlikely. And you've forgotten the most important thing." Atu was grinning.

"I have?"

Atu drew out the agony for a second. "What about Awena's book?"

Jaden couldn't believe he'd forgotten. "Yes!" In that moment, the words came back to him. "I think you nailed it! I just remembered what Zareh said, and it fits perfectly."

Atu raised an eyebrow. "Are you going to tell us?"

"Oh, sorry!" Jaden assumed a pose, trying to look like Zareh. "Your guide, it has been, since received it, you did."

Atu burst out laughing. "You sound nothing like him. Although the pose was believable."

Jaden grinned. "What do you think? Those words fit the book perfectly. The book has given us the names of the places we've had to travel to. It makes sense that it will provide the next location."

"You could be right. Where is it? Let's run through that baby with the ultramagnifier and see what we can find!"

Atu's uncharacteristic enthusiasm had Jaden doing a double take. Why was he being so optimistic? It was almost as if he were being overly jovial. One glance at Iri's face answered his question. "You needn't coddle me. I'll be okay. I believe we will get Kayla back. And when that happens, I need to be sure we have a map in hand so we can finish this without delay."

Iri studied him in that way of hers. Satisfied, she nodded. "Okay. Let's get the book and find that map."

CHAPTER TWENTY-ONE

Kayla stared at the woman, breathing hard and fighting back the nausea from the pain shooting up her leg. To think she and the others had originally told Sven hand-to-hand combat had no place in fighting this war! She'd have to remember to thank Sven for insisting they master it.

Glancing at the doorway, Kayla listened. No sounds of running feet—or skittering claws. *No one's coming to investigate. Excellent! I need to remove the implant and close that door.* Kayla retrieved the scalpel from the bandages around her leg. Deftly, she sliced across the bandages, and they fell away.

Kayla groaned when she saw the two tiny stitches. No wonder the cut hurt so much. Why the woman had used stitches instead of skin glue, she didn't know. But at least reopening the wound wouldn't be as painful. Gritting her teeth, Kayla carefully picked at the stitches with the tip of the scalpel.

Minutes later, coated in sweat and puffing like she'd run a marathon, Kayla stared at the microscopic chip on the tip of her bloody finger. For something so small, they could've injected it. *Why did they cut my leg open instead?* Examining the cut, she thought she knew.

The woman who now lay unconscious on the floor had no medical training. She'd been using Kayla as a guinea pig. The cut was too deep and at the wrong angle. The skin glue she had tried to apply to Kayla's arm hadn't worked, so the woman opted for stitches on her leg instead. With thread that had no place in a human body. Kayla was lucky she hadn't gotten an infection.

Sighing, Kayla buried the chip in her pocket, then limped to the door and quickly closed it. She rifled through cabinet. There was no time to remedy the woman's pathetic attempt at closing the gash on her arm. At any moment someone might walk in, and the game would be up.

Kayla settled for spray rather than skin glue, sealing the section of her arm she had torn open. When she'd applied the requisite two layers, she repeated the quick fix on her leg, wishing there was time to repair both areas properly with skin glue. But the spray and bandages would have to do. Expertly, she wrapped the bandages around her leg and arm, making sure they were tight. She prayed the spray would hold long enough for her to get away.

A quick assessment of the woman on the floor told her the head wound was minor. Not wanting to risk the woman waking and raising the alarm, Kayla found more bandages and used them to tie the woman to the bedpost. As an added precaution, she wrapped a few layers around the woman's mouth. *That should keep her quiet.*

With a last backward glance at the woman to make sure her position allowed her to breathe, Kayla crept to the door. Putting her ear against it, she listened. No sounds. Cracking the door, she peeked outside. The passage was empty.

Gripping the tools she'd stolen, she slid down the corridor, gritting her teeth against the pain in her arm and leg. Kayla paused and inspected every intersection and doorway before she crossed it. Getting caught now would ruin everything. She just needed to keep going until she hit that comm room.

When she heard clicking, she slowed. Stopping short of the doorway, she dared a quick glance inside before ducking her head back behind the wall. Two men, both of them facing their consoles, their backs to her. *Really, doesn't anyone here think they should be placed facing attack instead of away from it so people can't sneak up on them?* Then she answered her own question.

They thought they were invulnerable. No one would attack Slurpy's fortress, or whatever this place was. Come to think of it, Kayla remembered Taz saying that no one knew where Slurpy had disappeared to. No wonder they didn't bother with security.

But how are humans here? Isn't this Zareh's world? Or did Zareh or their gliders just not think to tell them humans also inhabited their world? Worse, how can humans stomach working with the usurper? Don't they know what his plans are?

Deciding the humans weren't working for Slurpy by choice was the only way to explain something so irrational. Although, considering what she had to do now, imagining they were willing participants would have been easier.

Kayla glided into the room, stealth in every step. Staying behind the men, she touched the tip of the tool to the first man's neck. She pressed the button. Kayla almost dropped the taser when it zapped him. She hadn't expected it to be so loud. The first man collapsed before the second man started moving. Kayla swung the taser in his direction, and the man froze. Not giving him a chance to reconsider, Kayla lunged, zapping him too.

With both men down, her eyes ran over the instrument panel. More than ever, she wished Jaden was here. He would know what all these buttons and dials were for. Since she didn't, she couldn't afford to skimp. Liberally spraying the console and monitors with the acetone she had snatched from the "surgery," she made sure anything that looked important was well coated.

Then she hurried to the edge of the room, leaving a trail of bandages as she did. She paused inside the doorway, peeking out to check the coast was clear. When there was no sign of movement, she lit the matches and tossed them onto the bandages. She only gave herself a split second to verify the bandages were leading the flames to the comm unit before she ran for all she was worth.

Thanks to the surge of adrenaline burning through her veins, blocking the pain in her leg was easier now. Kayla turned the corner and sprinted down the corridor, counting the doorways and cross passages. This time, she didn't bother confirming she wouldn't be seen. Soon enough, anyone who saw her would have better things to worry about.

Just before she reached the last corridor to that arch, that magical gate between worlds, the explosion ripped through the complex. Kayla ducked down, partly to shield herself from the force of the blast, should it have made it this far down the tunnel, and partly to hide. If she stayed small and in the darkest part of the corridor, those who came racing past to investigate might miss her.

She needn't have worried. The bearer of that voice she heard in the gateway room earlier burst out. She didn't even check the corridor, running in the opposite direction from Kayla.

Kayla waited a few seconds. When Tarise didn't emerge, she wondered whether the serpent had slithered out. *Or is she still inside?*

Erring on the side of caution, Kayla crept forward, sneaking a glance into the room. Empty. Crashing footsteps pounded her way, coming from the direction of the comm room. Time to move. Kayla sidled into the gateway room.

The most obvious thing was the arch, still pulsing with light. *Does that mean it's still on? Still able to send things back to my world? Or does it always do that?* Slashing the questions away, Kayla scanned the room. Several pieces of equipment were scattered along the walls lining the long, thin sides. The closest item was a console, most likely what the woman had been using to control the gate.

It was the only place Kayla could reach before those footsteps caught up to her. Scurrying behind the console, Kayla waited. She strained to hear over the whirr of the console's fans. Then the feet clattered past. The agitated voices told her they weren't looking for her, but a way to escape the flames spreading to other parts of the complex.

Kayla didn't care if the whole place burned to the ground. *Good riddance!* Before it did, though, she needed to figure out how to use that gate. She had to get back to Jaden. Risking a quick glance over the console, she saw no one. But she did spot something that might be of use.

Snatching the clipboard off the console, Kayla dashed toward the gate. A few feet from the pulsing arch, she hurled the clipboard at the opening. She didn't stop running but moved slightly off center. If the arch tossed the clipboard back at her, she wouldn't be a target. And if that happened, or the clipboard passed through the opening to the other side, she would know the gate wasn't functional.

Blinding light flashed as the clipboard entered the arch. Kayla slammed on the brakes, her hands lifting to protect her eyes. As quickly as the light flared, it disappeared. Kayla blinked at the bright spot blocking her vision, trying to clear the tears blurring them. The bright spot faded to dull red.

Then she could see. The clipboard was gone! Only the pulsing arch remained. She took a step forward. Tarise appeared in front of her.

"I wouldn't go in there."

Kayla's anger blazed. "Why not? Because it'll spoil whatever plan you have for me?"

"No, because you'll end up in the sky, hundreds of feet off the ground. With no glider, you'll crash down and die."

Kayla reminded herself she couldn't trust Tarise. "How do I know you're not just saying that?"

Tarise rolled her eyes. "When you saw the Gaptors coming through that gate, where were they appearing? On the ground or in the sky?"

The question made Kayla hesitate. She hadn't thought about that, but it was true. The Gaptors had popped through in the sky, way above Daxsos. Far too high for her to survive a fall. She wanted to hold on to her suspicions, but another memory slapped her: the way the Gaptors had always appeared out of nowhere while she and Taz and the others were flying. They really did pop up in the air in Kayla's world.

But the way Tarise was looking at her . . . like she was meat for a shark. Tarise had to have had a plan. "If that's true, how were you planning on getting us out of here? How were we going to escape?"

143

Tarise smirked. "Who said we were both getting out of here?"

The question confirmed everything Kayla believed, but it didn't make her feel any better. Kayla's voice was hollow. "You were just going to use me to get yourself out?"

"I needed someone to test the settings when I changed them. To make sure I didn't end up mangled or dead on the other side. What better use is there for a backstabbing girl who steals someone else's man?"

Kayla's anger flamed anew. "Jaden was never yours. In fact, he's no one's property, Not a piece of flesh you can own."

She would've said more—except Tarise barreled into her, teeth bared, eyes glittering with hatred. The impact knocked Kayla down. She panted for breath, the agony in her leg making it hard to think. As Kayla gasped to regain the air that had been forced out, Tarise jumped on top of her. She locked her hands around Kayla's throat and clamped down as she screamed.

"Why did you have to ruin everything? Why are you here? I haven't had time to coerce the correct setting from the tech yet. Now we're just going to have to figure it out on our own. And if you're dead before you go through, it doesn't matter."

Kayla's instincts kicked in. Using her legs to boost herself upward, she bucked Tarise enough to loosen the hold. As Tarise's arms flailed trying to find something to latch onto, Kayla rolled sideways, using the movement and her uninjured arm to shove Tarise off. Tarise hit the ground with an audible "oof," and Kayla scrambled on top of her.

Kayla's hands were going for her head when Tarise's knee punched her in the kidney. Pain shrieked along her nerves. Using Kayla's distraction, Tarise twisted away, lifting a leg and wrapping it around Kayla's neck. Then she rolled and pinned Kayla to the ground.

No way Tarise is winning this fight! Using her arm, Kayla shoved up on Tarise's leg, forcing the knee backward. Yelping, Tarise angled herself to relieve the pressure. Kayla was free. She scurried backward, a little disoriented. She stood, vaguely aware her leg had started bleeding through the bandage and of a buzzing near her. Turning her head a fraction, she confirmed the arch was directly behind her. Not good.

Even as she twisted back to face Tarise, she was a split second too late. Tarise hurtled forward, arms outstretched. Before Kayla could take evasive action, Tarise crashed into her, using her momentum and arms to shove Kayla backward. Backward into that buzzing.

Kayla's arms pinwheeled as she tried to regain her balance, tried to move away from the arch, tried to avoid that opening. But Tarise had pushed so forcefully, her attempts were futile. As she faced death, Kayla's mind went to Jaden. She would never see him again. He would never know what had happened to her.

Then there was a light so bright she had to close her eyes. *Is this the afterlife?* But air so cold it froze the tears on her lashes sliced into her. *No, I'm still alive. But how high up am I? Is there even air at this altitude?* Icicles pricked her airways, like they had that time running around the lake near home. It felt like forever ago.

Something was wrong. At this altitude, she shouldn't have been able to breathe. Something unyielding pressed against her face and against one side of her body. The cold was so acute, she could literally feel her blood freezing. *Ha, one way to stop the bleeding.* It was her last thought before the abyss claimed her.

CHAPTER TWENTY-TWO

Iri had always seen the warmth glowing from the book. The leather held an unnatural gleam. The colors were also abnormal. Typically, she saw only one color on an object. With the book, colors of every shade and hue churned over its surface. An anomaly she couldn't explain.

Jaden set it down between the three of them. Reverently, Jaden opened the book to the first page. Inch by inch, they inspected every tiny speck, splotch, and blot, page by page. But the only two words the ultramagnifier revealed were those they had already solved.

Jaden closed the book with a sigh. "Well, that was a waste of time."

Iri blinked at the sudden flash of color coalescing into a cohesive form. Something recognizable, but gone too soon for her to make out what it was. "Jaden, can you do that again?"

"What? Sigh?"

"No, no, go back to the last page and then close the book again."

Iri ignored Jaden's dubious look as he did what she'd requested. When the colors repeated their interesting fluctuation, Iri could hardly contain herself. This time, because she had been looking for it, she saw the tiny peaks and valleys on the leather itself.

Jaden's frown said it all. "Are you seeing something?"

She ignored his question, asking one of her own. "Do you feel anything when you close the cover?"

Jaden's confusion only increased. "You mean like one of those feelings I get?"

"No, I mean do you feel anything with your fingers?"

When Jaden hesitated, Iri grabbed the book. Asking him questions was getting her nowhere. She ran her fingers over the cover, tracing the shapes carved into the leather. As her fingers followed their paths, an interesting thing happened. The twisting colors came together, forming a line along the inner edge of the back cover. As long as her finger remained on the carvings, the line pulsed and blinked along the edge. The moment her fingers lifted, the line disappeared, allowing the colors to roil around the book as they had before.

"What are you seeing?"

Atu's quiet question demanded an answer. Iri glanced up. Both boys were staring at her as though she held the secrets to the universe in her hands. "I'm not sure. For the most part, this book doesn't have any definitive colors. That's unusual. Most things have one distinct color. But the book has multiple colors swirling around it. Unless we touch the carved images on the leather of the back cover. Then all the colors come together and form a line—here." Iri ran her finger along the inner edge of the outer cover.

"May I?" Jaden asked.

Shrugging, Iri handed the book over. She watched as Jaden repeated the motion, then gasped as his fingers began playing a pattern along the line. "What are you doing?"

Jaden looked as surprised as Iri felt. "Why don't you tell me?"

"It looks like you're playing music with the lights."

"Okay . . . I'm not sure I know what that means, but doing this felt like the right thing."

"It's beautiful. A symphony of color, pulsing with a beat, the colors intensifying from pastels to brights like the volume is changing. I wish you could see it." Abruptly, there was a flash, and all the colors disappeared. "What did you do?"

The question was unnecessary. Jaden was peeling the inner part of the back cover away. Underneath, a rectangle of silver shimmered.

"I think we found the map," Jaden breathed.

"Bro, you have the magic touch. First with the disc, then with the cube, and now with the book. We must patent those fingers of yours."

Jaden laughed, but as the oranges faded and pinks and then whites replaced them, Iri could both see and smell his relief. Then Jaden's colors changed yet again. Grey this time. "Something confusing you?"

"Yes, I have no clue what this is. I don't even know if I can take it out of the book." Gingerly, he dipped a finger into the silver. Like spaghetti running away from a fork, the silvery substance avoided his finger, forming a tiny hole. Jaden lifted his finger, and the hole disappeared. "I can't touch it."

"You answered your own question then," Atu said.

"I guess I did. New question: how is this supposed to help us figure out where we are going?"

When Jaden gazed her way, Iri knew he expected an answer. "My gift doesn't mean I have all the answers. What's your gut saying you should do?"

Jaden didn't even think. He placed his hand above the shimmering mass of silver. Closing his eyes, his fingers began moving. The silver lifted and began shaping itself into a small hill. When the top of the hill dropped away into a crater and tiny splashes of silver spouted into the air, it became obvious.

"Bro, open your eyes," Atu whispered.

As though coming out of a trance, Jaden did, blinking several times. Then focus returned, and he gazed at the mini diorama. "A volcano?"

"Isn't it amazing?" Iri's awe filtered through into her voice.

"Yeah, cool and all, but how does that tell us where we supposed to go?"

Iri didn't have to see the red tints flashing around him to know he was angry. Her own temper ignited. "Haven't you figured out yet that this is how it always goes? First, we get the clue. Then we have to find out what it means. Both the words and this image provided by the book are clues to a place. Now we just have to do some digging to find out exactly where it is."

Jaden opened and closed his mouth. The colors around him flipped from red to white to red to white as he struggled for control. When the colors settled on white, Jaden said, "You're right. You're no doubt all just as frustrated as I am. I'm sorry I allowed it to get to me."

Atu grinned. "You're getting better at handling your anger. You're going to impress the heck out of Kayla when she gets back."

Although Jaden smiled, the deep purple enveloping him telegraphed his sorrow. Iri put a hand on his shoulder. "She will return. Remember, 'live with hope.'"

"That's what I tell myself every day when I wake up and every moment when I think of her." Jaden sighed. "Enough of this melancholy. It won't help get her back any sooner. Let's enlist some help in figuring out which volcano we're supposed to be going to."

They found Jaden's childhood friends gathered in the control room. Markov noticed their arrival and waved them over.

"Jaden, you've got to see and hear this." His excitement was tangible.

Iri peeked over Jaden's shoulder as they studied the monitors in front of Markov. Markov took one look at them clustering around him before shaking his head and tossing the images onto the wall. The holoscreen magnified the images.

It was a social media site. Comments and posts were coming in so fast that the text was scrolling too fast for Iri to keep up. "Can you pause it so we can read what people are saying?"

Markov placed a finger on his console, and the scrolling stopped. When Iri heard the sharp intake of breath next to her, she knew she wasn't the only one stunned. "They want to form a resistance?"

Jaden, as if confirming that what he was seeing was real, began verbalizing snippets from the conversations. "Fight off this unnatural enemy . . . Where do we get more of those flying bats? . . . Does anyone know how we reach the people who fly on those bats? . . . We need to fight back . . . This is our world, not theirs." Jaden read countless more, all expressing the same sentiment. "It seems we have the rise of an army. We have the volunteers to people a resistance, but I doubt we have the gliders to match their numbers."

"That, a problem will not be."

They whirled to find Zareh standing in the doorway.

"Gliders, provide I will. More from our world, coming they are. Find their riders they will, when arrive they do. Your concern, that is not. Need you, your gliders do. Now."

With that, he vanished.

Iri was beginning to understand Jaden's frustration. Why did Zareh always come and go without giving them a chance to ask questions? Then she registered what Zareh had said. "Our gliders need us?"

The others were already moving. Iri chased them. The teens crashed out the front doors to find the gliders circling overhead. Shrill squeals and squeaks crackled through the air. Glancing up, Iri noticed their agitation. Its smell was powerful enough to make her take a step back.

Jaden scowled, his hands shielding his ears. "What's wrong with them? Don't they normally twitter when they talk?"

Iri wasn't sure why Jaden had asked her what was going on with their gliders. Perhaps he hadn't been addressing anyone in particular. Suddenly, Han loomed right above them, separating himself from the other anxious gliders.

"What took you so long?"

Jaden stared at Han. "You'd better start explaining. Zareh just made an appearance and disappeared before he gave any answers—as usual. And you're acting all crazy. What is going on?"

Iri could have laughed. *Is it just me, or have we asked that question about a hundred times today?*

Han bared his teeth, enough to sober Iri up. "Taz sensed Kayla. Will that get you on my back, or do you want to waste more time discussing this?"

Iri gaped. The wide eyes all around showed she wasn't the only one who was agog. Then everyone was moving. Jaden was yelling for people to get airborne. Gliders were swooping down. Jaden's friends swarmed around her. Iri felt lost in a whirlwind.

What should I do? She hadn't wanted to replace Tinks. But now, with all the gliders spinning around, would anyone even notice she didn't have a ride? Taz was too preoccupied with thoughts of Kayla to remember her. Iri clenched her fists. *Why, oh why, didn't I find a new glider?* Tears welled behind her eyes. On the verge of turning to go back inside the house, she heard someone hollering her name.

"Get ready for a pickup. We'll collect you on the next flyby," Atu called as he and Aren zipped past.

Iri grinned. She was giddy with delight. Someone had remembered her—and not just anyone. She bounced from foot to foot as Atu and Aren dropped for the connection.

It took a little jostling, but they eventually rearranged themselves so she sat in front of Atu. It made sense—he was taller, so he could still see over her head. Iri sucked in a surprised breath when his arms slid around her waist, and the desperate feeling that she was all alone washed over her again.

If they'd been on the ground, she would've pushed him away and stalked off. But they were soaring far from the ground, Aren cruising the breezes and chasing the others. For a second, Iri considered her old trick of pretending to fall off. *No, that'll only distance us from the others. I don't want to cause further delays.*

As if reading her mind, Atu leaned close and whispered in her ear. "There's no need to run. I understand what it feels like when you're left behind. There's no shame in feeling gratitude that someone remembered."

How does he know? Tears leaked out.

Atu's arms tightened around her. "I felt the same way after the usurper took my parents. I was alone in the desert with no one to help me. Then Jaden, Kayla, and their gliders appeared as if providence had heard my cry. I will be forever grateful to them for finding me that day."

Something in his tone was unsettling. Had he been considering a more desperate solution to his situation? Iri couldn't help herself. She glanced down and noticed his colors weren't their usual purple hues.

In fact, now that she thought about it, they hadn't been purple for quite some time. Ever since his parents had returned. Now, his colors were faint, but leaning towards blue. Iri shuttered her mind, refusing to think what that might mean.

There wasn't time, anyway. They had caught up to the others. She surveyed their surroundings, trying to work out where they were. Still near to Sven, but not in his valley. They must have been at a higher elevation because there was no snow, only pure ice encasing the massive mountains like a second skin. The reflected sunlight was blinding.

Taz's piercing cry drew her attention, and she peered ahead. Far enough in the distance to require the magnification lenses on her goggles, a crumpled figure lay on the ice. Iri's eyes remained glued on it as they sped closer. Female. A little nearer. Long, blonde hair spinning gold in the sunlight. Iri tried to suppress her worry at the lack of colors around the form. A moment later, there was no doubt. It was Kayla.

Iri marveled as every glider except Han, Taz, and Aren began circling the still form. Their gliders didn't follow the rest. Instead, they swooped down for the dismount. Except for Taz. She landed, her claws skidding where they hit the ice and skating her a little way past Kayla. She hopped back to where Kayla lay, repeatedly calling Kayla's name.

Iri and Atu executed the double dismount, then sprinted for Kayla. Jaden was already kneeling by her side. Blood frosted the surrounding ice.

"Jaden, don't move her," Atu shouted, running faster when Jaden bent over Kayla.

Jaden heeded the warning, but his eyes never left Kayla's face. He carefully laid a hand over one of hers, his eyes wide and pleading. "Help her! She's so cold!"

Blood and cold flesh didn't bode well. Trepidation squeezed Iri's heart in its iron fist before she saw the faint signs of life:

colors clinging to Kayla's still form. But the colors were dull—and fading.

Kayla looked like she had been through the wringer. Her face was pale, as white as the ice on which she lay, except for the purpling bruises around her eye and along her jawline. Red welts rose around Kayla's neck. Then there was her arm flung to the side, covered in a bloody bandage. But where had the rest of the blood originated?

Atu dropped next to Kayla. His fingers touched her neck, checking for a pulse. Using care, he unwrapped the bandage from her arm. A nasty cut, crudely repaired. Atu moved on, his hands flitting over Kayla. His face grim, he closed his eyes.

Was it her gift creating the golden light flowing from him, or was what she saw actually happening? *No, I've never seen colors like that before. Or light that moves in that way. It must be Atu.*

Awed, she watched as the colors around Kayla stopped fading. Then grew brighter. Actual color—not her sense color—seeped back into Kayla's ashen face. The exposed cut on Kayla's arm disappeared under that golden glow. When Kayla's eyes popped open, the bruises on her face also gone, Iri was beyond speech.

Atu had water at Kayla's lips before she could speak. "Hush now, you need your strength. We can hear all about your adventures once you've rested. You've lost blood, and you're dehydrated, so drink up."

Without a word, Kayla drank, but her eyes gleamed with gratitude as she touched Atu's hand. Then she had eyes only for Jaden.

Iri turned away. The blues between Jaden and Kayla were so bright and connected, she felt like an intruder.. Atu must've felt the same way because he joined her a second later. They gazed at the ice surrounding them, casting its mirrored light back to them so the world was unbearably bright.

"That's quite a gift you have," Iri commented.

Atu was quiet for a moment. "Thanks. We all do what we must on this mission."

"Was Kayla's condition what forced you to show that to everyone today?"

His scent was sharp, reinforcing the orange glazing his features. Iri took his hand. "You don't have to worry. None of us will tell anyone what we saw today. You can trust Jaden's friends. And I doubt the gliders haven't seen stranger things."

Atu glanced down at their joined hands. When he looked back up at her, his eyes glowed like black coals in his handsome face. "You don't find it disturbing?"

Iri snorted. "Yeah, because your gift is *so* much more disturbing than mine!"

Atu grinned. "I suppose that's true."

After so many years of oblique comments about her gift, Iri would've reverted to being insecure, except Atu's hand tightened around hers. She glanced at him a second time, surprised by the vehemence on his face.

"Never, ever apologize for who you are."

Just like that, she lost her tongue and every coherent thought. Without thinking, she leaned into him, resting her head on his shoulder. Appalled by her impulsive and irrational behavior, she began to pull back, but faster than a striking snake, Atu's hand shot up and eased her head back down.

She left her head there, feeling awkward, her posture stiff. When his arm slid around her waist and he drew her into his side, she gave in to the warmth and security Atu offered. There was nothing wrong with accepting help from a friend, and she had needed something to keep her on her feet as her mind reeled. *What's happening to me? I've never depended on anyone.*

Again, Atu spoke as if reading her thoughts. "There's a first time for everything."

Her breath hitched a little. "That's enough of that. It's like you've stolen my abilities."

Atu chuckled. "Not by a long shot. But if it helps, I think living on your own for so long never taught you to be conscious of your body language."

"Aha," was all she could muster as she relaxed into him further. That was a mistake. Abruptly, she keenly felt of every part of her body that touched his. A body, lean, strong, and warm, against her own. Her hands itched to run along those sinewy arms and up to his sculpted shoulders. Atu's sudden sigh crashed her wayward thoughts. "What?"

"We need to get Kayla back to civilization where she can get the warmth and rest she needs."

Even though Iri had been sure she was ready to back away from him a moment before, her reluctance to leave his arms shocked her. Just as well he moved first. She turned and watched him cross the short distance to Jaden, Kayla, and their gliders. Frowning, she followed, closing her mind to thoughts that could lead nowhere good.

CHAPTER TWENTY-THREE

Jaden had only seen Kayla that still once before. It was no less terrifying the second time around. When he spotted her on the ice, looking like a broken doll, his breathing had stopped. He was lightheaded by the time he reached her side. He couldn't stop seeing all that blood on the ice. And she was so cold when he touched her. What would they have done if Atu hadn't been there?

He tucked Kayla tighter against his chest, holding her like she might break at any second. Despite her weakness, she clung to him, her touch telling him how much she'd missed him. He brushed his lips against her hair.

"I know, I missed you too. You don't know how relieved I am that you're back."

Kayla squeezed his arm, agreeing. The touch was feeble, all strength gone from her hands. *What did she endure? Do I want to know? I do. But for her sake, I can't lose it when she tells me.* Jaden resolved to keep it together, no matter what she said about her time away. *It's the least I can do after I didn't rescue her.*

That thought stung. *What would've happened if she didn't find her way back? How is it possible she did?* The questions tumbled through his mind like drinking glasses juggled by an amateur, each one threatening to shatter and pierce him with answers he wasn't sure he could bear. *It doesn't matter what I feel,* he reiterated. *I have to think of Kayla. I have to give her the support she needs—and that means focusing on* her *needs and not mine. Why aren't we there yet?*

Jaden glanced down. They were just entering Sven's valley. At least another ten minutes, then. Had Kayla's parents heard the uproar presaging their departure? If they had, had they figured out what it meant? For a moment, he felt guilty he hadn't made the time to invite Sadie and Vicken to join them. Then Kayla shifted in his arms, and he was glad he hadn't.

By the time Sven's house came into view, Kayla's constant wriggling told him she was in pain. That the movements were feebler by the second spoke of her exhaustion. Worried, he glanced down and noticed her licking her lips. Cracked and dry, like she hadn't had water in days.

He cursed himself for not thinking to bring water. She had already drained the flask Atu had given her, even though she'd only been taking small sips as Atu had commanded. Without warning, Han veered violently. Jaden snatched at his neck fur to secure his grip.

Jaden didn't need to reprimand him. Taz was already snapping a long stream of twitters. At least they weren't screeching anymore. Then the tone of the twitters filtered through.

"What's wrong?"

"What's *she* doing there?" Han demanded.

Jaden noticed Han was avoiding the house. Engaging his magnifying lenses, he scanned the area. His arms tightened around Kayla. She wheezed, patting his arm. Both a request to relax his grip and a demand to know what he saw.

"It's Tarise."

Kayla went still in his arms. Then her sudden frantic beating on his arm alarmed him. "Hey, what's wrong?"

Kayla's mouth opened and closed, but the words were inaudible. Irritation sparked in her eyes as she mimed a pen and paper.

"Fine, I'll get Han to put us down. Then we'll set you up in a nice warm bed, with plenty of water and that pen and paper. Try not to stress. I've heard it's not good for healing."

But Kayla only bared her teeth and shook her head, her finger pointing as her hand bounced up and down.

"Okay, okay, I get it. Pen and paper as soon as we land."

Kayla slumped in his arms, looking for all the world as though that tiny demand had taken every ounce of her remaining strength. Jaden cradled her a little closer. *Oh yes, she'll get that pen and paper alright. But if she thinks she can stay awake past writing a sentence or two, she's in for a rude awakening.*

About to ask Han to take them down, Jaden realized Han was already banking towards Sven's home at a shallow angle. He was more surprised when Taz and the other gliders formed a protective circle around them. Had they seen Tarise, or was it that silent communication system of theirs?

It didn't matter. Jaden was grateful for the protection. When Han landed, the other gliders remained overhead. Taz touched down, placing herself between them and Tarise and flaring her wings to create a barrier.

Jaden dismounted and turned to allow Kayla to slide into his arms. Catching her, Jaden carried Kayla into the house, ignoring Tarise. However, he was amused when he caught Taz studying Tarise like a mouse ripe for pouncing.

His smile faded as Kayla's head turned to find Tarise. Then his mouth set in a thin line when Kayla's gaze never left Tarise's face. Kayla's eyes flashed for a split second. *In warning?*

Making a mental note to ask her about it later, he sought a room where she could be on her own. She began beating on his arm again. "I know, you want the pen and paper, but I have to put you down somewhere first."

She huffed, her only sign she would tolerate the delay even though it didn't please her. Jaden had barely settled her in the bed he found before she was gesturing for a pen and paper again. Jaden rolled his eyes.

"Hold your horses. I'm getting there."

Kayla motioned a circular gesture, which Jaden took to mean, "Hurry!"

Jaden did, and when he returned with the requested implements, she grabbed them out of his hands. "Steady on!"

But Kayla was scribbling furiously. She held the paper up to him. On it were the words, "Don't trust her."

Why would Kayla think he would ever trust Tarise again? After what Tarise had done, Jaden was beyond disgusted that she had dared show her face. Did she think they would all welcome her with open arms? Then Jaden's breath snagged. How had Kayla known they couldn't trust Tarise? They had kidnapped Kayla before Tarise confessed.

Kayla was writing again. This time, Jaden read as she wrote, "I think she followed me here."

Jaden was confused. "I don't understand. How could she have followed you? She doesn't have a glider and was here when we arrived."

Kayla shook her head, then groaned as the movement caused pain. This time, her penmanship was a little shakier. "Followed me here from the other world."

Jaden's eyes widened. "She was there with you?"

Kayla nodded. She wrote again. "She pushed me through the portal. I think she was trying to kill me."

Jaden went dead still. Even though he never thought he would be capable of killing another human being, his every instinct was to kill Tarise. But he had promised himself he would be here for Kayla, that he wouldn't allow his own emotions to hinder her healing. So he smothered the anger. Should he tell Kayla he already knew Tarise was a traitor?

The pen tumbled from Kayla's hand. Jaden lurched forward, catching Kayla as she fell. This was all too much for her. He eased her back onto the pillow. "Rest. We won't trust her. Before you sleep, have a little more water."

Thankful he had remembered, he held the glass to her lips. He waited while she took a few sips, then tucked her in when she nodded she'd had enough. "Now sleep. Don't worry about anything."

He stayed with her, watching as her facial features relaxed. She fell asleep almost instantly. He tarried, not wanting to leave her, just absorbing every line of that precious face. He was still trying to wrap his mind around the fact that she was here. Back with him. Safe. He jolted when the door burst open. Sadie and Vicken stood in the doorway, their eyes wide, their faces expectant.

Jaden stepped in front of them as they rushed into the room. "She's okay. Please, let her rest. She just fell asleep."

Sadie ignored Jaden, rushing around him to touch Kayla's face and smooth away the hair that had fallen across it. Jaden revised his assessment. Perhaps Sadie hadn't ignored him totally. At least she hadn't thrown her arms around Kayla and woken her up.

"She's alright?" Vicken's voice was terse as his eyes examined Kayla.

"A little dehydrated, but otherwise fine. You can thank Atu for that."

"Why's she so pale? Where did you find her? How did she get back?" The questions spilled from Sadie.

It would be unwise to tell them what little he knew—not here. "Why don't we talk outside? Kayla needs to sleep, and I don't want us waking her."

Vicken grasped Jaden's unsaid plea. With a curt nod, he side-stepped Jaden and took his wife's arm. "Let Kayla rest."

Sadie glanced up, panic in her eyes. "But she just got back. I don't want to leave her alone."

Vicken guided her away from Kayla's bed. "We'll be right outside. If she wakes, we'll hear her."

As Vicken led her from the room, Sadie still didn't look convinced. Jaden paused long enough to pick up the notepad before following them out and closing the door behind him.

When he turned to face Kayla's parents, Vicken's eyes glittered. "Start talking."

Jaden spared Sadie a glance. "Kayla had lost a lot of blood by the time we found her." Sadie's eyes widened again, and Jaden put a hand in the air. "Atu took care of all that and healed her. The only thing that's still a problem is the blood she's lost. Her body will need time to recover. As miraculous as Atu's healing is, it seems regenerating blood is not something his gifts cover."

Sadie sagged against Vicken's chest, and his arms wrapped around her. A muscle twitched along his jawline. "What else?"

Jaden could tell Vicken had plenty more questions, but all he wanted right now were the bare essentials. "Speaking was beyond her. She wrote this." Jaden handed the pad to Vicken. "That's about the sum extent of what we know so far."

Vicken's eyes flicked over the words. When he spoke, his voice was soft, only adding to the menace in his words. "Who is 'she?'"

CHAPTER TWENTY-FOUR

Jaden debated not telling him. Truly, he did. A man with Vicken's past could put Tarise down without a thought. And, deep down, part of Jaden wanted him to act on that impulse. That knowledge appalled him. But Vicken wasn't without self-control. And he *was* Kayla's father. "Tarise."

The glint in Vicken's eyes was terrifying. "We need to find her."

Vicken hadn't yet heard Tarise was here. This time, Jaden really did pause before passing along the information. "We don't need to. She's here."

"What?" Vicken's roar had Sadie shushing him with pointed glances toward Kayla's room. After his own look in that direction, Vicken said, "Tarise can't stay here. Didn't you see what Kayla wrote?"

"I'm hoping Sven has her in a holding cell."

Vicken's face snapped from anger to satisfaction. "One of his making?" Jaden nodded. "Outstanding. Let's go find out why Tarise has a death wish for my daughter."

The grim line of Vicken's mouth had Jaden wondering if talking was all Vicken intended. "I already know why. It's because she thinks Kayla stole me from her."

Vicken's face was comical as his mouth dropped open. "A crush on you made this girl homicidal?"

Scrubbing a hand over his face, Jaden said, "I know, it's ridiculous, right? But you didn't see how upset Tarise was the last time she saw Kayla and I together. If her eyes could shoot flames, she would've incinerated Kayla right then. Then Tarise and Kayla had it out right before Kayla disappeared."

"Why didn't you mention this before?"

Jaden blinked. "I thought you heard the conversation with Tarise after the battle. When Tarise said she had arranged for Slurpy to take Kayla away?"

Vicken's brow furrowed as he cast his mind back. "You mean that ruckus between you kids right before you left?"

It was Jaden's turn to think back. Only then did he realize Sadie and Vicken might've witnessed the confrontation, but they'd been walking away and were too distant to have heard anything. "I'm sorry. I just assumed you knew Tarise was the one who gave Kayla up. I should've checked with you sooner."

Vicken sighed. "It doesn't matter now. It only matters that we got her back. We should be thankful." Jaden nodded, but tensed when Vicken frowned again. "Now that Tarise is here with us, we should take advantage of it. Have a little chat with the traitor to find out what she knows about the usurper and his plans."

Chills snaked up and down Jaden's spine at the venom in the words. Much as he wanted Tarise to suffer for what she'd done, he didn't think he could live with Vicken's implied threat. "As long as we're just talking, I agree."

Vicken's hard stare had Jaden swallowing. Vicken growled his own terms. "As long as she's answering truthfully, I don't have a problem."

"Fair enough." Jaden couldn't say anything else. Any information Tarise might pass along could be useful. And she was smart. Smart enough to figure out what a father might do to get answers. Jaden only hoped she was smart enough to listen to her brain this time.

Vicken turned to Sadie, who had been quiet this entire time. "Honey, can you stay here with Kayla while I take care of this?"

"As long as you get answers, I can do that."

Whoa! Forget Kayla's dad. Her mom's more lethal, Jaden thought, shocked at her tone and its unspoken command that Vicken do whatever was necessary.

Vicken dropped a kiss on Sadie's head and then glanced at Jaden. "Well, what are we waiting for? Lead on!"

Jaden was a little cowed by the intimidating pair. *And I'm dating their daughter?* Noticing they were both looking at him like he would provide a meal, Jaden said, "Just to be clear, I don't know where Sven's keeping Tarise."

"Then let's find Sven," Vicken declared.

Leaving Kayla in Sadie's care, Jaden led the way to the front of the house, the last place he had seen Tarise. But only Taz and Han remained, their worry clear. Jaden went to Taz, feeling bad she couldn't reach the part of the house where Kayla rested. He rubbed her neck. "Kayla will be fine. She's sleeping now. You get some rest too. She'll want to see you when she wakes up."

Taz rubbed her delicate nose against Jaden's hand, the most astonishing thing she had ever done. Startled, Jaden looked to Han for an explanation. Han's smile told him this was a privilege Jaden should enjoy. So Jaden allowed her to express her thanks, then stepped back when she lifted her head.

"Vicken and I were looking for Tarise. Any idea where she might be?"

Han bobbed his head toward Sven's workshop. "They marched her in there, and we haven't seen them since."

"Thanks. You and Taz get that rest now. I have a feeling things are about to get exciting." When Han raised an eyebrow, Jaden nodded confirmation. "Yes, one of those feelings."

As he and Vicken strode toward Sven's workshop, Vicken asked, "Am I wrong, or do these feelings play a role in this quest you're on?"

Jaden sighed. "Yes, they have relevance. I've had them all my life, but it's only in the last few months that I've realized how important they are. That I've started paying attention to them. No doubt I'm more

attuned to them now than before. And before you ask, I haven't gotten
to the point yet where I can differentiate what the feeling means. Who
knows? That could happen before all this is over." Jaden smiled bitterly.

Vicken said nothing until they reached the door to Sven's workshop. "I would view those feelings as a gift if I were you." With that, he
pushed through the half-open door and went inside.

Jaden wasn't sure why it surprised him to find the workshop
empty except for Sven. "Where's Tarise?"

Sven grinned. "In her nice, comfortable, little room that you told
me to prepare for her."

Was Sven teasing him? "You mean you made a cage for her?"

Sven's grin turned to a scowl. "Why do you have to call it that?"

Understanding Sven's reluctance to refer to anything as a prison,
Jaden said, "Sorry. I trust you made her 'room' a space where she
could relax without going places we don't want her to go?"

The scowl didn't leave Sven's face. "That's hardly better."

Jaden remained silent, and Sven gave in. "Yes, her accommodations
are secure."

"May we speak with her?"

Sven threw a hand up in the air, a few garbled words expressing
his annoyance. "Must everyone know all my secrets?" Still muttering,
he stood and led the way to the back of the workshop. He touched a
tool hanging on one of the numerous hooks.

The door opened so silently Jaden didn't hear it. If Vicken hadn't
been standing in its way, neither of them would've noticed. As it was,
Vicken scrabbled out of the way, making Jaden turn. Sven's secret
entrances never disappointed. On the other side of the door, lasers
crisscrossed the area, glowing red. Flipping the tool around, Sven
disabled them.

When Jaden made to enter, Sven said, "Not so fast."

Jaden leaned against the nearby counter. "Is this going to take as
long as disabling all the devices guarding the tunnel to your valley?"

"You would have me make it easy for her?" Sven continued
adjusting various tools. Catching Jaden watching him, he said, "And

don't think you can memorize the pattern and sneak in here without me."

Jaden laughed at Vicken's incredulous face. "This is totally normal." Addressing Sven, he said, "A rolling combination?"

Sven beamed, his usual jovial nature returning. "I thought a few extra precautions wouldn't go amiss."

Jaden smirked. "You let us know when we can go in then."

Seconds later, Sven waved a hand. "Go ahead. I'll lock you in there. Buzz me when you're ready to get back out again." Noticing Jaden's open mouth, he interjected before Jaden spoke. "There's an intercom in there."

"Of course there is." Jaden muttered as he led the way, Vicken following.

The short passage leading to another door was cold. Jaden wondered what other mechanisms Sven had hidden to make it so and what those mechanisms would've done had they still been active. Even though Sven didn't like cages, he'd done a stellar job creating this one.

Steel reinforced the door at the end of the passageway. Jaden reached out to search for a hidden handle, but the door slid open. *There must be a sensor in the panel*, Jaden thought. He and Vicken remained on the threshold, inspecting the room.

Inside, an antechamber allowed visitors access to a small lounge area. On the far side, a sheet of glass—or some other transparent material—separated the antechamber from Tarise's room. *No attacking unsuspecting people entering her quarters. Sven really thought of everything.*

Relieved to find Tarise curled up on her bed and facing the opposite direction, Jaden took advantage of her inattentiveness and studied the room. He couldn't find a way into it. That didn't mean there wasn't one. Sven had to have put Tarise into the chamber somehow. A quick glance told Jaden Sven had crafted the room to provide comfort without sacrificing security.

He guessed Sven had made the soft furnishings of materials that could only be severed with a knife—if that. He had welded the furniture to the floor, so Tarise couldn't loosen any bolts and use them or the furniture as tools. The bathroom in the background had a metal sheet for a mirror. And Sven had molded the fixtures as part of the room itself. It was a veritable fortress.

Glancing at Vicken, Jaden noticed the man's appreciation as he reached the same conclusion. Catching Jaden's stare, Vicken said, "Shall we?"

CHAPTER TWENTY-FIVE

There had to be an intercom transmitting sound from the antechamber into Tarise's room because the moment Vicken spoke Tarise abruptly sat up and turned to face them. Hurriedly, Jaden stepped back into the passage. Ensuring he hid his mouth behind Vicken's body, he whispered so he would not convey the words to Tarise either by sound or lip reading. "Before we do, know Tarise is a genius. Don't underestimate her."

"Understood," Vicken murmured. "Anything else?"

The threat lurking in his eyes almost had Jaden feeling sorry for Tarise. Almost. Then he remembered Kayla so lifeless on that ice, and the thought of Tarise going up against Vicken was gratifying. "Nope. Take it away, boss."

They marched into the room. Jaden averted his eyes so Tarise couldn't make eye contact. It didn't mean he couldn't feel her tracking him into the room. When he reached the glass wall, he stopped and stared at her. Tarise's face was sullen, her body language belligerent. Jaden's blood heated.

Noticing Jaden was finally paying attention, Tarise sneered. "You're welcome."

Jaden's blood heated several more degrees. *How dare she?* "Weren't you the one who put her there in the first place?"

Tarise's eyes were calculating. Jaden was relieved Vicken was here. He had so much more experience with this kind of thing. Not wanting to sabotage whatever Vicken planned, Jaden stayed quiet, shaping his face into a bored expression. *If she thinks she'll get any attention from me, she's mistaken.*

His apparent disinterest had the desired effect. Anger flashed in Tarise's eyes. "I thought you'd be grateful I brought your precious Kayla back to you. I shouldn't have bothered. It seems you don't care for her as much as I thought you did."

The outright lie had Jaden fighting for self-control. That, and Tarise was baiting him. She knew his tendency toward losing his temper. She didn't know Kayla was helping him master it. And he would make Kayla proud. Sweet, precious, Kayla. Hardening his resolve, Jaden worked at maintaining his bored expression. To sell it further, he faked a yawn. "Vicken, do you have anything for her? I've seen enough."

Vicken grinned. "Yes, no point wasting time here. Let's go."

Jaden was so astounded by the grin he almost lost his tenuous control. Forcing the energy that would've given him away into walking back to the entryway, he heard Vicken following.

They were almost to the door before Tarise said, "Wait."

Jaden kept right on walking. If they were to succeed at selling this to someone as intelligent as Tarise, they would have to make it believable. When Vicken's footsteps didn't falter either, Jaden knew he'd played the hand as he should've.

"Please!"

This time, Jaden heard Vicken stop. "What do you want? There's nothing you could say that would help at this point."

His voice was colder than the ice they had found Kayla on. It cut the air, a knife intended to cleave whatever arrogance Tarise still possessed. It worked. Jaden heard the sob, even though his continued footsteps had taken him almost to the exit.

"Jaden, please! I realized I shouldn't have allowed Zubiaba to take her. I tried to help her. After she fell through the gate, I went after her with a Gaptor. But I couldn't find her. Please, let me help."

That she hadn't said sorry or apologized was uppermost in Jaden's mind. She had no remorse. She only wanted Jaden's attention. Reminding himself he couldn't trust her, Jaden allowed a pause before he turned. "Do you honestly think I believe you? After what you did, I doubt you'll ever have any of our group's trust again. Not for a long time—a very, very, *very* long time."

It was the straw that broke the camel's back. As though she couldn't bear to hear the disgust in his voice or see the condemnation in his eyes, her hands covered her ears, and she closed her eyes as the sobs heaved out of her.

"Enough of that," Vicken spat. "If you have something to say, say it. Or we're out of here."

With an audible, ragged inhale and between sobs, Tarise blubbered, "I can tell you where you're supposed to go."

Jaden froze. Of all the things she could've said, this was unexpected. Allowing himself a moment to school his face back to a neutral expression, he feigned disinterest. He leaned against the back wall, crossing his legs and folding his arms. "Is that a fact? And where should we be going?"

Tarise sniffled. "You're supposed to find the last artifact, right?"

Jaden didn't acknowledge that. The less she knew about their planned movements, the better.

Defeated, Tarise waved a hand in the air, her head drooping. "Okay, I know you have to. But you need a general location before you can find it, right?"

Somehow, Jaden swung himself off the wall and towards the door. He tossed the words over his shoulder. "If you're just going to ask questions and speculate, we're done."

"No, no, please!"

The shriek was desperate enough. Jaden faced her, his expression unyielding. "You have two minutes to convince us to stay."

Tarise looked undecided, as though she wasn't sure whether she should remind them she had "saved" Kayla or whether she should give up her only leverage. When she imploded on herself, her body shrinking, Jaden knew which way she had decided.

"Fine, you win. You're looking for some place with tons of volcanoes. Zubiaba referred to them as 'The Fire Lands,' but I worked out what we call it." She took a quick look at Jaden's face to gauge his reaction. Finding no mercy, she huffed, "Terratalunga."

Jaden turned to pace, the only way he could hide his shock. *It can't be that simple, can it?* Dipping his head, he hoped it would hide his relief that she had divulged the information. He marched back and forth several times as though considering her words, all the while composing himself.

When enough time had passed that Tarise would think he believed her, Jaden faced her. "When did you hear him talking about this?"

Tarise looked startled. She hadn't expected the question. Her eyes darted around the room as though searching for an answer. Jaden tensed. *What lie is she going to tell now?*

"It was right before I left. He was in the comm room, speaking to one of his minions here in our world. I've never seen him that angry. He was ranting about the medallions being taken. Saying you should never have been able to find them."

She paused. Was she trying to remember or stalling so she could fabricate more tales?

"There was a lot of cursing and yelling. All of it directed at the idiots who'd been unable to keep the medallions safe. Then he said something like, while you may have recovered the medallions, you hadn't yet worked out where the Fire Lands were."

Jaden's skin itched with all the lies she'd just told. How had Slurpy been able to talk to his minion if Jaden's team had destroyed all the Gaptors in that nest? Sure, Zareh's device might not have registered a lone Gaptor or two as a nest, but was that feasible? Then there was the part about the Fire Lands. If she had heard that right before she left, how had she been able to work out it was Terratalunga between then and now? Time to turn up the heat.

Jaden's face was implacable. "How is it you can now spill Slurpy's secrets without that brand on your hand burning a hole through you?"

Although she tried to hide it, that tiny quirk of her lips gave her away. That minuscule smirk that showed she thought she was superior. It had always warned Jaden when she thought she was pulling one over on the rest of them. A sure sign he couldn't trust whatever words came out of her mouth next.

Tarise waved an airy hand meant to encompass her prison. "Don't you know? In here, I can get away with anything. Sven designed the space so well, I don't think even Zubiaba can reach me in here."

While the explanation was plausible, Jaden listened to that inner voice that had sounded alarm bells. True, Sven was a genius in his own right. But those little warning signs spoke to Tarise having an alternate answer. One she didn't want them knowing. Like she was here on his bidding, pretending to give them information. Or for some other dark purpose.

Satisfied with his own answer, Jaden shrugged nonchalantly. "If you say so." Keeping his expression neutral, Jaden watched her like a hawk. The little nibble on her lip gave him his answer. She wasn't sure whether he believed her.

Jaden was so focused on Tarise he'd forgotten Vicken was there until he spoke.

"You've had your two minutes. We're done here."

So saying, Vicken marched to the door. As if by magic, the door slid aside, allowing them to exit. Jaden followed Vicken without a word or backward glance. Sven must've been watching them. Jaden hoped he'd recorded the meeting. It would allow Jaden to further analyze Tarise's actions.

Only when they were back in Sven's workshop, sealed off from Tarise and away from her too-keen eyes did Jaden allow himself to relax.

Vicken put a hand on his shoulder. "I'm impressed. You did well in there. I've said this before, and I'll say it again: if you're ever looking for a job, come see me first."

Jaden grimaced. "You don't know how difficult that was for me."

"Difficult or not, you pulled it off. Even I believed you wanted her to become a worm in the woodwork, fading into obscurity."

"What happened to you taking the lead?" Jaden croaked.

"You had the background with her to rile her up, which you did. After that, I thought I would let things play out. Seems it was a great choice. Because you've known her for so long, you read her like a book. I wonder if she's even aware of those micro-expressions of hers."

Jaden ran a weary hand over his face. Of course Vicken had noticed. But that only made his question more pressing. "If we had her where we wanted her, then why did we leave when we did?"

"She needs to stew on her uncertainty about whether you believed her. It will make her more desperate. Desperation leads people to say and do things they ordinarily wouldn't."

"And you think that might make her give up something else that's valuable?"

"What I know is Kayla told us not to trust her. I intend to take that advice. If you and the crew go to Terratalunga, I'll be going ahead of you to clear the way. Just in case Tarise has some other dastardly plan on the back burner."

Vicken's face was grim, and the set of his shoulders told Jaden he wouldn't convince the man otherwise. "In that case, thank you. I'll feel safer knowing someone with your experience has gone ahead of us."

Vicken's smile was pure evil. Jaden shuddered to think what would happen to anyone—or anything—that got in his way.

"Sure. Where else can I put my skills to such excellent use?"

The glee in his voice only reinforced Jaden's opinion of the man and his gratitude that Vicken was playing for their team. Repressing thoughts of Vicken's abilities, Jaden said, "Time to study a map, then, and set things in motion. Somehow we have to find the real place we're supposed to be going to. Ruling Terratalunga out if it's a trap is a start."

CHAPTER TWENTY-SIX

Kayla didn't want to, but it was time. For the last few minutes, she'd been enjoying the warmth and comfort of this bed. But now the weight, someone leaning on the bed, pressed into her again. Not that the person was heavy. It was that her leg wasn't hurting anymore.

Opening her eyes, Kayla found Jaden's head lolling against her leg. His mouth was half-open, his eyes closed under the strands of hair that had fallen over them and his handsome face relaxed in sleep. It only made the black rings under his eyes more pronounced. Had he not been sleeping? What had he been doing while she'd been gone?

Unable to resist, Kayla reached out and smoothed that dark blonde lock of hair away from his face. As if her touch was electric, Jaden's eyes snapped open. Those wonderfully deep blue eyes stared back at her, endless pools with their dark rims and dark centers. She had missed them. And that mouth, curving into a slow smile.

"Kiss me," Kayla breathed.

Jaden's astonishment was absurd, and Kayla laughed, but the sound died as she saw his gaze fly to the other side of her bed—and her parents. Awake and watching her. Heat suffused her face as color stained her cheeks.

"At least we know you're okay," her dad said dryly.

Even her mortification couldn't dampen her sheer joy. Kayla's grin was irrepressible. "Hi, Dad, Mom." She lifted her arms toward them and it didn't surprise her when her mother rushed in and embraced her. "It's wonderful to be home again." Over her mother's head, she saw her father's face. "What's wrong?"

Her father shook his head, then wrapped his arms around Kayla and her mom. Kayla didn't rush the hug. She wanted to feel every minute. Bask in this bliss of being loved. All so she could remember this moment and be thankful for it. Treasure it in her heart and hold it close as a reminder the next time she stepped into danger. Because this, their mission, wasn't over. She had glimpsed it on Jaden's face in the split second he let it slip, then again on her father's face before he held her and her mom.

Kayla turned her head when Jaden moved off the bed. He situated himself a respectable distance from it. Then he stood there, watching them, first scrubbing his hands over his face, then running them over his arms before looking like he wanted to pace. Kayla smiled, and his fidgeting ceased.

The way he stared at her told her he still didn't truly believe she was there. A moment later, Jaden's face split into a smile. That wonderful, gorgeous smile that made her bones melt.

As if her parents sensed her attention had wandered, they drew back. Kayla directed her eyes to them. "Dad, are you going to tell me what's burning through your mind?"

Sadie scowled at Vicken and smacked his arm. "I told you not to let her worry."

Vicken just smiled back at her. "With you as her mother, do you think anything escapes Kayla?"

Sadie gave Vicken an incredulous stare—then chuckled. "No, I suppose not. Sweetheart, before your father drops his news, how are you feeling?"

"Considering I haven't thought about that since I opened my eyes, I suppose I must be fine. Nothing in my body is screaming for attention. Nothing's hurting." Kayla glanced at her arm and put a hand under the sheet as she explored her leg. "Huh, it's healed. I'm guessing

Atu worked his magic on me?"

Since she had directed the question toward Jaden, he answered. "You bet he did."

As if speaking his name had conjured him, Atu appeared in the doorway. "I thought I heard your voice. How are you feeling?"

Kayla beamed. "For the second time, just fine. And I'm sure that's thanks to you."

Atu dipped his head.

"Really, thank you! Come here, so I can give you a hug," Kayla ordered.

Tossing Jaden an impish grin, Atu did as she'd asked. When Kayla had dispensed the hug, Atu stepped back. He glanced at Jaden, the smile still playing on his lips. "Now that Jaden is about to eat me alive, how about I make a run for it and get the others so you only have to tell your story once?"

Kayla chuckled, then sobered. "Before you do, how bad were my injuries?"

"Not as bad as they could've been." Atu glanced at her, his eyes holding questions. "Few people survive a 'pod crash. How did you manage that?"

Kayla frowned, trying to remember. Then it all came rushing back. "I think I almost didn't. When I regained consciousness after the crash —" Her eyes suddenly widened, and her hand flew to her neck. "My medallion! I lost it! I think Slurpy took it."

Jaden's hands reached Kayla before Atu's could. "It's alright. We'll get it back. Atu will tell you not to stress about things."

Atu rushed to reinforce his statement. "I shouldn't have to tell you how to take care of yourself after the trauma you suffered. You know what you should be doing. And Jaden's right. If you allow yourself to get stressed, it will cause problems. And how will Taz feel when I tell her you're sabotaging your healing?"

Kayla couldn't believe she hadn't thought to ask about her glider. Then again, in her defense, she hadn't been awake that long. Kayla moved again to sit up. "Where is she? Can I see her?"

Jaden put out a hand and eased her back onto her pillows again.

"You can see her if you behave. The sooner you get your rest, the sooner you can see her."

Kayla knew it was childish, but she stuck her tongue out at him anyway. It made her feel better. And she didn't have the strength to argue. She smothered the grin when Jaden's eyes flamed with warning of what he would do to that tongue when her parents weren't around. Heat tingled in her veins, but the thought of her parents had her gaze sliding back to them. Her mom was all worry, her dad . . . "What aren't you telling me?"

Vicken's smile was grim as he placed a hand on her arm. "Honey, I promise you'll hear what I have to say. But I want to hear your side of the story first. No, let me rephrase—I *need* to hear what happened to you."

Kayla studied him a moment before acquiescing. "Okay, but I'm holding you to that promise." Her dad's smile was his only acknowledgment. "Where was I? Oh yes, Atu asked about my injuries." Kayla was nervous. *What will they make of it all? But none of it was my fault.* And she was done lying. To anyone, about anything. "When I woke up after the crash, there wasn't a part of my body that didn't hurt. And I couldn't move."

Jaden, seated on the bed next to her again, went still. "Couldn't move as in Gaptors had zapped you?"

Kayla shrugged. "I don't think so. I still had my ring, so that should've countered the numbing effects, right?" Jaden nodded agreement. "In which case it's more likely that one of my injuries was causing temporary paralysis."

It was Atu's turn to interrupt. "Temporary?"

"Yes, just before they came to get me, I could move the tip of one finger. And then, a few minutes later, two whole fingers."

"Where did they take you?"

Jaden's voice was quiet, but his anguish ripped into her soul. Kayla took his hand in hers. "To surgery. Slurpy wanted me healed so I would be ready for the next part of his plan." When Jaden's face paled, she knew she was spilling details too fast, too haphazardly. One glance at her parents' faces confirmed it. "Okay, all of you take it down a notch. I feel like someone will combust at any moment. I'm fine! Nothing terrible happened to me. I'm here and nothing that transpired there will scar me for life. No PTSD, okay? Are we clear?"

"Okay," Jaden mumbled.

But his breathing was audible. Like he was using it as a tool to calm himself. Kayla observed as he concentrated on relaxing. Although his breathing settled and his face was rigid with control, the tension never left his shoulders, and his eyes remained haunted. She squeezed his hand. His eyes darted to hers, those incredible dark blue pools.

Kayla smiled. "You're getting better at managing your temper."

Jaden snorted. "I'm glad you think so."

But his eyes had cleared a little. "Isn't my opinion the only one that counts?"

This time, Jaden laughed, and the same emotion stirred the water in those pools. "I missed you."

The laughter bubbled out of Kayla, a pure expression of her relief that his eyes *could* still smile. She tried not to think of how much she had missed them. Those tiny crinkles at the sides, that never-ending blue she could lose herself in.

Her father cleared his throat. "Should we give you two some time alone?" His tone was dry, but he was smiling. As though he too didn't care what she did right now. Just cherished the fact that she was here to do anything.

"Let me finish my story. How about I tell it without interruptions so I can tell it in the order it happened and with none of you panicking every time I say something that might hint at peril?"

Her father nodded, and her mother grabbed the hand that wasn't holding Jaden's. "Sweetheart, you tell the story any way you want. Just tell it already."

Kayla caught her mother's implied plea to put her father out of his misery. "Here's the short version. I don't know how badly injured I was, but when they took me into surgery, Slurpy was there." She cringed as they all tensed again, but they kept quiet. "He wasn't there to hurt me. In fact, just before they put me under, I heard him telling someone else in the room that he would take care of my more serious injuries. The way he said it, I don't think he intended using traditional methods." Kayla paused. "Atu, is it possible he can heal like you do?"

Atu's face was grave. "We have passed this gift down through my family since the days of our forefathers. If the legend we transferred with it to each generation is true, then this gift came from Zareh." He smiled when he saw their shock. "I don't know why that surprises you. But I told you that to answer your question. If Zareh could bless us with this gift, who knows what power the usurper has? I would say it's in the realm of possibility that the usurper can heal like I do. Possibly better."

Kayla chewed on his answer for a second. "I'm going with that because when I woke up after the 'surgery,' only minor injuries remained. Except for my leg." She put up a hand forestalling the questions. "While they had me in surgery, they implanted a tiny chip in my leg that would transmit pain every time I moved a certain way. Its purpose was to stop me from thinking I could escape by making me believe I had broken my leg in the accident, meaning running would be impossible."

Jaden whistled. "That must be some chip."

Kayla grinned. "No, sorry, I didn't bring it with me."

Jaden returned the smile, and Kayla's heart lifted at the sight. But she needed to finish. She had to tell them. "Then Tarise appeared and warned me about the water." A giggle rippled out of her at their confusion.

"She warned you?" Jaden repeated as though he'd misheard.

"Don't get ahead of yourself. She only warned me because I was part of her escape plan. She needed me so she could get away." Kayla outlined all that had happened afterward, culminating in the way Tarise pushed her out of that other world and through the gate.

Vicken's voice was steel. "That's why you thought she was trying to kill you? Because she pushed you through, guessing you would fall to your death?"

"I believe so. Only I didn't end up in the sky. I think I was on the ground when I passed out on this side."

"We found you on the ice, a short distance from Sven's home," Jaden supplied.

Nodding, Kayla said, "Yes, that would make sense. I remember something frozen and hard against my face. And thinking the chill would slow the bleeding." She thought a moment longer. "Perhaps the way the gate works is it puts you though on the other side in the environment you're familiar with—water for fish, sky for Gaptors, land for humans?"

Jaden was following her logic. "That would explain why Tarise ended up in a different place." Kayla raised her eyebrows. Jaden shrugged. "She said she came after you when you 'fell' through the gate."

Kayla rolled her eyes. "I *fell* through?"

Jaden put his hands up. "I know, I know. We don't trust her. And I'll tell you more about that later. But let's finish with your story first. If she came through on a Gaptor, chasing after you like she says, your theory means she would've come through in the sky. That's why she couldn't find you. You weren't in the air. You were on the ground hundreds of feet below."

Shuddering, Kayla said, "I'm glad she didn't find me. I don't think she would've saved me."

"And when she couldn't find you, she came crawling back here like the maggot she is," Jaden hissed.

Everyone was silent, but their expressions told Kayla they were trying to comprehend what had happened. Kayla didn't want them dwelling on how close she had come to death—on more than one occasion. "You said you had your own reasons for not trusting Tarise. Is that what you've been keeping from me?"

CHAPTER TWENTY-SEVEN

Jaden smiled at Kayla. He was still trying to accept she was here. That she'd been returned to him. Then something she'd said made him sit up straighter. "Before I answer, can I go back and check on something you said earlier?"

"As long as you're not just procrastinating about answering my question, shoot."

"You said that you destroyed the comm room there?" At her nod, Jaden asked, "From what you said, I'm assuming Slurpy wasn't there?"

"No, and I didn't see him anywhere else while I was trying to escape. Why?"

Jaden glanced at Vicken. The man's icy expression confirmed he knew what Jaden was up to, and Vicken had reached the same conclusion. "We just paid Tarise a visit." When Kayla's eyes went to her father, Jaden rushed on. "Don't worry, she's in a cell Sven constructed for her." Jaden grimaced. "But don't call it that if you speak to Sven. You know how he is about prisons."

Kayla raised an eyebrow. "I'll heed the warning. What happened with Tarise?"

"She told us she had heard Slurpy in the comm room right before you left."

"That's a lie!"

"Yes, one of many she told us." Her father's voice was quiet and soothing.

"Why would she lie about that? What did she say Slurpy was doing in the comm room?"

"Ranting at his minions. I'm guessing she had to finagle a way to tell us what she knew without making it sound suspicious."

"Jaden, what did she say?"

Jaden grinned. "Now don't get impatient." When Kayla crossed her arms and glared at him, he chuckled. "Tarise told us she overheard the destination for the next part of our quest."

Kayla's expression was a combination of glee and suspicion. "It's possible she would know. She had free rein of the place. In her wanderings, she could've overheard Slurpy mentioning the location. But I doubt he would've been that careless."

"I agree. There are three possibilities that I can see: that she genuinely overheard him, that he told her to tell us where to go, or that she just made the whole thing up." Jaden caught the appreciative gleam in Vicken's eyes as he turned to him. "Did you have others?"

"No, I think you about covered it."

"But what would make you think there's even a chance she's telling the truth—either because she overheard or because it's what Slurpy told her to say?"

"Because she added a grain of truth to it. Isn't that the best way to lie?" Jaden squirmed under another speculative gaze from Vicken. Deciding to ignore Vicken's reactions, he focused on Kayla. She was glaring again.

"I've about had it with you two," Kayla warned.

"Sorry, I'll get to the point. A lot of things happened while you were gone, the most notable of which was recovering all the medallions Slurpy's been stealing over the centuries." Kayla gaped. "There's more, and I'll get to that in a second. But the reason there's a slim chance Tarise is telling the truth is because she also said she'd overheard Slurpy ranting about the cache being found and retrieved."

Kayla leaned towards him. "And?"

Jaden chuckled. She knew him so well. "What we aren't sure of is whether Slurpy also knows that we stole one of his communication devices."

Kayla blinked. "A communication device? There was one there?" She waved a dismissive hand. "No, never mind. I never heard about a missing communication device and Tarise never mentioned it. Neither fact answers your question either way."

Jaden rubbed his jaw. "Unfortunately not. We'll just have to pray he isn't aware of the loss."

Kayla wriggled against the pillows until she was more comfortable. "Why wouldn't he be?"

"It's time I caught you up on what's been happening here, starting with how Tarise betrayed you." Kayla's face paled, and Jaden wondered if he shouldn't have led with that.

But Kayla squeezed his hand. "Tell me," she breathed.

Jaden studied her face, finding resolve there. If he didn't tell her, she would wheedle it out of someone else. Better if he controlled the flow of information. He could parse it out so she only received manageable snippets.

Even with this approach and omitting large sections, by the time Jaden concluded with retrieving the cache, destroying the Gaptor nest and stealing the communication device, Kayla's face was wan.

"You know most of it now. It's a good place to stop so you can get some rest." Jaden squeezed her hand before releasing it.

"No, don't go, tell me the rest," Kayla begged, her feeble attempt at grabbing his hand failing.

Jaden raised his eyebrows. "And here I thought you were the one with the medical knowledge." As though she understood what he was saying, she slid her hands under the sheet. "Hiding your hands won't help. You're exhausted, and you know it. Get your rest, or we'll all walk out that door!"

"Like I believe you'd do that. Or that my parents would." She glanced at them, her half-smile fading when she noticed her mother's stern expression.

Sadie closed in on the bed. "Sit up a minute and let me fluff your pillows. Then you'll do as Jaden said and sleep. Or we will carry out his threat—and drag him with us if need be."

Her tone brooked no argument, and Jaden chuckled as Kayla sighed theatrically but did as her mother asked. With the pillows rearranged, Kayla obediently lay back down again. With a wink at them all, she closed her eyes.

Jaden guessed she probably only meant to close them for a second, but her ruse worked against her. In three blinks, she was asleep, her deep, regular breathing a comfort to them all. Catching his eye, Vicken gestured that they should speak outside. Jaden gave Kayla a quick kiss on her cheek, then followed Vicken out.

As soon as they were out of earshot, Vicken said, "Kayla won't want to wait. As soon as she thinks she's well enough, she'll be itching to get out of here. With that in mind, while she rests, I think I'll make that scouting trip I mentioned earlier."

Jaden blinked. "You don't want to stay here with her while she recovers?"

"She has you and her mother. Between the two of you, I think she'll have more attention than she wants."

Jaden wasn't sure whether Vicken was joking. "But you're her dad. If you're not there, she'll want to know where you are. And how do you think that'll play out when we tell her you've gone ahead of us to scout the area Tarise mentioned?"

Vicken's laugh was mirthless. "You won't tell her where I went. Sadie knows how to handle her. Kayla will just think I'm off on another one of my missions. Like I've been so many times before."

Vicken's tone was distant as he said the last part, his regret evident. "I'm sure she understood that was your work—" Jaden began.

"Work or not, I could've settled a long time ago. I wish we had." Vicken shook his head. "But better late than never, right? We've found a perfect place to call home. And when all this," he waved a hand in the air, "is over, we can settle into it."

"It's something we can all look forward to," Jaden murmured. He didn't add the part that nagged at him—if they survived.

Vicken put a hand on his shoulder. "There's no choice but to stay positive. Letting doubt in is not an option. We have to believe we can do this."

For whatever reason, his words made Jaden think of the two leather strips they had recovered and the messages written on them: "Believing with faith" on the first and "Living with hope" on the second. What did the strips mean? Were they simply meant to be encouragements on this journey? Or did they have some deeper purpose? Still pondering the matter, he nodded to acknowledge what Vicken had said but didn't speak.

"I'll give Sadie the specs. I plan to leave tomorrow morning."

That woke Jaden up. "You're going alone? Shouldn't you take some of the others with you?"

Holding up a hand, Vicken said, "I won't go alone. But I won't be taking any of the people here either. Although they've improved, they lack the skills I require. I'll take my usual team with me." He grinned at Jaden's obvious relief. "Yes, I don't plan on you having to tell my daughter you fed me to the wolves without backup."

Jaden laughed. "Thanks, I appreciate you considering my welfare."

Vicken chuckled. "It's her welfare I'm thinking about, not yours."

His comment only made Jaden laugh more. "Ouch!"

"You'll get over it." Vicken grinned. "Alright, let's go find that place on a map, and then you can get back to Kayla."

"You're not joining me?"

"I have arrangements to make, and I should do that while Kayla rests. My guess is she won't be waking up again until tomorrow, so I have a few hours to set things up."

CHAPTER TWENTY-EIGHT

True to what Vicken guessed, Kayla slept through the night and halfway into the next morning. Jaden expected Vicken to leave at first light—wasn't that what spies did?—but Vicken stayed until Kayla woke up. Then he and Sadie chatted up a storm with her while she ate a hearty breakfast.

As Jaden observed, part of him wondered whether Vicken had stayed so he could see Kayla one last time in case things didn't go as planned. But Vicken let no hint of any doubts slip as he conversed with Kayla.

Sliding his gaze across to Jaden as though aware Jaden had been watching him, Vicken said, "You're not eating?"

Jaden huffed a laugh. "Contrary to what everyone thinks, I don't eat *all* the time."

"Just most of it," Kayla said around a mouthful of egg.

"I'm not eating now, am I?"

Kayla's gaze was shrewd. "When did you last eat?"

"Okay, I give up with you and your lawyer mom!" Jaden wouldn't admit to eating while fetching Kayla's breakfast.

Sadie blinked her surprise, then giggled. "You didn't just say that!"

"I certainly did. Kayla learned from the best. She could squeeze a confession from a soda can if she needed to."

Now Kayla's dad was laughing too. "You're more like your mother than you realize."

Kayla's face was priceless. "I like to think I'm more like you."

"Heaven help us!" Sadie said between giggles.

The banter continued for at least another hour, Vicken showing no sign that he was in a hurry to leave. Jaden grabbed another cup of coffee from the pot someone had brought to the room. He had just decided that Vicken planned to delay his departure when Vicken checked his watch and rose from his chair.

"Much as I hate to go, duty calls. I'm sorry I can't stay longer." Vicken planted a kiss on top of Kayla's head. "Get your rest." He glanced at his wife. "Sadie, a word?"

Sadie cupped Kayla's cheek. "I'll be right back."

Jaden watched Kayla as her parents left. They had barely stepped from the room when she said, "Okay, what's up?"

Jaden choked on the sip of coffee he'd just taken. He used it to gain a little time to think. *So much for Sadie knowing how to handle Kayla. Did Kayla figure out something was going on from her parents' behavior or mine?*

Kayla crossed her arms. "Don't even think of lying. I know you're all hiding something."

Grabbing at straws, Jaden said, "It's Tarise."

The mention of Tarise had Kayla frowning. "What about her?"

Think, Jaden, think! He had given himself a little more time, but it wasn't enough. "She might know about the changes happening to the animals."

Kayla stared. "What changes?"

Jaden suppressed his guilt about Kayla not noticing that he hadn't said this was where her dad was going. But he had told the truth about Tarise—she might know what was going on. "Mutations."

Jaden settled into telling her about what had been happening in the world around them. The changes to the animals. The CDC's fear that it might affect humans despite the lack of visible evidence. The continuing EMP attacks. Their effect on the power grid. How people were getting angry enough to take action. The army rising in response.

Her silence as he spoke told him how shocked she was by how much had changed. When Jaden finished, she took his hand in her own. "I understand now why you didn't add this to what you told me yesterday. It would've been too much."

That she had admitted as much was scary. But her face wasn't as pale and drawn as yesterday. "It seems the rest you had last night was what you needed. Perhaps you need a little more?"

Indignation flashed in her eyes. "Why? Is there something else?"

A dangerous question. But one he was prepared for this time. "No, I've told you all that's been happening." *And not what's happening right now, not where your dad is or what he's doing*, Jaden thought, disgusted with himself. "Now that you know, it's time we worked on a plan. I just wasn't sure if you needed more rest before we started."

Kayla's gaze was incredulous. "Are you kidding?"

Raising his hands, Jaden said, "No need for condemnation. I don't know where you're at. I only wanted to give you the chance."

Kayla's gaze softened. "And I love you for that. That you care about those around you. But now's not the time for us to be sitting around. Time's running out. We have to act."

Jaden heard nothing past the first sentence. *She loves me?*

Kayla raised her eyebrows. "What? You're just staring at me."

"You love me?"

Kayla opened her mouth like she would say something but closed it again. Not what she had expected him to say. Jaden could almost see her mentally running over her words. Then she smiled her most glorious smile yet.

"Yes, you idiot. If you haven't figured that out by now, you're not as smart as I thought you were." She grimaced. "Of all the ways I could've said that, I'm sorry it just came out as part of the conversation." She eyed him nervously. "Say something, would you?"

Jaden inched closer, taking her face in his hands. "I don't care how you said it, just that you did. And I know it's clichéd for me to say it right back, but it's true. I love you, Kayla Melmique. I think from the first moment I saw you on that arrowball court. Not that I grasped it until we were at my gran's. But this thing between us—it's always been there. More than attraction, more than admiration. An understanding, the knowledge that you're the other half of me."

Kayla's smile was soft, her green eyes shimmering with unshed tears. "Jameson, I've said it before, and I'll say it again—you know how to sweep a girl off her feet."

Jaden leaned in then and kissed her. Her mouth was soft against his, her slight groan music to his ears. He hadn't been alone in his need. Jaden's hands slid from her face and over her shoulders as he pressed her closer. He needed her body against his. Needed to feel her close to him.

Jaden's eyes closed as he tasted her mouth, inhaled her intoxicating scent, ran his hands over her strong back. For a moment, he lost himself in the wonder of her. That she was back with him again. He deepened the kiss, her passion rising to meet his.

When he drew back, his breathing was uneven. Kayla's face was flushed, her eyes sparkling. "You've never looked more beautiful to me than you are now."

Kayla took a moment to steady her own breathing. "You're not so bad yourself."

Jaden chuckled, feeling lighter inside than he had in weeks. "You know, you're just what I needed to get my feet under me again."

There must've been something in his voice because Kayla took his hand and gazed into his eyes. Making sure he maintained eye contact, she spoke slowly and clearly, meaning for her words to reach him. "It's not your fault."

Jaden almost broke. *How does she always know?* Fighting the desperation that had plagued him since the battle, he said, "I miss her."

Kayla leaned into him then, wrapping her arms around him. She tucked her head under his chin, snuggling in so she was as close to him as she could get. "I miss her too."

Silent tears rolled down Jaden's face. He would've said more, but his throat was thick with grief. Kayla didn't need to hear the words.

She knew, as she always seemed to. She squeezed him against her, tightening their circle.

"You need to grieve. Let it out. There's no shame in mourning the loss of someone you cared for."

As Jaden allowed his grief to spill over, he could feel Kayla shuddering against him, giving in to her own sorrow. They stayed like that for a long time. Just holding one another, comforting each other, allowing themselves time to come to terms with their situation, the silence between them a salve to their battered souls.

When Kayla eased back, studying his face to gauge where he was at, Jaden said, "Thank you. I needed that."

"I did too."

Her unspoken words called to him. "Yes, there will be more time to reflect and celebrate who Bree was. This isn't the end. But now we need to make sure her sacrifice wasn't in vain. We have to finish this thing."

CHAPTER TWENTY-NINE

Kayla watched Jaden compose himself. She could almost see him compartmentalizing the grief, putting it in a box he wouldn't open again until he had the luxury of giving Bree the time and attention she deserved. When his intense blue gaze settled on her again, he was focused.

"Ready to hear what we think we know about where we're supposed to go?"

Kayla giggled. "That was a mouthful! But yes, thought you'd never spill."

His half-smile showed he hadn't entirely put his grief behind him. "Tarise said the place we're looking for is Terratalunga."

"The volcanoes?"

"Yes. Another part of the reason it may be true is because the third map seems to confirm this."

Kayla punched his arm. His wince told her it had hurt as much as she'd meant it to. "You *found* the third map and didn't think to tell me?"

Jaden rubbed his arm. "Why do you think I waited?"

Figuring it out took a split second. "Oh. Because I would've insisted we leave right away."

"Yes, and you weren't in a state to be leaving your bed just then."

Kayla squared her shoulders. "And you think I'm well enough now for us to pursue this?"

"I'll defer to Atu's judgement."

"Did I hear my name?" Atu ambled into the room, followed by Iri.

"Seriously, you've got to stop appearing out of nowhere every time someone mentions your name," Kayla laughed.

Atu's face brightened. "You're sounding chipper."

"I feel great. Yes, I admit all of you were right. I needed to catch up on my sleep. Even though I feel like a slacker leaving you three to figure things out on your own."

Atu glanced at Jaden. "You told her?"

"I was beginning to."

"Well, before we get Kayla all excited about getting out of bed, let's see how she's doing. Can you lie down for me, please?"

Kayla flopped onto her back. Atu lifted his hand and floated it along the length of her body. When he closed his eyes, Kayla guessed he was making sure nothing lurked which might escape him if he wasn't totally focused. A moment later, his eyes popped open, and he grinned, giving Kayla a measure of relief.

"I'm good to go, aren't I?"

"Almost," Atu pronounced.

Kayla scowled. "What do you mean 'almost?' I feel fine!"

"I mean you need at least one more night of sleep, preferably two."

Snorting, Kayla said, "I suppose I can live with that." Then her eyes brightened, and she rubbed her hands together. "Tell me about the third map. What is it this time? How did you find it?"

"Actually, we've had it all the time," Jaden replied.

"We have?"

"Yes, it's the book Awena gave us."

"Does the map have something to do with those weird curves and lines etched into the leather?"

"That was the start," Jaden said. "But why don't we show you?"

He was already moving towards the door. "Where are you going?"

"To get the book," Jaden tossed over his shoulder as he disappeared.

"He's a new man now that you're back with us." Iri curled up at the bottom of Kayla's bed.

If the extent of Kayla's longing for Jaden while they'd been apart was any clue, she didn't want to dwell on how much he'd missed her—or the pain it caused them both. "Was he an ogre while I was gone?"

Iri smiled. "No, actually, it seems working on managing that temper of his while you were gone kept him somewhat stable."

Kayla chuckled. "Let's hope it lasts. How have you two been?"

Atu perched next to Kayla, and the three of them chatted about nothing of consequence in the short time it took Jaden to retrieve the book. When he rushed back into the room, a grin plastered on his face, Kayla couldn't stop her own smile. His happiness was her happiness.

Jaden didn't wait until he reached Kayla before he started explaining. "Atu was the one who thought it could be the book, and Iri was the one who figured out how we got it to reveal its secrets." He beamed. "How's that for teamwork?"

Jaden reached the bed, and Atu scooted down so Jaden could be right next to Kayla. "Watch this. It's incredible!"

Jaden closed his eyes as his fingers began playing over the inside of the back cover, in the area along the spine. Kayla squeaked as the back cover separated from the book. Jaden peeled it back, revealing a shining, silvery substance.

"What is it? Can I touch it?" Not waiting for an answer, Kayla reached for the captivating element. When her finger dipped in, the silver parted like mercury. Intrigued, Kayla repeated the motion with the same result. Abruptly, she pulled her finger away. "It's not mercury, is it?"

"You think I'd let you touch something poisonous?" Jaden asked, his face sour.

Kayla grabbed his hand and kissed it, amused when a smile graced his face. "Never. But if it isn't mercury, what is it?"

"No clue." Excitement colored Jaden's voice again as he added, "But watch what it does!"

What she saw was about as unbelievable as many things they'd already experienced on this quest. When Jaden finished playing his fingers over the silvery pool, a miniature volcano spat tiny specks of lava from its cute spout. Kayla whistled. "Wow!"

"Right?"

Jaden bounced off the bed, unable to contain his excitement. "This is the reason Tarise could be telling the truth. She doesn't know about the book or that it gave us this diorama."

Kayla's mouth turned down. "Just because she mentioned Terratalunga doesn't mean it's the *right* volcano."

"Yes, yes, I agree. But there must be a way to figure that out." Jaden looked at Kayla. "Right?"

He had something in mind. But her brain was still processing all the other stuff he'd dumped on her in the last few days. Kayla sighed. "I enjoy these guessing games of ours, but I'm too tired to think right now. Why don't you just tell me?" Jaden's face clouded and Kayla wished she had just guessed.

Atu glanced at Iri, seated opposite him at the foot of the bed, before scooting up right next to Kayla. "How tired are you?"

Feeling trapped because Iri would know if she was lying, Kayla attempted a reassuring smile. "Tired, but not as wiped out as yesterday." As Atu studied her, his eyes intense and somewhat unfocused, Kayla squirmed. "Ziggety! Stop staring at me like that!"

"Sorry." Atu's eyes snapped back into focus. "I stand by what I said earlier. You need more rest."

Kayla flipped a hand in the air. "I already agreed. But I'm not sleeping again until Jaden answers my question. And maybe not even right after that! I only just woke up. You can't expect me to fall asleep again so soon?" Kayla knew she was whining, and when Atu said nothing, only gave her that knowing stare, she huffed. "Fine. But Jaden gets to finish that last thought first." When Jaden didn't answer but looked to Atu first, Kayla's irritation rose. "Really?"

Jaden didn't cave. Only after Atu nodded approval did Jaden say, "We've always been able to find the answer ourselves. It's something Atu and Iri have both pointed out a few times. First, we get the map. Then the book gives us the destination."

Kayla snapped her fingers. "But this time, the map and the book are the same. You're thinking there's something else in the book we've overlooked?"

Jaden smiled. "Not so tired after all."

Kayla rolled her eyes. "Tell that to the dictator on the bed."

Atu laughed. "You're welcome."

"For what? Insisting I sleep?"

"Because you'll thank me once we set out on our journey again and you can deal."

"Yes, Doctor. I suppose I will." Kayla angled a glance at Iri. "Really? No support from you? And here I thought us girls had to stand together."

Iri laughed. "Oh, I don't get in his way. And we all want the same thing. For you to be at your best again."

Kayla's eyes filled with tears. Her voice was gruff when she said, "Come here. I want a hug."

 · Iri blinked as though she wasn't sure she'd heard right. Then her face flushed with pleasure, and she came around the bed, knocking Atu off his perch. "My turn."

Tired though she might have been, Kayla didn't miss the way Iri knocked him off the bed. She dragged Iri into a hug. Holding her tight, Kayla whispered, "What's up with you and Atu?"

Iri stiffened. "What do you mean?"

Kayla pulled back and almost laughed when she saw how guilty Iri looked and how red her face was. But she resisted the laughter and the questions. Tugging Iri close again, she spoke so only Iri could hear. "You'll have to catch me up on things—later, when we can have some girl time."

When Kayla released her, Iri's expression was bemused. Iri nodded acceptance but said nothing and wouldn't look Kayla in the eye. Kayla grinned. Things really had been happening in the time she'd been away. That reminded her. Kayla lifted the sheets and shook them out.

"What are you looking for?" Iri asked, hopping off the bed.

"Awena's book. I thought Jaden left it here."

Jaden surprised her, flattening the sheets as he took Iri's place on the bed. His leg touched hers. Kayla identified with his need to be close. She took his hand, giving them an additional point of contact. Jaden smiled at her then, and all her thoughts went out the window.

Atu cleared his throat. "Shall we leave?"

She and Jaden weren't alone. Sighing, Kayla dragged her eyes from Jaden's. "No, we just needed a moment." Her brain fumbled for what she'd been thinking before Jaden sat down.

"Here." Jaden smiled, reached for the bedside table, and retrieved Awena's book.

"Oh, that's where it was. Thanks."

Iri frowned. "What are we doing?"

"Finding something in the book that might provide the volcano's name," Kayla muttered, already focused on the pages in front of her.

Sounding unsure, Iri asked, "Didn't we already do that?"

Kayla's head snapped up. "You went through the book for more splotches?"

Iri nodded. "We even used the ultramagnifier."

Kayla slumped back against the pillows. She glared at Jaden. "You didn't think to mention that earlier?"

Jaden shrugged. "No harm in fresh eyes looking, is there?"

Groaning, Kayla lifted a hand and flopped it over her eyes. "Ugh, I'm so tired of this. Why didn't Zareh just put things in plain sight?" She moved her hand and found concern swimming in Jaden's depthless blue eyes.

He lifted a strand of hair that had fallen across her face and moved it aside. "I think it's time you had a nap." Kayla opened her mouth, but he cut off her objection. "You got the answer you wanted. Now," he stood and took the book from her, placing it on the bedside table, "it's time to do your part."

Kayla wanted to grumble. But the urge to wipe that worry from his face was greater. And now that she was considering sleep, she was suddenly exhausted beyond words. Nodding her consent, she slipped down under the covers. *This bed is so comfortable. Not like that gurney they had me sleeping on before.* Jaden's hands brushed the thoughts away as he tucked her in. *Hmm, yummy! He smells wonderful. Spicy and clean. I'm . . .*

CHAPTER THIRTY

Kayla woke with a start and a horrible nagging feeling she had left something undone. Squeezing her eyes shut, she tried focusing on what had happened before she fell asleep. That thought was enough to send her brain careening down another path. *How could I fall asleep? Wasn't I only awake a few hours?*

Opening her eyes, Kayla glanced out the window. Sunshine painted the world in vivid colors. *How long did I sleep this time?* She glanced around the room. Empty. *Where is everyone? Did they decide I was well enough to leave me on my own? Even my parents? I can understand Jaden leaving. We were . . . oh yes! That's what we were talking about! The third map!*

Kayla's eyes skittered to the bedside table. The book was where Jaden had left it. Reaching for Awena's book, she smiled when the leather warmed her hands. When it felt like the book's very soul called to her. It never failed to amaze her, this connection she felt to it. *How did Zareh do it?*

She was spiraling again. Kayla grunted with annoyance, clenching her jaw and forcing herself to focus on one thing. The book in her hands. They needed to find something else in here. There had to be another clue that would confirm or deny Tarise's claim.

Running her fingers over the leather, she found the carved lines mesmerizing. A tactile euphoria urging Kayla to trace the patterns for hours. But sating that desire was a luxury they couldn't afford.

Concentrating, Kayla began examining each line, every whorl and indentation, allowing her fingers to explore as much as her eyes. Minutes later, she confirmed there was nothing to find. If it hadn't been for Iri, Jaden would never have found the opening at the back of the book either.

Kayla opened the book. It seemed years since she'd read Gedrin's story, since she had looked at the book for what it was. A cautionary tale. *Would we have carried on if we knew then what we know now? Come to think of it, did we even have a choice?* If Zareh had selected them centuries ago like he claimed, it was unlikely. Sighing, Kayla started reading the story again, remembering first time she and Jaden had laid eyes on this book. How much they hadn't known then. How much had changed since then.

Her eyes roamed the pages, absorbing the gorgeous artwork again, the written words that replaced a typed font. She reached the page where the splotch marked that first destination it had sent them to. And then, a few pages on, the second splotch. Somewhere in the back of her mind, she realized the splotches were chronological. So anything for the third destination should be from this point onward.

Paying closer attention, Kayla scrutinized everything on every page. She had given up on finding anything by the time she reached the last page. The one with no writing, only the image of Gedrin's headstone and the mountains in the background. *The mountains in the background!* Kayla squinted, trying to make them out more clearly.

"What are you looking at?"

Kayla about knocked the pen she was chewing on into the roof of her mouth. "Don't scare me like that!"

Jaden's grin widened. "Someone woke up cranky."

"No, I didn't. You gave me a fright. And I hate getting frights."

Sobering, Jaden nodded. "Sorry, you know that wasn't my intention."

Kayla reached a hand toward him, trying to soothe the irrational anger she always felt when someone scared her. She regretted wiping that smile off his face. "I know. I'm sorry too. Knee-jerk reaction." The smile returned as Jaden ambled over. Kayla noticed the chest in his hands. More like an insulated metal box to be exact. "What's that?"

"Something I'm hoping might cheer you up."

He took his time setting it on the bed. When he made no move to open it, Kayla reached for it.

"So impatient." Jaden's eyes brimmed with laughter.

Kayla ignored him, pulled the chest closer, and flung the lid wide. Her mouth dropped open when she saw all the medallions. There must be hundreds here. Raising her eyes to Jaden, she found him frowning. "What now?"

Instead of answering, Jaden put his hand in the chest and moved the medallions around. The crease between his eyes only deepened. Then he looked at her, his face grim. "I think you were right."

"About what?"

"Guessing that Slurpy has your medallion."

"Why would you say that?"

"Because, when we opened this chest before, the medallions floated out and found their owners." At Kayla's wide-eyed disbelief, Jaden explained how the riders who had been with them had received their medallions.

"Just because they floated out and found people to attach themselves to doesn't mean the medallions belonged to them," Kayla countered.

"I disagree. Zareh told us the medallions would always find their way back to their owners. Somehow, they would just reappear to the next person in that family if the previous family member tried to get rid of them—or lost them." He suddenly chuckled.

"You know, you're really starting to annoy me with all those things going on in your head that you aren't explaining!"

"Sorry," Jaden said, still grinning. "It just occurred to me. Remember how our moms were so adamant about us not losing our medallions—about taking good care of them?"

Kayla got it and giggled. "It wasn't necessary. The medallions would've found their way back to us, no matter what we did."

"Exactly."

Kayla glanced around the room. "If that's true . . ." She scooted towards the edge of the bed and swung her legs over.

"Whoa! What are you doing?"

The alarm in Jaden's voice made her snap at him. "Getting out of bed. I'm not an invalid!"

Jaden was shaking his head and pushing her back onto the bed. "No, you can't. Atu said you needed more rest. You have to—"

Kayla wasn't sure whether to sweep his arm away or laugh. The thought of her getting up made him so agitated, it was funny. No, it was endearing. Actually, it was annoying. She cut him off. "I've slept. I've rested like you asked. Now, I'm getting out of this bed!"

Eyes wide, Jaden stood motionless, looking like he had stopped breathing and not uttering a syllable. Kayla started laughing. It was too much. "Yes, you can help me get out of bed."

Relief washed over his face as he put his arms around her waist, bracing her whilst she stood. On her feet at last, Kayla took a moment to assess. No dizziness. No nausea. Her legs were a little shaky, but she'd expected that. Moving more of her weight off Jaden and onto her feet, she assessed again.

"You can let go." Kayla pushed off Jaden and took her first step in . . . days? It was a little wobbly, but the next step was firmer, and by the third, she was stable. Despite this, Kayla used slow, measured steps as she walked to the end of the room, then turned and did the set back to the bed a little faster. Jaden hovered next to her the whole way.

When she reached the bed, she knew she'd be fine. "I'm okay. You can leave me to walk by myself now." Jaden's face was pained, but he reluctantly agreed. Kayla began an even gait away from the bed and back again, increasing her pace for each circuit. By the time she'd completed three, the anxiety had left Jaden's face. Curiosity took its place.

"What made you get up?"

Jaden's unexpected question made Kayla pause. If she stumbled or looked even a little unsteady on her feet, Jaden would banish her back to bed, which was the last thing she wanted. *Why did I get out of bed?* Then she remembered what they'd been discussing. "I thought I would check the drawers and closets to see if my medallion had somehow found its way here." Kayla turned in time to catch Jaden's eye roll. "What?"

"You could've just asked."

"True, but then I wouldn't have raised your heart rate by getting out of bed and walking around."

A smirk touched his face, and Jaden's eyes glinted. "There are better ways of increasing my heart rate."

Kayla giggled. "There certainly are." She moved so she could wrap her arms around his neck. Lifting onto her toes, she craned her neck and kissed him. The moment his lips brushed hers, current sparked her blood and raced along her veins. Leaning into the kiss, her body melted into his when he deepened the kiss.

Coming up for air, Kayla again clutched at straws as she tried to remember what they'd been discussing. Catching sight of the sun outside when she snuggled against Jaden's shoulder, she dredged up one question. "How long has it been since you rescued me?"

Jaden's arms tightened. She shouldn't have reminded him she hadn't been here. His voice was gruff when he answered.

"Almost a week."

Kayla did the math. That meant she had slept for another day and night. "Aren't you tired of me sleeping yet?"

Jaden curled a finger under her chin and lifted her face towards his again. "Only when it means I can't do this." He kissed her again.

When he released her this time, Kayla sank onto the bed. Whether it was his effect on her or weakness after her ordeal, she wasn't sure. But she didn't want him worrying. "Whew, a girl's gotta sit after that!"

Jaden laughed. "Nice try."

Kayla shrugged. "It was worth a shot. I don't want you fussing over me all day."

This time, the laugh was heartier. "I didn't plan to. I brought the chest, hoping your medallion would be in there."

"But it's not. So—" Kayla made to rise but Jaden stopped her, shaking his head.

"Don't bother. I've checked this room, your backpack, and had someone check your room back home. There's no sign of it."

CHAPTER THIRTY-ONE

Kayla's blood ran cold. "Now I understand why you agreed with me about Slurpy having my medallion. What does that mean for our mission?"

"For starters, that unless we get it back, we can't use the medallions to finish this thing."

"Why?"

"We had hundreds of medallions in that chest. If that many together didn't make the Gaptors disappear, then it can only mean one thing—that we need *all* the medallions for their magic to work."

"We have to get mine back then. But how? How do we cross into that other world?"

Jaden grimaced. "I have no clue. But I've been wondering if there's a way to use the arcachoa to cross into that world. If it allows us to cross timelines, perhaps we can cross worlds."

"I assume you'll tell me what you're thinking if and when you figure it out?"

"I will. When I've had time to think about it more. When I've worked out whether it's viable."

Angling her head, Kayla studied him. "You're not going off on your own again, are you? I thought you'd learned that lesson."

This time, Jaden grinned. "No, ma'am. Learned and dealt with. I'll share any plans with you and the others. I just need to figure out some details. If it's even an option."

Kayla crossed her arms. "So much for 'learned and dealt with.' Last time you thought you had it all figured out, but you didn't. Why not share your thoughts now—uninformed as they are? More minds attacking the problem will yield faster results, and better ones at that."

A muscle along Jaden's jaw flexed, and his blue eyes flashed. But to Kayla's surprise, his voice remained calm when he answered. "Will you trust me on this?"

"Considering you're impressing me by not unleashing that temper of yours, I'll cut you some slack. But only for a day or two. Then I expect you to share."

"Fair enough."

Still preoccupied with thoughts about her medallion, Kayla wasn't troubled when his voice remained flat. "You'd think if Slurpy had all those medallions in that box, he would've taken them to his world long ago and destroyed them." Jaden studied her. Kayla slashed a hand upward. "Oh, for heaven's sake! I'm just wondering why he didn't take them—not fishing for what you were thinking!"

Jaden sighed. "I wondered the same thing. Since I've had more time to think about this, here are my thoughts. First, I believe that when Zareh created the medallions, he put some safety mechanism on them that would prevent them from crossing the breach—or rather, that someone other than a seeker couldn't take the medallion across. Which brings me to my second point: I believe you still had your medallion with you after the crash, when the Gaptors took you to their world."

"You don't think it's possible my medallion could still be at the crash site?"

Jaden paused and studied her. "No. Finding their way back to you, remember?"

"Oh. Yes, I suppose if I lost my medallion at the crash site, it would've turned up somewhere here." Kayla saw the tension in his face ease a little. She needed to think more before she spoke. Any more silly statements and he would chain her to her bed. "So, what else?"

"Hmm." Jaden still looked at her as though he was deciding about something.

"You were saying I still had my medallion with me when the Gaptors took me?"

Jaden resumed theorizing. "Yes. Third, you were still wearing your medallion, so that allowed it to cross the breach. That was what caused the safety mechanism to fail. It's how your medallion ended up with Slurpy and why it can't cross back."

"Because it has no seeker to carry it across the breach!"

"Exactly."

Jaden's grin was the happiest Kayla had seen today. She almost hated to ask her question. "Do you think Slurpy's experimenting with it? Trying to see if there's a way he can figure out what the medallions do—or a way to break their power if he already knows their purpose?"

As expected, Jaden's grin faded. "It's what I would do if I were in his position. We have to hope we can retrieve your medallion before he destroys it."

Jaden didn't need to complete the thought. If Slurpy succeeded, would they even have a chance of victory? That reminded Kayla. Picking up the book, she said, "Here's something that might cheer us up."

Taking a seat next to her, Jaden glanced at the book. "You found something?"

"Perhaps. I was looking at it when you walked in with the chest." Flipping the book over, Kayla opened it from the back, to the page she'd been examining. "Tell me if I'm crazy, or if you see the same thing I do."

Jaden peered at the page. "I don't see any splotches."

"You're not looking for splotches. Look at the picture." His sudden sharp intake of breath had her grinning. "I'm not seeing things, then?"

"I never noticed that before."

"I know, right? They were just mountains in the background. Or so we thought. But you agree they're volcanic mountains?"

"Yes." Jaden's voice rose with excitement. "Those tiny little dents at the top aren't noticeable until you really look. Why didn't the artist have lava spouting from the top? It would've made it so much easier to recognize."

Kayla laughed. "Yes, right! Zareh—remember?"

At her repetition of his words from earlier, Jaden chuckled. "How could I forget?"

Taking his hand, Kayla said, "Then again, just because they're volcanic mountains doesn't mean they're the ones we're looking for."

Jaden squeezed her hand before releasing it to lean in closer and inspect the volcanoes again. "Actually, I think they are." When Kayla frowned, he pointed at the most prominent volcano. "See that little kink along the side there?"

Kayla squinted. "I suppose. It's tiny."

"I bet if I got the ultramagnifier, it wouldn't be the only differentiating factor we'd see. Hold on. I'll fetch it."

"Bring Atu and Iri along," Kayla called after him as he dashed out the door.

Minutes later, Jaden returned, the ultramagnifier in hand and Iri and Atu in tow.

"Jaden says you might've found something," Iri said.

"We'll see," Kayla replied as the four of them crowded around the book and watched Jaden run the lens over the volcano.

"Here," Jaden pointed, "and here." He pointed at another spot. "And here."

Atu frowned. "Curves on the side of the volcano?"

"Yes, notice the way they kink. Not like those on any of the other volcanoes around it." To prove it, Jaden moved the lens over the other mountains. Moving it back over the kinks, he had pointed out, he said, "Remember those."

Jaden flipped to the back cover. Running his hands along the spine, he pulled up the silver rectangle, then opened the map using that finger trick of his.

Kayla gaped. All the kinks and curves were in exactly the same places. She raised her eyes to the others. They were as astounded as she was.

Jaden grinned. "I'd say we've found the place."

"Not quite." Atu scowled.

"What do you mean?" Jaden asked.

"Well, the map and the image in the book are the same. But did you forget where you found this book?"

Kayla's excitement was doused as thoroughly as a bucket of water dumped over a fire. "In the myths and legends section of the library."

"Meaning it might be impossible to figure out where this story took place," Jaden concluded miserably.

Kayla couldn't take the disappointment. Not again. "We're saying we can't find it before we've even tried? Didn't Awena appear when we needed her last time? I say we go to the library in Daxsos and see if she appears again! We have nothing to lose."

A quiet knock on the doorframe startled them. Markov stood there, his face set. From the way Jaden reacted, Kayla knew something was wrong. Terribly wrong. She suspected it had something to do with whatever Jaden was keeping from her. When Jaden exited with Markov and returned a few minutes later, his face pale, her apprehension grew. "What?"

"There's something I have to tell you."

"Something you should've told me yesterday—or first thing when you walked in this morning?" Kayla couldn't help snarling. She had known he'd been hiding something, but she hadn't wanted to push. Now she wished she had.

"This is news I only just heard." Jaden took her hand in his as he sat next to her on the bed again.

"But it has something to do with what you've been hiding from me since . . ." Kayla went still. "Since my dad left." Her eyes flew to Jaden's. And she knew. "This is about my dad, isn't it?"

This time, Jaden didn't make her wait. "He left that day because he wanted to scout Terratalunga—wanted to make sure it was safe. That it wasn't a trap. That Tarise hadn't lied to us."

Kayla held her breath. "He went alone?"

"No, he took some of his coworkers with him."

"But?"

"He said he would check in every two hours."

Kayla wanted to scream. "And?"

"He just missed his third check-in."

CHAPTER THIRTY-TWO

Iri wished she couldn't see the colors or smell the fear on Kayla. But it was what it was. Kayla's dad was missing; in the place Tarise had told them to go looking for the next clue. Which meant Tarise had probably lied to them, and Terratalunga had been a trap.

For want of something to do, Iri said, "Are we going to find Kayla's dad or go back to Daxsos to find this Awena person?"

The peach tones around Kayla flickered at the distraction. Then Jaden's teal overlaid the peach as he moved even closer and took Kayla's shoulders in his hands.

Focusing all his attention on Kayla, Jaden said, "This is your call."

Fascinated, Iri watched as the colors around Kayla died down, like a fire reaching the end of the coals. The fiery oranges mellowed to lemon. Before Kayla said the words, Iri knew what she had decided. "Scary as it is when he misses check-ins, my dad's done it before. Usually because he's been held up by something."

Kayla didn't expand on her statement, but Iri watched the lemony hues solidify into the bright sunshine of determination.

"Because I believe in my dad, we'll go to Daxsos. We'll find the information that will confirm exactly where we should be going. And if it's not Terratalunga and my dad hasn't checked in by that time, then we'll swing by Terratalunga first and collect him on the way to wherever we *should* be going."

Jaden studied Kayla carefully before he answered. "If you're sure . . ."

"Jaden, have you thought about where Terratalunga is relative to where we are and where Daxsos is?"

Iri ran the map in her head. She saw Atu and Jaden reaching the same conclusion she had. But Jaden balked at answering, so Iri said it instead. "Daxsos is on the way to Terratalunga. If we go to Daxsos first, we wouldn't have lost anything if Terratalunga's where we should be going." *And we'll be closer to your dad if he needs us.*

"Can we go now?" Kayla asked, maroon sparks betraying her impatience.

Despite this, salmon undertones still throbbed below the dominant buttery yellow. Kayla wouldn't admit to being worried.

Jaden leaped to his feet. "Yes, we don't have a moment to waste."

Iri completed the sentence again. *Because if something has happened to Kayla's dad, we need to get there sooner rather than later.* Iri realized everyone was moving. Not wanting to be left behind, she rose and dashed to her room, grabbed her gear, and then sprinted toward the front of the house. She stopped dead when she exited and saw what was there.

A new glider waited with the other voyagers' gliders. Suddenly, breathing was difficult. Her grief was suffocating. Iri closed her eyes against the image of Tinks being torn apart. She'd been helpless to stop it.

"I understand it's difficult. But you'll need your own ride. And Tinks wouldn't want you to be without someone to watch over you."

Atu's voice was soft so only she could hear. Iri turned, finding his rich brown eyes full of understanding. When Atu touched her arm, her eyes followed the movement, her body leaning towards his. When she raised her eyes to his again, something different shone there. She wasn't sure what.

"Come on, let's go find out who they thought worthy enough to follow Tinks." Atu turned before Iri could fathom what she had seen.

Iri wasn't sure whether it was frustration that she couldn't read Atu like everyone else, or that Pallaton had decided to give her another glider without asking first, or the grief still filling her soul, but she wanted to scream. And hit something. Lash out against anything to vent her emotions.

As if sensing her brewing eruption, Atu faced her again, this time easing her hand into his so he could lead her toward the gliders. The moment his hand touched hers, Iri's emotional slate was overwritten with a more powerful feeling. One she thought she recognized but didn't care to name.

Still staring at their joined hands, she allowed Atu to steer her toward the waiting gliders. Not surprisingly, Taz spoke when they reached them.

"I know it's too soon after we lost Satinka, but she would've wanted us to make sure you were taken care of."

Iri glanced up, her neck craning to find Taz's face. Iri found sympathy there. And under it, steel. Sighing inwardly, Iri realized she would not escape a new glider, however much she wished it.

Taz must've recognized her resignation because she said, "Iri, this is Rozene."

Iri wondered whether she could pull off the wild girl routine and pretend she'd never learned any manners. *Will that allow me to get away with ignoring this bat?* But she couldn't do that to the glider. Then she smelled it. Sorrow. Despair to the core.

Daring a glance at Rozene, Iri found her own grief echoed on the bat's face. "Satinka was my friend. I miss her too."

Rozene's voice was gentle, her posture anything but. As though she dared Iri to say anything negative about Tinks. Iri warmed to her—instantly. Without thinking, she moved right up to Rozene and put her hand on the bat's warm chest.

"Then let's finish this thing and make Tinks proud."

A flash of amber temporarily drowned Rozene's aubergine. "Yes, let's do that."

Both of them would need time to grieve Tinks's loss. But they could do it. Together. Feeling lighter than she had in weeks, Iri grinned. "Let's mount up then."

As one, the gliders lifted into the air, returning one at a time to collect their voyagers. Taz slipped in first, as usual. When Iri saw Atu gazing at Kayla instead of her, she felt a twinge of something unpleasant. *Am I jealous? What a ridiculous idea! And there's no need. Atu's only watching Kayla because he's assessing her health.*

Then Iri remembered Kayla hadn't seen Taz since her return. Their behavior evidenced their elation at their reunion. Kayla grinned like a loon as she aerial connected with Taz, and Taz's face was almost fiendish with her fierce grin.

Iri was so busy watching them she would've missed Rozene descending if Atu hadn't nudged her. The slight action had her turning to him and then whirling as he pointed behind her.

"Better get ready." Atu grinned. "She looks like a glider on a mission."

Iri only just managed the jump in time, but Rozene compensated for the slightly late take-off, and Iri slid into position as though she and Rozene had been a team from the start. Iri immediately felt guilty.

"She would've approved," Rozene said, glancing over her shoulder.

Smiling slightly, Iri rubbed the fur along Rozene's neck. Rozene leaned into the touch. "Yes, Tinks enjoyed that too."

They flew in silence for a while. Then Rozene snuck a glance over her shoulder. "Why did you call her Tinks?"

The question had Iri smiling. "Because that was her nickname."

"Nickname?"

"A shorter version of someone's name, used when we like someone. Like you. I think we can call you Rozie."

Rumbling under her told Iri Rozie was laughing. "If you say so."

They flew on, tailing the others as they sped towards Daxsos. Interesting how different Rozie was compared to Tinks. Tinks had been so formal and almost horrified at the use of a nickname. Probably why she and Rozie got along so well. *Don't they say opposites attract?* Iri glanced to her left, to where Atu flew. *Is he my opposite? Is that what's developing between us?*

Her thoughts lingered on the question. When they landed for the evening, Iri still had no answer. She'd never been close to anyone before all this had started. This mission had given her her first true friends. Now, it was potentially giving her something more. Something she wasn't sure she was ready for.

Swiping the thoughts away at last, she decided she wouldn't make a thing of it. So she made light of things, joined in the banter, and tried to act normal. But she was suddenly intensely aware of where Atu was at all times, like she couldn't escape it. Even when she tried to ignore the pull, it wriggled back, making her even more aware of Atu than before.

Finally, exhausted by her own mental gymnastics, Iri said goodnight and crept into her sleeping shell. When she woke the next morning after a deep, dreamless sleep, the first in weeks, she took a moment to ponder. She hadn't expected to sleep a wink, let alone sleep so well. Whether it was this thing with Atu or meeting Rozie, she gave up on guessing. For now, she was refreshed and grateful for it.

Travel that day passed quickly. When twilight loomed, they were close enough to Daxsos to press on regardless of the risk. If they hurried, they would make it to the library before its nine o'clock closing.

Their gliders provided the speed needed for them to arrive thirty minutes before the doors shut. Dropping them in the large, derelict square outside the library, their gliders took to the air again as the four voyagers hurried inside.

CHAPTER THIRTY-THREE

Iri wasn't impressed. She'd seen a fair number of libraries while she roamed to find a place she could call home, and this was one of the worst. Her attention shifted to Jaden as he marched up to the circulation desk.

"Is Awena in?"

As the librarian shook her head, the vague whites around Jaden turned scarlet. Annoyance. Like he'd been expecting the rebuttal.

"I'm sorry, no one by that name works here."

Jaden turned to Kayla. "I'm sorry. We should've thought to call before we came." The scarlet muted to tangerine, and Iri caught the scent of uncertainty. "We might've wasted time coming here."

But Kayla smiled, the soft aquas around her intensifying as she took Jaden's hand. "Nothing's ever wasted. Just because Awena's not here doesn't mean we can't find answers."

Iri giggled at Jaden's surprise. He spared her a derogatory glance before looking back at Kayla. "What do you suggest?"

"We found the book in the legends section. That's where Awena took us. Perhaps we should pay those shelves another visit."

Jaden grinned. "You're thinking something else might magically appear on the shelves?"

Laughing, Kayla said, "If only we could be that lucky. But it's a place to start."

Jaden and Kayla led the way. When they reached their destination, their faces showed confusion. "Is something wrong?"

Kayla hummed. "Last time, all the books in this section were on the bottom. Now, they're up here." She pointed at the top three shelves. Kayla glanced at Jaden. "You don't think she somehow arranged the shelves differently for us last time?"

"The question would be why," Jaden muttered. He thought a moment, his eyes going distant. "Do you remember how she wouldn't let me help her get the book?" Kayla nodded. "Is it possible the book wasn't even on the shelf? That she had it with her and just made it look like she was taking it off the shelf?"

Air whooshed out of Kayla. She looked stricken. "I bet she did."

The air around her friends turned mauve. If Iri could see colors on herself, hers would be the same shade of dejection. "If Awena didn't take the book from this shelf, what are the chances anything else can tell us where Gedrin's story took place?"

Once again, buttery yellows flowed from Kayla, drowning out the mauve. "We won't know there's nothing here until we've looked. Let's get started. We only have about twenty minutes until the library closes."

Hands reached for shelves, and the four of them began pouring through the books. In fifteen minutes, they'd cleared every book on the three shelves. Not surprising considering each shelf was only half full.

"What now?" Iri asked, turning to Jaden.

She noticed crimson blooming around him. Iri could relate to his anger. At every turn, something blocked them.

Kayla studied Jaden and then took his hand in hers as she answered. "There must be another way to find this place. We know it's a volcanic area. Why don't we go to the geography section and see what we can find about areas with volcanoes—or any reference to 'Fire Lands?'"

The colors around Jaden cooled to a morning sky, and his scent was as grateful as the glance he directed toward Kayla. Iri had detected his annoyance before, when everyone kept asking him what they should do next. She'd also noticed how often Kayla stepped in to share the burden.

"I've already searched for 'Fire Lands' on the web." Jaden frowned when he saw Kayla's hopeful expression. "No, nothing. You don't think I would've confirmed all this before if we had concrete evidence to back up what Tarise said?"

Spying Kayla's faltering yellows, Iri said, "The geography section it is, then. Who knows the way?"

After looking up the Dewey number on his PAL, Jaden led them to the appropriate aisle. Closing in on the number he had pulled up, Iri saw the familiar lilacs rising to the surface again.

Kayla stared at the shelves and shelves of books. "How are we going to get through all those?"

Pulling a random book out, Jaden glanced at the title. "*Mountains of the Northern Quadrant.*" Shoving the book back in, he pulled out another. "*An In-Depth Review of Mountain Ranges.*" Jaden slammed the book back into place. He paced down the shelves, reading titles aloud as he went.

A pointed "Ahem" sounded behind them. Whirling, they found the librarian from the circulation desk. "The library is closing in five minutes. Is there anything I can help you find?"

Kayla glanced at the stacks of books around them. Her sigh was audible. "Not unless you know a quicker way to find a very specific volcano."

The librarian smiled, dimples sweetening her face. "If it's volcanoes you're looking for, you're in the wrong section. This section is for mountains."

The blinding flash of a rapid, instant color change had Iri turning toward Jaden. Fuchsia replaced the lilac, and joy shone on his face. "What just occurred to you?" Jaden gave her that look she was all too familiar with. His incredulity that she knew he'd had a revelation before he said anything.

"We searched for the term before. But we didn't know there was a shape we could look for. A very specific volcano will have a very specific shape."

They all understood what he was getting at. Smiles broke out all around, except for the poor circulation lady, who just blinked at them.

Jaden smiled at her. "Is there a place where we can access the internet? I promise, we won't take more than the few minutes we have left."

Casting glances at them over her shoulder as though she wondered what they were up to, the lady led the way to a bank of computers against a far wall. Iri glanced at the relics, wondering if they would suffice. They were so old they didn't even have holoscreens, just antiquated monitors. And keyboards!

Unfazed, Jaden sat down and pulled the keyboard closer, his fingers flying. Despite the antiquated equipment, the internet connection wasn't lacking. Information began scrolling on the monitor in front of Jaden. As one, Iri, Atu and Kayla leaned in to see what he'd found.

"There!" Kayla squeaked, pointing at a result that was just disappearing off the top of the screen.

With a few keystrokes, Jaden stopped the scrolling, then reversed it, landing on the image. The kinks and curves matched perfectly. Clicking on the reference, Jaden brought up the article. He read the headline. "*Terratalunga Receives National Park Status.*"

"It is Terratalunga," Kayla breathed.

Jaden grinned. "And that came from a terrain overlay search—not from the name."

"So, no doubt then?" Atu asked.

"No doubt. Although I am a little surprised the terrain overlay search worked for something on this mission. Remember how unsuccessful our previous attempts were?"

Kayla nodded, her eyes still on the screen as she read. 'This says the volcano's been dormant for centuries. They only establised the park a few decades ago. Look, there's a link to a map."

Jaden clicked on the link. The map came up, and as one, they stared. Their combined shock was a sharp sting biting Iri's nose. Because, at the very bottom of the map, in the park's logo, was something they recognized. *The medallion!*

CHAPTER THIRTY-FOUR

While not identical to their medallions, the colors and shapes were unmistakable. The ink pot had been cleverly transformed into an obsidian mountain, the quill magically presented as golden lava spewing from the top, and the beautiful mother-of-pearl surface was depicted as smoke swirling around the volcano. If all that didn't seal the deal, the familiar octagonal shape of the logo was a dead giveaway.

"Wow, I would never have believed the image on our medallions could be a volcanic mountain," Kayla breathed.

They continued staring at the images as though trying to make sense of them.

"Did you find what you were looking for?" The librarian's question reminded them she was still there.

Jaden glanced at his PAL, confirming the time. "Yes, thank you. And we're so sorry to have kept you past closing time. If we can print a few things, we'll be out of here."

"No problem. Old as it is, that computer connects to the printer downstairs." She smiled at them. "Yes, I know, we're a little outdated here. But if you print, it will make its way to the printer near the circulation desk."

Jaden hit the print command, then closed the browser and wiped the history. "Shall we?"

They trailed the librarian downstairs finding the multiple print-outs waiting for them. He snatched them up and stuffed them into his pack. "Would you like us to wait with you while you lock up?"

The librarian's smile covered her whole face. "What a nice young man you are! I don't believe anyone's offered to do that in at least a decade."

Jaden smiled. "More's the pity, then. And it's the least we can do after keeping you past closing time. Can we do anything to help you?"

The librarian moved behind the counter, flipped a few switches, and then lifted her purse. "That's all the 'closing' this place requires. It's old, I know, but they have made some things easier. It's just the main doors now."

Jaden and the others preceded her to the exit where Jaden held the door for her. Once she had locked the doors, he asked, "How are you getting home?"

The librarian turned and pointed at a 'pod just dropping into the square outside the library. "My ride just arrived. Thank you for waiting with me. I'll be on my way now."

The four of them watched as she trotted over to her 'pod and disappeared inside. The 'pod lifted and vanished seconds later.

As if their gliders had been waiting for just that, they appeared.

"Ready to leave?" Han asked.

"Yes. Time to head for Terratalunga," Jaden replied.

Their gliders disappeared as they circled around and then dropped back down one at a time to collect their voyagers.

Once they were in the air but before he had connected his comm system, Jaden said to Han, "I think Rozie's an excellent choice for Iri." Han rocked under Jaden as his glider laughed. "What?"

"You and your nicknames. Who came up with that one?"

"Iri. And I think it's a good sign that she's already given Rozie a nickname."

Han sobered. "It is. It seems the feeling is mutual. Rozene seems to like Iri as much as Iri has apparently taken to her." Han was quiet for a moment. "Where is Terratalunga?"

Jaden sniggered. "And here I thought you gliders were all-knowing!" He flicked his comm system on. "I'm assuming we're agreed on heading for Terratalunga with all haste?"

The confirmations came back. Then Kayla asked, "Have you heard from Markov?"

Jaden knew what she was really asking. Had Markov heard from her dad. "No, I haven't spoken with him yet. But I'll call him now."

"No, let's wait until we find somewhere we can rest for the night." When Jaden remained silent, Kayla sensed his question and answered it. "My dad's next check-in is only due in another hour. We may as well wait until then."

Some tension left Jaden. Kayla had sounded like herself for the first time since leaving Sven's. Happy, even. There was no worry marking her voice. Since they'd confirmed Terratalunga as their destination, the stars were lining up. Maybe her dad was only having communication issues rather than something more dire. Yet that small, quiet voice in the back of his mind nagged at Jaden.

The sensation grew the longer they flew. Something was off. Jaden wasn't sure what, just that something was. "Han, we need to land."

Han dove, twittering to Taz and the other gliders. Without argument, they followed. Shooting a glance over his shoulder, Han asked, "Are you going to tell me what's wrong?"

Jaden frowned. "I don't know. There's just something. And I have a feeling we need to be on the ground for this."

Han nodded, his focus on the terrain below. He drifted for a short while, then angled toward a dark spot. "There's a safe place for us to spend the night."

Jaden engaged his night vision lenses, telling the others to do the same, so no one hurt themselves on the landing. It was just as well because short bushes, only ankle height, but with branches thick enough to hurt or cause injury if they landed on them by mistake, covered the place Han had picked.

When they had all dismounted without injury, moving against the side of the small hill, they waited for their gliders to join them. Their gliders landed and hopped closer, Taz taking charge—as usual.

"I thought we were in a hurry to get where we were going. Why did we stop?"

"Jaden had one of those feelings of his," Han replied.

Weight crashed down on Jaden as everyone turned to look at him. "No, I don't know why we had to land. Just that we needed to."

Banging drums and a screeching electric guitar pierced the air. They all jumped, the sound extraordinarily loud in the silence of the empty landscape. Jaden needed another second to get past the fright and recognize it as one of his PAL's defining ringtones. He slid his gaze toward Kayla. "It's Markov."

Her face immediately radiated strain. "Well, answer it!"

Jaden tapped his CC. Markov's face floated up on the holoscreen, bright in the darkness around them.

Markov peered past Jaden. "Are you alone?"

"No, the others are here," Jaden said, turning so Markov could see them in the background.

Jaden read the uncertainty on Markov's face. "Does this have to do with Kayla's dad?"

"No."

Jaden's impatience rose. "Spit it out." Something in his tone had to have conveyed the seriousness of the conversation. As one, Kayla, Iri and Atu drifted closer.

Noticing them converging on Jaden, Markov's eyes darted toward Kayla. "Maybe we should open a private line?"

"Too late," Jaden replied as the others huddled around. "Not that it's necessary. We don't have time to keep secrets these days."

Kayla mouthed, "Dad?" as she glanced at Jaden while Iri and Atu exchanged greetings with Markov.

Jaden shook his head. He had no clue what this was about.

Kayla switched her attention to the holo and added her greetings. "So, what's up?"

Once again, Markov dared a quick glance toward Kayla. Jaden suddenly understood Kayla was why Markov had wanted the private line. Jaden eased his hand into Kayla's, giving it a reassuring squeeze when she raised her eyebrows at him.

Markov sighed. "Fine. I was hoping to not have to tell you like this, but since you and the others disappeared on us, I don't really have a choice."

Hearing the unspoken accusation in Markov's voice, Jaden said, "Sorry, dude. We didn't think we'd be long. Just a short trip to Daxsos to confirm something. I guess we're so used to flying off and doing things with no one knowing we'd taken off that we didn't think to tell people. But since the time freeze broke when the Gaptors and gliders became visible to everyone, we need to adjust our thinking."

When Markov nodded without pressing the issue, the pit in Jaden's stomach yawned wider. Whatever Markov had to say, it wasn't good. The only thing that kept Jaden from snapping a second time was knowing this didn't have to do with Kayla's dad. "Why are you calling?"

As if realizing he couldn't put the answer off any longer, Markov looked directly at Jaden. "Tarise escaped."

Kayla stiffened beside Jaden. His hand tightened around hers. Of all the things Markov could've said! "What? How?"

"See for yourself." Markov swiped across his screen, and a video showing footage of Tarise's cell replaced his face.

Jaden and the others observed Tarise pacing in her cell. Then she halted, looking up as if there was a taller person blocking her path. She stared up, her lips moving. Her lips stopped for a short while before moving again. Then she turned so her back was to the camera.

"What's she saying?" Jaden asked.

"That first sentence was, 'What are you doing here?' The second sentence begins with, 'You know I can't.' Then it's impossible to know what she says after that."

"Why not? Sven had the room wired for sound."

"He did, but it didn't pick up anything, even that first part. He had to lipread to tell us what she said. Tarise appeared to have a whole conversation."

"Conversation?"

"Just watch," Markov muttered. Something in his tone had Jaden thinking this wasn't the worst of it.

Indeed, it seemed Tarise was speaking to someone. Even though her back was to them, her gestures supported a conversation. When Tarise turned and began pacing again, her lips moved and stopped, then moved again.

Horror crawled through Jaden. "Markov, what else did Sven lipread?"

Markov's face was grim. He knew Jaden understood. "Only bits and pieces, but from the little he could glean, Sven said she was arguing with someone."

There it was. Jaden felt Kayla's eyes on him. Looking at her, he saw the question in her eyes. "Yes, I think she was talking to Slurpy. I don't think she's lost it enough yet to for us to call her crazy. But she wasn't talking to herself."

"You think that's why we can't see who she's talking to—or why there's no audio?" Kayla croaked.

"I do."

"But if the usurper is there, why didn't he black out the screens like he usually does?" Atu asked.

His normal quiet entry into the conversation with something none of the rest of them had considered made Jaden glad Atu was there. "Why do *you* think he did it?"

Atu considered. "Maybe there was something he needed us to see —even though he didn't want us hearing what they discussed?"

"Huh. I suppose that could be true." Speaking to Markov again, Jaden asked, "Did Sven notice anything unusual about this interaction?" Markov was silent for so long Jaden wondered whether he had heard. "Markov?"

"Yeah, I'm here. Just watch to the end, and then I'll answer your questions."

There it was again. That odd tone. Jaden's earlier impatience returned, but he knew his friend well enough to know Markov meant it. Reining in his impatience, Jaden watched. No, he scrutinized. Every little gesture. Every facial expression. There had to be something.

He almost reeled back when Tarise suddenly clutched at her hand, her face twisting into a silent scream.

Despite his anger towards Tarise for betraying Kayla, Jaden couldn't help feeling sorry for the anguish she was suffering. She clutched at her hand, tears streaming down her face. Then she collapsed in a heap on the floor, as though the pain was severe enough to rob her of the use of her legs.

Jaden felt sick. He was about to order Markov to fast forward to the next part when Tarise slumped to the floor, unconscious. Watching unseen hands shake Tarise was almost surreal. Her eyes snapped open as she was pulled from unconsciousness. Jaden didn't want to know how Slurpy had done that. He braced himself, waiting for the torture to begin anew, but he wasn't the only one breathing a sigh of relief when Tarise only blinked at the unseen person standing over her. Her lips moved once. Then her head snapped sideways as the blow struck.

Jaden cast a quick glance at the others, finding them equally appalled. When Tarise twisted back, a clear red imprint marked where the hand had hit. She snarled something, evidenced by the way her lips twisted. Jaden didn't need Sven to lipread that one word. "Fine."

What had she agreed to? Jaden's insides curled as Tarise continued glaring up for a few seconds. Then her gaze dropped to the floor, and her shoulders shook as she sobbed, her hands over her face.

"Did he leave?" Atu asked, peering at the screen.

"It's hard to tell," Jaden murmured.

But as they continued watching, it became clear Tarise was on her own again. No words crossed her lips, just a forlorn expression when she stopped crying and rose to her feet. As she made her way to the desk provided for her use, she looked like she was in a trance. She began tapping on the desk's integrated screen, her back to them, shoulders stiff.

When she rose again, her face was impossible to read. Was it determination? Resignation? Despair? Or all of them rolled into one? Jaden couldn't work it out as Tarise strode to the door of her room. As if by magic, the door popped open. She exited her cell and made for the passage that led to Sven's workshop. Again, the door slid open at her approach, as though Sven himself had operated the controls.

Jaden's eyes never left the screen as Tarise traversed that danger-laden passageway. None of Sven's traps activated. The door to the workshop opened, and Tarise disappeared beyond it.

When Markov's face suddenly reappeared on the holo, replacing the video, they jerked back.

"I'm assuming Sven wasn't opening all those doors and preventing the traps from stopping her?" Even to his own ears, Jaden's voice sounded strained as he asked the question.

"No."

The one syllable answer had Jaden wondering what Markov wasn't saying. Then he knew, and his gut confirmed it. He didn't want to ask. But he had to know. "What did Tarise type?"

Markov's mouth thinned. "None of this was your fault. She made her own decisions. And she didn't think to discuss this with any of the rest of us, even though we're her friends."

Jaden heard the disappointment in Markov's voice, but he was weary beyond words. "Just tell me what she wrote."

Instead of answering, another image flashed onto the holo: the note Tarise had written. Jaden skimmed over it. Dread coalesced in a tight ball in his chest, making it difficult to breathe. Kayla's hand tightened around his own.

"Markov's right. Tarise even said not to blame yourself." When Jaden remained silent, Kayla pressed. "Say something."

"I have a terrible feeling about this."

Markov's eyes were instantly alert as he snapped back onto the screen. "What do you mean? You think she'll betray us again?"

"I don't know. But whatever she plans to do isn't something we'll like."

CHAPTER THIRTY-FIVE

Minutes later, Markov signed off. They were all too shattered by the news to do anything except stand there. After what felt like an eternity, Jaden sighed. "Shall we spend the night here?"

Surprisingly, Atu answered. "I'm too hyped after that to sleep."

"I agree," Iri muttered.

"Me too," Kayla added, her voice bleak. "I say we press on. We can always rest if we get tired later."

Their gliders took to the air, returning for the pick-up and then speeding onward. News of Tarise's escape had smothered them with desolation again, like they were all waiting for the next blow.

Jaden's mind kept returning to the words Tarise had written. More than that, he wished he could shake the feeling she would do something stupid. Genius that she was with some things, she was clueless in others, as though whatever had added to her intellect had taken from her common sense. Why wouldn't she come to them with her troubles?

"Do you think she knows we have Slurpy's comm device?"

Kayla's question cut into his musings. It confirmed she was also still thinking about Tarise. "I can't see how with Sven isolating her. Then again, who knows what else she might've been doing in her cell?

She's smart enough to take that sound system Sven installed and reverse it so she could listen in on what was going on around her."

"You think she's capable of that?"

Jaden heard the shock in Kayla's voice. He wished he could see her face, but they were hundreds of feet in the air, their masks and goggles covering their faces as they sped toward Terratalunga and whatever fate awaited them there. Jaden sighed loudly, since she couldn't see his face any more than he could see hers.

"Yes, she's capable of that. Whether or not she did it, only Sven can tell. I'll ping him as soon as we finish talking." Kayla's silence wasn't reassuring. Jaden pulled himself from thoughts of Tarise. "How are you holding up?"

It was the most generic way he could think to ask with all the others able to hear their conversation. *Is it even worth asking Sven to add a channel switch so people can have private conversations? No, we're almost done with this.* Or at least, he hoped so.

"Hanging in there," Kayla replied. "I'll know better after the next check-in."

When she would find out if her dad had in fact checked in. Jaden wanted to ask if her dad would contact them outside a check-in time if he'd missed his previous connections but decided against it. It would only have Kayla hoping for something that might not materialize. There was nothing he could say to make things more tolerable for her. The best he could do was get them to Terratalunga as quickly as possible.

A short while later, Jaden pinged Sven as promised. When Sven's face paled at the possibility that Tarise hadn't somehow manipulated the intercom, it didn't reassure Jaden. Signing off, he decided worrying about it was pointless. Tarise either knew they had one of Slurpy's comm devices or she didn't. She would either betray them or she wouldn't.

As the time and miles stretched on, Jaden's concern shifted when he sensed Kayla's rising stress. Like an elastic thread stretching so thin it could only snap violently. Jaden was sure they would all be casualties when it did.

Vicken missed that check-in. And the next one. But still the thread held. Jaden was in awe of Kayla's ability to keep it together. It only highlighted his own heightening apprehension. Was Vicken okay? Was Terratalunga a trap, regardless of it being their true destination?

Jaden glanced at Kayla, wishing he could see her face. Even her posture was stiff and unyielding, as though she were bracing herself for the worst. What was the longest time Vicken hadn't checked in for and still been okay?

Jittery, Jaden leaned forward so Han could hear him over the roaring wind. "How long until we get there?"

"We're close."

It was all Han said, his energy focused on getting them to their destination with all due haste. Jaden didn't ask more questions. He glanced at Kayla again. Just the way she held herself made him tired. It was a wonder none of them had wanted to stop for rest.

With his own brain slowing a little, something nagged at the back of his mind. Jaden tried to latch onto it. *Kayla? No. Our group? No. Something Markov said . . . Yes.* Closing his eyes, Jaden mentally replayed the conversation. This time, he focused on Markov and not Tarise. He had been . . . Jaden's eyes flew open. Sitting up straighter, he scanned the surrounding skies.

"What's wrong?"

Han had picked up on the change in his mood. Jaden used one hand to turn his comm off while the other rubbed the side of Han's neck. "Nothing bad. I believe we may have some welcome company soon."

Jaden mentally saw the eye roll he was sure Han made. "Care to elaborate? And why are you turning your comm off?"

"Because I don't want to get the others riled up—either excited or anxious."

"Well, now that you've made me both, spill."

Jaden ginned. "I think Markov and the others may be on their way to Terratalunga too."

Han bucked under him. "What makes you say that?"

"I didn't notice it earlier, but when Markov sent that transmission, he wasn't at Sven's. I just assumed he was. But the sky in the background wasn't Sven's starry blanket. It was a hazy orange, as though the lights of a compound were near."

"What do you think it means?"

"I'm not sure. Could be Kayla's mom raised the alarm when she didn't find Kayla in her room. Or that Sadie asked them to go to Terratalunga to find Vicken. Or both."

"Perhaps Tarise's escape prompted this?"

"No, I don't think so. I think Markov and the others had already left when they discovered that little gem."

"Then why didn't Sven say something when you called him? And why did he send the information to Markov and not to you?"

"Maybe because Sadie's traveling with them and Sven wanted to update her first?" Jaden rubbed a hand over his face, finding the smooth material of his face mask there. It only irritated him further. "What's with the questions?"

"You're all too quiet," Han grumped.

"Ah, friend, don't worry about us." Jaden rubbed him along his neck again. "We have you to scare off the big spooky monsters." Han's snort of laughter had Jaden grinning. "Seriously, though, how would we have gotten this far if it hadn't been for you and Taz and the other gliders?"

"Okay, enough already. I'll try not to worry about you. Pipsqueak that you are."

Jaden laughed. It must've been loud enough for the others to hear even without his comm connected. When he saw their inquiring glances, he flipped his comm back on. "Han thinks I'm a pipsqueak."

General cackling over the comm. Even from Kayla. She caught him studying her and raised a hand, putting it under her chin and miming a lifting motion. Torn between pride at her optimism and worry for her struggle, Jaden gave her a thumbs-up signal. It wouldn't be long now. Then they would find out for themselves what had happened to Vicken.

Not quite an hour later, they reached the mountains that formed the outer rim of Terratalunga. Jaden stared, their starkness unexpected. Nothing like the Shadow Mountains. Where the mountains hunched over his home had snow and trees and shimmering lakes, these hills were black, barren, and boiling, coated with thousands upon thousands of tiny onyx pebbles. Heat pulsed up through them, wreathing the air with mist as the heat hit the cooler air above and steamed.

Jaden had never seen a more severe landscape. After the light conversation following Han's comment, the comm went silent again. Jaden wasn't the only one stunned by the foreboding landscape before them.

Jaden almost told Han to get a move on before he realized Han hadn't stopped. These mountains were so open, Jaden didn't feel movement the same way he did in the Shadow Mountains.

They banked towards a ridge hiding the rest of the range from them. As they crested it, Jaden grinned when he saw the gathering ahead of them. "How in heck did you beat us here?"

"We didn't have to make a detour to Daxsos," Markov replied. Jaden could hear the smile in his voice. Markov's glider peeling away from the group and heading their way. The other gliders followed suit, circling toward them.

"You knew Markov would be here?"

Kayla's question was quiet, but Jaden heard the unspoken recrimination. "I suspected they might join us. I never thought they would be here, waiting for us."

Before Kayla could reply, a glider sidled up to her. Alarmed, Jaden opened his mouth to warn her. Then he realized who it was. With that, he understood why Markov and the others had come.

"Mom!" Kayla's greeting rang out, her joy and relief tangible.

Sadie's glider settled as near to Kayla's as their wingspans would permit.

"I couldn't wait anymore. It was killing me to sit around doing nothing. I had to come see what was keeping your father. He's never been this late with a check-in before."

Well, that answers one of my questions.

"I understand." Kayla's soft reply did nothing to dim her own distress. "I'm so glad you're here."

"Me too. Let's go find your father."

As though the gliders heard the conversation, they formed up again, and the group plowed deeper into the hissing steam that was Terratalunga.

CHAPTER THIRTY-SIX

Kayla's heart pounded. With every flap of Taz's powerful wings, they were one step closer to finding her father. Her mother's presence only increased her dread. Her father had never been gone this long before without checking in.

Trying to keep her fear at a manageable level, Kayla caught glimpses of the landscape through the mist surrounding them. Not that there was anything to see. It was a lunar landscape: just rock, rock, and more rock.

Taz banked so suddenly Kayla would've fallen, had her smart suit not corrected her position. "What was that?"

Before Taz answered, a plume of water shot up next to Kayla. Then another, this one so close it sprayed Kayla with water. *Hot* water. Another spout gushed up. Then another, releasing from the smoldering earth below with a whoosh.

Geysers? She never would've guessed there was enough water in this barren wasteland for such a phenomenon And yet Taz swerved again as another one shot up in front of them. Taz twisted and turned as she guided them through.

Then it was silent again, the land below them asleep once more. No more fountains shooting up around them.

Kayla wiped the spray from her eyes. While the water had been hot, it hadn't been unbearable. Between the mist and steam now swirling around them, visibility was zero. "Can you even see where you're going?"

Taz snorted as though the question were ludicrous. "Do you think I'd be flying at this speed if we could crash into the mountain?"

The uncharacteristically sharp comment made Kayla realize Taz was just as nervous as she was. Not about the perils that faced them, but about Kayla's state of mind. About how Kayla would react if something had happened to her father.

Reaching forward, Kayla massaged a soft spot just behind Taz's ear. "I'll be alright. As soon as we get there and find my father, I'll be fine." Kayla didn't add not finding her father would be devastating. Although that possibility always lingered, along with something unthinkable.

Shoving the dark thoughts aside before they formed fully, Kayla steeled herself. Whether or not they found her father, whatever state he was in, she and the other seekers had no choice but to press on. Delays would only increase the risk that the usurper's invasion of their world would harm others they loved.

Kayla gazed at her mother, flying next to her. She was thankful her mother had come. If Kayla had to leave before they found her dad, her mom would find him. Of that, she was sure. Sadie never failed when she put her mind to something. Her mother looked at her, and Kayla waved, trying to hide the dismal thoughts tracking through her mind.

Needing to know the plan, Kayla asked, "Jaden, do you know our destination? Or are we just flying around until you get one of those feelings of yours?"

"Yes, we have a plan."

Jaden's voice was sour. Kayla smiled despite the heaviness in her heart. He didn't like it when she referred to those feelings of his like they were something he controlled. "Care to share?"

"I studied that map of the park we printed at the library."

"When did you have time to do that?"

"Flying here with nothing to do for hours, hello?"

Kayla loved that he was trying to keep things light. She could do no less. "I thought you'd fallen asleep, leaving Han to do all the work!" Han's laughter rumbled in the background.

"Yeah, he says to say thanks for the support," Jaden grunted.

"Are you going to tell us where we're going?" Sadie interrupted.

Kayla glanced at her mother, who shrugged. Kayla supposed they had drifted off topic. And she could relate to her mother's need to get an answer on *something*. Anything. Anything to make Sadie feel she was getting closer to finding her husband.

As though Jaden realized it too, he answered, "We're headed to the mountain with the kink."

"The kink? What does that mean?" Sadie asked.

Realizing mother wouldn't know the relevance of the spot, Kayla explained.

Sadie was quiet for a moment. "Yes, that's probably the best place to start."

Swift as the gliders were, it still took a while before Taz said, "This is the one."

Kayla peered into the mist. Since it had taken them so long to get here, the distance from the outskirts, where they'd met the rest of the gliders, was significant. That, or the gliders had been flying around in circles trying to pinpoint the location. "Are you sure?"

Taz sighed. Instead of answering, she leaned to the right and slowed, turning toward the black mass of the mountain lurking under the mist.

Kayla saw it. The kink they had been looking for. The place marked by the map in Awena's book. Confirmed by the terrain overlay search at the library. Their final destination. It was almost surreal how accurately the kink mimicked the map's.

Taz growled. "We need to find a better place for your dismount. That space isn't large enough."

Kayla had to agree. The kink was a jagged outcropping, only six feet by four feet, with empty air below if they missed the landing. A quick slip to a sure drop. Deadly if the gliders couldn't get close enough to mountain side to catch them.

Kayla studied the outcropping as Taz circled, scouting for a safer place. The swirling mists made it difficult to establish what the terrain around the ledge looked like. The ledge itself, from the glimpses Kayla managed, appeared to be a solid slab of stone. *How odd. A slab of stone amid all this gravel.*

Then Kayla realized what she wasn't seeing. "Taz, can you get us a little closer?"

"Why? The winds that close are treacherous. If we're not careful, they'll slam us into the mountain."

"I can't see my dad. If he's not there, there's no point trying to land."

"Hold on, I'll get us as close as I can."

The moment they were within ten feet of the ledge, the winds battered them. Kayla tightened her grip on Taz, peering through the infernal mist. A gust of wind swept the ledge clear for an instant. Kayla's hopes were dashed. No sign of her father.

Trying to keep it together, she said, "We can go."

"No, I thought I saw something," Taz said through gritted teeth. "Look beyond the ledge, to where it meets the mountain."

Kayla hung on, wondering how Taz wasn't being flipped over as the wind continued its assault. Then another gust, and she could see the entire ledge this time, not just the part sticking out of the mountain like a thorn from a finger. This time, Kayla spotted what Taz had glimpsed. A cave yawned at the end of the ledge, its opening dark enough against the ebony trim of the mountain to make it invisible—unless you were this close and specifically looking for it.

Taz suddenly tucked her wings and dove. Kayla's breath burst out of her. Thankful for her smart suit, Kayla yelled, "What are you doing?"

"Saving us from being smashed against the mountain," Taz tossed back. "Hold on, I'm pulling out."

Kayla did. When Taz spread her wings, oxygen returned as the crazy dive ended and they swung away from the mountain.

"That was too close," Taz muttered.

"What were you thinking?" Han growled, speeding in to take up a position next to them. "You can't take those kinds of risks. That's what I'm here for."

"My apologies, I didn't know I had to ask *you* first," Taz snapped.

Kayla glanced at Jaden. What was it with their gliders? Jaden shrugged as though he had no clue either.

Han huffed but said no more, following Taz until they were far enough from the mountain to be safe from the winds. The rest of the gliders followed, and when Taz began circling, the others did too, agitated twittering spiking the air. Kayla had had enough.

"Okay, what's with all the twittering? Speak to us."

Taz turned her head. "Sorry. We're trying to figure out how to get you onto that mountain."

"Just drop us further up or down—it doesn't matter," Kayla answered.

Taz cocked an eyebrow. "It seems you're not considering all that loose gravel. If we drop you anywhere on that mountain, chances are you'll slide all the way down."

Kayla *hadn't* thought of that. If that was true, how had her father done it? Or had he?

Jaden's shocked voice cut in. "We're supposed to land there? It's nothing but a slab of rock. And a tiny one at that. If we miss the landing—"

Kayla interrupted before he could continue. "There's a cave behind it."

"Oh."

It was all Jaden said as the gliders continued their twittery conversation.

"Did you see your father down there?"

Sadie's question had Kayla turning as her mother's glider slid up alongside Taz. "No, he wasn't on that ledge. But you might've heard via the comm there's a cave behind it."

Neither of them wanted to voice the other option. That he had tried for the ledge and missed. Fallen all the way down the mountain.

Kayla caught Jaden glancing between her and her mother, trying to interpret the underlying conversation. When she heard his sharp

DUEL OF DEATH

intake of breath, then saw him glance to her for confirmation, she nodded.

Jaden's voice was brittle when he spoke, his words going out over the comm. "Han, let's do another circuit of the area."

Han's complaint was loud enough for Kayla to hear it from where she and Taz hovered. Jaden's hand went up to his comm. His lips moved under his mask, their words silent without the comm. Abruptly, Han turned, and he and Jaden disappeared into the eddying mists.

Biting her lip, Kayla couldn't decide between telling Taz to chase after them and staying to see what the verdict was. Then she realized that, without Taz, there would be no verdict. Her head ached. Kayla began rubbing her forehead, trying to ease the pain growing worse with each minute. She wasn't thinking clearly. She couldn't allow that. Her mind had to be clear.

Rustling on her left prompted Kayla to open her eyes. Iri, her mask drawn back, smiled tentatively. "I hate to intrude on people's private agonies, but I can't stop my gift. I'm sorry. Forgive me for sharing your pain with Atu. He thought this might help."

Kayla ogled Iri. The words didn't register at first. When they did, Kayla realized Iri was offering one of Atu's ubiquitous tubes.

Kayla smiled. "You don't know how wonderful that looks. Thank you!"

Iri's smile was dazzling. "If it's like any of the other things he gives us, it'll take care of that pain in an instant."

Kayla grinned. "Are you going to just tease me with it or toss it over?"

"Oh, sorry!"

The tube sailed across the gap between the gliders, landing right were Kayla's hand waited for it. "Nice throw."

"You didn't think it would be?" Iri smirked. "What do you think I spent all my time on whilst I was in the forest?"

"Reading."

"Touché," Iri laughed, tipping a hand to her brow. "Come on, use

239

the stuff that's in there already so we can roll as soon as Taz and her cohorts finish plotting."

A movement to Iri's left drew Kayla's attention. Jaden and Han were back. *Already?* Kayla's courage faltered.

Jaden touched his comm. "The cave it is."

CHAPTER THIRTY-SEVEN

Kayla steadied the mad beating of her heart. Her father wasn't at the bottom of this mountain. He wasn't on the slopes. There was still a chance he had survived this. Perhaps he was too deep inside the mountain for his comms to reach beyond the stone.

Jaden flipped his comm switch again, this time pulling his mask off as he gazed at her. His concern made those little creases between his eyes she'd come to recognize. And hate.

"Are you okay?" Jaden mouthed, a sidelong glance at Sadie telling Kayla why he hadn't used his comm.

Flipping her own mask up, she sent a weary smile his way. "I've been better."

Jaden nodded, letting the rubber of his mask snap back over his face. He touched the comm again. "Ready to go," he announced to no one in particular. "Kayla, ask Taz when they'll quit jabbering. We need to get into that cave."

Smiling at the thought of Taz's reaction, Kayla conveyed the message. She wasn't disappointed.

"Unless you want to tear yourself to shreds on those sharp little crystals down there, you'll have some patience," Taz snapped.

"But why would I want to be on the sides of the mountain when I can be on the ledge?" Jaden reached behind him and held up a hank of rope.

Kayla saw Taz's mouth open as though she would've sniped something else. Then Taz went still. "You think that's how Vicken made it down there?"

"I don't see any other way." Jaden's voice was calm as he described how they could do it. Kayla wondered how long he'd been noodling the idea. "That is, of course, if it's not too undignified for you to have us dangling from your talons," Jaden concluded.

"We'll live with it," was Taz's dry answer.

"This won't hurt your leg?" Kayla asked as she held the loop at the end of the rope out for Taz to grip in her talon. She had already secured the other end around her waist.

"It'll only hurt if you miss the landing and I have to catch you," Taz muttered. "So stick the landing."

"Yes, ma'am," Kayla murmured, hiding her smile. It was endearing the way Taz tried to hide how much she worried about Kayla's welfare.

"Ready?" Taz's one-word sentence was the only indication of her nerves.

Han zipped past. "You two don't get to do this before we've tried it first," he called over his shoulder.

Kayla gaped. She couldn't find words. Then she sputtered, "What makes you the heroes here?"

Even though she yelled, she wasn't sure they heard. In fact, she hoped they hadn't. She prayed all their attention was on the landing Jaden would have to nail. Han's wings rippled where the winds lashed them. From the way Han kept tilting this way and then that, it was all he could do just to keep his wings level. Closer and closer they crept, the mountain an obstacle that would not be forgiving if they made any mistakes. Kayla held her breath. *Closer. Closer. Now!*

As she thought the word, Jaden leaped. Kayla's shoulders hunched, and her eyes scrunched up as she tried to hide while still looking. Jaden sailed through the air. The rope between him and Han, initially slack, began to stretch. Jaden hit the ledge. Kayla leaned forward on Taz, waiting for his momentum to take him over the edge.

Jaden tumbled forward. Then he planted one foot in front of himself, regaining his balance. But the rope was almost at its limit. Jaden waved frantically at Han. At the signal, Han dropped his end of the rope. Not a moment too soon. If he'd held on for a second longer, he would've dragged Jaden off the ledge. Jaden took a moment to catch his breath before he turned and faced Kayla, his face grim.

"I won't lie. It will be difficult to get this right. The rope we brought is too short. It won't give us a lot of play. Make sure you don't linger between the drop-off and Taz letting go. But make sure you're steady before you give the command."

"Anything else?" Kayla asked, swallowing hard.

"I'll be here to catch you. Just give me a moment."

Kayla watched, amazed as Jaden pulled more rope from his backpack and disappeared inside the cave. *When did he figure all this out? In fact, where did he get the extra rope?* She looked around and then felt silly. *Duh, we all have a rope in our packs. He could've gotten it from anyone.*

Kayla waited for Jaden to return, her jaw beginning to ache. Realizing she had clamped her teeth together, she opened and closed her mouth a few times, trying to soothe the pain. Then there he was. A taut figure on the ledge. She saw his face. White as a sheet.

"What's wrong?"

Jaden looked like he would be sick. He bent over and put his hands on his knees, gulping down air as though his life depended on it.

"Jaden, speak to me," Kayla ordered, her panic rising.

He waved a hand at her. Kayla waited impatiently, watching Jaden like a hawk. When he rose, his face was haggard. "Markov?"

"Yeah, dude, I'm here." Markov's glider slid up next to Kayla's.

"I need you to come down next."

"What? No wait, I'm next," Kayla argued.

Jaden turned and looked directly at her then. "Kayla, I *need* Markov to be next."

Staring back at Jaden, Kayla tried to figure out what it was he wasn't saying. When she realized what it was, her breath stuttered. "No!" Kayla shook her head violently. "No, Jaden please tell me, tell me that . . ." Kayla couldn't finish the sentence. Jaden swam in her vision as her eyes filled with tears.

Holding her gaze, Jaden motioned she should turn her comm off. Sobs rising, Kayla did as he'd asked. Then he mouthed something. Kayla blinked to clear her eyes. "What did you say?" she mouthed back.

"Your dad's alive. I need help getting him out."

Kayla's breath came in little gasps. *He's okay! Jaden just needs help.* Her sluggish brain took a few seconds to reach the next realization. And she knew. Kayla just knew. Kayla had to work to form the words through frozen lips. "The others?"

Jaden shook his head, his face drawn.

Markov's glider slid even closer so he could speak to Kayla without her mother hearing. *Mom!* Kayla swung her head, finding Iri engaging her mother in a conversation on the other side. Iri darted a glance at Kayla past her mother, and Kayla understood that too. Iri had seen—or smelled—or used whatever sense she had to tell her Kayla's mother couldn't be looking at Jaden now that he had exited the cave. Kayla dipped her head in thanks. Then she turned back to Markov.

"Sorry, I didn't hear what you said." Frazzled, she swiped a hand through the air. "No, I mean, it was loud enough. I just didn't comprehend what you said."

Markov's face was as grim as Jaden's. "I said, let me go down and help Jaden. You stay here with your mom."

Numb, Kayla nodded. She didn't think she'd be able to land, anyway. Not with limbs that were paralyzed, her body frozen in shock. *Dad's team! None of them survived? What happened? They were all so skilled.* Horror clawed at Kayla, digging in and creating fear so intense, it robbed her of air. Gasping, she hoovered air, halting the spots dancing across her vision. Kayla concentrated only on breathing. *In. Out. In. Out.*

Kayla didn't see Markov make the jump—or his landing—or

whether he had to do it more than once. Keeping her eyes glued on the same spot in front of her, Kayla's brain drummed out the words her body had to obey. *In. Out. In. Out.*

"Kayla!"

Taz's sharp cry cut through the mantra. Dazed, Kayla shook her head. "What?"

"Your mother. You need to think of your mother."

Kayla's eyes felt like balls rolling in a too-large channel. Like they would spin right out of her head if she moved them too fast. Maybe if she moved her head instead of her eyes . . . Her gaze fell on her mother. Kayla blinked, trying to focus. Relieved to find Iri still talking to Sadie, Kayla sucked back sobs again. This wouldn't do. She had to get herself under control. Her mother knew her too well. She would take one look at Kayla, in the state she was in, and start panicking herself.

Taking a deep, steadying breath, Kayla closed her eyes. She could do this. She took another breath. And another. The terror, the fear, the anguish, she shoved them deep down. Way down, where she put a shield around them. Relegating them to the box she had crafted to keep them there. Contained. Where they couldn't come out. Where they couldn't be seen. Not until she was ready to open that box again. Settling her face into a calm mask, she opened her eyes.

Her mother was just turning her way. Kayla smiled. She didn't know how, but she did. "Seems you and Iri were having a nice conversation?"

"We were! Did you know she lived in a forest all by herself? And that . . ."

Kayla didn't catch the rest of it. It was a garbled mass of sound. She had to get her mother away from here. From whatever was in that cave. From whatever Jaden was bringing out. Because while he had told her her father was alive, his tone said there was more to it.

Kayla kept the vacant smile plastered on her face until her mother stopped talking. "Mom, we'll need more rope." Her voice sounded strange to her own ears. Kayla ignored the fact. "Can you and Iri please see what you can round up from the other riders?"

For a moment, Kayla thought her mother would question her. Would say no. But then Iri spoke.

"Come on, Mrs. M. Let's gather that rope so we can get down there, explore that cave, and find your husband."

"Well, if you think it will help," Sadie said.

I'm not the only one with an addled brain, Kayla thought as Iri dragged her mother away. Atu had somehow convinced the rest of the riders to move out of sight. Around the side of the mountain if she had to guess, based on where Iri was leading her mother.

Bless you both. Then she gripped the rope around her waist, checking it was secure. "Taz, let's get down there."

Taz cast a glance over her shoulder. "Are you sure?"

Kayla was grateful Taz hadn't tried to talk her out of it. "Yes. I need to see what's there. I need to get to my father. And I have you to catch me if I don't stick the landing."

Because, Jaden and Markov were nowhere in sight. They had to be in the cave. Kayla held on as Taz took them closer, the winds pummeling them every inch of the way. Taz's muscles bunched under Kayla as Taz worked to get them close enough for the dismount without smashing them into the mountain.

Thankful for her goggles keeping the wind out but cursing the mist making judging the distance tricky, Kayla concentrated. She and Taz recognized the perfect moment at the same instant. Kayla leaped right as Taz shouted, "Now!"

Never had anything seemed quite so small as that ledge. Kayla scanned for uneven bits which might throw her off-kilter. But the rock was rushing up to meet her so fast, there wasn't time. Aware of the rope trailing behind her growing taut, Kayla tucked her legs, bracing for impact. Then she hit. The force of the wind knocked her to her knees. Her hands went out in front of her to stop the face plant. They almost slid over the edge.

Scrambling backward on all fours, Kayla fell back onto her butt. The rope bit into her waist. *Taz! She has to let go!* Kayla waved, her arms flopping around in the air in front of her, too weak from adrenaline to give a proper wave.

It was enough. Taz let go, arcing away from the mountain like it was on fire. Kayla watched, tense, as Taz fought the winds that hammered her wings. Then she broke free of the gusts running up and down the side of the mountain, and the ripples along the edges of her wings smoothed.

Kayla wanted to melt into the ledge she sat on. But her need to establish what had happened to her father drove her to rise on shaky legs. Stumbling forward, she entered the cave.

CHAPTER THIRTY-EIGHT

Jaden closed the man's eyes. Glancing at Markov, he asked, "Ready?"

A grim nod was Markov's only answer. Together, they bent over the man. Markov took his legs, and Jaden gripped the man under his shoulders. Heaving, they lifted him and staggered to the side of the cave, the dead man's weight a burden between them.

Setting the man down, they stood. Then they gazed at the men lining the side of the cave, all dead. Except for Vicken. Even that was debatable. With a loud sigh, Jaden trudged back to where Vicken lay.

"Any idea what happened to him—or any of the others?"

Atu's face was grave. "No. And I'm not able to heal him."

Jaden linked his hands behind his head as he began pacing. That Atu had snuck down here without Kayla noticing was a miracle. *But if Atu's magic isn't working, what is this?*

Jaden glanced back at Vicken. Condensation formed on the mirror Atu had propped in front of his nose, showing he was still breathing. His chest still rose and fell. Beyond that, though, there was nothing. No marks on his body to explain what might have befallen him. No bruises. No cuts. No visible wounds.

Jaden stared at the dead men along the wall. It was the same with them. Nothing on them, but they were dead. *Is Vicken just taking longer to die?* His heart squeezed in his chest. Vicken couldn't die. It would forever change Kayla. *How am I going to tell her about her dad? Or Sadie?*

Scuffling at the entrance to the cave made Jaden whip out his DD. Twin flares of light behind him confirmed Atu and Markov were also ready.

Kayla was the last person Jaden expected to see. She stood still, adjusting to the light. She probably couldn't see into this dim interior after the bright mist outside.

Cursing under his breath, Jaden sheathed his DD and strode over to her. "What are you doing here?" His words sounded harsher than he'd meant. He regretted it when he saw Kayla's face. He had never seen fear like this on her. Her lower lip quivered, biting back tears, and her soft green eyes were shimmering fields in a face whiter than the mists outside.

Jaden enveloped her in his arms, hers sliding around his waist and curving up his back as she leaned into him. She took comfort for only a second before pulling back enough to look up at him. "Is my dad really alive?"

Jaden didn't have words. "Come see for yourself."

Leading her into the darkness, he understood why she had stayed on the edge of the cave rather than entering. He stopped for a moment, letting his eyes readjust to the dark. There was a reason he didn't want to use his PAL's light. Jaden didn't want her seeing the dead men lined up along the opposite wall. She only needed to see her dad.

Jaden hurried on as soon as he could make out shapes again. By the time they reached Vicken, they could both see. Thankfully, her eyes were only on the man in front of her. She fell to her knees before him, taking his hand in hers.

"Dad?" When he didn't answer, she repeated it. When there was still no answer, she looked up, her eyes wide. Then she noticed Atu. Kayla gasped. "When did you get here?"

"Right after Markov."

"What's wrong with my dad?"

Atu's sigh was heavy. "I'm sorry, but I have no clue. I'm not getting any results from anything I've tried. And I'm not getting any feedback from him either."

"Feedback?"

Atu frowned. "That's what I call it. When I run my hands over someone who's sick, an energy flows up to my hands from them. It's what allows me fix the exact issue." One look at Kayla's face had him hurrying on. "He's alive. No doubt about that." When Kayla still said nothing, just stared at her dad, Atu said, "Perhaps Iri might see something I can't."

On cue, footsteps sounded behind them. Then a bright light shone in their faces. "Why are you all huddled in the dark? There—"

Iri trailed off as she saw the men on the side of the cave. She snapped her light off. Too late. Kayla had seen them. Her eyes widened in horror.

"Iri, turn the light back on." Kayla's voice was quiet, but commanding.

Iri huffed but did as Kayla asked. When light suffused the small space, Kayla stared at the men for so long, Jaden wondered whether they should've allowed it.

"They were good men." Kayla's voice broke. "My dad will miss them." Facing Atu, she said, "How did they die?"

"We don't know. There's nothing on them revealing a cause."

"I suppose there's nothing on my dad either?"

Jaden's heart was shattering into tiny pieces. The sorrow in Kayla's voice was unbearable. He crouched next to her, but he didn't take her hand. Hers were both holding her dad's, and he couldn't separate Kayla from her father.

"No, nothing on your dad either," Atu confirmed. Glancing at Iri, he said, "Can you find anything that might help?"

Kayla's eyes flew to Iri. Jaden didn't know how she did it. How could she face this head on? He kept his own eyes on Kayla, watching for the slightest reaction. But Kayla's face was a stony mask. Even her eyes were dead. Finding no answer in Kayla, Jaden turned to Iri too.

Iri was staring at Vicken in her way that always made Jaden squirm. Then Iri sniffed the air. First, near Vicken, then walking over to where Vicken's team lay and sniffing there. Finally, she turned to Kayla.

"I'm no expert, but I'm smelling the same thing on these men as on your dad." When Kayla whimpered, Iri held up a finger. "But not to the same extent. These men were exposed to whatever it was in varying degrees. My guess is that they were in a line, and your dad was at the back—he had the least exposure. While his colors are muted, they're stable." Iri thought a moment before adding, "Not draining away."

A sob escaped Kayla. "You think my dad will be alright, then?"

Iri closed the distance between them, knelt down, and squeezed Kayla's shoulder. "I can't say. All I can say is it seems his condition is stable for now."

Kayla sniffed, tears spilling down her face. She nodded. "Okay, that's good. I can deal with that." She hiccupped, trying to compose herself. "Atu, do you think if they took my dad to a hospital, they might find out what's wrong with him?"

"I don't know."

Kayla's throat bobbed, and her forehead crinkled as she shook her head. "No, no, what I mean is . . . do you think modern medicine will be more effective at healing my dad than your gift?"

Atu sighed. "I'm sorry, I can't answer that one either."

Jaden understood what Kayla was getting at, and that she needed someone else to decide. He would take that responsibility. Jaden only hoped he was making the right decision. "Keeping Vicken here isn't helping. Atu already said he can't heal him. I suggest getting Vicken to a hospital." Jaden *really* hoped he was right about this next part. "Atu stays with us so he can make sure you remain healthy to see your dad on the other side of this—and we get on and finish this thing!"

Jaden said the last words with such vehemence, it was a wonder they didn't flame on their way out. The others ogled him. "What? I'm done with those we love suffering because we haven't ended this yet. It has to end."

Silence. Then Iri said, "I can't think of a better plan. Kayla?"

Kayla gripped her father's hand so hard her knuckles turned white.

"Just because I'm leaving you now doesn't mean I don't love you. Because I love you I have to let you go. I have to let you get the care you need. You fight, you hear me? Fight! Just like I'll fight for you. Be awake when I get back to you." Kayla's head dropped as she kissed her dad's cheek. "Fight!"

Jaden had never felt more helpless. Even when Kayla was missing, there had been hope he'd get her back. This situation was infinitely worse. Jaden swallowed the lump in his throat as Kayla rose and faced them.

"Let's get him out of here. Markov, can you go with him and my mom to the hospital?"

Markov didn't hesitate. "Sure." Then he glanced at Jaden. "If that's okay with you? You don't need me down here with you?"

If Kayla trusted Markov to get Vicken where he needed to go, Jaden wouldn't stand in his way. "We'll be fine. Even better knowing you're taking care of Vicken and Sadie."

Markov read the unspoken request and nodded. "I hear you. Will do. Now, how are we getting Vicken out of here?"

Getting off the mountain was a far simpler process. By the time Kayla spoke with her mother, some other riders had returned with longer ropes., Markov having dispatched them on that errand before he had descended to the cave. Kayla herself tied the ropes to hold her dad as Taz hovered overhead, haranguing Han, who held the other end of the rope in his talons.

Jaden spared a moment to give Han a sympathetic glance. Han only shook his head, holding onto the rope as though his life depended on it. Jaden hid his grimace. *Poor guy! Taz will make him suffer if he lets that rope slip even a fraction of an inch.*

In under ten minutes, Vicken was off the mountain. Taz glanced at Kayla. "We'll get your father to the hospital. Then we'll get back here as soon as we can." She looked at Jaden. "Don't do anything foolish while we're gone."

Jaden wanted to laugh. Han wouldn't be the only one paying if something happened to Kayla. "Yes, ma'am."

Taz sniffed. "Stop with that nonsense. Just . . . be safe."

Jaden could've sworn her eyes and voice softened on those last words. They said all she couldn't. He'd have to hug her the next time he saw her—if that was even possible. "We will. You be careful too."

With a final nod, Taz turned, and Han followed, several riders and their gliders trailing them. Jaden and the other seekers remained on the ledge, watching until the posse was out of sight. Then Jaden turned and faced the cave. It was time.

CHAPTER THIRTY-NINE

A few steps into the cave, Jaden's skin crawled. Like a thousand creepy, squirming millipedes had fallen onto him from the roof of the cave, their millions of spiky legs bristling against his skin as they wriggled. It was a sensation he hated. The one his weird feelings invoked. If they provided direction, it would've been bearable. But they never gave answers. Just pricked and pricked at him until he was bleeding. He froze.

"What's wrong?" Kayla asked.

Jaden held up a finger. But Iri answered. "He's having one of those feelings of his."

Jaden really wished she couldn't tell—or wouldn't tell—the others when it happened. "Can a guy have some privacy?" Iri looked morti-fied, and Jaden regretted the barbed comment. "Sorry, Iri, I didn't mean it like that."

Although Iri nodded, she remained reserved. Jaden couldn't take back what he'd said. His irritation rose as the crawling intensified. There was something nagging at the back of Jaden's mind. He fumbled for what it was. It also had something to do with Iri. Some-thing she said . . . back then when she was talking to Kayla.

Jaden turned to where Iri had stood, as though he could still see her there. He replayed the scene in his mind. Iri had been talking about Kayla's father. In a flash, it came back to him. Something he had wanted to question when Iri spoke but hadn't had a chance to. Now, it was imperative he had an answer.

"Kayla, I'm sorry I have to ask, but is your dad usually at the back of the line?"

In the dim light, he saw Kayla's frown. "No. But Iri said that, didn't she?" Kayla turned to Iri. "That is what you said, right?"

Iri nodded, her rising uncertainty clear in her voice. "Sorry, should I not have?"

Jaden crossed to Iri, and, taking her hands in his, he gazed into her eyes. He wanted her to hear him—really hear what he had to say. "Don't you ever doubt your gifts around us. Again, I'm sorry I snapped at your earlier. Forgive me?" Iri nodded, a tentative smile gracing her face. "Thank you. And the reason I say never be scared to voice what you see and smell around us is because your observation could've just saved our lives."

Iri's eyes widened. Jaden nodded at her before turning and stalking back to the cave entrance. "Markov, can you still hear me?"

"Yeah, dude, what's up?"

"Hurry back. I have a feeling we'll need you. Who did you leave in charge?"

"Stovan."

Hearing his name. Stovan asked, "You need me to escort the group to the hospital instead?"

Jaden glanced at Kayla. She had been the one who had wanted Markov to take her dad to the hospital. Take care of her mom. Kayla stared back, her gaze wavering. Jaden waited. It was her decision.

Kayla sighed. "I trust you have a solid reason—make the switch."

Jaden's nod was an answer to both her questions. "Yeah, dude. I need you to take over from Markov. Let me know when it's done."

They waited in silence. Minutes later, Markov said, "Stovan just arrived. I'm on my way back."

Grateful Markov knew him well enough not to ask questions, Jaden waited a few more minutes, all the time wishing he could just move. The longer he stood here, the worse the crawling sensation became. When he felt like he would explode, he tested the distance. "Stovan?" No reply. "Stovan, can you hear me?" Silence.

Markov's voice came back. "I figured you didn't want them to hear. I believe they're out of range. Speak to me."

Feeling Kayla's eyes on him, Jaden turned to face her as he answered. "I think there's more lurking around these mountains than just mist."

"Why?"

"Let's just say that whatever happened here in the cave came from outside." Jaden didn't want to blab over the comm about the dead men. Although word might've already spread to the rest of the riders.

"Any evidence you're basing that on?" Markov's question was as oblique. The other riders didn't know, then.

"Kayla's dad always leads the group. He was the least effected."

Jaden didn't have to say they had been in a line. Markov understood how things worked. He probably didn't understand how Jaden figured out the specifics, but that was the beauty of their friendship. Not everything had to be explained.

As if reinforcing Jaden's train of thought, Markov said, "I can work with that. Go, get on with what you have to do. We'll take care of things out here."

"Thanks. And Markov?"

"Yeah?"

"Stay alert. Be safe."

"You too."

Jaden clicked his comm to mute it. "Do you understand now why I wanted to make the switch?"

Kayla nodded. "Yes. Markov's the better strategist. If there are . . . things out there, he's better equipped to deal with them."

Jaden held her gaze. "And you're okay with Stovan taking care of your parents?"

"Yes—he has Taz and Han with him too. I don't doubt my parents are in capable hands."

Jaden had been worried Kayla's focus might return to her parents' safety. He was wrong. She seemed equally eager to finish this. "Time to move on, then?"

Grim nods all around.

"You take the lead and I'll bring up the rear," Atu said.

Jaden blinked. Atu wasn't usually so forthcoming.

Atu rolled his eyes. "Yes, I can make decisions and speak up when I need to."

Soft laughter rippled from the girls.

"Whatever you say, dude." With the girls still giggling behind him, Jaden took the lead.

Passing the poor souls lined up along the wall, Jaden prayed none of the voyagers would end up the same way. Then, putting thoughts of everything except what was in front of him out of his mind, Jaden strode toward the back of the cave.

Only when the tunnel showed itself did Jaden wonder why he'd been so sure there was more than a cave. Nothing hinted at a path deeper into the mountain. And yet, somehow he had known he would find it there.

Chalking it up to another thing he couldn't explain, Jaden flicked on his flashlight. The powerful beam cut through the darkness, its light so bright it carved a path far down the tunnel. Jaden played the light along the walls, floor, and ceiling of the tunnel, not spotting visible dangers. That didn't mean there weren't any. "Iri, are you sensing anything in that tunnel?"

"No, I was checking while you were. Nothing to see or smell that would hint anything's amiss."

Clink! The sound of the pebble hitting the stone floor was enough to make them all jump. All except Atu. He grinned.

"It worked in the Buried Forest. Thought it was worth a try here."

Jaden chuckled. "Good man! Rather safe than sorry." He glanced back at the tunnel. "And it seems there is nothing there. Best we all stock up on a few stones just in case. Doesn't look like there'll be too many down there."

Indeed, the floor of the tunnel looked like someone had swept it with a broom. There wasn't even dust on its glossy black surface.

Jaden stilled. *Why is there no dust?* He turned from where he'd been selecting stones, peering back into the tunnel. Taking his time, he shone the light around the space again.

"Did you hear something?"

Kayla's voice next to him made Jaden jump a second time in as many minutes. "You should all wear bells or something," Jaden muttered.

Kayla studied him. "Someone's jittery. What's got you spooked?"

Jaden didn't miss Iri and Atu padding up to them. "Bells! Bells!"

Iri glanced at Kayla, a smile on her face. "What gives?"

"He thinks we like to slink up behind him and give him frights." Kayla slapped Jaden on the back. "But it's his own fault for being too focused on other things to pay attention to his surroundings."

Jaden scowled. "You'd think your friends would have your back." When the others laughed, it only enraged him further. "Seriously, I'll buy bells and put them on all of you. Then you can't sneak up on me."

The smile left Kayla's face. She put a hand on his arm. "Jaden, lighten up. What's wrong?"

His revelation was too disturbing for Jaden to dwell on making Kayla lose her smile once more. *Dang it, if something happens to her, I won't be able to live with myself!*

"Jaden?"

With a start, Jaden realized he hadn't answered Kayla's original question. He gestured down the tunnel with his flashlight. "What don't you see in there?"

Atu was the one who got it. "There's no dust. It's like the tunnel's used often enough for there to not be any."

Atu's words settled on the others, a hefty weight squashing the air from them. Jaden nodded. "Kayla, would your dad or his team would've cleaned the tunnel like that?"

Kayla shook her head. "No, they try to be as invisible as possible. It's inadvisable in their line of work to leave anything that could trace back to them."

"I thought so. The only answer is there's something alive down there. Something that comes up here often enough to prevent the dust from accumulating. Something large or numerous enough to sweep the entire floor clean."

If Jaden thought there hadn't been enough air before, it was a complete vacuum now. He drew his DD. Its light flared, outshining the flashlight, the current running along the blade sizzling into the stillness. "Let's go face our fears then."

Jaden smiled when the others drew their blades, ready to follow, steely determination their only expression. All that he had to do was lead the way.

CHAPTER FORTY

Iri paced behind Jaden and Kayla. It was slow going. And quiet. None of them made a sound as they descended into the depths of the mountain. All Iri's senses scanned for the danger they expected. Ultimately, a sense everyone had heralded . . . something.

The group halted. They all heard it. Claws skittering across stone. Iri tightened her hold on her DD, ready to cleave any approaching enemy. But the sound remained constant. Whatever it was, it scuttled about in the same place, not drawing any closer.

A second later its scent wafted up the tunnel, punching Iri's nose, the invisible odor enough knock her over. Fetid. Decaying. Like what waited below wasn't alive. It reminded Iri of how the Gaptors smelled.

"Whatever it is, it's something Slurpy created," Iri warned in a whisper.

"What makes you say that?" Jaden breathed, his voice matching hers.

"Same sort of smell, but not like the Gaptors. Rotten. Artificial. Not of this world, that's for sure."

Jaden glanced at Kayla and Atu. "The rats or spiders? It doesn't sound like the snake."

Iri perked up. They had told her the stories of the horrendous mutant creatures they'd encountered in the desert. None sounded like critters you wanted to cross in a dark tunnel. But Iri wasn't anybody. And the thought of besting one of Slurpy's creations only made her savor the fight more. Glancing at the others, Iri decided she probably shouldn't mention that the monsters lurking below might be something they had encountered before.

Bouncing from foot to foot, Iri waited as Jaden scanned the part of the tunnel they were in. It was as empty as what they'd already traversed. Not a stone or boulder to hide behind. Nothing on the floor. Nothing they could barricade themselves behind. Nothing to close the tunnel off or at least reduce the opening to limit the number of foes attacking them simultaneously.

Sweat trickled down Iri's brow. Was it her imagination, or did it seem hotter than before? She swiped a hand across her forehead. When another bead of perspiration trickled down not even a second later, Iri knew she wasn't imagining it.

"Is anyone else feeling the heat?"

"Haha," Jaden commented sourly. "But not funny."

"No, I didn't mean that. I mean real heat. The temperature in the tunnel is higher than it was a few minutes ago."

The colors swirled around her friends as Iri surveyed them. Jaden's aura was the first to glow yellow. "You have a plan?" Iri smiled, feeling his grimace. But he didn't berate her this time.

"Iri, anything indicating any side tunnels up ahead?"

Iri stopped her bouncing and closed her eyes, focusing on the surrounding air. The acrid smell of those aberrations made her gag. Swallowing the bile, she focused on what lay beyond. The brush was so light, so fleeting, she almost didn't recognize it before it disappeared. Her eyes snapped open.

"Yes, there's another path. Fresher air coming from another place. Except I can't tell how close it is to where those . . . things are gathered. And it's impossible to know if it leads anywhere. It may just be another cave. Also, in case it's relevant, that's also where the heat's coming from."

Jaden's sunny hue only intensified. "Alright, then this is what we do."

Minutes later, Iri grinned maniacally at Kayla, waiting across the cave from her. Racing back up the tunnel to just inside the cave entrance as Jaden ordered hadn't taken long. They waited, the light coming from the ledge outside muted by the mist. In the cave's dim interior, Kayla's face glowed blue from the light of her DD. Between the light, the blade, and Kayla's stern expression, she looked like an avenging angel.

Kayla lifted her chin at Iri. "What are you smiling about?"

"We get some action."

Kayla rolled her eyes. "You sound like my dad. Remind me to reintroduce you two when we get back."

Iri didn't miss the tangerine tinge touching Kayla when she mentioned her father. "He'll be alright. He's a fighter. Like his daughter."

Kayla's smile didn't reach her eyes. "I'm concentrating on crushing one obstacle at a time."

"The next one's almost upon us," Iri said when she heard the commotion coming their way.

Iri spared a quick glance beyond the ledge. All she saw was mist. There was no sign of Aren, who had collected Atu only seconds before and spirited him away. Markov and the others waited just out of sight, above and below the opening. Iri checked the rope around her waist. Secure. Rozie fretted at the other end. Iri could feel her glider's tension running along the rope back all the way back to her.

"We'd better be strong enough," Kayla muttered.

"We don't have to be—just quick enough."

Kayla nodded but said nothing as she peered into the darkness of the tunnel. The tangerine glow around Kayla intensified as the clamor of claws clicking on stone grew louder. Then they heard Jaden shouting.

"Almost there!"

A second later, Jaden burst into view, streaking up the tunnel like his life depended on it. When Iri saw what chased him, she realized his life *did* depend on it. Her arm already raised to prepare for what she had to do, Iri swung the second rope.

At the exact moment Jaden cleared the tunnel, Iri tossed the rope. The loop landed perfectly. Not that she had thought it wouldn't. Although, if she was honest with herself, the pressure of the situation might have made her miss. Not that she would ever tell the others.

Yanking on the rope to tighten it around Jaden, Iri leaned out of the cave and yelled, "Now!"

With a jerk, the rope around Iri's own waist tightened, and she was airborne. She glanced back in time to see Jaden and Kayla dragged clear of the snapping jaws and claws chasing them.

As Rozie swung them away, Iri stared at the spiders. *Horrid things. How didn't I hear the electricity running along the hairs coating their bodies —or see the light as they came up the tunnel?*

Iri only had another second to glimpse their fire-engine red bodies beneath that sparking current before Markov and the others descended on the spiders. The spiders hadn't anticipated an enemy outside and were piling up on the ledge.

As Markov's glider's claws dug into the first spider, it exploded like a ripe tomato. Iri's eyes watered when the acidic odor of its blood spiked the air. She glanced at the glider's talons, expecting them to be smoking as the blood ate into them.

But Markov's glider's claws were fine. The same could not be said for the ground beneath them. Where the blood sprayed onto the dark pebbles lining the sides of the mountain, smoke curled up as the stones melted. *Melted!* Iri's gaze flew to Markov. But his glider had been smart enough to keep the blood away from his rider. Iri opened her mouth to call a warning to those attacking the spiders, but Markov beat her to it.

"Watch out—their blood's acidic!"

Then Markov's glider was diving back down for another spider, even as two other riders reached the group before he did. The spiders sensed the approaching danger and scuttled up the side of the mountain, racing upward so fast Iri could only track them because of their size. Enormous. Bigger than her bed. Iri doubted she'd ever get a peaceful night's sleep again.

Iri analyzed the spiders' upward trajectory. How did they not slide down on that graveled surface? As soon as the spiders were above the gliders, they whirled, their abdomens lifting. Underneath, a silvery liquid pulsed. Horrified, she yelled, "Back off! Avoid their webs!"

Iri's shouted warning came too late. Thin strands of steel shot out, knocking riders from their mounts. Senseless, they tumbled into the air below. Iri held her breath as their gliders remained motionless for a second, trying to comprehend what happened. Then as one, they dove after their riders.

Iri didn't wait to see if they caught them. Her attention was back on the spiders, who twisted their heads at an unnatural angle, allowing them to stare at what was behind them. *Stare* was the only word to describe the hundreds of blank, shiny black slates that glinted her way. Their way. Toward the three humans dangling at the ends of the ropes that had whisked them beyond the spiders' reach.

While that may have been true seconds ago, it was no longer the case. "Rozie, fly!"

But Rozie was wheeling away before Iri finished her sentence. A cable whipped behind her, and Iri ducked. The spider's webbing whizzed past her ear, a high-tensile strand instead of silk. Deadly if it had hit her. *Were the other riders that were hit just unconscious, or dead?* Rozie angled her wings, dipping them perpendicular to the ground, and Iri focused on hanging on.

The whistle of air preceded a second strike. Again, Rozie took evasive action, all the while moving them further from the spiders, beyond the reach of their deadly webs. Then the mist enveloped them.

"Can you even see where you're going?" Iri called to her glider.

Rozie chuckled. "We may be larger than our counterparts in this world, but we have the same ability to sense our surroundings."

Sonar? Iri wasn't sure if it was rude to ask, so she didn't. The squelch of another spider going belly-up made her realize they were closer to the mountain than she had thought. The squelch sounded like the noise those old arcade games made when you played whack-a-mole. For an instant, the mist cleared, and Iri saw exactly that. Whack-a-mole. Or rather, stab-a-spider.

The spiders had realized they had no defense against the scores of attackers outside and had retreated into the cave. Every so often, one was tempted to race out and attack a glider hovering too close. Except they weren't factoring in the other gliders hidden in the mist, just waiting for the chance to stab them.

"They're not too bright, are they?" Iri muttered.

"Possibly a flaw with all the usurper's creatures, engineered as they are," Atu replied.

Iri had forgotten he could hear her through the comm. "Are you alright?"

"How would you feel if they kept you out of the battle?"

Iri had no reply. Evidently, Atu wasn't taking his forced abstinence too well. She couldn't say she wouldn't feel any different in his position. More squelches. Iri didn't see if it was one spider or more.

"Are we going back down there, or are you keeping me away too?" Iri demanded of Rozie.

Rozie cast a baleful glance her way. "I'm waiting my turn. There are others ahead of me in the line."

Iri would have to take her word for it. She peered into the mist. It was getting thicker. As though her thought struck a chord with Jaden, his strident voice came over the comm.

"Back away! I need everyone to get away from the ledge! Now!"

Iri couldn't see him, but she was sure the color surrounding him represented those feelings of his. Iri tightened her knees around Rozie as her glider veered away from the mountain.

Jaden's voice came over the comm again, even more urgent. "Get away! Get out of the mist!"

CHAPTER FORTY-ONE

Jaden's command had Rozie's wings beating faster. The mist brushed against Iri, touching slivers of exposed skin. The tiny droplets of condensation stung. At first, Iri assumed it was because Roxie was flying so fast. But then her nose crinkled.

Something was not quite right with the air. A taint marring its purity. Iri glanced at the tiny space left open between her gloved hand and suited arm. The narrow band of exposed flesh at her wrist was abnormally pale, as if exposed to a can of white spray paint. At last, she understood.

Glancing at Rozie's wings, Iri's heart skipped a beat when she saw the same film coating them. She leaned forward and found it on Rozie's face too.

"Sit back," Rozie ordered, her voice scratchy, like she hadn't had a drink of water in hours.

"Rozie, we have to get out of the mist. It's poisonous."

"I'm aware," Rozie replied tersely.

Iri heard what she hadn't said. Rozie was struggling to find clean air. *Are my senses better than Rozie's?* Iri doubted it, but anything was worth a try. About to close her eyes again, Iri noticed a spot of brighter white, glimmering through the dirty white of the mist. *Is it possible?*

"Rozie, head—" Iri faltered. She couldn't work out their direction. "Go left!"

"Why?"

Rozie sounded beyond irritated. *Is Rozie as disoriented as I am?* The thought was disconcerting. The bright spot beckoned. "Just . . . trust me. If you don't hit clean air in seconds, we can turn and go back in the direction you were heading."

Muted sounds emanated from under her. *Is Rozie cussing me out?* Despite this, Rozie complied with Iri's request. A split second later, the brilliant white patch loomed in front of them. They barreled into it. Or tried to. Rozie flapped furiously, struggling to smash through the invisible barrier holding them at bay. Iri tugged and pulled against the stickiness coating her, making movement difficult. With a loud thwack, Rozie snapped free, and they burst through.

Iri could see. For miles ahead, the air was clear. No hint of mist. Tentatively, Iri dragged air into her lungs. Fresh, pure. *Clean air!* Rozie came to her senses first and started twittering. Iri should do the same.

"Tell your gliders to find Rozie. We found a way out. Know that it takes a little struggling to get through the barrier, so persevere."

Seconds later, gliders began breaking through the filmy barrier, exiting with audible pops. As Rozie backed away to allow the other gliders space, Iri noticed the mist formed a dome over Terratalunga. It reminded Iri of a clear Christmas bauble filled with smoke.

Soon, the gliders exited in greater numbers, all of them coated in the same white film. Remembering Rozie's wings, Iri glanced at them. The winds whipping around them had wiped the coating away.

Just as Iri decided they had dealt with the strange mist, Rozie wheezed. Then Rozie's entire body seized up. Her back arched, her head snapped back, and her wings crumpled against her sides. They dropped twenty feet in an eye blink.

Iri shrieked. "Rozie, what's wrong?"

But Rozie was coughing. *No, she's hacking her lungs up.* From the way Rozie's wings remained curled at her sides, the coughing was all-consuming. Taking all Rozie's energy, all her attention.

"Rozie!" This time, Iri kept the fear from her voice and inflected a level of command.

Rozie's head lifted ever so slightly. However, more coughing swallowed any reply she might've given. Iri didn't know what to do. She glimpsed the ground racing up to meet them. If Rozie didn't snap out of it, they were both dead.

Iri was unprepared for the water blasting them upward. Gushing under, over and around them with such force it swamped her before shoving its way through her face mask and up her nose.

Choking, Iri coughed, trying to clear her airways as the water pounded them. Then it vanished, as suddenly as it had appeared. Iri's wet hair dripped down her neck. A sudden hissing nearby had Iri swiping water from her goggles.

Before she found the source, they were dunked again. This time, the water was piping hot. Iri yelped as it stung the places not covered by her smart suit. Not submerged for as long this time, Iri moved as soon as the water disappeared. Coughing up what felt like an ocean in her lungs, she dashed the water from her face.

One glance told her where they were: the field of geysers. And Rozie was flying directly at the next spout in their path. Iri barely had enough time to suck down air before they plunged into the water again. *What is this crazy bat doing?* She answered her own question. *Washing away the poison. That's why she can fly now.*

They hurtled clear once more, and Iri gulped down air. "Rozie, glad you're feeling better and all, but could you test the water before dashing in? I have no desire to be cooked like a lobster in a pot." Rozie jerked under her. "What? You are feeling better, right?"

"Sorry! I forgot humans weren't built for extreme temperatures. I'll be more careful."

Rozie sounded so forlorn, Iri giggled despite their situation. "No harm, no foul. I'm not boiled yet. Just . . . be more selective about which geysers you take us through? If you can?"

"I can and I will. And I'll pass the information along to the other gliders."

"How would they know to go through . . . oh, you already communicated that to them?" Iri still hadn't figured out how the gliders communicated without a sound. She hadn't seen colors or scented anything on Rozie to show she'd been conversing with the others.

Another geyser loomed and Iri shelved her contemplations, sucking in air. Three geysers later, Rozie streaked upward. Iri grabbed for purchase as Rozie shot high above the geyser field. Then, just as suddenly, Rozie dove back down, the wind battering Iri as they zoomed for the ground far below. *Now what?*

Sensing Iri's unspoken question, Rozie shouted, "The wind will wipe away any excess water and dry my wings."

"There wasn't another way?" Iri managed through clenched teeth. She needed all her strength not to get tossed off by the force of the wind rushing past.

"This is the fastest way—and the most fun."

Iri heard the smile in Rozie's voice. "Oh yeah? How about this for fun?" With no small degree of relief, Iri released her death grip on Rozie. Tumbling into open air, Iri loosed a jubilant holler. It was just what she needed. Joyous, unfettered freedom, the air a wide open space around her after the confines of the tunnel.

Rozie cut the luxury of floating short by catching Iri. There was no reason she couldn't enjoy it a little more. Iri rolled off again. Rozie got the message because she left Iri to drift for a while, flying alongside as Iri soaked in the freedom.

Moments later, Rozie darted under Iri again, catching her. Below them, other gliders and their riders were drenching themselves in the cleansing water of the geysers. Iri and Rozie hovered above, observing as they exited the field with their ability to fly in a straight line restored. While the gliders were in their element again, their riders were drowned rats.

Iri grinned. "Who would've thought the water in the geysers would counteract the poison?"

Iri noticed Atu and Aren closing in on them. She waved a hand in greeting. Using her comm, she asked, "Do you think the geyser water is the antidote, or was it effective because we washed the poison off before it had been on our skin for too long?"

Atu rubbed his chin. "I honestly couldn't say. But I sent a glider and rider with the information on to the hospital where they took Vicken. Along with a sample of the water from the geysers here. Perhaps some mineral in the water is the elusive element I was looking for."

Iri noticed the lack of colors around him as usual. But something in his tone had her asking, "Is everything alright?"

Atu glanced at her askew. "What makes you think anything's wrong?"

For a second, Iri doubted herself. But it was there again, in his question. Fainter this time, but there. "Stop hedging and spill."

Atu sighed. "If we don't know how to counteract the poison in the mist, how are we going to get into the mountain? Because that's where the map was leading us."

The way he said it triggered something in Iri's mind. "Hmm, was it?"

Now Atu just looked irritated. "What are you babbling about?"

"Remember how the first map had those floating lines, and then they converted into an *X*? Then how the second map used the stars to show us where to go, and when we arrived there was that burst of light which was absorbed into the book to give us our actual destination?"

Atu was nodding. "You're saying the book gave us the volcano as the general area, but we should look for something more specific now?"

"Yes!"

Atu's face brightened. Iri still saw no colors communicating his improved outlook. "How do you do it?"

"What?"

"Keep the colors from showing."

Atu blinked. "I didn't know I did."

"Huh," was all Iri said as she considered his answer. Not for the first time, she debated whether his even temperament kept the colors away.

"Is it unusual?"

"You're the only person I've ever met who doesn't give off colors and scents like a walking billboard."

"That's how it is for you with everyone else?"

"Yes."

It was Atu's turn to think the anomaly over. Apparently, it didn't merit much attention because seconds later, he said, "Shall we find Jaden and Kayla and tell them the good news?"

Iri had to process his words. "Oh, right, the second part of the map. Yes, let's find them."

CHAPTER FORTY-TWO

Kayla couldn't contain her relief. She threw her arms around Atu and hugged him. He'd just told her he'd sent explanations and samples of the geyser water to her father's hospital. A load she hadn't known she'd been carrying lifted from her shoulders.

Atu grinned at Jaden over her shoulder. "It's just a hug."

Kayla turned in time to observe Jaden's smile. That gorgeous smile that lit his whole face and turned her to mush.

"I'm just waiting my turn." The wicked glint in Jaden's eyes dimmed Atu's smile.

"What are you thinking?" Atu's words were tentative and his expression apprehensive. He didn't seem excited about the prospect of a hug from Jaden.

"I should thank you just as effusively for making Kayla so happy."

Jaden's grin was pure evil. Atu read his message and backed away from Kayla. "No need. Kayla's hug was enough."

Iri chuckled, and they all turned to look at her. "Jaden, there's no need to be territorial."

Jaden rolled his eyes, and Atu looked pained.

"I can look after myself," Atu muttered.

Kayla grinned. *Trust Iri to put them in their places.*

"Now that Atu's given you the first piece of good news, how about more?" Iri asked.

That got Kayla's attention. "What more is there?"

Sparing a quick glance at Atu, who nodded, Iri explained what they had deduced about the maps.

Jaden hummed. "You're saying there should be a second part of the map—hidden in the first?"

"Yes. I think you need to open the map in Awena's book again. Let's see if anything has changed."

Despite shaking his head, Jaden took the ancient book from his pack and opened the back spine. His fingers played over the pool of silver. Kayla saw his eyes were closed as usual. It only accentuated his thick lashes. Lashes so gorgeous they didn't belong on a boy. The envy of every girl ever.

The silvery liquid sparkled as it rose once more. Before the shape even half-formed, Kayla knew it was different. There was no hint of the sides of the mountain painting the miniature volcano.

This shape started with numerous indentations, tiny holes in a pocked landscape. Kayla jumped back when one hole spewed tiny jets of silver. She gasped as more miniature fountains sprayed up intermittently. Unlike the volcano where the lava had belched out the vent and then oozed down the side of the mountain, these jets flew up, spouting into the air and then subsiding for a while before repeating their mini explosions.

Iri and Atu crowded closer.

Atu pointed. "Is that what I think it is?"

Kayla glanced at the geyser field. The correlation between the image generated by the book and the surrounding landscape was unmistakable. "Jaden, open your eyes."

He did, staring at the tiny, animated diorama before him. Then his eyes widened, his gaze flying to Kayla. "The geyser field?"

"Yes. The shapes and patterns are consistent. See this spot?" Kayla pointed at a hole towards the far right on the book's "field." "Look at the hole on the very edge over there."

Jaden did, his gaze whipping between the book and the geyser. He swiveled the book so its orientation matched that of the field behind them. His eyes traced the other geyser spouts on the field, matching them to their counterparts in the book.

Every single geyser matched perfectly. The tiny variances in shape and heights of their waterspouts were identical to the book. Kayla started when the entire animation portrayed by the book suddenly rose upward.

She wasn't the only one. Jaden, Atu and Iri all backed away, their faces mirroring Kayla's apprehension. Despite this, they stayed close enough to see the image. A new part appeared. Kayla watched, holding her breath as the image filled out. She whistled. "A tunnel!"

"Yeah, but do you see where it starts?"

Jaden was less than enthusiastic. Kayla traced the tunnel to its source. She swallowed. "Oh, great!"

The source was a geyser spout. Even as they stared at the book, the precise geyser opening to the tunnel sprayed a teeny silver fountain into the air.

"From bad to worse," Kayla muttered. "We have to go into that geyser to access the tunnel? What if it's filled with water?"

When Jaden didn't answer, Kayla glared at him. But he wasn't watching her. Engrossed in the tiny geyser, he stared at it until it spouted, then his eyes flew back to the actual geyser on the field behind them, repeating the process over and over. His lips moved, but Kayla couldn't hear what he was saying. "Jaden?" No response. "Jaden!"

This time, he held up a hand. Kayla drummed her fingers on her legs. After a few minutes, she rounded on Iri. "Any idea what he's doing?"

Iri shook her head. Pointing at Atu, she mouthed, "He's doing it too."

Shocked, Kayla realized Iri was right. Not only was Atu's head bouncing between the book and the geyser field, his lips moved the same as Jaden's. Fear snaked through Kayla. *Are the boys under some spell?*

She shrieked when Jaden and Atu shouted at the same time. "Three minutes!"

Kayla's gaze went to Iri who was just as stupefied. "What's three minutes?"

Jaden grinned. "The intervals between eruptions."

Wanting to throw something at him, Kayla fumed. "So what? It only proves there's water in the tunnel. I might be wrong, but that tunnel leads under the field all the way back to the mountain—not a distance I think any of us can hold our breath for. And that's not accounting for any increases in water temperature along the way!"

Jaden cocked his head at her before taking her hand. His smile was gentle, his eyes crinkling around the corners in that charming way she loved. Kayla knew she was giving in to his coaxing. She rolled her eyes. "Okay, what am I missing?"

Jaden pointed at his smart suit, then his aerolator dangling from the hood that hung off to one side. She felt like an idiot. *Duh! Sven's smart suit will protect us from any temperature extremes, and the aerolator can filter air from the water. We won't have any problems breathing.*

"It would be better if water *does* fill the tunnel," Jaden said.

He lost Kayla again. "Why?"

"Because there won't be any spiders."

Pouting, Kayla countered. "Not unless Slurpy gave them a way to breathe underwater. Which, knowing him, is possible."

Jaden grimaced. "You just had to go there, didn't you?"

"Oh, that's not all I've got. While the smart suit may protect most of our body, what about the exposed parts—wrists, hands, ankles, feet, and neck—where the smart suit doesn't reach?"

"The lotion we use for the cold can protect from heat too," Atu interjected.

Kayla turned. She had forgotten he and Iri were there. "It's waterproof?"

Atu nodded.

"If there are no other obstacles then?" Jaden said, arching an eyebrow.

Kayla sighed. "I just don't want us going in there unprepared."

Jaden squeezed her hand. "You're awesome to think of those things. But no matter how many problems we come up with before we go in there, I hate to say there'll no doubt be at least one thing we didn't consider."

"You're right," Kayla conceded.

"But I did genuinely want to know if there was anything else anyone else," he glanced at Iri and Atu, "might want to question before we venture in?"

Silence as they contemplated possibilities. After a few minutes, Jaden said, "I think we're about as ready as we will ever be. Let's go tell our gliders the good news."

"They won't like that they can't come with us," Kayla murmured.

Taz ranted as Kayla had expected. Kayla waited the tirade out. It was the only way to deal with Taz when she was like this. Taz would not listen to reason if she thought the chosen course of action was likely to place Kayla in more danger than another option. Taz took a full ten minutes to slow down. Even then, Kayla had to give it another five minutes before she attempted speaking again.

Putting a hand on Taz's neck, she gazed into those angry eyes. Those angry, *worried* eyes. "I care about you too. I don't plan to leave you in this world without me. If there was another way, a safer way, don't you think we'd take it?"

Taz's eyes shone silver. "You're sure we can't use the mountain?"

Kayla had to explain again about the two parts of the map and how using the mountain had been wrong the first time. There was no way they would risk it a second time. "Even if you think all the spiders are dead, there's no guarantee some of them didn't flee when they saw we outnumbered them."

Taz drew in a ragged breath. The sigh that escaped was heavy and resigned. "I really wish there was another way."

"Believe me, so do I. But the map is showing this is the route we need to take. Since the maps haven't been wrong so far, we should follow them this time too." Kayla didn't add that even though the map showed this was their path, it didn't mean there wouldn't be danger.

She just had to trust this path posed less danger than any alternatives they might've pursued.

Taz guessed where her head was at. "Be careful." They were the only words Taz could offer at this point.

"We will." Kayla reached up and planted a kiss on the soft fur along Taz's neck. To say she was astounded when Taz dropped her head and wrapped her neck around Kayla's shoulders to nuzzle her was an understatement. Kayla smiled and rubbed Taz's ears. "I know, I'll miss you just as much. You stay safe too. With the way things go on these missions, we might need a quick extraction at the end."

Taz nodded. "I'll be tracking you with our link. We'll be close at all times. Pop out of any openings along the way and wave to us if you can."

"We'll do our best."

With one last nudge against Kayla's shoulder, Taz lifted her head. Kayla stepped back and gave what she hoped was a reassuring smile. "See you on the other side."

"Make sure you do. Now, I assume you need a ride to that hole?"

Kayla grinned. "Yes, please."

Taz smiled as she took to the air. "I'll be back."

Aerial connecting seconds later, Kayla glanced behind her as the others followed. It was only the four of them. Before summoning their gliders, Jaden had told them he still had that feeling the others should remain in the area. Outside. Not in the tunnel with them. So they had agreed to keep their plans to themselves, their gliders, and Markov.

Kayla shivered when he confessed he didn't know why the others had to stay aboveground. Hopefully, nothing lethal would come of it. But the feelings Jaden had rarely yielded positive results. She prayed Taz would be alright.

Taz glanced at Kayla over her shoulder. "Stop worrying about me."

"Like you should stop worrying about me?"

Taz shook her head and turned her attention back toward the geyser. Minutes later, she dropped Kayla off with more warnings as she departed. Kayla watched her disappear into the sky, hoping it wouldn't be the last time she saw her glider.

As she waited for the others to dismount, Kayla observed the other riders and their gliders darting through the air above them, healed of the poisonous effects of the mist. Kayla was beyond glad Markov was leading them. Keeping him here instead of going into the tunnels with them had taken some convincing, but Jaden had conveyed the gravity of the request.

Markov had eyed him for a long time before nodding his consent, telling them he would keep the air above them safe while they traversed the tunnel. He'd dispensed almost as many warnings as Han and Taz. Now, Markov's glider lined up next to Taz and Han. If anyone could keep Taz safe, it was Markov.

A tap on her arm brought her back.

"Here you go," Iri said, passing her a tube. "Atu said to cover every piece of exposed skin."

Iri rubbed the lotion over her neck. Kayla noticed Jaden and Atu were already doing the same. Taking the tube, Kayla squeezed a little onto her palm and followed their lead.

It wasn't long before lotion coated them. *Just as well it feels and smells good. It would've been nasty if it was sticky and smelly.*

She was tired of waiting. She wanted to get on with things. Apparently, Jaden did too. "Let's go," he said, activating his mask and aerolator. Without another word, he dropped into the hole.

Kayla's heart stopped when he did. She froze, expecting the geyser to spit him back out. But it wouldn't. It had erupted only seconds ago. Kayla stiffened when Iri jumped in after Jaden. When Atu nudged her towards the hole, she still wasn't ready. She glared at him, unsure whether he could even see her expression past her mask and aerolator.

"We only have three minutes," Atu said, prodding her again.

Here goes nothing, Kayla thought, dropping in. Sudden panic consumed her when she fell into nothing. And fell. And fell. *We should've checked the drop before we jumped! Are Jaden and Iri okay?*

CHAPTER FORTY-THREE

It was pitch black in the hole. Kayla reached up to activate her goggle's night vision. Her teeth smashed together, the impact jarring through her as she hit the water. Before she could curse, the water covered her. No discernible heat. Soft hissing from her aerolator. For a moment, she doubted it really would filter breathable air from the water. But then she took a deep breath and found air in the tube.

Kayla finished activating her night vision. Her limbs jerked in the water when she spotted dark blobs close to her, but it was Jaden and Iri. Her heart stuttered back to its normal rhythm. Jaden gestured, and Kayla turned in time to find Atu right behind her.

Jaden moved his aerolator aside long enough to speak. "Let's get to the other end of this tunnel. Keep your eyes peeled for anything unusual." Popping the aerolator back over his mouth, Jaden turned and swam away.

It surprised Kaya the comms worked underwater. But considering Sven's genius and that he'd made the suits and masks to withstand the elements, it would've been more unrealistic if the comms hadn't worked.

Scanning her surroundings, Kayla followed Jaden and Iri, Atu bringing up the rear. The water was remarkably clear, revealing a symmetrical tunnel. No narrow pieces to get stuck in. Or, at least, not as far as she could see. If they could believe the book's generated image, it would stay that way.

Stay that way it did, all the way to the end. There, the tunnel curved upward, its elevation rising steeply as the book had shown. Minutes later, Kayla's head popped above the water. She remained where she was, studying the space and alert for threats. The others were doing likewise. None of them were eager to rush onward without establishing the associated risks first.

The tunnel opened into a high cavern; the water ending where it lapped against a rocky shelf. The shelf extended backward, disappearing into blackness beyond—an ominous space at the opposite end.

Something glinted on Kayla's left, and she turned her head. The walls sparkled in the dim light, a result of crystals caught in the rock itself. The walls were intriguing. Ribbed, with subtle, smooth curves between hard ridges.

Kayla spat her aerolator out. "It looks like a giant, sparkly worm burrowed through here and left half its skin behind."

Iri giggled, but Kayla's comment didn't amuse the boys.

"Let's hope it's long dead," Jaden muttered, wading forward until he reached the rocky shelf.

Shrugging at Iri and then pulling a face at the boys' backs that had Iri giggling again, Kayla followed Jaden out the water. Once Kayla was on the ledge, she realized it was also part of the tunnel; a flat part leading away from the water and deeper into the mountain.

Iri loped out the water and abruptly stopped next to Kayla, going still. Kayla tensed. "What?"

Iri sniffed the air. "It's the same thing I smelled in the tunnel—right before the spiders appeared."

Four blades of blue light lit the air instantaneously. They waited, Kayla's ears straining for any hint of skittering claws. Silence echoed back to them from the darkness beyond. They gave it a few more minutes.

Jaden spoke, his voice soft. "Waiting here is getting us nowhere. We press on. But slowly. Be alert for spiders overhead."

Kayla could've done without that last piece of advice. Spiders weren't her favorite creatures, and Slurpy's abominations only made her hate them even more She followed Jaden's lead, behind him this time. No way was Iri going to be protecting his back. If anything attacked Jaden, Kayla wanted the first shot at it.

Unlike the tunnel higher in this mountain, fallen boulders littered this pathway. Some small, some large, each posing its own danger. Kayla was careful not to twist her ankle on the smaller ones rolling away under her feet even as she checked where she put her fingers when scrambling over the larger ones.

Their progress was slow. Every little sound had them pausing to listen. Each fallen boulder that blocked their way was a potential threat. They scrutinized every dark space overhead. They'd only been in the tunnel for about fifteen minutes when Iri's hand shot to Kayla's shoulder.

Kayla turned and noticed Iri's frantic gesture—a chopping motion across her throat. Kayla tapped Jaden's shoulder. He glanced at her before Iri's hand motions drew his attention. Iri motioned they should go back the way they'd come.

Iri only took them back far enough to allow them to whisper. "The smell just got worse. And there's heat too."

Jaden scrubbed a hand over his face. "What do you think the heat means?"

Iri shivered. "Combined with the smell, maybe a nest?"

Kayla smothered her shriek. "A nest? You mean spider babies?"

Iri's eyes were wide as she nodded. "It's the only thing I can think of that would generate so much heat."

Kayla braced herself. "Well, we've come this far. May as well see what the lion's den holds."

Jaden nodded grimly, looking to Iri and Atu for consent before he said, "Let's be smart about this. Proceed as though they could be around the very next corner. When we find them, if we're outnumbered, we back up as quietly as we can and call for reinforcements. Okay?"

When everyone murmured agreement, Jaden led the way. Kayla kept close, not wanting to be too far away in case he stumbled into the nest. None of them knew what to expect. *What will a nest look like for these spiders? Eggs in a sling overhead? Trapdoors made of steel threads covering holes stuffed with eggs? Will they even be eggs or a gazillion baby spiders?* Kayla shivered, trying to wriggle free of the thought.

Shaking off her imaginings, Kayla concentrated on what she could control. Keeping quiet. Protecting Jaden's back. Putting one foot in front of the other. The closer they got, the hotter the air became, until it was almost suffocating.

Just when Kayla was thinking she couldn't take it anymore, they rounded a boulder larger than any of the others and almost fainted from the heat. What they saw was unexpected.

A river of lava crawled across their path, wide enough they couldn't jump across it. Hot enough Kayla didn't think either their smart suits or Atu's lotion would protect them if they tried wading through, assuming it was shallow enough. By the looks of it, it wasn't. The lava boiled down, carving a path that seemed to reach all the way to the earth's core.

Involuntarily, Kayla's feet stopped. She stared. There was something fascinating about the way the lava flowed. Fiery oranges rolling over cooler yellows, melding with spots white enough to incinerate you before you even knew you'd been burned alive. Now and then, a black rock, glowing red at its edges, would bob to the surface, thrust up by the molten rock flowing over it. It would linger on the surface for a short while, smoking and shrinking until it melted and the deadly river swallowed it.

Kayla was so riveted by the lava flow, she almost didn't hear Iri's shouted warning. At the last second, it registered, and Kayla's eyes snapped to her surroundings. She wanted to gag. Wanted to scream. Wanted to run. But this was not the time.

On the other side of the boulder, hundreds of bulbous sacs glowed, a pearlescent mass glued between the boulder and the wall of the tunnel. If the sacs were still, it would've been okay. But they were wiggling and jiggling as tiny spider claws sliced against the thin film keeping them inside. Thousands of teensy spiders began crawling out of the sacs, their millions of beady eyes on the four voyagers.

Kayla was already reaching for Jaden, trying to pull him back down the tunnel. But he twisted out of her hands, running towards the lava flow instead. Nearing the edge of the scorching river, Jaden turned and grinned at her. Grinned at her! "Are you insane? What are you doing?"

Jaden pointed to a spot overhead. "Provoking Mama Spider."

He didn't wait for Kayla to answer. Raising his DD, he flicked his wrist, shooting a fatal bolt into the middle of the pearly sacs. Usually, the light accompanying the demise of Slurpy's creatures was bright enough to make Kayla shield her eyes. Here in this black domain, it was blinding.

Despite Sven's dampeners, spots danced in front of Kayla's eyes. The acrid smoke curling through the air didn't help. Her eyes watered, and Kayla blinked rapidly. A high whistling sound forced her eyes open and Kayla peered past the dots still blotting her vision. Glimpsing something shiny overhead, she looked up—in time to see the horrid spider perched above the eggs shooting another strand of steel at Jaden.

Kayla gaped, her gaze flying back to Jaden. But he was dancing around, avoiding the lethal projectiles. Dancing . . . the way he did on the arrowball court. Like he had that day they had first met. Kayla grinned. She knew how good he was at that game. Bounding over to him, she joined in.

Jaden spared her a quick glance, his grin devilish. "You figured out what I was doing?"

Kayla grinned, sure her face was just as maniacal as his. "Arrowball won't be much fun after this."

Jaden's laughter rolled out of him. He flicked another bolt of current at the emerging baby spiders while dodging a steel strand streaking his way. Kayla had time to check where it landed before releasing her own bolt. "Nice going, Jameson. Almost a bullseye."

"Do you two care to fill us in on what you're doing? This mind reading is a little tedious for us mere mortals," Atu complained.

Kayla's laughter joined Jaden's. "Ever played arrowball?" She dodged the cable snapping at her, ducking as it soared over her head and latched onto the wall behind her.

"No, but I don't think you have either, considering the way you're 'playing' it," Atu snorted.

"Yes, we changed the rules a bit." Jaden flicked his wrist again and shielded his eyes as more itty-bitty mutants were annihilated. "Kayla and I are playing against Mama Spider."

With a gleeful shriek, Iri jumped over to join them. "I get it! I get it!"

Atu moaned. "Why am I always the last one in on these things?"

Iri explained. "We're getting Mama upset enough to shoot her webs at us. The dodging is the same as what you'd do on the arrowball court. Except, instead of the usual target, the wall behind us is what we're trying to get her to aim for."

"But why would . . ." Atu's voice trailed off as he figured it out. "You're planning on using those cables to cross the lava river! Brilliant!"

In a flash, he joined them, his DD sending its own devastating shafts. With four of them firing at the jiggling sacs, they completely eradicated the threat in a few seconds.

With the last batch's disappearance, Kayla altered her target. She released the spitting current, watching it stream through the air. It hit Mama Spider squarely. Another flash of vivid light. Kayla shielded her eyes, then checked the spot. Mama Spider was history, along with all her babies.

Still, Kayla didn't want any little critters that might've crawled away, creeping up on them. Closing in on the side of the boulder, she checked all its nooks and crannies, then the area around the boulder, up the walls, and the roof. She even backtracked down the tunnel a bit. Only when she was satisfied they had incinerated every single one of those ghoulish little babies did she return to the others.

Jaden had an enormous grin on his face. "You missed the one on your smart suit."

Kayla shrieked and began dancing about as she tried to find it. When Jaden laughed, she realized what she'd seen on his face. "You were teasing!" She punched his arm so hard he winced, but it didn't stop the chuckles. She smacked him a second time. Once hadn't been enough.

Jaden backed away, his hands in the air as he tried to smother the laugher still rocking him. "Okay, okay, bad joke. Sorry!"

Kayla huffed, crossing her arms as she glared at them. "Now that you've had your fun, should we cross the river?"

That sobered the lot of them. Kayla smirked. *Nothing like a dose of reality to calm the hysteria.*

Jaden sighed. "Well, it would be wasteful to not use the excellent bridge the spider gave us. We should use it before we lose it."

"Lose it?" Kayla echoed.

"Looks like the heat from that river is already too much for some of those cables."

Kayla turned. True enough, the bottom cables were drooping, leaning ever closer to the lava. "Huh. I guess they may look and feel like steel, but perhaps it is just webbing after all."

As they watched, the lowest cable dissolved in the middle. Instead of a snapping twang as Kayla would've expected, it was more a sigh as the two pieces on either side wilted into the smoldering river.

Kayla crossed to a cable higher than the rest already bending toward the heat. When she gave it a solid yank, it held before yielding a little. "These cables in the middle are also getting soft. We'd better use the highest cables if we don't want them sagging into the river while we cross. And we'd better hurry."

CHAPTER FORTY-FOUR

Jaden had no time to resent the fact he was deciding. Again. His mind raced at light speed, factoring the calculations. Then he made Atu go first. Atu countered it should be one of the girls and Jaden almost lost it. "We don't have time to argue. I need you to go first because if any of us reach the other side with burns, you'll need to fix us—preferably with no burns of your own!"

Atu stared at Jaden for a moment. "You know, I'm starting to resent this healing gift! You're treating me like my life is worth more than any of yours."

Iri intervened, putting a hand on Atu's arm. "That's not what we think. And never, ever begrudge your gift. It's incredible. And exactly what we need to get us through to the end of this quest in one piece."

Iri's words soothed Atu. Jaden nodded. "She's right, dude. If you're not around to heal us, how are we ever going to survive?"

"I can't bring you back from the dead," Atu muttered.

But his tone held no heat, and when he shoved his backpack around to his front, then leaned toward the cable, Jaden tried not to sigh his relief too audibly.

They had climbed up onto Mama Spider's rock. It had been the launching point of all her cables, and, for whatever reason, she had tethered them to the tunnel wall behind her. It was the only spot they access the highest cables from.

Atu pulled the sleeves of his smart suit down to cover his hands. With one last recriminatory glance at Jaden, Atu turned and wrapped his hands and legs around the cable, hanging under it so his body formed a basket. Without further ado, Atu alternated shifting his hands and legs to inch along the cable.

Satisfied he was underway, Jaden directed the girls to their cables. They clambered on in the same fashion, beginning their own path across. He kept one eye on the progress of his friends and the other on the knot of cables attached to the wall beside him. He hadn't been sure whether they should chance two people crossing at a time. But events decided for them.

As they had reached the top of Mama's rock, a second and third cable dissolved into the lava in quick succession. When Jaden glanced back at their anchor knot, it was smoking. He had dumped his water bottle over it, unsure whether it would make the situation worse or better. The hissing and steam subsided to reveal the knot no worse for wear.

Reaching out his hand, Jaden had hovered it over the knot, gauging the temperature. The heat rising from the river and attacking the cables was traveling along them back to their source. It would only take a few more cables before the heat compromised the knot, and then any chance they had would literally go up in smoke.

A sharp cry made Jaden turn his head. A hiss was all he allowed himself. Kayla's cable was dangerously low, almost as low as the cables that had melted. The lava spitting up from the river was only inches below her. A stray globule must've jumped higher than the rest and nicked her.

"Are you okay?"

"I will be when I get to the other side of this cable," Kayla ground out.

Jaden couldn't take his eyes off her. No surprise she was already looking like she would take first place in the race to reach the other side. She was already past the midway point. He chanced a glance back at the knot, finding it smoking again. He dumped more water on it. When he turned his head again, Kayla was dropping on the other side. She faced him.

"Your turn!"

"Ow!" Jaden wished he could turn the volume of his headset down. "No need to yell."

"Jaden!" Her eyes were wide and pleading through the heat warping the air between them.

"Yes, on my way." He shouldn't have been teasing her. She was right. There was no time. Dumping the last of his water over the knot, he pulled his smart suit over his hands. He could already feel the heat coming off the cable before his hand touched it.

Jaden braced himself and placed a hand on the cable. Warm, not hot. Still, if it was warm through the smart suit, it was hot enough to burn uncovered skin. Hooking his legs over the cable, he felt the heat there too. *I shouldn't have wasted those seconds teasing Kayla.*

Jaden backed along the cable, thankful for his time spent climbing in the Shadow Mountains. Despite his speed, the decreasing tension on the line was unmistakable. That meant . . . Pain seared into his back. Sharp, fiery, intense.

Almost losing his grip, Jaden pulled himself closer to the cable even as another drop of heat burned its way into his skin. The agony was so severe, Jaden had to fight to keep his mind in the game. And he wasn't even halfway. Which was where the cable would sag most.

As he scurried along the cable, he glanced backward over his shoulder to the lowest point. Only four feet above the molten lava, and that was without his weight, meaning the cable could drop lower. Even at four feet Jaden wasn't sure his smart suit wouldn't combust from the heat. He stopped moving.

Kayla's voice was a shriek in his ear. "What are you doing? You don't have time to stop! Hurry!"

Jaden knew she'd be mad at him for not answering, but he had no bandwidth for that now. He assessed the surrounding cables. The one Iri had used was still high above him. Two cables hung about seven feet below Iri's, and then two more were slightly higher than his. A final two were already below him.

Those two and his cable would be the problem. Once those cables dropped into the river, he couldn't stop the heat from reaching the knot. It would start smoking again. And with no way to cool it down, how long before it caught fire and dropped all the cables into the river broiling under him?

Judging distances, Jaden decided it was his only chance. Shoving a hand inside his backpack, on his stomach for the trip across, Jaden rummaged for the rope. Extracting it without spilling the rest of his pack's contents was difficult. After some frantic wiggling, he wrested the rope free just as another blob of lava leaped high enough to scorch its way through his smart suit and into his skin.

Growling against the pain, Jaden used his teeth and one hand to tie a thick knot at the end of the rope. He leaned sideways. Concentrating, he aimed for the two cables slightly above him. The rope hooked over both cables, and the knot swung back down toward him. Grabbing the knotted end, Jaden passed it through the loop he had made with the rest of the rope. Then he pulled on the loose end, relieved when the knot slid up to the top and secured itself against the two cables above.

He didn't waste time. The next spurt of lava was encouragement to scramble up the rope. Even as he reached the cables above, the rope began smoking. Jaden had guessed this might happen. He increased his pace. Curling his knees around one cable, he ripped the smoking rope free. As he bundled it around his arm, he hoped it wouldn't catch fire. The rope secure, he placed his hands beside his knees.

It was now or never. Letting go with his hands, he flung himself backwards, extending his arms to generate momentum. When he was almost doubled over backward on himself, he let go with his legs. His body continued its arcing trajectory, and Jaden hoped he had timed it right.

Arching his head, he searched for the next two cables. *There they are!* Jaden grabbed at them. His body was at an angle, and so his left hand hit first—and slipped onward. He had to catch with his right hand, or he would be toast. Jaden didn't see the cables, just felt one biting into his hand. Reflex had him gripping the cable, rather than intention. A second later, his arm screamed in agony as every joint complained at having to halt the momentum of his body weight.

He heard cheering from his friends waiting on the other side of the river. Wincing as pain lanced his shoulder, Jaden levered himself upward until he straddled the two cables. That done, he snatched the rope off his arm and wound it around the two cables.

The rope neared its end and Jaden tied it off. He didn't waste time inspecting his handiwork. Smoke was already rising from the rope again, and he heard faint twanging as strands snapped. Using his hands to keep him steady, Jaden maneuvered his feet onto the tiny square platform of rope.

Balancing, Jaden let go with his hands and rose to his feet. He had never felt more vulnerable. Jaden took a moment to make sure his balance was perfect. Then he took a deep breath. With a quick snapping motion, Jaden bent his knees and jumped.

Jaden hadn't even been sure it would work. When the cables and ropes worked together to trampoline him upward, it was with such force he missed latching onto the highest remaining cable.

The cable zipped past his eyes, already level with his waist before he registered his moment had passed. Pure luck was the only reason his legs were still bent. They hit the wire, spinning him around so violently Jaden's legs ended up on the wrong side.

As he flailed through the air, it reminded Jaden of a trapeze artist changing direction on his swing. His body floated backward over the cable until his hands hovered over it for a second time. He didn't waste this opportunity. His hands snatched at the cable, finding purchase, and Jaden secured his hold.

For a moment, Jaden could only hang there, breathing raggedly. He almost hadn't made it. He became conscious of noise. Warbled words from the others. Still dazed, Jaden glanced at them, noticing their panicked hand gestures. Reality crashed down, and the words made sense.

"The knot's on fire!"

"Hurry!"

"Come on, Jaden, you got this!"

Groaning, Jaden locked his hands and legs around the cable. With focused movements, he scuttled backward along the cable, relieved when hands touched him. When he released his legs from the cable, Jaden would've fallen if Atu hadn't supported him. Dropping his hands to his knees and sinking his head, Jaden gulped down air.

It took a few minutes for his breathing to return to normal and for his legs to stop quivering. Feeling like he could stand again, he rose. The stinging slap caught him by surprise. Kayla followed by leaping into his arms, knocking him over. Stunned, Jaden lay there as she pummeled his chest.

"Don't you ever do that to me again! I thought you were going to die—a few times! Never, ever again, you hear me?"

Jaden finally had the wherewithal to grab her hands. "Hey, stop that! I'm sorry. You think I *wanted* to do that to you?"

Tears streaked Kayla's face. She stared at him like he had grown mushrooms on his head. Then her face crumpled, and she dropped onto his chest, hugging him so fiercely Jaden felt like he couldn't breathe again.

"Easy."

Kayla's grip only loosened a little, but it was enough to take in some air. Jaden wrapped his arms around her, breathing her in. "I know, I'm sorry. I didn't have a choice."

As his hands ran up and down her back, soothing her, he didn't say his actions were preferable to the slow, tormenting death he would've suffered if his cable had dipped into that molten rock. *No, there's only so much a brain can take.*

Some time later, Atu said, "Let me look at those burns."

Kayla reacted like she had been electrocuted. She jumped back and Jaden felt her absence acutely. His arms felt empty. Reaching for her, he found Atu blocking his way.

Atu's face was stern. "I need to take care of those burns."

Jaden sighed. "Always so serious."

A giggle from Iri diluted the tension. Jaden rolled onto his stomach, allowing Atu access to his back. When the golden light flowing from Atu's palms swirled over him, Jaden experienced immediate relief.

"And you were the one who didn't want to go first. What would we have done if we didn't have you to heal us on this side?" Jaden murmured when the light faded and Atu allowed him to sit up.

Atu rolled his eyes. "I suppose I can let it go. Can you? Or is this going to be something you harangue on and on about?"

Jaden laughed. "It's behind us, dude." His laugher subsided. "Time to see what's ahead."

CHAPTER FORTY-FIVE

Kayla needed something to do. Despite their embrace, Kayla was still mad at Jaden for taking risks. Understanding his reasons didn't nullify her anger. He hadn't told them what he was doing before he'd acted on his own. Again. He hadn't asked for help. He'd taken matters into his own hands as he had so many times before. *Will he ever learn?*

Turning so Jaden couldn't see her expression, Kayla peered into the gloom of the tunnel leading away from the river. The bright light from the fiery lava made discerning anything deeper in the tunnel impossible. Kayla was debating activating her night vision feature again when there was a loud plop behind her. The hissing and crackling that followed had the others whirling too. While it wasn't something attacking, it was a problem.

Kayla sighed as the lava flow absorbed the knot and cables. "There goes any chance we had of getting back across."

"Not that it was an option after we all made it here," Jaden muttered.

Kayla glanced at him, unsure whether he was attempting to make her feel better about the situation. His scowl didn't help. She had no way of discerning whether Jaden was holding resentment toward her or if it was anger at the predicament they were now in.

Jaden caught her staring and turned away. His reaction made Kayla think he had directed his scowl at her after all. Jaden stared at the tunnel, his face shadowed. "At least we know the spiders never made it across to this side."

Too exhausted to stay angry, Kayla crossed to him. She placed a hand on his shoulder, feeling him tense as she did. If she could've reached his neck, she would've planted a kiss there. But their height difference made that impossible. Sighing, Kayla ran the hand down his back instead, then stepped next to him as her hand slid further down to grasp his.

When she looked at him, she found those fathomless blue pools staring back at her. "Am I forgiven yet?"

"I'm getting there." Kayla pointed at the tunnel. "What made you say the spiders didn't make it this far?"

Iri and Atu joined them, having decided it was safe to approach, considering Jaden and Kayla weren't yelling at each other.

Jaden pointed at the floor. "Dust."

And not just a thin layer. She moved her foot, and a small cloud swirled up. "I suppose we have the tunnel to ourselves then."

"For now anyway," Jaden muttered. "Keep your eyes open for any sign of that changing."

Without another word, he let go of Kayla's hand and marched down the tunnel. Kayla stared after him, feeling deserted. It wasn't only how he let go of her hand. It was the way he spoke. Like something inside him was dead.

Iri nudged her. "Better get going. I don't think he's waiting for anyone."

And there's the problem. Her anger returned, and she stomped after him. Catching up, she grabbed his arm and swung him around. "What fly crawled up your nose?"

Those cold, blue eyes flared, ice replaced by heat in a flash. "Why do you always have to judge me? Can't you accept that sometimes I don't have time to explain things? If Markov were here instead of you, he'd know I'd already have considered all the angles!"

Kayla drew back like he'd slapped her. She sucked in air, not feeling like it was reaching her lungs. Then her eyes stung. "What's wrong with you?" Kayla warbled, shoving him aside and taking the lead. She didn't want him to see the tears.

Jaden remained where he was for a moment. Then Kayla heard him running to catch up. His hand touched her arm.

Kayla wrenched it away. "Don't touch me!"

Jaden's footsteps faltered. Kayla didn't care. She was done. *He can fall back down the tunnel into the river for all I care.* The thought stopped her in her tracks. The tunnel had been rising. They had been climbing since leaving the river, and she hadn't been watching the ground. Wiping away the tears blurring her vision, she sniffed as she glanced at the floor. Relief washed through her. There was still dust.

A realization tempered her relief. *Now is not the time to indulge our emotions. We have to focus, have to work as a team. If we don't, our chances go way down.*

Composing herself took a good few minutes. While she did, she remained where she was. She sensed the others stopping when they reached her, silently questioning why. Squaring her shoulders, Kayla rounded on them. Or, rather, on Jaden.

"I realize your analytical brain is probably way ahead of the rest of us with weighing the options. But—and you need to hear this—we are a team. Things don't work when you do things without telling us." Jaden opened his mouth, and Kayla raised a finger. "No. You had time to explain what you were doing back there. Our comms work fine down here, and even if you didn't know exactly how you would handle it, you knew you were aiming for Iri's cable. How difficult would it have been to deliver that one sentence?"

Kayla heard the rising hostility in her tone. "And I'm sorry if that sounded accusatory. I don't mean to judge you. I just like to be kept informed, as I'm sure the rest of the team does. If you don't include us in your decisions, how do you know there's not a better option?"

Jaden said nothing. Kayla glared at him. He was staring at her, arms folded, his mouth set in a thin line. "Well?"

"I'm allowed to speak now?"

Kayla wanted to punch him. Smash that condescending look off his face. Her arms were already rising when Iri blocked her path.

"Don't," Iri breathed.

"Why not?" Kayla demanded. "He—"

Iri cut her off. "This isn't you. It isn't Jaden. And considering I'm seeing anger on Atu when he's normally a blank slate, something in this place is affecting us."

Kayla had been about to push Iri out of the way so she could get at Jaden when Iri's words registered. At that moment, a wave of heat washed over them, followed by what was coming up the tunnel. "Oh, you've got to be kidding! Not again!"

The others spun, following her gaze. Little spiraling dust motes danced across the floor, swirling together to form funnels. Whirling funnels increasing in size and velocity as they moved up the tunnel, getting closer by the second.

"Aerolators on!" Jaden ordered, grabbing Kayla's hand. "Run!"

They took off. "Atu, grab Iri's hand. I don't want you two separated.," Jaden called, barreling up the tunnel.

Kayla followed, not given much choice. Jaden's grip on her hand was steel. At least he wasn't running at his usual breakneck pace. His long legs easily outpaced hers. That his first instinct had been to get her to safety and then he'd been considerate of her shorter legs mollified Kayla. *Not now!* She was focusing on the wrong things again.

Their pace didn't slow. Gradually, they left the mini dust tornadoes behind them. But Kayla still feared a strong wind might shove them back onto their group. In this place, anything was possible. *What caused the dust storm in the first place? Heat rising from the river? But there hadn't been a wind before . . .*

"There's fresh air ahead," Iri squeezed out between breaths. "And more tunnels . . . I think."

"You think?" Jaden queried.

Iri stared into the gloom ahead, sniffing. Kayla wondered what she was seeing or smelling with her gift. Iri frowned. "If they are tunnels, they're tiny compared to this one—or perhaps short. Either way, they're different."

Kayla supposed that could explain the sudden breeze, but only if those tunnels themselves were newly opened. "Jaden," Kayla panted, "what are the chances those tunnels weren't there before?"

Jaden shook his head. "Slim to none."

"Great!" came Iri's muttered response.

They had only run a few more minutes when Kayla noticed the tunnel wasn't as wide as it had been before. She and Jaden had been running next to one another. Now, she was scraping against the tunnel walls, trying to stay at his side. Seconds later, Kayla had to release his hand and run behind him. "Jaden?"

Jaden nodded, his face stony. "I'm aware."

On cue, Iri called out. "The source of the fresh air is close."

At last, Jaden slowed. Kayla had been wondering how much longer she would last. She stopped, gulping air down as Iri and Atu reached them. Kayla flopped onto the tunnel floor, and they took a few minutes to rest and hydrate. *Or was it only one minute?* It felt that way when Jaden ordered them all back to their feet again.

They had gone another twenty feet when the tunnel closed in on itself. Completely. It ended in a cave. Or perhaps *culminated* was a better word because lining the walls of the cave were several octagonally shaped tubes, each leading out.

Kayla stared at the tubes. "How are we supposed to escape using those? They're far too small! Even for me."

Iri arrowed toward the tubes, her hands drifting in front of a few. "This one, and this one and this one—these are the ones leading to fresher air."

Desperate to escape this mountain, Kayla darted over to join Iri. Putting her own hands out, Kayla felt the air rushing past. Out of the cave. To the exterior part of the mountain. Kayla wished she hadn't felt that freedom. It only made her feel more trapped. "A lot of good the air does us. There's still no way we're squeezing through those tubes. That's assuming we're supposed to use them to get out of here."

Jaden spoke so abruptly, Kayla wondered whether he'd even been listening to their conversation. "I think we're supposed to use this."

Kayla turned to see what he was looking at. The moment her eyes fell on the wall behind him, she dropped her pack and scratched around in it for a pen and paper.

"Oh, goody. Time to take a load off and wait while she translates." Atu plonked himself down.

Kayla spared a second from her frantic scribbling to cast him a disparaging glance. "No offers of help?"

"Nope. Just like healing's my thing, that's all you, baby." Atu grinned at Jaden's scowl. "Sorry, let me correct that to 'Kayla.' Guess I'm not allowed any endearments."

At Kayla's exasperated glance, Jaden protested, "Well, he's not your boyfriend. I'm the only one with those privileges."

Grinning and shaking her head, Kayla let it go. She had to focus. Of all the translations she had had to do on this mission, this one was the trickiest. Some of the little lines showing which parts of the word should be stressed were so faded Kayla had to stand up and step closer to be sure she was capturing them correctly.

Just as she was nearing the end, she heard it. The soft whooshing of air moving along the tunnel. Her gaze connected with Jaden's. He didn't have to confirm what it was. His mouth thinned into a harsh line.

"Are you almost finished?"

Kayla nodded and copied the last few characters. She sensed the others moving in the cave behind her and had to trust they were doing what they could to keep the mini tornadoes from following them.

Concentrating, Kayla began crossing out characters, replacing and switching letters as she worked on the actual translation. When the air moving across the back of her neck stopped, she vaguely acknowledged the fact. The accompanying silence replacing the whooshing was another indicator something had changed. But when the temperature began rising, Kayla turned to see what was happening.

Using whatever they could scavenge from their packs, they had plugged up the three tubes where air had been rushing out. If Kayla wasn't mistaken, Iri's pack itself was plugging the last tube. Instead of looking relieved, the others stared at her, tension radiating from them.

"What?" Kayla asked.

Instead of answering her question, Jaden asked, "Do you have the translation?"

While he kept a calm expression on his face, there was no mistaking the urgency in his voice. "Yes, here it is. Want to tell me why you're all freaking out?"

Just then, Kayla's ears popped, like they did during a change in altitude. She put it together in an instant.

Iri nodded. "Yes, it won't be long before the pressure in here squashes us likes bugs."

Kayla was already hurrying over to them. As soon as she reached the hole covered by Iri's backpack, she began tracing her fingers around the edges. Almost at once, she found what she was searching for. To verify, she ran her hand around the edges of the other two holes. There was no doubt in her mind now. Her birthmark had itched unbearably when she had touched *that* tube, only serving as additional confirmation.

"I believe this is the tube that will get us out of here. But you might want to check my reasoning before we try what it says."

CHAPTER FORTY-SIX

Kayla offered the translation to Jaden. He grabbed it, his eyes wary thinking of the implied threat in the last riddle. *Funny how he doesn't remember he was the object of that threat in the first riddle. I wonder what he'll make of this one.*

Iri and Atu peeked past Jaden's shoulders so they could read too. Kayla knew the lines by heart already:

> *In the cave that ends it all*
> *Chart the bottom third on wall*
> *Decimate the veins*
> *Break the binding chains*
> *That deepest emotion find*
> *To negate what makes you blind*
> *Not if you should love*
> *But when you should love*
> *Stop the boy from choking*
> *Stop the girl from smoking*

Kayla was more interested in Jaden's reaction. Watching him closely, she saw his face only showed confusion. No anger or fear.

Jaden grunted. "What am I looking at here? Can you explain?"

Kayla would only explain what was essential. "The pattern is the same as the others. The first line tells us where we are, the second what they did here, and the third what we have to do now."

"And the last few lines?"

"We don't need them right now. Getting out of here is more important than analyzing them."

Jaden gave her a strange look. Kayla guessed he thought she was hiding something, something concerning those lines she didn't want to discuss. She threw her hands up, exasperated. "They're not important! But since you won't let it go, the fourth line is a warning or encouragement, and lines five through eight relate to what's written on the leather strip."

Jaden's mouth was a thin line. "What about the last two lines?"

"I don't know—I've never been able to relate them to anything. Can we get on with it now?"

Jaden sighed. "Okay, explain your logic."

"Lines two and three give it away. Line two directs us to this tube," Kayla said. "'Chart the bottom third on wall' could mean the third tube from the floor. See, the tubes are all over the walls. But they're at differing heights. If we count the tubes from the floor to the ceiling, this tube would be the third from the bottom."

Jaden scrubbed a hand over his face as he was prone to doing. "Okay, assuming that's the logic they used, this is the correct tube. But how do we know they didn't mean for us to look at all the tubes in the bottom third?"

"They didn't." When Jaden opened his mouth to argue, Kayla cut him off. "My birthmark started itching when I touched that tube."

Jaden stared. "You're sure it was that tube?"

"Yes. Not only that. I believe line three confirms this tube." She didn't wait for Jaden to object. "It reads, 'Decimate the veins.'"

"A sentence that makes no sense," Jaden grumbled.

"Only if you don't know what you're looking for." Kayla grinned at his annoyance. "So how does it feel when someone strings you along?"

The flash of irritation on Jaden's face melted in an instant. "Yeah, I suppose I deserved that. Okay, Sherlock, tell us what we're missing."

Kayla took Jaden's hand and held his palm flat against the rock wall. She moved his hand until she saw realization on his face. When she released his hand, and he moved it himself, she knew he'd found her clue.

"Grooves! There are grooves in this wall!"

His excitement prompted Iri and Atu to join him, their hands roaming the wall as they explored too.

"Not grooves," Kayla corrected. "Veins."

"They run over the whole wall," Atu said. "How do we know the grooves relate to the tube you pointed out?"

Kayla knew she probably looked smug, but she *had* found the answer. "Run your hands along the edges of any tube. I'll bet anything the only tube with grooves around its edge is the one covered by Iri's pack. The grooves run around the mouths of the other tubes, but never quite reach their edges."

Kayla waited for them to test her theory. She had only checked the other two tubes air had been passing through, not any of the others. Minutes later, Jaden nodded and justified her choice.

"You're right. This tube is the only one where the grooves run into the edge. You're thinking these grooves are the veins the riddle is referring to?"

"I do."

"But why hide them?" Iri muttered. "If they meant for us to find them, why cover them up?"

Kayla shook her head. "I don't think they were—at least, not when they created this place. You saw how thick the dust on the floor of this tunnel was when we first entered. I'm guessing the grooves accumulated dust in the same way until they were no longer distinguishable from these uneven walls."

"How are we supposed to 'decimate' the veins?" Jaden asked.

Kayla grinned. As usual, his brain was already on the next problem. "That was the part I needed help with."

"I can think of something that decimates," Atu offered. When they all looked at him, he pointed at Jaden and Kayla's rings and then their DDs.

Kayla gaped. "You don't think that's a little drastic?"

Atu shrugged. "They're the only things we have that destroy those abominations Slurpy created. Utterly 'decimate' them." He grinned.

Jaden hummed. "I don't know, dude. Zareh created all these clues and containments for the artifacts. If Slurpy had been the one in charge, sure, I could see using our relics stones or DDs. But not Zareh."

Iri jumped in. "Along that line of thinking, didn't Zareh say our medallions were the key?" She didn't wait for agreement before rushing on. "Perhaps we should try fitting our medallions into the grooves before we do something as drastic as trying to cut into them with our DDs."

They digested her words. Kayla had to agree. Iri's plan had merit. "I second that. The medallions led us into the final area last time. And this approach isn't as final as applying our DDs to the grooves. If we're wrong on that one, we could bring the whole mountain down on ourselves."

"Alright, let's go with that," Jaden said. "Kayla, any hidden clues in that message on where we place our medallions? And all four or just one?"

Kayla grimaced. "I think all of you keep forgetting I don't have my medallion anymore."

Jaden's face fell. "So we can't finish this?"

"I didn't say that. I was just reminding you I don't have a medallion. Partially because that was an answer to your previous question." Jaden looked confused. "You asked if we should use all four medallions?"

"Ah, yes, so I did."

"Last time, we only needed one, so I think one will suffice. Also, if we're not supposed to use the medallions, and the grooves swallow them like the keyhole did last time, we'll only lose one medallion, not all three. As for placement, I'd say anywhere the groove meets the edges of the tube?"

Without acknowledging Kayla had phrased that last suggestion as a question, Jaden pulled a knife from his pack and crouched down, gently scraping the sand away from the grooves leading into the tube.

"Are you just going to use your medallion, or were you thinking of asking what everyone else thought?" Kayla knew her tone was snippy, but she couldn't help it. Frustration boiled anew within her.

Jaden picked up on her tone. He stopped clearing the groove. Wearily, he glanced at her. "I'm happy to waste more time discussing whose medallion we should use. Considering I was closest, it seemed the most logical and efficient course for me to clear the groove and use mine."

Liar, Kayla thought. *You want to protect Iri and Atu from being exposed to the same danger of the Gaptors' EMPs that I am, should they lose their medallions.* She shouldn't have been upset with him. His heart was in the right place. *But still . . .* It took an effort of will, but Kayla applied herself. *Jaden is worth it. And I shouldn't be hinting that I doubt his leadership skills now. He got us this far, didn't he?*

"You're right. We don't have the time to waste. Thanks for thinking ahead and getting started."

Jaden searched her face. Finding what he was looking for, he nodded, then went back to clearing the groove. That he hadn't smiled spoke volumes. Tentatively, Kayla touched his shoulder. He stilled. Kayla sensed him soaking in the contact. It only made her feel worse about hurting him.

Crouching next to him, she put her arms around him. It was an awkward attempt at a hug, but it was the best she could do, given his position. "I'm sorry. Will you forgive me?"

Jaden turned then and rose to his feet, pulling her up with him and into his arms. He gazed into her eyes. "Yes, I forgive you. I know I don't have a great track record for including others in my decisions, but cut me a little slack, would you?"

"I'll try."

"Thanks." Jaden kissed her forehead and released her. "Sorry, no time to make up properly. We need to get this done."

Kayla had to agree. Her ears were feeling the rising pressure more acutely. They didn't have long. Seconds later, Jaden had all the grooves around the tube cleared of accumulated dirt.

"Maybe you two want to join us in standing here?" Jaden suggested to Iri and Atu, who still hadn't come any closer.

Kayla suspected Iri had been the one to hold Atu back so Kayla could clear things up with Jaden. Kayla confirmed it when Iri approached, her blue eyes, far lighter than Jaden's, dancing between Jaden and Kayla. Satisfied, she smiled at Kayla and Kayla grinned back. *Yes, there was no fooling Iri.*

Iri and Atu had barely reached them when Jaden pressed his medallion into one of the grooves. They waited. Nothing happened. Jaden tried another groove. Then another a few seconds later. When he tried the last groove without results, he said, "Perhaps we all need to use our medallions. Does it strike anyone else as a little too coincidental that there are four grooves and four of us with medallions?"

"Again, I don't have mine anymore," Kayla pointed out.

Jaden groaned. "Oh, yes."

"Shall we try with three?" Iri suggested.

They did. In many combinations. None of them yielded results. The pressure was unbearable now, and Kayla felt a headache building behind her eyes. "Enough! We tried the medallions. And I'm fresh out of any other ideas besides our DDs. You up for trying them?"

Three blades burned to life in answer. Kayla's grin was feral as she loosed her own DD. She glanced at Jaden. "Any guidance on where to put these?"

Jaden's smile told Kayla he had forgiven her, and he understood what she was doing. "Nope. Your guess is as good as mine. Have at it."

Kayla lifted the tip of her DD, about to place it in the groove closest to her when she heard something. She paused, noticing the others had stopped to listen too. Soft clinking, like pieces of metal sliding over one another. Soft and faint at first, but louder as it drew closer. A second later, the smell bowled them over.

Kayla yelped. There was no mistaking it. "The snake!"

"Spiders, now snakes! I hope the rats aren't following," Jaden mumbled.

Kayla suddenly laughed out loud, startling them all. Jaden raised an eyebrow.

"It's the riddle come to life. How Zareh knew there would be snakes coming down this tube is anyone's guess. But he did. And decimate their veins, we will."

The others chuckled, placing themselves strategically around the hole. They staggered their positions. If a snake got past Jaden (first, naturally), then it still had to run the gauntlet of three more DDs before it was free to attack. Providently, this placement was just as much to protect themselves from each other's blades. Win-win for them. Not so healthy for the snakes.

The clanking was so loud now that there was no doubt the snake was close. Kayla relaxed her stance, raising her DD into position. She blinked. One moment the tube was empty. The next, the snake's hideous head oozed through.

Slashing down, Jaden chopped the head off. Light flared, brilliant in its intensity, accompanied by a deafening roar—way more sound than usual. Kayla slapped her hands up to her mask, checking the ear protection. It was there, but this time, it did nothing to mute the racket.

Bits of rock began raining down on them, tiny pieces too small to cause damage. However, the accompanying dust was suffocating. Kayla felt rather than saw the breeze washing the dust away. Cool, clean air. Her ears popped at the sudden change in pressure. Working her jaw, she tried to clear the second pop from her ears. It was more painful than the first, and Kayla pressed the button in her mask deactivating the sound suppressors.

Kayla was still using her fingers to ease the ache in her ears when she realized where the wind was coming from. The other two tubes! Instead of sucking air up as before, they were now blowing wind into the cave. Or what remained of the top of it.

While everything below to the left and right of the tube remained, the explosion generated when Jaden chopped the mutant snake's head off blew the section of mountain directly above it to smithereens. A perfect semi-circle had been carved out of the side of the mountain like someone had used a giant ice cream scoop.

The stars glittering in the night sky beyond the rim of the semi-circle were the most wonderful thing Kayla had seen in days. The fresh air lifting her matted hair from her sweaty neck was the sweetest thing she had ever smelled. She closed her eyes in relief. Being freed from the depths of the mountain was bliss.

Kayla's eyes snapped open again. She surveyed her surroundings. *Not the depths of the mountain.* The tunnel from the lava river had led them up far enough so a thin shell of rock had been the only thing confining them.

Turning to Jaden and the others, Kayla saw the awe and wonder on their faces too. She opened her mouth to speak, but the wind blasting through the other two tubes ceased. Kayla wasn't sure what she expected. More snakes. Rats Even the return of the spiders. Her DD blazed in her hand, prepared for whatever came out the tubes.

It was not what any of them expected. Twin soft plops. Then a single object appeared in the mouth of each tube. A glass bottle (shaped exactly like those on their medallions) sat in the first tube, filled with a liquid so black it swallowed the light. The inkpot!

In the mouth of the second tube was the usual strip of leather. Kayla glanced at Jaden. He understood. Even though she was closer to the leather strip, she couldn't touch it. Not without her birthmark burning a hole through her arm.

Jaden leaned in front of her and carefully extracted the strip. He unfurled it on the rock wall so Kayla could see the ancient text. But the strip itself distracted Kayla. It was the piece that completed the puzzle, the piece that had prevented her from reaching this conclusion as Slurpy's prisoner. The revelation was enough to knock the breath from her.

"Kayla?"

Jaden's face radiated concern. Realizing Jaden and the other were still waiting for a translation, Kayla waved away his concern. She'd have time to dwell on this discovery later. She quickly rearranged the ciphers in her head. These messages were always easier to translate than the riddles. "Conquering with love."

"About as useful as the others were," Jaden grumbled. Rolling the leather strip up again, he put it in his pack before reaching for the inkpot in the tube in front of him. "Did anyone else think that delivery system was cool? Like one of those old postal tube systems they had back in the day." They met his comment with blank stares. "Never mind."

Kayla grinned. The disappointment on his face when no one shared his passion for old tech was downright adorable. She strolled over to him and wrapped her arms around his neck. "Ah, don't worry. We love you just the way you are. Just because we don't get—"

Kayla's words cut off mid-sentence. With her face upturned, she saw them over his shoulder. Black shapes blotting out the stars. Black shapes too large to be birds. Black shapes heading toward them. "Gaptors!"

CHAPTER FORTY-SEVEN

Jaden heard Kayla's warning at the same time he registered Markov's urgent calls buzzing through his comm.

"Jaden! Jaden! Are you there? Can you hear me?"

"Here. We were under the mountain and—"

"They ambushed us! We're under attack! Get your asses up here!"

"On our way."

"No need. That little explosion you set off has them all riled up. The battle's coming to you."

Sure enough, when Jaden looked to the cries of the battle, far to their right, countless dark shapes blotted out the stars. The boom when they first found their relic stones and accidentally activated them had been a Gaptor magnet too. Jaden searched the sky overhead. *Where's Han? How are we going to deal with such a vast enemy army?*

"Kayla, Atu, I want you to stay here." Kayla's glare had him rushing to finish his explanation. "This time we're seriously outnumbered. Their ambush means we don't have the advantage. We don't have Sven's cannons. Chances we'll survive this assault are slim to none."

Resolve glittered through the tears rimming Kayla's eyes. "Don't say that. There's always a chance. Look at what happened last time."

Jaden gripped her arms, tugging her to within an inch of his face.

He stared directly into her eyes. She had to understand how important this was.

"Look behind me. See those shapes falling from the sky?" Kayla nodded. "Those are our friends. Our army is being slaughtered. And you no longer have a medallion to protect you from those EMPs. Don't act in denial."

Kayla scowled. "Okay, I get it."

Relieved he had sparked her anger, Jaden hoped it would sustain her for what he had to say next, even though he dreaded speaking the words. "You know I love you and I'll do anything to protect you. But this time, I'm also asking you to stay because if something happens to Iri and I up there . . . you and Atu have to finish this. If you two don't, Slurpy wins, and the world goes to hell. Do you get that?"

A muffled sob escaped Kayla's mouth, and she clapped a hand over it. The tears streamed down her cheeks now, but her face hardened. "I do."

Jaden crushed her to him, holding her like there was no tomorrow. Because it was likely, there wouldn't be.

"Any day now!"

Han's growled words reached Jaden over the commotion around them. He pulled back. "I have to go."

Kayla grabbed his arm. "Wait! Before you do, there's something I have to tell you."

Jaden glanced up at Han and then back at Kayla. "Make it quick. Han's looking like he might snatch me up with his talons at any moment." Jaden's mood improved as a slight smile touched Kayla's lips.

"Tell the old man to cool his heels."

That made Jaden laugh out loud. "Only if you tell Taz the same thing."

Kayla looked up then, as if only realizing Taz was there too. She sighed, putting her hands to the side of her head. "How to make this quick . . . um, okay. I think the leather strips have something to do with my birthmark."

Jaden frowned. "Didn't we already establish that?"

Waving an agitated hand, Kayla said, "No, no, that came out wrong! I mean, I think the leather strips form the shape of my birthmark. You know, like they're puzzle pieces we have to put together?"

Too shocked by her revelation to say anything, Jaden stared at her. From the matching expressions on Iri and Atu's faces, she hadn't shared this with them either. Jaden's mind sifted possibilities. "Even better."

Kayla's eyebrows shot up. "Not the answer I was expecting."

"I mean it gives you another reason to stay here." Jaden wrenched his pack off and shoved it into her arms. "This contains all the artifacts. Use your time here to piece that puzzle together. Atu, can you help her move them?"

Atu was already nodding. "Yeah, yeah, I know she can't touch them."

Jaden was out of time. "Let us know via the comm what you find. I love you!" Snatching her into his arms one last time, Jaden kissed her fiercely. "Live!"

Then he sprinted for the edge of the semi-circle that opened into the abyss that was the edge of the mountain. Han was ready for him. He caught Jaden and immediately gained elevation.

"Han, please tell Taz Kayla is—"

"We know. We heard your conversation. Taz is staying with Kayla. She, Aren, Pallaton, and some of the Legion's best will patrol overhead, protecting Kayla and Atu from aerial attacks. Can I count on your full attention for this fight now?"

"You can." Jaden firmly shut the door on thoughts of Kayla. It was the only way he might survive another day to see her again. "Iri, you close?"

"Right next to you."

Jaden glanced to his left and found her and Rozie there. His gaze drifted from them to the approaching battalion. "That's a lot of Gaptors."

"And not a lot of gliders left fighting them. Do you have a plan?"

Jaden grinned. "I think everyone's been a little too preoccupied to notice *that*." He laughed at the way Iri's face changed when she saw it on the mountain closest to the one that had trapped them. It glowed, brilliant orange against the dark shape of the mountain.

"Is that—"

"Yes. I'm guessing the explosion set off a chain reaction in the fires under this mountain range. That's lava. And it's exactly what we need to get an advantage in this battle."

Iri looked dubious. "If you say so."

"I do. Markov, you there?"

"What took you so long?" Markov's panting was audible.

Ignoring the question, Jaden outlined his plan.

"I hope it works." Markov set about complying with Jaden's request.

Gathering the Gaptors was more difficult than Jaden had thought it would be. They were determined to stay near the site of the explosion. *Were they ordered there, or is this just some unnatural homing instinct Slurpy bred into them?*

When the gliders and their riders raced away from the battle, the Gaptors continued milling around the explosion site. Jaden was worrying about Kayla and Atu's safety when the Gaptors finally registered their prey had moved to the next mountain over.

Slowly, the Gaptors followed. Jaden figured that in their puny minds the new spot wasn't that far from where the explosion had occurred. *Let's just hope they keep thinking about that first explosion and don't start wondering about others.*

The Gaptors' tardiness worked in the Legion's favor. The riders had time to join Jaden, waiting on the opposite side of the volcano's vent. It was still dribbling lava over the rim, as though doing more would be too much effort.

Iri's voice, breathless, filtered through the comm. "I have it."

"Any problems?"

"No."

"Are you in position?"

"Yes, ready whenever you are."

"About another minute."

Jaden had no need for his night vision goggles. The light from the lava provided all he needed to see the approaching Gaptors. Closer and closer, until they crossed the foothills of this volcano. Jaden tensed when a few Gaptors slowed and glanced down. But he relaxed again when they continued onward, deciding the lava posed no threat.

The lead Gaptors were only a hundred feet from Jaden and the others when Jaded murmured into his comm. "Here goes nothing. Let's do this!"

At the same moment Han darted toward the approaching enemy, the other riders and their gliders backed away—enticing the Gaptors to advance further, to position themselves exactly where Jaden wanted them.

Abruptly, a few of the Gaptors noticed Jaden and streaked his way. *Perfect!* Jaden allowed himself a smile. *As long as it's just a few and not the whole crowd, we're golden.* Tracking the Gaptors racing after him, Jaden darted glances toward the other side of the mountain and located Iri, waiting exactly where he'd told her.

"I see you," Iri said, waving her arms.

"Aim for the Gaptors trailing me. Remember, wait until they're between us, or this won't work." *It if works at all. Then again, if it doesn't work, we've lost nothing and moved the Gaptors away from Kayla and Atu.*

This next part would be the trickiest. "Han, let's get the Gaptors trailing us lined up over that vent. Work it so we're angled about forty-five degrees down from where Iri is."

"You already explained this."

Jaden heard the complaint in Han's voice. "Sorry, buddy. We only get one shot. I know they're not the brightest, but this might be enough to scare them from attempting it twice."

"Nag, nag, nag," Han muttered as he spiraled downward.

The abrupt change in Han's trajectory had the pursuing Gaptors screeching. Agitated, they picked up speed.

Jaden grinned. "Yeah, you think you'll be heroes—just keep chasing us, suckers!"

Han placed them at the perfect elevation below Iri. Tilting his wings, Han arced around the night-dark curve of the mountain, forcing their pursuers to dive under the bulk of the Gaptors now bunched directly over the vent.

"Iri, get ready—three, two, one!" Jaden threw his hand up, catching sight of Iri above them as she did the same.

Crackling light blazed between the relic stones, blinding white slicing through the dull red glow rolling off the mountain. For a nanosecond, stark white outlined the Gaptors chasing them. Then light erupted as the Gaptors were incinerated, the reverberating boom of their demise cracking over the surrounding mountains. Right over the vent oozing lava.

"Iri, clear out!" Jaden cried as he saw the first fracture shoot down the spout.

Han saw it too and sped away from the mountain. Jaden swiveled on Han's back to see if his plan worked. That first crack split into several. The lava squeezed through the new spaces, no longer restricted to flowing upward.

One moment, the lava was seeping along the lines, the next a thunderous blast rocked the upper part of the volcano. The force ripped the top off and the glowing chunk rocketed diagonally into a group of unsuspecting Gaptors. More light and sound as it obliterated them. Then, what Jaden had been hoping for, happened. The sudden release of pressure catapulted lava skyward, high enough to catch the Gaptors right above it.

With screeches that had Jaden slapping his hands over his ears, his sound suppressors not enough to deaden the raucous cries, the lower ranks of Gaptors burst into flame. The next level of Gaptors weren't distant enough to avoid the leaping fire. Whoosh! It consumed them too. The chain reaction continued up through the ranks until it seared an enormous hole through the middle of the Gaptors' army.

The Gaptors on the outer edges of the circle of fire bashed into one another as they scrambled to escape, panic blinding them. *Yeah, not the brightest creatures.* Their wings became entangled, and Gaptors crashed down to earth. Those that didn't burn up as they dropped perished in the lava flow below. Light strobed the sky, and constant booms echoed up and down the valley, confirming none who fell would pose a future threat.

Jaden's attention settled on those who *had* escaped. While the ranks had been thinned substantially, the Gaptors still outnumbered them three to one. Time to get their hands dirty.

Han read his mind, already aiming for the remaining Gaptors. With a start, Jaden realized where they were. Kayla and Atu were far below, waving their arms and jumping up and down. Jaden grinned. *Yes, I'm just as excited my plan worked. We would've been in real trouble if it hadn't. If . . .*

That familiar, hateful chill raced down his spine. In slow motion, Jaden realized four things simultaneously.

Kayla and Atu did not have joy or excitement on their faces.

Their mouths were moving, but he couldn't hear them through his comm.

The Gaptors around them had gone rigid, as though afraid of something.

And a shadow blacker than the night, far too large to be a Gaptor, had fallen over him.

Han dove as Jaden glanced up. It *was* a Gaptor, two or three times the size of the usual monster. And sitting on its back, his incredibly handsome face wearing a wicked grin, was the last person Jaden ever expected to see. The usurper.

CHAPTER FORTY-EIGHT

Horrified, Kayla watched Slurpy's abominable brute latch onto Han. Its talons were long enough to clamp all the way around Han's waist. Overhead, Taz growled. "What?" Kayla asked.

"It will crush Han's chest!"

Panicked, Kayla engaged the magnification aspect of her goggles. *If that thing has its claws around Han, what happened to Jaden?* The pain on Han's face was obvious as he struggled to escape, but the Gaptor had a death grip. Han's wings were pinned against his sides. His neck was too short for his teeth to reach the talons.

Blue light blazed, so bright against the inky sky Kayla had to avert her gaze. The Gaptor's shriek pierced through the other battle sounds. A Gaptor's severed, gnarled leg suddenly floated across the lens, making Kayla gasp.

Then Han reached across his body and sank his teeth into the Gaptor's other leg. It was too much for the monster. With an even louder shriek, it released Han. Han dropped like a stone, Jaden clinging to his back.

"What's happening? Why isn't he flying?" Kayla demanded.

Taz's eyes were slits as she studied the falling pair. Then she grinned, her sharp teeth glinting in the moonlight. "He will."

Kayla took the smile to mean she shouldn't worry. But as Han and Jaden continued falling, her worry boiled up again. She was so focused on them she wasn't paying attention to Slurpy and his beast. Out of nowhere, they appeared.

The Gaptor's stump where Jaden's DD had sliced off its leg trailed a significant amount of the odious black blood Kayla knew all too well. Her nose wrinkled. The blood loss didn't seem to impede the Gaptor. It aimed for Han and Jaden, its path unerring.

Kayla's heart dropped to her feet. "It's going after Han again!"

Taz snapped out a command. "Pallaton, take two others and go help Han and Jaden!"

"It's my duty to protect—"

"That's an order!"

Pallaton looked torn between duty and obedience. With a heavy sigh and a reproachful glance at Taz, he streaked away. Two of his Legion followed. Kayla didn't wonder how he communicated with them.

Her eyes darted back to Han and Jaden. In the two seconds of Taz and Pallaton's exchange, Slurpy's Gaptor had reached its target. Instead of ramming Han as Kayla expected, the Gaptor sailed past. She blinked. *What just happened?* It hit her so forcibly Kayla crumpled to the ground. *It took Jaden!*

Atu appeared beside her. Crouching down, he cradled her in his arms. Even if they had wanted to, they couldn't peel their eyes away. They watched, helpless, until Slurpy's beast passed beyond range of their magnification lenses and took the choice from them. Slurpy and his beast had vanished. And he had taken Jaden with him.

"Why did he do that?" Kayla couldn't keep the tremor from her voice.

"I don't know. Why snatch Jaden off Han when he could've just—" Atu trailed off.

Kayla knew what he'd been about to say. She couldn't say it either.

"Han and Pallaton will retrieve Jaden. There's nothing we can do from here. I believe there are other matters you should attend to."

Taz sounded so matter-of-fact, Kayla wanted to hit her. Only she wasn't within reach. Kayla glared up at Taz, prepared to give her a piece of her mind, when she saw Taz's eyes. Sorrow. Anger. Frustration. It came to Kayla then. Taz was just as devastated. But she was trying to do what Jaden had asked. She was doing what every leader—what every ruler—had to learn to do. Make the tough choice. Put the mission ahead of personal feelings.

Taz cleared her throat. "We have no way of knowing how what you do here will help. Let's not waste time. Our army is dying."

Gliders and riders were tumbling from the night sky. Whether they would survive to fight another day might depend on her. With shaking fingers, Kayla ran her hands through her hair. "Atu, I think it would be better if you left me sitting here on the ground."

Atu stared at her as though she'd lost her marbles. "Why?"

"Because when we do what we have to with those strips of leather, I won't have far to fall if I pass out." Kayla didn't mention the pain she might have to endure. She winced just thinking about it. Every time she'd touched those leather strips in the past, her birthmark had burned with such intensity she believed her arm was on fire.

"You okay?"

Ziggety! Atu noticed that wince. Kayla had to remember he was a healer trained to observe. "Yup. Just a reaction to thinking about touching those strips."

"Lucky for you, then. You don't have to. Where are they?"

Kayla smiled. It was so like Atu to cut to the chase. "In Jaden's pack. Here." She handed it over.

"Interesting."

"What is?"

"That you could tolerate having the pack on your back with the strips inside."

"Not really. They only cause that violent reaction when I touch them directly."

"Hmm," was Atu's only response as he retrieved the strips. He glanced at them and then Kayla. "What do you want me to do with them?"

Kayla scooted over to a flatter part of the mountain. "Spread them out in front of me." Atu did. "Now, take that one and move it to the bottom."

"This one with the odd bite out of it?"

Kayla grinned. It was actually an excellent way to describe the missing chink. "Yes. Position the bite to the right." Kayla used her hands to show which "right" she meant. "Yup. Now take that one," she pointed, "and fit it to the top left of the bite piece. It should fit together like a jigsaw."

Atu had to jiggle it a little to make it fit. The leather had stretched over time. He glanced at the other piece. "I'm guessing this last one goes here?" He pointed toward top right of the bite piece.

"Yup. Just be careful when you put that last strip in place. I have no clue what will happen, and I don't want you getting hurt."

Atu wiggled his eyebrows at her. "What *would* Jaden say?"

Kayla giggled. Even though her heart ached and despair squatted on her like a brooding cobra, the sound escaped.

Atu grinned in return. "Whatever happens, remember, we're in this together. This is where we chose to be."

So saying, he lifted the last piece of leather. This time, instead of fitting it on the ground, he angled it in the air until he was satisfied with the position. "I think I have it. Ready?"

Kayla nodded, unable to speak. Her eyes were wide as Atu crouched down. Gingerly, he lowered the piece a fraction of an inch at a time. When it was barely above the pieces on the ground, he dropped it and jumped back.

This time, the light was golden, a soft glow as opposed to the dazzling, white flash usually accompanying things from that other world. And instead of the quick release of energy, the golden light hovered over the strips. As it did, the strips melded together, forming a single large piece.

It confirmed the strips were the product of someone ripping the larger piece apart. Kayla could guess who might've been responsible. *But is it possible Slurpy got his hands on this piece of leather? If so, why didn't he just destroy it?*

The golden light coalesced into a wand weaving over the leather, an unseen hand guiding the pointed light. Wherever the point touched, symbols appeared.

Incredulous, Kayla dared crawling closer. The words on the individual strips had vanished, leaving no sign of the symbols forming the original three messages. As the new symbols appeared, Kayla's birthmark itched, but it wasn't the severe burn of before. Not even remotely painful. Just itchy, meaning she should pay attention.

Snatching up her pack, Kayla found her pen and paper and began transcribing the symbols. She didn't wait for the wand to finish before she began the tedious process of crossing out and rearranging.

By the time Kayla reached the last few lines, the wand was drawing a familiar shape to encompass the symbols. When the shape was complete, the wand stopped scribing. Kayla waited, eager to discover what the wand would do next. But with its assigned task complete, the wand had no further purpose. It faded slowly, and the golden glow gradually disappeared with it.

"That was something to behold," Atu breathed. "Jaden and Iri won't be happy they missed that."

"Yup. That was incredible."

"What does it say?" Atu asked, gesturing toward her notepad.

"I'm not quite done yet. Give me a minute." Hurriedly, Kayla translated the last few lines. Although she'd noticed the words subconsciously while writing them down, she hadn't comprehended their meaning. Not until now, reading the whole thing.

Something in her face had to have given the importance of the message away because Atu bounded over. "What?"

Kayla glanced from the paper to Atu and back to the paper, then at Atu again. "These are instructions for using the medallions to eliminate the Gaptors forever!"

CHAPTER FORTY-NINE

Jaden squirmed in the Gaptor's grip. *No, Gapzilla's grip. He's stronger than a gorilla and the size of Godzilla, so why not?* No matter what he tried, he couldn't gain an inch of freedom. Gapzilla's grip only tightened the more he struggled. Breathing was becoming difficult, so Jaden stilled.

He glanced up, finding Slurpy grinning down at him. About to make a rude comment, something shiny caught his eye. Jaden couldn't hide his sharp intake of breath. Quickly, he averted his eyes. Slurpy couldn't know he had seen it—or that Jaden knew who it belonged to.

"You can look. I know what you were staring at," Slurpy said. "She brought it to me, you know."

Jaden gritted his teeth. To say something would acknowledge he'd been looking. *Kayla's medallion!* If Kayla's intricately crafted holder hadn't confirmed it, Slurpy just had.

But why does Slurpy have it with him? The answer came to him clear as day. *As long as he has at least one medallion, we don't have them all. If we don't have them all, we can't use them to get rid of the Gaptors like we're supposed to.*

In his peripheral vision, Jaden caught Slurpy leering. "Yes, without this, you can't defeat me. You can't become the Gatekeeper."

Is that what destroying all the medallions will make me? The Gatekeeper? Jaden's teeth ached from grinding. Opening and closing his mouth a few times, Jaden tried relaxing the muscles in his jaw. It gave him a few extra seconds to think. "Why do you keep calling me 'Gatekeeper?'"

An incredulous bark of a laugh. "If you don't know, then I'm in a better position than I thought."

"Care to explain?"

"Do you take me for a fool? Without knowledge, you can't fulfill your purpose." Slurpy suddenly roared with laughter. "Yes, this little conversation has been highly illuminating. It's becoming clear that you'll never achieve that goal. You might have all the artifacts, but evidently you're ignorant about what to do with them." Another raucous laugh. "After all this, Zareh's plan fails!"

Something beyond menace lurked in that last sentence. Then Jaden made a fatal mistake: he looked directly into Slurpy's eyes, wanting to read what he could see there. Instead, all he saw was red. Red hot eyes like pokers searing into his soul. Red eyes glowing hotter than the embers of hell. They were bewitching. Jaden tried to look away, but something about that gaze held him, hypnotized him.

Jaden flung a hand out to stop himself from falling. But his hand was still wrapped in Han's neck fur. For a moment, something nagged at his mind. As quickly as the niggling thought pricked him, it went away. He thought he'd almost toppled off Han, but no, Han's heart still thumped below his own.

The beat intensified, pounding through Jaden's brain and compounding Slurpy's hateful red stare. When Slurpy spoke, Jaden jumped. "Behold! See what I am doing to your world!"

Jaden glanced down. His shock was so severe he almost lost his grip on Han. He lurched across Han's side and spewed the contents of the stomach. Still heaving, he stared at what he saw.

The world was ablaze! Malicious lava sprayed death from every mountain top. Fires flared and flames crackled, devouring any place untouched by lava. Worse, their army, all those riders and gliders, lay scattered across the lower levels of the mountains.

They were all dead. The thought crushed Jaden. They had been here, fighting for him. Despair seized him. These people, these gliders whom he'd barely gotten to know . . . all dead. He would never truly know any of them now.

Their bodies littering the mountain resembled broken and discarded toys in a maniac's game. And they were directly below the lava gushing down the mountain, gobbling everything in its path. As the lava poured over them, consuming them forever in its hissing, spitting maw, Jaden's soul shriveled inside him.

Kayla! The thought punched Jaden so hard it was almost a physical blow. His gaze darted toward the mountain where he'd left her and Atu.

He fell to his knees, too distraught to wonder where Han had gone. *What does it matter?* There was nothing left of the place where Kayla and Atu had been. The entire mountain had melted into the lava flows below. Jaden's heart constricted, the pain unbearable.

Then his mind caught up. Jaden shook his head. *This can't be right. No way an entire mountain dissolves in minutes! Was it mere minutes? Or is Slurpy powerful enough to speed up whatever processes he wants to destroy in seconds instead of days or weeks or months?*

Jaden retched again. Sick to his stomach, dealing with Slurpy was the last thing he wanted right now. *But since when did I ever have a choice in any of this?* A fact that was more repugnant by the second.

Swiping a hand across his mouth and wishing he had some water to rinse away the vile taste, Jaden righted himself on Han's shoulders. *Huh, Han's back again.* "Sorry, dude. Hope I didn't spray you."

Han said nothing. Didn't even acknowledge that Jaden had spoken. Jaden's spine tingled. He didn't need that sense of his to know something was terribly wrong.

"He can't hear you," Slurpy said. "I've blocked his ears. In fact, he doesn't even remember the peril he's in."

Peril? Why is Han in peril? The more Jaden tried to remember, the less he felt like himself. Something was definitely off.

He squeezed Han's ribs with his knees. A movement too subtle for

Slurpy to notice, yet enough for Han to feel. Han didn't react. *This is bad. Really bad!* Jaden scanned the area.

"If you're looking for your friends, they're over there." Slurpy motioned toward a small hill Jaden hadn't noticed in his frenzied scan earlier. It remained unscathed in the midst of the chaos below.

Jaden blinked, trying to find a visual path through the acrid smoke belching from the surrounding mountains. A fortuitous breeze allowed him one quick glimpse. Kayla, Atu, Markov, Stovan, and Shianna balanced precariously on a tiny ledge far too small to hold them all.

Shianna's arms flailed, and if Stovan hadn't grabbed her, she would have toppled into the blazing lava below. Those Jaden loved balanced there safely for only a second before the heat rippling from below created another gust of wind, rocking them once more.

"How long do you think they'll last?"

Slurpy's question held malice and suppressed glee at his own cleverness. Before Jaden could answer, Slurpy spoke again.

"They're at least a little more robust than that other friend of yours. What is it with the women in your life? They can't stay away from me." Slurpy chuckled, tickled by the thought.

Jaden's brain was in overdrive. He had the overriding sense he was missing something. Jaden panted. *Get a grip!*

"What, nothing to say? Well, I suppose she wasn't worth your time, anyway. And after what she did, who can blame you for choosing the living instead of the dead? Still, she was a pretty little thing."

Jaden's face contorted in rage. "Who are you talking about? None of the women in my life have ever willingly come to you."

Slurpy waved a dismissive hand in the air. "Think what you must so you can feel better. You know, it was your fault she did what she did. If you hadn't kicked her to the curb, she would never have taken her own life. You're no better than I am."

Jaden froze. Nausea returned with a vengeance. "Tarise?"

Mocking laughter. "Who else would I be talking about?" Slurpy snapped his fingers. "Now you've put that together, come on, you have to agree . . . *she* came to *me*."

Jaden reeled. Guilt. Shame. Rage. Sorrow. All mixed, forming cement to seal his mouth.

"You still have nothing to say?" Slurpy tutted. "I would've at least thought you'd show some remorse. But didn't I already say you were no better than me?"

Blind rage consumed Jaden. He wanted to smack that smirk off Slurpy's face. He wanted to break something. Smash it to pieces. Tarise had followed through on what she had threatened in her letter. Only it wasn't what they'd thought.

Jaden,

I wanted things to be different. Don't blame yourself for what I do now. It's the only way.

Tarise

Jaden never imagined Tarise would take her own life. Shame filled him. *What made me think Tarise would betray us to Slurpy for a second time?* Anguish followed. *Why Tarise? Why? Why didn't you just let us help you?*

Then again, what other choice did she have faced with Slurpy's power? Regret coated anguish. Tarise died thinking she could never cross the chasm created by her betrayal.

Jaden ran a hand through his hair. He wished he had followed Markov's advice. Wished he had given Tarise another chance. Wished he hadn't been so harsh with her. *Was it Kayla who said my actions have consequences? Or did someone else say it—or did I read it?*

With a concerted effort, Jaden reined his thoughts in. He was spiraling. Probably exactly what Slurpy wanted. Jaden focused on something besides Slurpy. Their uncompleted mission. *Is there still a chance we can win?* Jaden's soul was so battered he wasn't sure he could even summon the desire to pick up the mantle again.

Driving the nail home, Slurpy said, "Oh, and look, here come your parents. I guess they were worried about their precious son. How unfortunate for them. They should've considered the danger before venturing closer."

With a flick of his finger, Slurpy made jets of lava burst up directly under his parents. Their gliders veered, narrowly avoiding the plumes.

Slurpy tittered. "Let's see how high those gliders can fly. And how long your parents last before they lose consciousness and fall off."

He lifted his hand this time, dragging a stream of lava from the lake below and literally pulling it through the air to form a flaming, hissing, smoking pillar. Its fingerlike tip reached for the pair of gliders. They were frantic, weaving through the air trying to dodge the fiery finger chasing them.

There was nothing left of Jaden's heart. It was an empty spot in his chest. His parents' faces were bone white, their fear palpable. "Please, stop!" Jaden's plea wrenched free.

Slurpy raised an eyebrow. "But why? This is so much fun."

"Please, tell me what you want! Leave them out of this."

Slurpy focused all his attention on Jaden then. "Do you really think I'll make this painless for you? After everything you've done to ruin the plans I've been perfecting for centuries? You and that loathsome Zareh! Why can't the two of you just play ball and die like you're supposed to?"

Jaden tried not to show how relieved he was that the pillar of rock and flame had collapsed back into the lava lake. "That's what you want —for me to die?"

Slurpy's face went slack. Clearly, he hadn't intended to let Jaden know that. Or not yet anyway. "I don't just want you to die. I want you to suffer. I want you to feel the worst kind of agony before your demise. I want you to endure years of torture for every bit of the rejection and failure you've laid on me with your little adventure."

Now that Jaden knew what Slurpy wanted, a spark of rebellion kindled. "Sorry for yourself much?"

His words only incensed Slurpy. "You think this is funny? That it's a game? I'll show you sport."

Before Jaden could stop him, Slurpy threw his hand out and snatched at the air. His power expanded like a ripple, flowing outward. The air smashed into the gliders carrying his parents, sending them plummeting.

CHAPTER FIFTY

Jaden's parents spun like debris in a tornado. Even from this distance, Jaden heard the bones in their gliders' wings cracking, snapped like inconsequential twigs. His parents screamed, the cries drawn out as they fell and fell and fell. Their gliders fell faster, though. Heavier than his parents, the damage to their wings rendered them helpless to save themselves, let alone his parents. They plunged into the lava lake.

With no sound at all, the lava embraced them, tiny flickering fires the only sign of the gliders' passing. Jaden's parents weren't far behind. An anguished wail escaped. "Mom! Dad!" His parents jerked to a stop, held in the air a few feet above the splashing lava by invisible hands. Jaden's eyes flew to Slurpy.

"What are their lives worth?"

Jaden had no words. He had no clue what Slurpy wanted to hear.

"Ready to beg?"

Jaden still said nothing, his eyes glued to his parents. Suddenly, they slipped a few inches. "No!"

"No?"

"No! I mean yes!" Jaden couldn't get the words out fast enough. They came out on a half-sob. Slurpy had twisted Jaden's words to his own ends. Before Jaden could say more, his parents dropped a little closer to death.

"I'm waiting."

He's waiting? For what? Jaden realized what, but not before his parents dipped too close to the fiery lake. A random drop of lava sizzled into his dad's back, and his shriek forced Jaden to his knees.

Vaguely, Jaden registered Han had vanished again. The flagstone floor under him was so cold it burned. Pain seared his shins where they met the floor.

It didn't matter. His parents needed his help. He couldn't lose them!

"Please, please, let them go!" Jaden's words were strangled. He would beg if that was what Slurpy wanted. His tears flowed freely, blinding him. A good thing. He wouldn't survive witnessing Slurpy dipping his parents in and out of the lava. The thought had Jaden shuddering.

Like a sword piercing him, Jaden registered what he was sensing from Slurpy. Pure delight. Pure evil. Pure control. That last one was the infinitesimal piece that kick-started his brain.

Fear. It's fear Slurpy craves! The more fear Slurpy invoked, the happier he was and the more in control he felt. *Sheesh, talk about a self-image problem! Making others less so he can be more. That's just sick.*

Jaden prostrated himself in front of Slurpy, pretending obeisance. The frigid floor scorched his hands, and Jaden didn't bother dampening his wail of agony. If nothing else, the ability to scream his lungs out was cathartic.

Expressing his torment had another effect. Slurpy drooled at his anguish. And while he was still beyond worried about his parents, he sensed the executioner's hand had been stayed. Slurpy was too busy soaking in Jaden's distress. Jaden had to play this to full effect. "Please, let them be!" Injecting supplication into his voice wasn't difficult.

As soon as Slurpy heard the words, he purred. Purred! Pure pleasure rippled through every decibel.

Keeping his head bowed meant Slurpy could neither read the emotions on Jaden's face nor guess what Jaden was thinking. Because thinking he was. Somehow, his brain regained normal functionality when he wasn't looking at Slurpy. When he wasn't gazing into those blood-red eyes. Jaden's mind raced. First, he couldn't look at Slurpy; those eyes of his were treacherous. Second, his "spidey sense," as Kayla called it, was screaming at the top of its lungs. He suspected he knew why. But that brought him to his third conclusion. And had him asking a question. *What do I fear most?*

Answering that question was simple. Since all this began, the thought of something happening to those he loved because of this quest had plagued him more than anything else. If he could just let go of that fear . . . could he? Or at least make Slurpy believe he had?

Jaden swallowed the bile threatening to propel itself from his mouth again. What he was planning made him sick. If he was wrong, he would condemn those he loved to death. However, if he was right, and he was sure he was, he might gain the upper hand.

Jaden spent another crucial second weighing the evidence. *Is this what the clues have been hinting at all along?* "Believing with faith." Meaning he had to trust what he couldn't see. Or that what he was seeing wasn't what it appeared to be. "Living with hope." Meaning what he was hoping was true was, in fact, true and not a vain hope. "Conquering through love . . ." That one was more difficult.

Was Kayla's love strong enough for her to forgive him for what he was about to do? For taking a leap of faith that would allow Jaden to let Slurpy kill them? Would she and the others understand why? Why he'd been willing to risk their lives on a gamble?

Could they ever forgive him? Surely, if he loved Kayla, his family, his friends, he wouldn't want to hurt them? But the opposite was true too, and this piece outweighed all the others. Because of his love for them, he could conquer his fear. He could live with hope. Believe with faith.

Done arguing with himself, Jaden went for it. Pulling his arms back and putting his hands under his chest, he pushed himself off the floor. Sitting back on his knees, he slowly raised his head, keeping his eyes closed.

Reaching this place had taken Jaden a long time. To realize no man was truly an island. He was the sum of those around him, in his case, his closest friends and family. And Kayla. Hadn't they told him he couldn't take responsibility for other people's actions? Hadn't Jaden himself said they would need to work as a team if they were to succeed?

With desperate hope and blind faith, he released a long, slow breath. As he did, he let go. Of his family and friends. Of Kayla. Of his fear that harm would come to them because of him.

The effect was instantaneous. Sudden waves of anxiety rolled off Slurpy. Before Jaden uttered a word, the anxiety morphed into fury.

Jaden grinned and kept his eyes shut tight. "Kill them if you must. Or kill me. I choose not to fear you or what you might do. Those I love will understand this is what I must do. This is *my* choice, *my* decision."

The shriek had Jaden cringing. "Who told you? How did you know?"

The garbled questions almost pried Jaden's eyes open. *What color is Slurpy's face? Red to match his horrid eyes? Purple to complement his black heart?* Jaden suddenly found it difficult to breathe. Something was squeezing his chest in an iron grip. Cracking an eye open, he peeked down.

A wizened talon clamped his torso. Jaden dipped his head further and saw another leg just to the right, ending in a bleeding stump. His memory returned with blinding clarity.

Scarcely daring to believe, Jaden looked past those horrid legs. The world was just as he had left it. Only one mountain trickled lava. His friends still battled the Gaptors in the surrounding skies. And Kayla and Atu—

Big, fat tears rolled down his face when he saw them hunched over something. *They're alive!* Everything Slurpy had showed him had been an illusion. Some form of hallucination. It was time to show Slurpy who he was tangling with.

Though his arms were pinned to his sides, his hands were free. Jaden twisted his wrist. His DD was still in his hand. He would have to time this perfectly. Curling the fingers of his free hand around a single claw, Jaden flipped the switch, and his blade sizzled to life.

A vengeful joy coursed through Jaden when Gapzilla flinched. But the brute didn't let go. It would need some motivation. Jaden rotated his wrist, slicing off the tip off a claw. The screech was so loud it overwhelmed Jaden's sound suppressors, but his action had the desired effect.

Gapzilla let go. His arms abruptly freed, Jaden scrambled for a hold on the leg above him, releasing his tenuous grip on the claw. Latching on, Jaden leaned forward. The current slid off his blade, spitting and crackling, and severed the remaining talon.

Gapzilla squawked and bellowed, flipping sideways, trying to dislodge Jaden. This wasn't quite how Jaden had envisioned it, but it was close enough.

Using Gapzilla's leg as a springboard, Jaden launch himself upward. Slurpy's eyes widened as Jaden barreled into him. Jaden's free hand snatched at the medallion, his fingers looping through the chain holding it. Wrenching the medallion free, Jaden toppled back into open sky. He arced his other hand over his head. With a flick, Jaden sent a current of light racing toward Slurpy.

CHAPTER FIFTY-ONE

Kayla handed the paper with the translation over to Atu, waiting as his eyes flew over the message.

His eyes widened. "You're sure this is what we have to do?"

"Yup. I've spent years on that language. Sometimes the translation is iffy because of the tenses, but not this time. This is the perfect translation. Exactly what we should do."

"Jaden's mom wasn't too far off the mark, then."

"What do you mean?"

"What she found when she went back into that vision of hers."

"She didn't see any animals. How's that relevant?" Then Kayla understood. "Oh! It's not about the animals! It's about where she was sitting—what she was running her hands through."

"Exactly. Problem now is how do we gather all the medallions?"

Kayla's face fell. "We can't."

Atu groaned. "Right! You don't have your medallion anymore."

Kayla squared her shoulders. "There's no way we've come this far for such a stupid barrier to defeat us. There has to be a way to retrieve it. We have no choice. I know Jaden had some ideas about getting to Slurpy's world to find me that he never acted on. Perhaps we can raid those."

Kayla was so focused on their conversation that she didn't initially notice Taz's strange cry. When it registered, Kayla's eyes flew up in time to see Jaden throw a beam off his DD. Right at Slurpy!

Everything became a blur of motion. The crackling current flying through the air. The enormous Gaptor's remaining talon tumbling through the sky. Jaden falling. So fast. Too fast!

Kayla's heartbeat sped up. He would plummet into the lava bubbling below!

Before Kayla could react, Han scooped Jaden up, streaking away with him. Then light split the night sky, so bright Kayla had to turn her back. The accompanying boom rattled her teeth. Thundering echoes clattered up and down the valley.

As soon as the light dimmed, Kayla whirled, scanning the sky. The gigantic Gaptor had vanished, but a figure was cartwheeling and twisting through the sky. Kayla used her magnification lenses to verify her suspicions. *Slurpy!*

From the way he dropped. Kayla realized he was unconscious. *Is that even possible for someone with his power?* He was headed for the unforgiving rocks covering the canyon below. *Will his body break when he hits them? Will that, finally, be the end of this impossible mission?*

Kayla gasped as a rider and glider swept under Slurpy and caught him. *Traitors!* The thought flitted through her mind before she realized who it was. Iri and Rozie!

"Iri! What are you doing?"

"You really think he'll die?"

"Can't we just wait and see?" Kayla couldn't believe she had said that. How had she turned into a bloodthirsty, revenge-filled maniac?

"No." Iri's voice was firm. "I don't want what happened to him happening to any of us."

Kayla didn't think she'd heard right. She glanced at Atu, who was just as confused. "What are you talking about?"

"Clear a space down there. Rozie and I are bringing him down."

Kayla couldn't decide whether to curse Iri, clear the space, or jump on Taz to finish the job herself. That last thought made her realize she was out of control. Since when was killing people alright?

But Slurpy wasn't just a person. He was a monster. With unbelievable power. But did that mean it justified Kayla killing him before redeemed himself?

Kayla remained rooted to her spot. Atu was clearing a space as Iri had asked. "How can you be so calm about this?"

"I have a feeling Iri sees something we don't."

Kayla kept forgetting Atu's proclivity for profound statements. He didn't say much, but when he did, it carried weight. The thought of weight, its other meaning . . . Kayla suddenly remembered. "Jaden! Jaden, are you there? Tell me you and Han survived that Gaptor's death!"

"Gapzilla? Yeah, he couldn't take us down even in death."

"Gapzilla?" Kayla choked out through tears. *He's alive!*

"Cross between Gaptor, gorilla, and Godzilla."

"Who's Godzilla?" Jaden's laughter made Kayla smile.

"I forget you and the others don't share my penchant for old movies. Never mind. I'll explain another time. See you in a sec."

Iri and Rozie descended, Jaden just behind them. *Did he see what Iri did? Does he agree?* Rozie touched down. Atu ran forward to help Iri with the unconscious Slurpy. Rozie didn't leap back into the air again. Instead, she remained right behind Iri. Apparently, Rozie shared Kayla's misgivings.

A soft thud made Kayla whirl. *Jaden! Safe!* Air bubbles suddenly infused Kayla's whole body, all bursting to the surface simultaneously. She was so light she could float up into the sky and drift there forever.

With a joyful shriek, Kayla raced to him, flinging her arms around his neck. He caught her up and twirled her in circles, laughing all the while. The sound soothed her soul. The instant he set her back on her feet, she yanked him close and kissed him. Not a peck on the lips. Not a quick show of affection. A deep, passionate kiss, demanding Jaden's full attention.

She got it. Kayla smiled through her kiss, her happiness complete. Jaden's touch erased the pain, the anxiety, the desperation of the last few hours. Kayla lost herself in the kiss and this man who could invoke such bliss.

Abruptly, Jaden drew back, breathing hard. Her eyes still closed, Kayla reached for him again. One kiss wasn't enough.

Gently, Jaden wrapped his hands around her wrists, placing their hands between them. Keeping them apart. Kayla's eyes flew open. Her green gaze met his blue one, her question clear. But Jaden didn't need to answer. Every ounce of him told her he hadn't wanted to end the kiss either. He yearned for her as she did for him. Yet he held back.

"Kayla." Jaden's voice was hoarse. "I want to give you the quality time you deserve. But we will never have that time, never have that freedom, unless we finish this mission."

Kayla's face crumpled. She didn't want him to be right. But he was. With a sigh, she dropped her head. Running a thumb over his hands where they touched her wrists, she sighed again. "Let's get on with it, then."

Jaden feathered a kiss on her brow. "If it's any consolation, I have a surprise for you."

Kayla perked up. "You do?"

Jaden grinned, then released her wrists to pull something from the inside pocket of his smart suit. Kayla tried to see what, but his hands obscured it.

Jaden's grin widened as she tried to pry his fingers open. "Close your eyes and open your hand."

Obediently, Kayla did. Something cool dropped into her palm. Her eyes snapped open. Sparkly. Silver. Familiar. She gasped, and her gaze flew to Jaden. That incredible smile hadn't left his face. His wonderful, gorgeous, handsome face. The face she loved so dearly. A face she hadn't dared hope she might see again.

And he had brought her medallion back to her. She was ecstatic. "You did it! How?" Kayla hugged the medallion. "Thank you!"

"Shall we join the others now?"

CHAPTER FIFTY-TWO

His question reminded Kayla where they were. What they had to do. Who it was that waited with Iri and Atu. How could she have forgotten about Slurpy? Kayla turned and stomped to where Iri and Atu waited.

"Care to explain yourself?" There was so much hostility in her tone Kayla barely recognized her own voice.

"Whoa, ease up." Jaden took her hand and squeezed it. "Iri's on our side. We're all part of the same team."

Kayla didn't acknowledge his touch. "Why didn't you just let him fall?"

Iri leveled her gaze at Kayla. "Because that would make us no better than him. Because that might turn us into him."

Kayla tossed her hands in the air. "*What* are you babbling about?"

Iri's attention reverted to Slurpy. "He used to be like us once. Used to be someone with hopes and dreams and ambitions. But he allowed the cruelties and disappointments of life to poison him. He allowed the roots of bitterness to take hold. They bound him in chains so unbreakable they twisted him into the monster he is now."

Kayla gaped. "You're on *his* side?"

"I'm not on anyone's side. I'm simply stating what I see in him."

"What you *see* in him?"

"Yes. Here." Iri touched Slurpy's chest where his heart would be. "And here." She touched Slurpy's head. "Chunks of black, like hunks of coal."

Jaden's mouth fell open. "That's why you stopped him from falling to his death? Because you saw black pieces inside him?"

Iri's voice remained calm, a soothing stream to cool Jaden's rising anger. "We have no way of knowing for sure he would've died if he'd hit those rocks. With his power, I wasn't prepared to take a chance. I think there's a better way. A way to ensure he's never a threat again."

Jaden's laughter lacked mirth. "You think there's a way to stop him without killing him?"

Iri nodded, her face solemn. "Whether it's because of the power he wields or because it's been a part of him for so long, the bitterness has become a sickness, a malady. Like a cancer eating away at his soul, leaving tumorous pieces." Iri glanced at Atu. "A disease someone with a very special gift can cure."

Atu gaped. "You think I can heal *that?*"

"We won't know unless you try. I would suggest trying sooner rather than later. He will not stay unconscious forever." Iri stepped away, indicating Atu should take her place at Slurpy's side. "You need to remove those black cores."

"You're telling me that if I do that—and that's a big 'if'—it will get rid of the bitterness, hatred, envy, rage," Atu threw a hand in the air, "heck, whatever other negative emotions made him the monster he is? That it will make him more 'human' again?" Atu half-laughed.

Kayla shared Atu's incredulity. Jaden was on the same page too.

Iri shrugged. "Jaden, haven't you always maintained we should work as a team? This is a fulfillment of that. My ability to see the problem. Atu's ability to heal. What's the harm in trying?"

"If that's true, what part are Jaden and I playing?" Kayla shot back.

Iri flashed that smile of hers. "Oh, I believe you have your part to play. That little secret you and Atu are sharing no doubt has something to do with it."

Kayla inhaled sharply. *Iri knows we've worked out how to destroy the medallions?*

Iri focused on Jaden. "You have your part too. Whatever the usurper said to you while you were his captive, those words cling to you like a second skin."

Jaden looked like he'd been sucker-punched. "He said a lot of things."

Iri smiled. "But only one thing that would leave that aura of responsibility glimmering around you. What did he say you had to become?"

Kayla wanted to whack Iri for making Jaden looked so uncertain, so unsure of himself. But then Jaden's face cleared. "He said I had to become the Gatekeeper."

Iri nodded. "Then that's the role you have to play in this."

"But I don't know how!"

Kayla felt Jaden's exasperation. She had to admit to a level of annoyance herself. Had Iri been holding out on them? Only showing them part of what she was capable of?

"You'll figure it out," Iri said. "If anyone can, you will."

Her statement didn't convince Jaden. "I'll remind you of that when I can't work it out. I'll make you help me."

Iri smiled sweetly. "And isn't that what Kayla wanted all this time? For you to learn that we're a team? Which brings us full circle—and is a reminder we don't have a lot of time." She faced Atu again. "Well?"

Atu looked totally put out. He huffed. "I don't know how you think I can do this."

"You're our healer, aren't you? I believe Zareh gave your family this gift for this specific purpose."

Atu rolled his eyes. "Fine, I'll do my best."

Kayla was suddenly aware of the hand Jaden had wrapped around hers. For no reason she could place, she had wanted comfort. And there it was, in Jaden's touch. She squeezed his hand. His gaze swiveled her way, and he smiled, squeezing her hand back. His eyes, however, still held uncertainty.

"As Iri said, we're a team. We'll figure it out together," Kayla reassured him.

Jaden only nodded before turning his attention back to Atu. Kayla snuggled closer, putting Jaden's chest against her back. Then she settled in to watch.

Atu knelt, his eyes closed, his hands hovering a foot above Slurpy. That golden light appeared, flowing from Atu's hands, washing over Slurpy. Abruptly, Atu's face went rigid.

Kayla made to leap forward, ready to snatch Atu away from whatever Slurpy might do to him. But Jaden wrapped his arms around her, keeping her where she was.

"I think Atu found what he was looking for. I don't believe he's in any danger," Jaden whispered into her ear.

Kayla remained alert, in case Jaden was wrong. The golden light fanning over the length of Slurpy's body shrank, gathering into a tight, shimmering golden ball right over the place Iri had pointed out on Slurpy's chest.

The ball dropped lower, then sank into Slurpy. The golden light vanished when the ball was completely absorbed. A quick glance at Atu showed perspiration running down his forehead. Kayla saw no sign of distress, only Atu's fierce concentration.

A soft glow drew Kayla's gaze back to Slurpy. Ever so slowly, the golden ball was reemerging. It eked its way out. It was suddenly obvious why its exit was so laborious. It dragged something black and solid out of Slurpy's chest, the black piece secured in the center of the ball.

Kayla gaped. "He's doing it!"

Her words were barely about a shouted whisper, but the golden ball faltered. Neither Jaden nor Iri said a word, just directed meaningful stares her way. *Okay, I get it! I'll be quiet!*

The golden ball resumed its path. It took a full two minutes before the ball was completely out of Slurpy's chest, floating a few inches above Slurpy. Abruptly, Atu slapped his hands together. The snapping sound was so loud in the unnatural silence that Kayla jumped. She jumped again when the ball flashed—and vanished.

Atu fell backward, breathing heavily.

"Help him!" Iri shouted.

Jaden's arms dropped from Kayla. He was at Atu's side with a water bottle snatched from his pack before Kayla could react. She rushed over to join them, panning an analytical gaze over Atu. His face was pale. His hands trembled. No sign of fever, though.

"He needs more than water. Jaden, do you have any of those protein drinks?"

Jaden raced to his pack and returned. Bending down next to Atu, Kayla gently lifted his head and pressed the bottle to his lips. "Drink!"

Atu's mouth opened, and he swallowed as Kayla allowed small amounts of the liquid into his mouth. After a few sips, she picked up the water bottle. "Jaden, do you have more water if we need it later?"

When Jaden nodded, Kayla carefully poured the water onto a clean shirt taken from her own pack. She wiped Atu's face and the back of his neck with the cloth. Then she used the dregs remaining in the water bottle to wet Atu's hair.

Atu's eyes popped open at the same moment his mouth did. "Aargh, that's cold!"

Kayla grinned. "You needed a little refreshing."

Atu scowled. "I do all the heavy lifting, and you give me grief."

Chuckles all around. Kayla offered him the protein drink. "I think you need more of this before you attempt the next one."

Atu groaned, and he flopped a hand over his eyes. "Don't remind me."

"Iri, your attention here."

Rozie's interruption was unexpected. Kayla and Jaden turned with Iri. Kayla's blood curdled. Slurpy was moving!

CHAPTER FIFTY-THREE

Iri was closest. She didn't stop to think, just snatched up a rock and bashed it into Slurpy's head. It made a sickening crunch, and Slurpy slumped. *Did I hit him too hard? Oh no, have I killed him?*

About to lean forward to put a hand under his nose, Rozie's darted between Iri and Slurpy. "He's still alive. I can hear him breathing. But it's not deep like it was before."

"He's not unconscious!" Kayla yelled. "Hit him again—on the jaw!"

Iri screamed, striking Slurpy again. She hadn't hit him too hard. It hadn't been hard enough. This time she put her weight behind the blow.

There was no artifice to Slurpy's slump this time. Just to be sure, Iri checked with Rozie. "Is he out?"

"Yes."

"Splendid!" Iri glanced at Atu. The musty scent of fatigue still rolled off him. Not as sharp as before, but unmistakably there. "I know you're tired, but do you think you can pull it together to finish this? I really don't want to have to bash him a third time."

Atu's smile was weary. "I suppose I can relieve you of that burden."

Kayla helped Atu sit up. She glanced at Iri. "I think your senses are better than my medical judgment here. How exhausted is he?"

Iri studied Atu. The lavender hues of fatigue were fading quickly, as was the musty odor. "He's on the mend." She glanced at Slurpy. "If we can give Atu another five minutes, it'll help."

Jaden nodded emphatically. "I'm not sure we have five minutes. The blast that killed his Gaptor was impressive, but it only knocked Slurpy out for about ten minutes. No offense, Iri, but I'm not sure how long your blow will keep him under."

Atu had had enough. "I'm sitting right here. If anyone knows what I'm capable of, it's me. I'll take another minute, then attack the next one."

None of them dared disagree, but Kayla made him eat the dried fruit she retrieved from her pack. Iri, sneaking glances his way, saw the lavender tones wink out, replaced by neon yellow. If nothing else, Atu was determined to succeed. That she could see colors on him when she typically couldn't, made her worry though. Iri wasn't sure it was even a minute before Atu knelt next to Slurpy again.

"Last one," was all he said as he closed his eyes and focused.

This time, the golden light didn't stretch out along Slurpy's body. It formed a smaller glow around Slurpy's head. Then, as before, it shrank into that shimmering, golden ball.

This black spot was smaller than the last. Hopefully, removing it would be less difficult. Atu's strain removing the last one had almost made her stop him.

Anxiously, Iri noted Atu's rising stress. The lavender hues had returned. Iri couldn't be certain, but it seemed this ball was taking longer to sink into Slurpy. A horrible suspicion assailed her. *Is Slurpy waking up?* She glanced at Rozie, whose eyes were honed on Slurpy.

Rozie sensed her attention and darted a quick glance her way. Iri mimed breathing. Rozie shook her head. *Does that mean Rozie doesn't know? Or that nothing's changed?* Iri mentally shook herself. *Stupid question. If anything changes, Rozie won't hesitate to tell us. So why is the ball sinking so slowly? Is Atu more exhausted than I can tell?*

The lavender hue hadn't changed. The musty odor was at about the same level. It was something else. Iri studied Slurpy again. Then clarity! This piece was somehow entwined with part of Slurpy's brain.

What she had taken to be a few holes were actually spaces where Slurpy's brain had meshed with the black.

Iri wanted to throw up. While this piece might have been smaller than the last, retrieving it and healing the aftermath would be a far more intricate endeavor. Slowly, so as not to disturb Atu, she sidled over to Jaden and Kayla, motioning for them to follow her.

When they had removed themselves a safe distance, Iri hastily explained. Turning to Kayla, she said, "Is there anything we can do to give him more energy?"

"Short of giving him an adrenaline shot, which we don't have, I can't think of anything. Besides, when I just whispered earlier, he paused. What do you think he'll do if we touch him?"

Iri sighed. "Nothing we can do then?"

Kayla shook her head. "Not that I can think of."

"Me either," Jaden added.

Quietly, they crept back. Perspiration beaded on Iri's forehead, then trickled down as Atu worked far longer than he should. The golden ball finally submerged in Slurpy's brain, but Atu's lavender tones had darkened. They were pale violet. *Not good.*

Trying to keep her apprehension at bay, Iri noticed the rising tension in Jaden and Kayla. She wished she had said nothing. But it was too late now. She had had to take the chance Kayla might have another way to boost Atu's health. Apparently, Atu was the only one capable of miracles.

A miracle it was when the golden light suddenly shimmered on the surface of Slurpy's skin again. Ever so slowly, the ball retracted from his skull. Iri darted glances between the ball and Atu. Pale violet had turned to dark violet. If he didn't hurry, he would pass out before the ball was completely removed. *If that happens, will the black piece sink back in?*

Seconds ticked by. A minute. Ninety seconds. At almost two minutes, the golden ball popped free. Atu clapped his hands together. The sound was feeble. The ball contracted but didn't disappear. The colors around Atu were slate gray now. Iri raced toward him before he opened his mouth.

"Help."

Jaden and Kayla rushed forward, looking confused. But Iri was already there. She understood what Atu meant. Leaning down carefully so she didn't touch Atu anywhere else, she encased the back of Atu's hands with her own. Using her thumbs and little fingers, she supported Atu's hands, sliding her middle fingers between his to brace them. Then, careful to ensure her fingers didn't touch his palms, she slapped Atu's hands together.

Thwap! Iri wasn't sure whether the sound or action did it. The golden ball flashed and vanished. The black piece disappeared. Iri was still crouched around Atu when he went limp in her arms.

"Atu!" Her voice rose with her panic as Atu collapsed sideways. She noticed the charcoal tones swamping him. Covering him. Claiming him! Iri jolted when Kayla shoved her aside.

"Move!"

Iri scrabbled backward on all fours, getting out the way. Kayla knelt next to Atu, listening for breathing, tilting his chin back. Tears blurred Iri's eyes.

"Jaden, I need help!" Kayla barked. "Bring that wet cloth."

Iri sat frozen, too stunned to move. She stared at Kayla. Blinked. Then Jaden was there. Kayla directed Jaden to wipe the cloth over Atu's forehead. Kayla moved to Atu's feet and lifted them, holding them about twelve inches off the ground.

Iri remained frozen. *Why did I think this would work? Did I just kill Atu?* Iri heard her own ragged breathing.

"Iri!"

The sound caught and held. Iri turned her head, seeking the source.

"Iri!" Kayla's voice. "Yes, that's right. Look at me. Nod if you can hear me."

Iri nodded.

"He's okay. Probably exhaustion that made him pass out. He'll be back with us in—" Kayla broke off as Atu moaned. "Hello, soldier! We lost you for a moment there." Atu tried moving. "No, no, just stay where you are." Kayla flicked her chin at Jaden, and he obligingly placed firm hands on Atu's shoulders, keeping him down.

"Easy, dude." Jaden smiled.

Atu grimaced. "Okay, I get it. Can I have some water?"

"Iri, can you get that?"

It dawned on Iri that Kayla had asked her to do something. That Atu was not dead. Or dying. She leaped up. "Yes!"

Iri bent to put the water to Atu's lips, but his hands arrested hers. Iri's eyes darted to his.

His brown eyes were steady as they gazed back. Speaking softly so the others couldn't hear, Atu said, "It wasn't your fault."

Iri averted her gaze. "You could've died."

Atu's hand brought her chin around so she faced him again. "But I didn't. Your plan worked. We didn't have to blot our souls to save him."

"That's what you meant when you said we'd become like him?" Kayla's voice behind her had Iri tensing. *How much had Kayla heard?*

Oblivious to Iri's lack of an answer, Kayla continued her musings. "Because if we let Slurpy die, if we killed him, our darker emotions would've had a place to take hold? And if they did, we could've become just as twisted as he was?"

This time, Iri answered. "Yes. For some people, the slope is a lot more slippery. And who knows how slick one's path is until you're so far down the slope you can't stop?"

Nodding thoughtfully, Kayla glanced back at Slurpy. He was still unconscious.

Jaden said what they were all thinking. "We'd better figure out what to do in case Iri's plan doesn't work. In case he's still a monster with demons driving him instead of a more humane version of himself, difficult as that might be to believe after seeing Atu extract those pieces."

Using every rope in their packs, they trussed Slurpy up, but he'd probably just snap the bindings with his power. So, as an added precaution, they aerial connected with their gliders and waited overhead.

They didn't have long to wait. When Slurpy came to, it wasn't with roaring and power. Rather, it was a whimper. His eyes rolled violently, studying his surroundings. Then swept up to where they hovered. Then careened further afield to the battle between Gaptors and gliders, still raging. He began screeching. "What have you done? Why did you take it?"

The voyagers glanced at one another. Was he talking about the pieces Atu removed?

Slurpy continued ranting. "It's gone! All gone! How can I face them now? I won't survive. They won't obey me. They'll turn on me." On and on he rambled, his words nonsensical.

"You think he's still speaking about the pieces Atu took out of him?" Jaden asked.

Kayla and Atu shrugged, but Iri was deciphering colors and scents. Despair. Regret. Guilt. Fear. Oranges and purples clashing so vividly they hid the man beneath. "I could be wrong, but I think he's sorry he created the Gaptors."

"You're not serious?" Kayla half-laughed.

Iri nodded. "More than that, I think he's afraid." The oranges tones were taking over, turning coral and suppressing the purple.

Slurpy was squirming in his bonds. His eyes darted wildly from side to side. "They have me. I can't do it. They won't let me live. Without my power, I am nothing."

Jaden flinched. "Is he saying what I think he is?"

Abruptly, the rich coral hues were snuffed out, replaced by violet streaks quickly morphing to mulberry. "Something's happening."

"What?" Jaden's voice reeked of alarm.

"I don't know. I'm not sure. He's . . . shrinking."

"Iri, are we in danger?"

Jaden's barked question made Iri jump. Her gaze bounced back to Jaden. "No, I don't . . . I don't think so. I've never seen anything like this. But no, I believe it's the opposite of dangerous."

"Are my eyes failing me, or does Slurpy seem . . . less?" Kayla sounded like she couldn't believe she had said the words.

They stared at Slurpy. Iri couldn't take her eyes off the colors swamping him. They were condensing, becoming more intense, and they formed a more concentrated aura around Slurpy.

Jaden's yell startled them all. "He's fading!"

"Yes, he is!" Atu exclaimed.

Kayla whispered, "He's not solid anymore!"

Iri squinted, trying to make the colors go away so she could see what the others did. But they wouldn't go. They became stronger, like clouds going from wispy, opaque cirrus to solid, dense thunderclouds. Except, instead of growing, the colors were contracting. She had been right. Slurpy *was* shrinking!

"I don't want to live if I can't be in control. I won't!" Slurpy's mutterings remained incoherent, his voice fainter with each word. "They can't make me go back. I refuse. I won't live if I don't have my power."

The last sentence ended on a wail. The colors compacted further, and the wail dwindled, then faded to nothing. A black flash! Iri stumbled away, staring. Nothing remained. Slurpy was gone.

CHAPTER FIFTY-FOUR

Kayla wasn't sure what to believe. "Did he fade back to his own world? Or fade away?"

"As in fade away and die?" Jaden asked.

Kayla shrugged. "How would I know?" She glanced at Iri. "What's wrong with you?"

"That black flash—it was . . ."

"What black flash?"

Iri stared at them. "None of you saw a black flash right before Slurpy disappeared?" Three nods. "It's real, then. If I was the only one who saw it, it was my gift. Not something he generated."

Kayla frowned. "You're sounding as addled as he did. Care to explain? Maybe with full sentences?" Iri's sudden smile was not what Kayla expected.

Iri hopped foot to foot. She threw her hands in the air, then did a happy dance and sang, "He's gone! Truly gone! Dead! And not because of anything we did!"

Kayla grinned at Jaden's quirked eyebrow, but he was right. They needed confirmation. "Are you sure about that?"

"I am!" Iri squealed, still leaping about like a magic bean.

Jaden tried. "Iri, could you stop a moment and explain?"

Iri paused, noticing the others weren't joining her in her exuberant celebration. "I only ever see that black flash when someone dies suddenly."

"But how did he die?" Aware of everyone else's shock, Atu hurried to add, "Not that I'm sad he's gone."

Iri finally stopped dancing. Her eyes rolled up to the left, recalling events that had only taken seconds. "I believe he surrendered his will to live."

Jaden guffawed. "Slurpy? Giving up? I don't think so!"

Iri returned his ridicule with a glare. "And how would you know? Did you see the despair on him? The fear?"

Jaden stopped laughing. "Sorry. It just sounded so preposterous. I don't doubt your abilities."

Kayla stepped in before Jaden put his foot in his mouth again. "I think what Jaden meant was we still don't understand. Can you elaborate?"

"Sure. Think about the words he spoke. He regretted something. I think that was creating the Gaptors. I think the only reason they obeyed him was because of his power. And I believe when Atu removed those black pieces, Slurpy's power went with them. Slurpy's rantings were all about not having control if he had no power. And his last words were something like, 'If I don't have power, I won't live.'"

Kayla replayed what she had heard. "Yup. I believe you're right. He chose death rather than living without his power."

"I disagree." Atu's rebuttal was mild. He studied Iri. "Were you able to see Slurpy past your gift?"

"No."

"If you had, you would've seen how he faded away. Not only faded, but *aged*. I agree with Jaden's observation—Slurpy didn't give up. Without his power, he could no longer sustain his considerable age. That's what killed him."

Iri shrugged. "Does it really matter? He's gone, and we don't have to deal with him anymore."

"He's really gone?" Kayla still couldn't believe it.

"Yes," Iri confirmed, "he really is."

Markov's voice cut over the comm, ice dousing their emerging jubilation. "If you're done jawing down there, we could use some help up here!"

The tension in his voice rocked Kayla to her core. *How did we forget there's a battle going on?* They had been so absorbed in dealing with Slurpy they'd abandoned their friends.

"On our way," Jaden replied.

"Hurry!" Markov urged.

Jaden shouted to Han, flying overhead. "Ready to take on some Gaptors?" He glanced at Kayla. "Are you and Taz joining us? You have your medallion now."

The mention of her medallion reminded Kayla she had news of her own. "Oh, yes! Yes, oh, um, there something was, I mean . . ." Kayla stopped, the words still jumbled in her mind. *Ziggety! Get it together, girl!*

"Having a little trouble there?"

As he took her hand, Jaden's grin was wicked. Kayla rolled her eyes. "What I meant to say was we can eradicate the Gaptors."

Jaden's grin vanished. "What?"

"You heard right." A harrowing scream echoed over the comm, reminding Kayla time was precious. "I'll explain later. Short version is those leather strips joined into that large piece over there - then a magic wand wrote instructions on it." It sounded inconceivable, and Kayla wanted to giggle at Jaden's gaping mouth, but another scream pierced the comm. "What I need right now is all the medallions!"

"You do know that without them our riders are vulnerable?"

Kayla smiled sweetly. "You're the logistics man. I'm sure you'll think of something."

Jaden growled. "You know I hate being in charge!"

"I do. But getting the medallions will rid us of those Gaptors more effectively than fighting them. They're also our best chance of winning with the odds stacked against us."

"Fine. I'll figure something out." Jaden crushed Kayla to him, snatching one last, brief, passionate kiss. He drew back, leaving Kayla's head spinning. "Stay alive!" Then he raced to the edge of the mountain and leaped. Han caught him and wheeled toward the raging battle.

Kayla watched them leave, her hand on her chest, still trying to find her breath. "You too." Jaden acknowledged only with a hand wave before disappearing into the maelstrom of war. Iri and Rozie followed him. Kayla prayed they would survive.

Now, she had business of her own to attend to. "Atu, you read the instructions. We need a place to collect those medallions. Any suggestions?"

"How about that nice little bowl carved out of the mountain?" Atu pointed at the spot the explosion had left them standing in.

Kayla studied it. The indentation was large enough so riders could fly past and drop their medallions into the bowl without having to dismount. "Perfect! I'll start clearing a section here—"

She broke off so abruptly, Atu whirled, his DD blazing. His mouth dropped open. They both stared at the flat piece of ground used only minutes before to piece the leather strips together.

The single large piece of leather was still there. But its markings were obscured by dozens upon dozens of medallions materializing out of thin air. The medallions solidified and dropped onto the leather with soft thuds.

Kayla gawked at Atu, who was staring back at her, dazed. His mouth opened and closed a few times before he got the words out. "Where are they coming from?"

Shrugging, Kayla activated her comm. "Jaden, do you still have your medallion?"

A moment's silence, then Jaden's terse response. "A little busy here. Yes. Why?"

"This might sound crazy, but medallions are appearing out of nowhere. Atu sees them, so I'm not imagining things."

"You're not making sense."

"It's like the medallions are manifesting from somewhere else. Squeezing themselves through a hidden dimension from wherever they were and appearing here. It's bizarre. And if you have your medallion, I don't know where they're coming from. Why are they just showing up like this?" Jaden was silent for so long Kayla tensed. "Jaden?"

"Yeah, here. Hold on."

Kayla glanced at Atu, staring at the medallions again. They drew her gaze too, just popping into existence as they were. The thought sparked a memory, and she suddenly understood. "Oh, never mind! I know what's happening."

"What?" The question burst from Atu and Jaden simultaneously.

Kayla grinned. She had the answer before Jaden. "Zareh told us the medallions would find their way to their owners. I think these medallions don't have owners anymore. I'm positive they're from the cache at Sven's. The ones still left in that box you stole from the Gaptor camp."

"But how?" Jaden sounded out of breath.

Kayla wished she was up there with him, watching his back. But not answering would only distract him. "This is where they were needed, so this is where they're appearing. The same way Zareh appears of out nowhere."

"One less thing to worry about," came Jaden's tight response. "Get ready for more. Riders and medallions incoming."

Mystified, Kayla began stacking the medallions, still plopping onto the leather piece. She hadn't heard Jaden giving any orders over the comm. Then again, she hadn't been paying attention. But as she looked toward the other mountain, she made out a steady stream of gliders coming their way.

Something else occurred to her. "Atu, can we mark that bowl so they know where to drop their medallions? It's so dark they might not see it."

Atu's teeth glinted in the dim light. "Done and done." With a snap, twin bars of light illuminated the space. Atu moved quickly, placing the glow sticks on two sides of the bowl. Hurrying, he snapped two more, placing them on the remaining two sides so the four lights formed a roughly rectangular barrier around the hole.

Flashing a thumbs-up at Atu, Kayla spoke into her comm. "Incoming riders, can you hear me?" Numerous replies on top of one another. "Excellent! Drop your medallions into the area between the lights. Can you see them?"

A dozen or more replies in the affirmative. Then the gliders and their riders were upon them, and medallions rained down. Kayla and Atu scurried out of the way. As the gliders passed on, Kayla noticed them heading for a mountain on the opposite side of the Gaptor battle.

Curious, she engaged her night vision lenses. What did Jaden come up with?

CHAPTER FIFTY-FIVE

It was simple, actually. While Jaden and the remaining riders kept the Gaptors occupied, small groups rotated out of the battle and dropped their medallions. Once their riders relinquished their medallions, the gliders delivered them to the far mountain before circling back to join the battle. Either the Gaptors didn't notice or didn't care more and more gliders without riders were fighting against them.

Kayla snapped off her goggles and returned to her task. When she looked up again a while later, Jaden was leading the final group toward them. And it *was* the final group. From what she could tell, all the gliders remaining in the battle were riderless.

Doubly pleased she hadn't tarried after noticing the rotation Jaden had set up, Kayla surveyed their work. Everything was ready. As soon as they had the last medallions, carrying out the instructions wouldn't take long.

"Jaden, Iri, we'll need you down here to finish this," Kayla advised via the comm.

"I figured as much. Iri and I will be the last two coming through," Jaden replied.

The group swung past, dropping medallions before the gliders carried their riders to safety. Iri and Jaden hung back until the group had left. Then they dismounted, landing next to Kayla and Atu with practiced accuracy.

Glancing skyward, Kayla noted their gliders overhead. They remained there, protecting their voyagers from any threats the skies might bring. She called to Taz, pointing as she did so. "You might want to make sure you aren't directly under that pile!"

Taz surveyed the medallions on the leather strip. She nodded, and their gliders rearranged themselves, forming a perimeter around their voyagers without being in the line of fire. Kayla snorted.

"What?" Jaden's eyes sparkled in the reflected light from the glow sticks.

"Nothing. Just me being silly. Thinking the gliders wouldn't be in the line of fire—not sure whether it's a pun or literal . . ." Kayla saw his confusion. "Never mind. Let's finish this."

Once more, Kayla bent forward over the newly reformed piece of leather. "Jaden, Iri, please help Atu bring me the remaining medallions."

They obliged. The others took care not to disturb her work when adding the new medallions. Kayla nimbly positioned the medallions on the piece of leather according to its instructions. Even though she was going as fast as she could, getting the placement of the pieces correct took time. Time filled with the cries of injured gliders and Taz's leashed misery over the fate of her friends.

Kayla reached for another medallion, but there wasn't one. Glancing up, she saw the others gathered around, gazing at the carefully stacked pile.

Jaden was the first to comment. "I should've guessed." His smile was wry, making those little crinkles around his eyes that Kayla loved.

"Yup. I suppose we could've all guessed—then again, how many times do we have to repeat the pattern?"

"One more," Iri murmured. "Zareh said our medallions were the key."

"It would've been more precise to say the *shape* of our medallions was the key," Atu observed.

The four of them stared at the pile, perfectly arranged on the leather in the familiar octagonal shape.

Kayla cocked her head. "Without this piece of leather, though, and the guidelines that wand drew, we wouldn't have known how large to make the medallion . . . pyramid?"

"Yeah, I'd call it that," Jaden agreed.

For it did look like a pyramid. With the outer medallions starting along the lines on the leather, Kayla had filled in the center and then kept spiraling the medallions upward, each exactly on the halfway mark of the last per the instructions. The distinct pattern made it obvious that four medallions were missing.

"Shall we?" Kayla asked.

Jaden hesitated. "Do we have to do this in any particular order?"

"No, just as long as we form the rectangle, it doesn't matter whose medallion goes where."

Removing his medallion from his wrist pouch, Jaden stared at it. "I'm almost reluctant to part with it."

"Stop wasting time! Act!" Taz's commands startled them. Kayla glanced up at her glider. "My people are dying while you tarry!"

"Sorry!" Hurriedly, Kayla placed her medallion on the pile and motioned for Iri and Atu should do the same. Jaden's was the last, his medallion forming the final piece in the rectangle, ready to support the second-to-last item that went on the pile.

Carefully, Kayla carefully balanced Awena's book on the four supporting medallions. Breathing a relieved sigh when the pile didn't fall over, Kayla glanced at Iri. "I need my relic stone back."

"Oh, sorry!" Iri snatched the ring off her finger and handed it to Kayla.

"Thanks." Kayla didn't put her ring on. Instead, she addressed Jaden. "See those little dots on either side of the pyramid?" Jaden nodded. "That's where our relic stones go. I'll do this dot, and you do that one."

"Are you sure?"

Kayla grinned at Jaden's bereft expression. "Here I thought only girls got attached to their jewelry."

"It's not jewelry. It's a weapon! No surprise I'm attached to it."

"Either way, let's do this." Kayla spared another glance at their gliders hovering overhead. "Our friends up there are getting more antsy by the second."

Sighing, Jaden pulled his ring from his finger and placed it on his dot.

Kayla placed her ring on her dot. "Now for the final piece. I would suggest you all take a step back. I'm not entirely sure what will happen, but Ruby's key is the trigger."

"Really, that too? We have to surrender everything?"

Jaden was so distraught, Kayla would've laughed if the situation weren't so desperate. "Not everything. This is the last piece for whatever it is Zareh had in mind for the medallions."

"Banish the Gaptors." Atu's quiet statement only highlighted the huge impact this tiny action would have.

"Here goes nothing." Kayla placed her hand above the medallion pyramid, gripping the key tightly. She angled it so the ends pointed directly at the relic stones on the outer edges of the pile. Holding her breath, she placed the key on the book.

When the key glowed white-hot, Kayla jumped back. Hissing, it burned its way through the book and burrowed down into the pile of medallions, melting all the way down to the leather piece. The instant the key touched it, a fierce wind gusted up through the hole left behind.

The wind didn't dissipate. It spun around the medallions, gathering momentum. One, then two medallions were caught by the wind. In a bright flash, the rest followed, the wind licking the medallions up in a line that spiraled into the heart of the vortex. The wind intensified, giving voice to its velocity with an otherworldly howl.

Kayla shivered. Still, she couldn't take her eyes off the swirling mass. Glints of pearly, shimmering white and sparkly obsidian on the outer edges were the only sign the raging wind still held the medallions within. Then even those disappeared as dazzling light blasted through the center of the funnel. With a wailing shriek, the wind morphed into a brilliant line streaking straight up.

The four voyagers watched, awed, as the streak darted toward their gliders, then veered away, swerving this way and that, searching, searching, searching.

When the streak of light found the first Gaptor, the light wrapped around it, forming a bubble of pure energy. The bubble popped. Audibly. The streak reappeared and speared onward.

After the brilliance of the light, it was difficult to see. Kayla waited impatiently for her eyes to adjust. No sign of the Gaptor remained. Kayla's eyes tracked back to the streak.

Finding another straggling Gaptor, it wrapped itself around the monster. Once again, when the bubble popped, there was no trace of the Gaptor. The light darted toward a group and wrapped around them, like it was no more challenging than a single monster.

The bubble formed, burst, and thinned into a ribbon again, leaving empty sky. Silent, swift, fatal, the streak flowed from one group of Gaptors to the next, dismissing them all with the same ambivalent ease.

"Do you think it's killing them or just sending them back to Zareh's world?" Atu breathed.

Jaden grunted. "We've always associated their deaths with the light and sound the relic stones or DDs generated. This streak isn't doing either." He glanced at Iri. "Can you tell if they're dying?"

Iri shook her head. "No. The Gaptors are there before the light gets to them, and then they're gone. There's no trace of color that might confirm their fate. And it's too far for me to smell anything."

Kayla squealed. "Look!"

They did. The streak flared golden, splitting into countless ribbons. The ribbons weaved through the entire battlefield and grew impossibly brighter. Not even Sven's goggles could block out the light. The voyagers turned their heads. Popping sounded all over the sky, like hail on a tin roof, drumming to a crescendo. Then silence. Darkness. And all was still.

CHAPTER FIFTY-SIX

A single ray of light lanced the sky, making Jaden think the deadly ribbon had returned. A second ray joined the first. Then a third, and a fourth, and then too many to count, bursting forth, stunning and unique. Painting the sky gold and tangerine and lavender. Surprised, Jaden realized what he was watching. Sunrise.

Dawn had broken. Jaden stared at the sky. Not a single Gaptor against that glorious backdrop. Gliders wheeled about, chittering excitedly. Jaden knew better than to rely on his own eyes. "Han, are the Gaptors really all gone? What are the gliders saying?"

Han shot him a familiar, toothy grin. "Yes, the Gaptors are truly gone." He listened to the surrounding twittering, then interpreted. "The Legion never thought they would see the day where their obligation to this world would end. But you did it—you and Kayla and the others." Han stopped, listened again, and then laughed out loud. "They're looking forward to going home after being away for so long. They're already planning the celebration party."

Boom! The roaring sound crashed against the surrounding mountains, reverberating up and down the valleys between, generating more noise and shaking the ground. Jaden glanced up at the source—far to his right, but unmistakable. Another ring had opened.

A gate. He'd only seen one once before, when Slurpy sent his army through.

His nerves on edge, Jaden leaped back when Zareh flashed into existence beside him. Jaden wasn't sure where to look—at the giant hole in the sky or at Zareh, the annoying gnat. His gaze settled on Zareh. "What are you doing here?"

"Your mission, unfinished is. Achieved ultimate victory, you have not."

"What do you mean? Slurpy's gone. We destroyed the Gaptors."

Zareh only pointed at the sky. Jaden turned, muttering. But the sound cut off when he saw an all-too-familiar blackness creeping around the rim of light defining the circumference of the circle. Oozing past the radiant barrier and leaching into his world. Bringing death with it. Jaden held his breath, expecting Gaptors to pour through.

"Become the Gatekeeper, you must, if forever your world to save you are. Restore this world, you must. Sealer of the breach, be."

Jaden glared at Zareh. "Really? After everything, you spout more nonsense?"

"Nonsense, it is not. Already within your grasp, the answers are. Your mission, complete! When gone we are, understand, you will."

"Gone?"

"Leave the gliders in this world, believe you I would?"

Jaden froze. "Han's leaving?"

"Take up his own mantle, he must. The princess's consort, officially become."

He was losing Han? Jaden squeezed the words past the lump in his throat. "And when you say 'princess,' you mean Taz?"

"Referring to who else would I be? Yearn for their princess, her people do. Return she must, now that her role here fulfilled she has."

Jaden couldn't stop the chuckle, garnering a sharp stare from Zareh.

"Funny, it is not."

"Oh, but it is. Do you think you can make Taz do anything she doesn't want to?"

It was Zareh's turn to laugh. That annoying chittering sound. "Know her well enough, you do not. Her duty above all else, she places."

Things suddenly weren't so funny anymore. Jaden *did* know Taz. Zareh was right. All Jaden had to do was think about the way Taz had protected Kayla. *Kayla! It will devastate her when she realizes Taz is leaving.*

Jaden realized Zareh was studying him, curiosity coating his beady little eyes. "What?"

"Understand, she will. Fret not. Your goodbyes, say. Leave we must, before taint your world irrevocably the usurper's device does. For your service, thank you, we do. Once beyond sight we are, close the gate, you must!"

Jaden's gaze flitted back toward the gate when Zareh mentioned Slurpy's device. Expecting Gaptors, he was relieved to find none. But the blackness oozing from the gate was spreading across the sky. A dark stain, oily and foul, marring the beauty of the sunrise. "Is that the same thing that made the animals here start changing?" No reply. Jaden turned. There was no sign of Zareh. "Ugh, how am I supposed to close the gate, you nitwit? Couldn't you just tell me?"

Kayla appeared at his side. "Was that Zareh?"

"Yes. Where've you been?"

"Checking on the medallion pile."

"And?"

"Everything's gone."

"Did you really expect that wind would leave anything?"

"I suppose not. I was hoping, though . . ."

Jaden grinned. "That it might've spared your medallion?" Kayla nodded. "Now who's the one getting sentimental about their jewelry?"

Finally, Kayla smiled. It lit Jaden's world and brought joy to a desperate situation. Jaden sighed.

Kayla eyed him. "What's wrong?"

"We have to figure out how I'm supposed to close that gate. The last time I came into contact with that thing, I didn't do so well." Jaden scowled. "It was a rather shocking experience."

Kayla's voice was calm, but Jaden saw her apprehension. "That's not all. What else aren't you telling me?"

Jaden sighed again, then took her hands in his, facing her squarely. "Our gliders are leaving. Going back to their world."

Kayla's face was a palette of varying emotions. Shock. Disbelief. Anger. And finally, sorrow. "I suppose it was inevitable."

Her voice was so small. Jaden pulled her into his arms, embracing her, wanting to ease the hurt. "I can't remember life without them," Jaden murmured into her hair.

Tears wetting her face, Kayla nodded, pressing herself into his embrace, her own arms wrapping around him.

"What's wrong with you two? You look like we lost instead of won," Atu commented.

"It's not the quest. It's something . . . personal," Iri noted, joining them.

Jaden shook his head at Iri, struggling to tell them what they needed to know. He didn't let Kayla go. "You could say that. Personal to all of us. Our gliders are going home."

Atu frowned. "Home?"

Jaden clarified. "Back to their world."

Iri overshadowed Atu's crestfallen expression by crashing to her knees. Giving Jaden a last tight squeeze, Kayla extricated herself from his arms. She hurried to Iri's side, crouching next to her and cradling her friend. Iri's shoulders shook. She glanced up at Kayla with a tear-stained face.

"I was just getting over Tinks. Now I'm losing Rozie too?" Sobs rocked her again, enough to break Kayla's own resolve.

Jaden surveyed the distraught girls, his own grip on his sorrow wavering. *We can't all lose it! Or can we? If we don't grieve now, then when?* Much as he wanted to give in to his own heartache, he couldn't. He glanced at the gate again. The black patch was growing at a steady rate. Not huge, still confined to the area directly around the gate. *But if it's caught in the jet stream, will it spread beyond containment?*

Soft plops near them made Jaden turn. He had been so engrossed in his own thoughts he hadn't noticed their gliders coming in to land.

"You already know what we've come to tell you?" Taz's voice was soft. Nothing like her usual imperious tones.

"You're really a princess?" Jaden asked, more to stave off the avalanche of emotion threatening to bury him than because he didn't know.

"I am."

"Not just a princess. The future queen," Han added, as though they should be aware.

Jaden raised an eyebrow. "And that makes a difference?"

Taz shot Han an irate glance. "It's why we can't stay. If there was someone else to lead my people, perhaps they might've permitted me to stay. But since I am the only one . . ."

"They might have allowed you to stay?"

Kayla sounded so hopeful, Jaden almost hated Taz for giving Kayla false hope. "Taz, don't lead us on. You're not staying. Nor is Han. Or any of the others."

Taz deflated. "I wasn't trying to mislead you. From the moment we arrived, I hoped there might be a way for us to stay in contact. That when this ended, we might continue to spend time together. That the end of the quest wouldn't be the end of our friendship."

"But it's not to be, is it?" Jaden's tone was clipped.

"No." Taz sighed, her massive wings drooping. "Zareh said that once you close the gate, all contact between our world and yours will be forever severed. There will be no way our worlds can interact ever again. It's the only way to ensure the safety of your world."

Taz's forlorn expression had Jaden backing off. The humans weren't the only ones devastated by the news. Swallowing his grief, Jaden glanced at Han. "I guess that means you get to be king?"

Han's muted laughter rumbled across the mountainside. "I suppose I do." He stopped laughing and glanced at Taz. "That's if Taz will have me."

Taz batted him with a wing. "Who else could ever take your place?"

Jaden grinned. "Dude, if that's her way of showing affection, then perhaps you might be better off with someone else."

Taz turned stony eyes on him. "That's not amusing."

This time, Jaden wasn't the only one laughing, even though tears stained their faces.

Kayla went to Taz and wrapped her arms around her glider's neck. "I will miss you—terribly." She leaned closer, her lips moving but her words too soft for any of the rest of them to hear.

It was time he said his own farewells. He placed a hand on Han's shoulder. Han's neck dipped, and Jaden rubbed the soft ridge near his ear. "Who will do this for you once you're back home?"

"With any luck, Taz."

Han's unexpected response had Jaden chuckling. "I hope so." Jaden wound his arms around Han's neck. "I don't know if I remember how to live without you."

"You will."

Han's voice was gruff. He wrapped a wing around Jaden's back. Jaden nuzzled his face against Han's neck. "It won't be easy. Words can't express how much I'll miss you." Jaden's voice broke. He had to try a few times to get the rest of the words out. "Thank you for always having my back. For making sure we reached the finish line. For risking your neck for our world."

A rumble from Han that Jaden had never heard before. He raised his head, searching Han's face. Jaden found his own sorrow etched there. The sound came again, and Jaden noticed Han's throat bobbing.

"Sorry, clearing my throat." Han's voice was even rougher now. He straightened his shoulders. "It was an honor to share this quest with you."

"Likewise," Jaden answered, his own voice shaky.

Han cocked his head. "Zareh is summoning us. Take care, Jaden Jameson! I will never forget you." Han removed his wing, stepped back, and launched himself skyward.

"Nor I you!" Jaden yelled.

His vision blurred. Jaden swiped a hand across his eyes. He couldn't—wouldn't—miss their last flight. His eyes remained glued on Han, now joined by Taz, Aren, and Rozie. Jaden felt Kayla's comforting hand slip into his own.

Hand in hand, they watched their gliders join the Legion, then take their place in front, along with Pallaton. The gliders circled the area once. Han dipped his wing in a final salute. Then the gliders were flying away. Not streaking away and gone in an instant, like the first time Jaden and Kayla met them. Slowly, as though they too were savoring every minute of the sight of their voyagers.

Their gliders grew smaller and smaller and became indistinguishable from the others until the entire group was just a tiny pinprick in the azure sky. Then the sky was empty. Between one blink and the next, their gliders vanished.

Jaden's heart cracked in two. He glanced at Kayla. She clutched Iri's hand, with the one that wasn't holding Jaden's and Iri's other hand gripped Atu's. The four of them. Together. Supporting one another. Still a team, even though they would never see their other halves again.

A shadow flitted over the group, then thickened and solidified. Jaden glanced up. Horror soaked him.

The poisonous cloud blotted the sun out. What had been a contained pool of blackness oozing around the gate now gushed out in great black waves, rolling into their world.

CHAPTER FIFTY-SEVEN

Jaden heard Kayla's sharp intake of breath.

"It's growing. What do you think it is?"

"A failsafe Slurpy left in place in case he never made it back to his bunker—where he could've deactivated it."

Kayla's green eyes were wild, ocean waves worked into a froth by a storm. "Unless we close the gate, that poison will continue leaking into our world until it destroys our whole planet!"

"I guess Slurpy decided if he couldn't have it, neither could we," Jaden muttered. "Vindictive man." He gazed at the rapidly expanding toxic pool. "Yes, time to close the gate. Any ideas now that we can't fly up there?"

Flinches from the others told Jaden he wasn't the only one still grappling with losing their gliders. Their distressed faces made Jaden wish he'd thought before speaking.

Kayla surprised Jaden with her response. "Did Zareh tell you what you had to do?"

Considering a snarky comment, he nipped it in the bud. "No. All he said was we had everything we needed." He remembered something else. "Oh yes, Zareh also said that we had to close the gate after they left. I guess that means we need not go up there to do it."

"You were with the usurper for some time. Did he hint at anything?"

Jaden cringed at Atu's question. It touched on the edges of him confessing the lengths he'd been willing to go to.

Kayla's sharp eyes didn't miss his discomfort. She rolled her eyes. "Now what? Jaden, when will you learn that sharing everything with us, with this team, is the only way we finish this?"

Jaden winced. "It's not that I don't want to tell you. It's that . . ."

"He's afraid of how we'll react," Iri finished for him.

For once, Jaden was grateful for her gift. He nodded affirmation when Kayla raised an eyebrow. But he couldn't put this off any longer. They were out of time.

Taking a breath, Jaden plunged into the core. "Slurpy hinted I was the 'Gatekeeper'—the same term Zareh used. Perhaps that was Zareh's way of telling me I had to share what happened while I was up there with Slurpy."

Kayla's tone was mild. "And that was?"

"Slurpy somehow gained control of my mind. He made me see things—abhorrent things—things that weren't real for the sole purpose of torturing me. He used the love I have for all of you against me. He made me doubt myself, made me believe I was inadequate. He took away any hope I had that we might still win this thing."

"Hmm," Kayla said, looking thoughtful.

Iri interjected. "If Slurpy had control of your mind, how did you free yourself?"

Jaden dreaded this part, the part he wasn't sure the others could forgive him for.

"Well?" Kayla pressed. Her eyes were guarded.

"Remember, I love you." Jaden snatched Kayla's hand up with his own. "You're precious to me." Noting Kayla had accepted his words, Jaden turned to Iri and Atu. "You're both special to me too, as are my other friends and family. I wouldn't have done what I did if I had another option."

Iri put things in perspective. "If you hadn't done it, we wouldn't all be standing here. Because of what you did, Kayla got her medallion back giving us the only way we had any chance at all against the Gaptors. So tell us what you did. It might be the piece Zareh wanted us to focus on."

Jaden sighed. "I doubt it, but here's the crux of the matter. I realized Slurpy craved our fear. My fear, the fear of what he was showing me, was pumping him up. Making him more menacing than he truly was."

Iri's giggle was unexpected. "You're saying he wasn't scary?"

Jaden had to smile. "Not entirely. He was still formidable—just look at what he did! But he became invincible when we added fear to the mix."

Iri's smile was knowing. "You still haven't told us what you did to escape."

"Fine!" Jaden took a deep breath. "I had to let go of my fear that something would happen to all of you because of me. Fear imprisoned me in that artificial world. So I relinquished everyone I loved in the only way I could think of to keep you all safe."

Jaden waited for a response. He could see them working through his words. Kayla's eyes widened. "You had to let us go? You mean allow him to kill us to escape his trap?"

Kayla's agitation was too much. Jaden's gaze fell. "If he believed I didn't care what happened to you, he'd have no hold over me. He was only hurting you because he wanted to torment me. If I released that fear, I freed myself. That meant I could get back to the real world where I might actually save you."

When Kayla's arm wrapped around his waist, her other hand nudging his chin up so she could gaze into his eyes, Jaden stiffened. But love shone there. There was no sign of the accusation he'd dreaded.

"That must've been incredibly difficult. Thank you for being willing to do that for us." Kayla leaned in and kissed him gently before pulling back. "But that wasn't the part Zareh wanted us to focus on."

Jaden gaped. "I spill my guts, and you tell me I didn't have to?"

Kayla's laughter was the balm his bruised soul needed. It lifted his spirits, filling him with that she could still laugh. That she understood.

"All bullies are really cowards in disguise. Why do you think Slurpy wanted to keep you afraid?"

The revelation floored Jaden. "He wanted me distracted. He didn't want me thinking about the quest—or how I could finish it."

Nodding, Kayla said, "What he didn't realize is that you've learned a thing or two since all this started. That no matter what we do in life, there's no way to avoid pain or loss forever. Like life, we can't escape loss. For that reason, we have to face it. We have to deal with the pain."

Jaden knew she was speaking about Bree. She didn't know about Tarise. *Or is that true?* Slurpy told him about Tarise while Jaden was under his spell. A tiny spark of hope flared.

Kayla smiled. "Yes, hope. Slurpy didn't want us having that. Or faith to do the impossible. I'll bet he also never bargained on the power of love—that it's strong enough to drive out all fear."

Kayla's understanding was almost too much to accept. Gratitude shone in Jaden's eyes. "You know I would never have left you behind if there was another way?"

"I know." Kayla's voice was as gentle as her kiss. Her eyes, however, danced with repressed mischief.

"What?"

Giggling, Kayla said, "You still haven't worked it out? I thought you were analytical."

Jaden was even more annoyed when Iri and Atu suddenly laughed too. He glared at them.

Iri sobered. "Jaden, stop worrying about letting Kayla down. She's already forgiven you. Forgive yourself and move past that. Focus on what she said."

Huffing, Jaden mentally ran through the conversation. Shock rippled through him. "The words on the leather strips!"

"Yes!" Kayla's eyes glittered with victory, reminding Jaden of Vicken. "And of all the things we found or were given on this quest, what are the only things we have left? The only things not consumed when we destroyed the Gaptors?"

"The artifacts!"

Kayla grinned. "There's hope for you yet."

Jaden ignored her. Now that he knew the answer, he wanted to get on with it. "Where are they?"

"Before I give them to you, do you know what to do with them?"

"Yeah, it's pretty obvious. I have to become the 'Gatekeeper.'" Jaden smiled wryly. "Now that we're at the end of this, I'm realizing Zareh must think we're all idiots. It's so simple."

"Let's hope so." Kayla reached into Jaden's pack.

The moment she produced the artifacts, the remaining light vanished. Jaden darted another glance upward. The darkness spewed past the shimmering rim of the gate, charcoal billows pumping out like they couldn't move fast enough.

"We have to hurry," Jaden urged.

Atu produced a flashlight, and Kayla placed the three artifacts on the flat rock. Then she, Atu, and Iri stepped back, allowing Jaden access. Sinking to his knees, Jaden gingerly lifted the ink pot. It was so tiny and delicate he was afraid he might crush it. Ever so carefully, he twisted the cap off. Picking up the quill, he dipped it in the ink, then handed the pot to Kayla.

"So it doesn't spill," Jaden said. He glanced at his friends. "Everyone in agreement about what I should write?" They all nodded.

Jaden felt a sense of awe as he put the quill to the paper. The ink was the bond between them. The same way love was the thread linking their faith in him to his hope he could finish this for them.

> *Believing with faith*
> *Living with hope*
> *Conquering though love*

An earsplitting explosion rocked the darkness. A sliver of light danced across the dark mountain. Jaden's body jerked.

The last time—the only time—he touched the gate, it sent some kind of power surging through him, rendering him unconscious when the gate snapped shut. The same power coursed through him now, that terrible sensation of expanding beyond his body's limits. *Am I going to die after all? Is this the delicious secret Slurpy was salivating over? Or was it the failsafe he left for us?*

Jaden was struggling to think. He forced his eyes open. He had to say goodbye. His eyes snagged on the obsidian clouds overhead. They were being sucked back into the gate. As they diminished, the power within him swelled. Spots danced in front of his eyes. Something would have to give, and soon.

Jaden tried to speak but found he couldn't. Stared at the ominous blackness disappearing back behind the gate. Like someone was holding a suction hose at the other end. Abruptly, the sun's heat warmed his face. Its light blinded him. He couldn't hold it back. The rising tension could not be contained.

He struggled to say something. To reach for Kayla. The world exploded.

CHAPTER FIFTY-EIGHT

Kayla held Jaden. Beyond words, her mind raced. *How did this happen? How did we not consider closing the gate might kill Jaden?* She glanced down at him, his head supported in her lap. There was no color in his handsome face.

Atu's hand hovered over Jaden. His eyes were closed and there was no sign of that golden light that had been so prevalent when he had examined Slurpy. Kayla studied his face for any sign as to Jaden's fate. All she saw was exhaustion. *If it comes down to it, does Atu still have enough strength to heal Jaden?*

Atu exhaled, then sat back, opening his eyes. "He'll be fine."

Kayla didn't think she'd heard right. "He'll be okay?"

"He will."

"You're sure?"

"Absolutely."

"But how do you know?"

Atu scrubbed a weary hand over his face. "Because this is exactly the same as last time. All the symptoms match up perfectly. And he woke up last time, didn't he? None the worse for wear and not remembering anything."

"What about brain damage, though? Surely a brain can't keep taking such punishment and not suffer trauma?"

Atu sighed more dramatically this time. "For any normal brain injury, I would say that was true. But that gate isn't of this world. And I doubt its effects work on the brain in the way you'd expect."

Kayla opened her mouth to ask another question, but Iri placed a hand on her shoulder. Kayla stared at the hand, trying to make sense of it. Iri leaned down so her face was directly in front of Kayla's. "Kayla, Jaden's fine. Atu said he is. If you don't trust his diagnoses, hear what my gifts are saying. Jaden's colors and scents are normal. He's just in a deep sleep, not unconscious. That means no effect on the brain, right?"

Kayla's face crumpled. "I don't know." Appalled when it came out as a wail, Kayla tried to calm down. *Girl, get it together!* Kayla ran her fingers through his hair. *Why won't he wake up already?* Aware she was on the verge of a meltdown, Kayla kept one hand wrapped around Jaden's and the other on his chest. Closing her eyes, she meditated.

Three breaths in, something distracted her. Kayla struggled to identify it. Movement under her hand!

Her eyes flew open. She gazed down into impossibly blue eyes. Dark blue like the deepest part of the ocean. Clear and sparkling and wonderful. A slow smile spread across Jaden's face. A sob burst free as Kayla wrapped him in a hug. "Jaden!"

He laughed, hugging her fiercely. "Yes, I'm happy to see you too." He savored Kayla loving on him a second longer before pulling back. "What happened?"

Atu's laughter was pure exultation. "Didn't I tell you?"

Jaden's smile widened. "Tell her what?"

"That you'd wake up and not remember anything," Iri supplied.

Jaden's head turn to find Kayla. She really should let him go. Dragging her arms away from Jaden was an effort. Not wanting to lose contact entirely, she kept gripping his hand. Jaden grinned at her. Kayla basked in that glorious smile that lit his whole face. That lit her from within. That made her own joy burble to the surface.

"That's better," Jaden murmured. "You needed to smile." His hand squeezed hers. Then he glanced at Atu. "And what was it I wouldn't remember?"

Atu grinned. "What's the last thing you *do* remember?"

"Let's see. The medallions vaporizing all the Gaptors. Then . . . Zareh coming and—" Jaden's face fell. "Our gliders!"

"What else?" Kayla prompted, her voice raw.

Jaden frowned. "Brightness. Darkness. Smashing together. Ow!" His hand went to his head.

Immediately, Kayla was alert. She glanced at Iri, then Atu. They both shook their heads, confirming it was nothing serious.

"My head! It felt like it exploded." Jaden's fingers probed his scalp. A second later, he grinned. "I guess it didn't. I'm not even sure why I thought it had." His hand went back to his neck, massaging along the side and then around the back. "It sure feels like it blew the back of my head off, though."

His hand moved his long hair aside, and Kayla gasped. He'd been lying on it before, and when he sat up, his hair covered it. But now, with his hand lifting his hair out the way, there it was.

Jaden continued massaging as he looked at her quizzically. "What?"

Leaning forward, Kayla moved his hand out the way, using her other hand to lift his hair. Atu whistled.

"What?" There was alarm in Jaden's voice.

"It's nothing to worry about." Kayla rubbed a finger over it. No raised or inflamed skin she would've expected. No tenderness. Just the brand on his skin, a perfect replica of their medallions, in full-color detail.

"Can you all stop gaping and tell me what you're seeing?" Jaden demanded.

"It's an image of our medallions—right here," Kayla said, still running an incredulous finger over the spot.

"Like a tattoo?"

"You could say that."

Jaden growled. "Get a mirror and show me!"

Iri giggled but dug in her pack and produced one. She handed it over.

Jaden angled it so he could see the brand. "Aw, man! Why did it have to have colors? It makes me look like a girl!"

Kayla burst out laughing. "You get a magic tattoo, and that's what you have to say?"

"Well . . . look at it!" Jaden blustered. "It's all sparkly and shiny!"

It wasn't only Kayla collapsing into uncontrollable laughter this time. The more they laughed, the more Jaden's face scrunched up, and the redder it grew.

"Fine for you lot! It's not on your skin!" Jaden touched the brand, angling the mirror back and forth. "I'm doomed to long hair forever."

That did it. Kayla took the mirror away. "Stop obsessing. Be grateful you survived closing the gate."

"Not that I'll ever be able to forget." Jaden rubbed his neck again.

Kayla didn't think any of them would forget. What would've happened if Jaden hadn't been able to close the gate? Hadn't been able to stop the blackness from poisoning their world?

Jaden quirked an eyebrow. "Now what's on your mind?"

"Do you think it would've affected people eventually?"

"What?"

"Whatever was coming through the gate."

Jaden shrugged, noticing Atu and Iri were paying attention. "Does it matter? It would've affected all the animals, then possibly the plants. Which begs the question—would the plants and animals have remained a food source, or would the roles have been reversed?"

"Ugh, Jaden!" Iri objected.

Kayla grimaced. "I agree with Iri. A chilling thought I don't care to dwell on. Now that the gate's closed and with it the chance for further contamination, let's hope Shianna and the people she's working with can find a cure for the mutations."

"Let's hope." Jaden's face soured. "If they don't, those poor beasties face termination."

"Delightful," Iri murmured. "Can we try and stay on the positive side of the scale? I've had enough negative experiences this week to last a lifetime."

"Yup, it's been grueling for all of us," Kayla agreed. It was several minutes before she broke the silence, standing as she spoke. "If I've learned one thing, it's that time is not something we can count on having indefinitely. Life is precious. I need to get to the hospital and check on my dad."

Jaden rose and took Kayla's hand. "I'll come with you."

"Us too," Iri said after an inquiring glance at Atu. "Except how do we get there?" Iri hadn't added *because we don't have gliders anymore.* But they all felt the words.

"Luckily, I have an answer."

Jaden's face lit when he heard the voice on the comm. "Stovan? I thought you were with Kayla's parents."

"I was until Sven arrived and took over. You know how he is—wanted to make sure Kayla's parents were secure. When he said he didn't need me, I came back here. Thought I might help."

"Glad you did, bro. It's good to hear your voice."

"Relieved to hear yours too, dude. You had us all worried there."

Kayla saw the flash of emotion across Jaden's face. "I'm fine. You're all . . . okay?"

"Yeah, we're all here."

Was it Kayla's imagination, or had those last words been a little somber? Then she remembered. Bree. She hadn't imagined it. Kayla glanced at Jaden.

He hadn't missed that note in Stovan's voice either. "She'd be proud of all of us."

Stovan's voice was infinitely quieter this time. "She would be, wouldn't she?" No one spoke for a while. Then Stovan cleared his throat. "It's time we got out of here. To answer Iri's question, I remote-commanded our family's terraporter as soon as you closed that gate. It should be here any moment."

"Dude, you rock!" Jaden's shout made Kayla smile.

"I do, don't I?" Stovan replied, sounding smug.

"Don't let it go to your head." Markov's voice this time, followed by chuckles from whoever else was on the comm.

"Exactly how long have you all been listening?" Kayla asked.

"The whole time," Markov replied. "It's not our fault you guys never remember to mute your comms."

Kayla would've questioned the strain she heard in Markov's voice, except embarrassment overrode her concern. Color flooded her cheeks. They must think she was a basket case, considering the way she had fallen apart earlier. The hand holding hers squeezed, and Kayla caught sight of Jaden's grin.

"Just something they can use to tease you—nothing more. And you know they'll only tease you because they like you."

Kayla rolled her eyes. "Thanks, I could've done without giving them ammunition."

More chuckles from the comm, interrupted by the roar of approaching engines. Kayla glanced up to see not only Stovan's terra-porter, but several other transports.

"I thought you only summoned yours," Jaden commented.

"Yeah, for us. But there are other riders here that need to get home. A bunch of them RC-ed theirs too."

"RC-ed?" Iri echoed.

"Remote-commanded," Kayla explained.

"We're finally leaving this accursed place. Not a moment too soon, and good riddance!" Jaden exclaimed.

Kayla watched as 'pods and terraporters dipped and rose, collecting those who had summoned them. Finally, only one terra-porter remained. It descended, and Jaden's lifelong friends clambered aboard. The terraporter lifted, making the short trip across to where Kayla waited with the others. It hovered next to the spot where they were stranded. Then the door opened, and a ramp dropped, crossing the distance between the ship and the rock ledge.

As Kayla scrambled across after Iri and before the boys, she noticed the lack of wind. *I should've expected no wind now that we've finished this thing.* Then she was inside the transport, Jaden and Atu on her heels. The ramp withdrew, and the door shut.

Kayla turned, almost bowled over by Shianna. Her exuberant hug was followed by several others, and Kayla noticed she wasn't the only one crying. After countless hugs, Stovan finally ordered everyone to find seats. Kayla dropped into a chair, and Jaden plopped down next to her. She grinned at him, unable to contain her elation. Their mission was over. They were going home.

CHAPTER FIFTY-NINE

The trip home was quicker than Kayla thought it would be. She had expected things would drag, like they usually did when she was anxious. But time sped by, starting with the "excitement" of Markov's injury.

When Kayla greeted him on her way in, she'd thought he looked a little gray but she'd attributed it to fatigue. That was until they'd been sitting only a few minutes when Stovan suddenly cried out.

"Help! A little help here!"

Jaden, on the aisle, reached Stovan first. He took one look and called for Atu. Kayla tensed. She crept to the edge of the group now encircling Stovan. On her toes, she could just see past the shoulders of the others. Stovan was supporting Markov, slumped sideways in his chair.

Atu caught her gaze. "Care to do an initial assessment, so we know if we can lie him down?"

The group parted to allow Kayla access. A little bewildered that they were trusting her to tend to one of their own, Kayla hastened forward. Her fingers and eyes made short work of checking the crucial points.

"Yes, we can lay him flat. I think the problem's here." Kayla gestured toward the spot where her fingers had detected a slight, irregular squishiness.

Between them, Jaden and Stovan carefully lifted Markov and laid him on the floor. As soon as he was flat, Kayla lifted Markov's shirt, revealing the dark purple splotch. She glanced at Atu. "Have your reserves built up enough for you to heal him?" She didn't have to add that if Atu couldn't, Markov was in a dire situation.

Atu shrugged. "I can only try and see how far I get." He glanced at Stovan. "As a precaution, might I suggest increasing the transport's speed to maximum?"

Amid faces depicting consternation, Stovan nodded, pulled up his PAL, and keyed in the commands.

Kayla braced herself against the burst of speed, then glanced at Iri once she'd regained her balance. Iri subtly lifted a hand in front of her, rocking it side to side. Kayla acknowledged with a subtle nod of her own. Even chances that Atu could pull this off.

A hush descended as Atu closed his eyes. Iri sidled over to stand next to Kayla. One glance told Kayla Iri was more worried about Atu than Markov. She squeezed Iri's hand. "He'll be okay."

"I hope so."

The familiar golden glow leeched from Atu's hands and settled on Markov's chest, rippling along the surface without sinking in. Awed, they watched the angry purplish-red patch along Markov's ribs shrink.

It was still golf-ball sized when Kayla noticed the slight sheen of perspiration on Atu's forehead. His breathing had become more labored. Her eyes darted to the spot on Markov's chest, now smaller but not yet gone. Alarmed, she glanced at Iri. "How's he doing?"

Iri's mouth was a thin line. "If you mean Markov, he's almost healed."

Kayla gently punched Iri's arm. "Who do you think I mean?"

Iri's voice wobbled. "Atu's holding up. But his colors are fading. If he doesn't stop soon . . ." She turned pleading eyes on Kayla. "Why didn't we think to ask him before he started if we could intervene?"

Kayla had just been asking herself the same question. "It's the first thing we'll ask him when he's done."

Iri nodded. A moment later, she clutched Kayla's hand so hard Kayla yelped, garnering a sharp glance from Jaden. Atu's departing strength hadn't escaped Jaden's attention either. He looked just as worried as Kayla felt. She glanced at Iri, now white-faced. "What?"

"Atu's colors are fading faster. He's going to—" Iri broke off as the golden light abruptly vanished, leaving the interior of the terraporter feeling colder somehow.

Iri let go of Kayla's hand and rushed to Atu. He was leaning back after tending to Markov, opening his eyes. He sighed when he saw Iri and gave her a weak smile, then collapsed sideways.

Suddenly, everyone was moving and talking. Kayla tried to reach Atu but Markov was in the way. She made to move around him, but his eyes fluttered open. Kayla glanced at his chest. There was no sign of the ugly bruise that had signaled internal bleeding.

Torn between tending to Markov or rushing to Atu, she looked at Atu. Jaden and Iri were with him. She should stay with Markov. "You gave us quite a scare there."

Markov attempted a smile. "I thought I'd last until we reached the hospital. Apparently, I was wrong." He glanced down and blinked, then stared at Kayla with wide eyes. "Is this your doing?"

"No, that would be Atu's gift." Kayla glanced in Atu's direction. Jaden had him lying down, and Iri was placing a rolled-up shirt under his head as a pillow.

"Is he . . . did he—" Markov began.

"He'll be alright," Kayla interrupted. She didn't want to think what Markov might've asked. They had come too close to losing Atu more than once today. "He just needs a healthy dose of sleep."

Markov took her hand, surprising Kayla. "Thanks."

Kayla shrugged. "It's not me you should thank."

Markov shook his head. "Not what I mean. Thanks for keeping Jaden safe."

"Oh." Kayla couldn't think of anything else to say. She was still searching for words when Jaden joined them.

He gazed at the hand Markov still held, then fixed Markov with a hard stare. "Dude, you should've said something."

Markov grinned. "About me and Kayla, you mean?"

Jaden threw his head back and laughed. "No, you idiot. Nice try, but you won't get a rise from me."

Markov raised both eyebrows and turned to Kayla. "You've tamed the beast. Before, he would've had me on the ground in a rear naked choke."

Kayla giggled. "That's probably an exaggeration."

Jaden grinned. "I'm glad you're still with us."

"Kayla said I can thank Atu for that. He will be okay, right?"

"Yeah, he'll be fine. Poor guy just needs some serious rest."

"Markov! You should've told us!" Shianna's worried face was streaked with the grime of battle, the same as everyone's. There would be time to clean up later. For now, Kayla was content to rest.

Leaning back against Jaden, Kayla listened as Markov and Shianna shared snippets of their experiences over the past few days. Stovan joined them, adding his adventures. Soon, the group maneuvered their chairs so Iri and Atu (still asleep) could be part of the conversation. Before she was ready, Kayla felt the sudden deceleration as the terraporter slowed. She glanced at Stovan, checking his PAL.

His eyes met hers. "Yes, we're at the hospital. Time to see how your dad's doing."

With minimal fuss, the terraporter landed, and Jaden arranged for a gurney to carry a still-sleeping Atu inside. They made quite the crowd marching down the halls, the gurney in their midst and Markov being pushed along in a wheelchair at Kayla's insistence.

As soon as they landed, Kayla pinged her mom, so she knew exactly where to go. When they arrived outside her dad's room, Kayla stopped. "My mom didn't comment on his condition. Okay if I go in alone first?"

They agreed vigorously, then told her they would be in the waiting room down the hall and she should hurry back with news. Kayla smiled. When she'd arrived in Daxsos, she had never dared believe she would make even one friend, let alone a group who would make her part of the family. "I'll update you as soon as I know."

The crowd rolled back down the hall, and Kayla grinned as Atu and Markov caught the attention of a passing doctor. *Where's Jaden?*

"I'm here."

Jaden's quiet voice behind her made her jump. "Oh, there you are!"

Taking her hand, Jaden said, "I'd like to come in with you, if that's okay? Give you and your mom some moral support?"

Kayla threw her arms around him. She whispered against his neck. "Yes, please. I'm so grateful you stayed."

Jaden dropped a soft kiss on her lips before stepping back, using one hand to hold hers and placing the other on the door handle. "Ready?"

Kayla nodded, and Jaden opened the door. Kayla wasn't sure what she had expected. The rowdy group inside was disconcerting. *Do I have the wrong room?* Jaden's parents were laughing. Then she found her mom. And then Kayla saw her dad. He was sitting up in bed, laughing with the rest of them. No signs of any illness. His color was excellent, and his eyes sparkled.

Kayla's legs wobbled under her. Jaden's arm went around her waist. Though she was grateful for the support, she had eyes only for her dad. *He's alive!*

Vicken noticed them then. "Kayla!"

One word was all it took for the other adults to turn their way. Then they were swamped with hugs and kisses and cries of joy. Kayla waded through them, intent on reaching her dad. She still couldn't quite believe her eyes. Only when she touched him and felt his warm hands curl around hers did she let go.

Sobbing uncontrollably, she hugged her father as he hugged her in return. Tears ran down his face as freely as they did hers. When she could manage the words, she asked, "How?"

Vicken understood. "They don't know. One moment, I was still in that coma-like state. The next, monitors and alarms were blaring, and doctors and nurses were rushing around, removing tubes and checking my vitals. In less than five minutes, I went from zero to hero." He stopped and laughed. "See, I'm even back to my usual, terrible sense of humor."

Kayla laughed through the tears. "I'll survive it."

Arms went around her shoulders, and Kayla turned to find her mom. She hugged her. Over her mom's shoulder, Kayla witnessed Jaden reuniting with his family. They were all okay. They had survived. For whatever reason, her dad had made a miraculous recovery. She wouldn't question it. She would . . . "Mom, how long ago did Dad wake up?"

Sadie looked surprised. "A few hours ago. Why?"

"Could you be more specific?"

Sadie considered. "At around six this morning."

The room suddenly went silent. Kayla's eyes met Jaden's. That was about the time Slurpy had faded away.

"Are you thinking what I am?" Kayla asked Jaden.

He nodded. "I'll go tell the others the news about your dad and get Shianna to check in with her contacts."

"Need me to come with you?"

Jaden smiled, understanding how torn she was. "No. Stay with your dad. I'll return with answers."

He left the room, and Sadie stared after him. "What on earth were you two talking about?" She faced her husband. "Did you understand that?"

Vicken laughed and pulled Kayla onto the bed next to him. "I'm sure if they wanted us to know, they would've been a little more communicative." He studied Kayla. "Although I suspect we'll find out when Jaden gets back. Now, how about that tea we were discussing?"

Sadie's hand went to her head. "I completely forgot. I'll go see if I can get a nurse—"

"You stay with your family," Clara ordered. "I'll see to the tea."

Kayla smiled. She wasn't the only one who had found friends she could trust and rely on in their new town—the town they would stay in, the town only a few hours from this hospital. No more moves. No more boxes. No more moving angst. Her heart bloomed with gratitude. Taking her dad's hand, she said, "I'm so relieved our nomadic days are over."

Her dad's face was serious when he replied. "As am I. We've found a wonderful place to call home, haven't we?"

Kayla nodded, aware more tears were leaking out. She needed something less emotional right now. "What's news?"

Her dad chuckled. "I'd think you have more to tell us than we have to tell you. Want to catch us up?"

"Wait for Clara," Ty interjected. "You know how upset she'll be if she misses even one word."

For whatever reason, this had all the parents laughing again. Kayla soaked it in, still struggling to accept it was real. That she was here. Safe. Her father well. Her mom happy. She curled into her dad's shoulder and listened as Ty and Vicken began tossing sports stats about. Clara bustled back in with the tea. She had barely set the tray down when Jaden burst in.

His broad grin supplied Kayla's answer before he spoke the words. "It's all gone. The mutations have vanished. No manifestations remain."

Jaden's mom stared at him like he had grown green horns and a third eye. "What are you talking about?"

"I believe he and Kayla are about to explain," Vicken guessed.

Jaden grinned. "Remember when the gate opened in the sky the first time and that Gaptor army came through?" All the parents nodded. It seemed they had been doing their own "adventure" sharing. "And remember how we started seeing changes in the animals? Strange mutations that initially couldn't be explained?"

Vicken nodded. "That's the last thing I remember you discussing before I left Sven's base."

"Exactly. Well, they're all gone."

"Gone?" Clara repeated.

"I mean, the changes reversed themselves. All the animals the researchers were studying just regained their normal form. Literally, in the blink of an eye."

"Exactly like what happened to me," Vicken murmured, understanding. "I'm guessing this occurred the same time I magically recovered?"

Jaden nodded. Vicken eyed him and then Kayla. "What did you two do to render that kind of effect?"

Jaden smiled that gloriously wicked smile Kayla loved. "It wasn't just us. It was the whole team. We cut the head off the snake!"

Kayla couldn't have phrased it better herself. Without Slurpy and his power to keep things together, the evils he had inflicted had been neutralized. With an audible sigh, Kayla flopped back down onto the bed, unaware of when she had even risen. This day had been too long already.

Sadie rushed forward, pressing a hand to Kayla's head. "Are you alright?"

"It's just been an extra-long day, Mom. I could use a hot bath, some food, a long drink of something cold, a fluffy bathrobe, and a bed to wallow in."

Her mother grinned. "Is that all?"

"No, perhaps a masseuse, a pedicure, some—" Kayla broke off with a laugh as her mother batted her arm.

"You're just fine without those things," her mother said with an eye roll.

Vicken nudged Kayla. "I'm still waiting to hear how you cut the head off the snake."

That lit the fuse for the stories to start up again. Kayla tucked herself against her dad's shoulder. The whole scene was so surreal. She closed her eyes, intending to open them again, but it wasn't to be. Sleep claimed her, and Kayla finally surrendered to oblivion.

CHAPTER SIXTY

Iri shifted in her position next to Atu's cot in his hospital room. A doctor had examined him, proclaimed he was suffering from exhaustion, ordered a drip hooked up, and told her Atu would be fine when he finally woke up. But she was not to wake him. She was to allow his body as much rest as it needed.

As soon as he left, Iri passed the news along to the rest of Jaden's friends. When the doctor told her they were outside Atu's room, waiting for his diagnosis, it had surprised her. She had been even more surprised when they'd invited her back to the terraporter to bunk with them while they waited for everyone to heal up before the trip back to Daxsos.

While the offer was generous, Iri was reluctant to leave Atu. She wanted to be there in case he woke up. A familiar face would squash any concerns he might experience. Expecting rebuttal, Iri had asked the nurses if they could wheel a cot in for her use. To her surprise, they'd obliged.

After Jaden's friends confirmed Iri didn't need them, they told her they would be right outside the hospital. If she needed *anything*, she had only to ping them. She was still marveling at the way they had included her and Atu as part of their group when she called Atu's parents.

Despite telling them Atu was okay and just needed some well-deserved rest, they had insisted on making the trip from Sven's. But without gliders, their trip would take far longer. Iri assured them she would stay with Atu until they arrived. She didn't tell them the arrangement suited her just fine. It would give her and Atu time alone before his parents arrived.

With a longing look at her cot, Iri turned and forced herself into the shower. While she was dead on her feet and would've loved to crash, being dirty would've bothered her subconsciously and affected her sleep.

Admittedly, the hot water rushing over her skin was bliss. She stepped out a good thirty minutes later, not even the slightest bit guilty she had taken so long. Being clean again was divine. Padding back into the room, it surprised her to find a food tray waiting. She dived in, thankful for the person who had thought to bring her a meal.

Her lunch gobbled up, Iri pushed the tray aside and finally allowed herself to flop back onto the pillow. She didn't even remember falling asleep. Hours later, she woke, the room dark and the hallway outside quiet. *What's the time?* She checked her PAL. Nearly dawn. She had slept the rest of the day away and almost the whole night.

She lay on the cot, abruptly wide awake like a second round of adrenaline had shot through her. She was having trouble assimilating everything that had happened. The trip to the mountains, the attacks, the tunnels, the ambush, the last artifacts, Slurpy's demise, closing the gate. At every stage, death crouched at the door, waiting to pounce. But it had claimed none of the voyagers. And none of their precious gliders.

Her heart pinched thinking of Tinks and Rozie. *Is Rozie safely back home? Will she ever think about me again? Did the gliders forge bonds the same way we did as voyagers?* Iri smiled in the dark. Jaden had been right. Everyone had played a role in bringing the ultimate victory. And they hadn't shunned her gifts. They hadn't shunned *her*.

"What are you smiling about?" Atu was grinning at her, his teeth a white line in the dim light of the growing dawn.

Iri jerked up. "You're awake! How do you feel?"

"Darn good, actually. Where are we?"

"Kayla's dad's hospital. Do you remember what happened?"

Atu nodded. "Every last painful second of it. How's Markov doing?"

"Just fine thanks to you. The docs checked him out when we arrived. Other than the residual weakness, they couldn't find anything wrong with him."

"Excellent. Toward the end, I wasn't so sure I'd be able to finish the task."

"You could've died, you know!"

Atu nodded, his face solemn. "Yeah, I'm aware how close I came." He studied Iri's face. "Sorry, I didn't mean to scare you."

Iri closed her eyes against the memory. "You don't know how awful it was to see your colors fading." Iri abruptly stopped. "Hey, I just realized something."

A slow smile spread across Atu's face. "What?"

"I saw colors on you!"

"Don't you see them on everyone?"

"You know I see them on everyone *except* you. How was it I could see them around you when you were healing Slurpy and Markov, but not any other time?"

Atu shrugged. "I had nothing to do with it. Perhaps it's something Zareh set in place when he gave this gift to our family. So someone else could tell if we were going over the edge and yank us back."

"And we can do that? Yank you back, I mean?"

Atu looked surprised. "Yes. Did you think you couldn't?"

"We weren't sure. Twice now, once with Slurpy and then again with Markov, your colors were so dim they were edging toward black. Kayla didn't know if snatching you from your . . . state would harm you. We didn't dare try in case it did."

"Well, now you know. It wouldn't have been an issue. In fact, next time, can I ask that you do?" Atu ran a hand over his torso. "Then I won't have to feel like a truck ran over me."

Iri jumped up. "I thought you said you were fine?"

Atu put out a hand. "I am! Don't get all excited. Just a little bruised and battered. It's normal. Nothing out of the ordinary."

Iri still called for the nurse. A few minutes later, the nurse assured Iri Atu was fine. Still a little dehydrated, but nothing else of concern. The nurse left, and Atu studied Iri.

"Didn't you believe me?"

"I, uh . . ." Iri tossed her hands in the air. "Forget it! I just needed to be sure you were okay. I can't see colors on you anymore, so I don't know."

"And we're back to what we were discussing before. Does it really bother you that much?"

Iri suddenly realized how close he was to figuring out the real reason it bothered her. A little flustered, she fished for an explanation. "I promised your parents I'd look after you until they got here. I can't do that if I can't see or smell how you're doing."

Atu's grin reappeared. "You can't smell me either? I think I smell pretty ripe after our adventures."

Iri was about to say something snarky, then burst into giggles. "You know what I meant. But now that you mention it, a shower before your parents arrive probably wouldn't be a bad idea."

"I suppose it would present a better front." Atu noticed the way Iri was regarding him. "What?"

"You're lucky you have parents." Atu blinked. Only then did Iri realize she had told none of them about her parents. "Before you ask, I don't have any. Do you think I lived out in the forest all by myself because it was fun?"

Atu shook his head. "I'm sorry, I didn't know. I thought it was because of your gift." He smacked a hand to his forehead. "And now that I'm saying it out loud, I can't believe how stupid it sounds."

Iri waved it away. "That won't change." When Atu frowned, Iri clarified. "I mean, people will still shun me because of my gift. It's still there. As is yours. I'm thrilled you can still heal people."

Atu sputtered. "What made you think I wouldn't be able to?"

Iri felt a little silly. "It's just something I wondered about. You know, afterward. With the threat to this world vanquished, would our gifts disappear too?"

"You thought perhaps we only received them so we could use them in the war against Slurpy?"

"Yeah."

"If you'd lost your gift, would you have mourned the loss?"

Iri had been wrestling with this question. She sighed. "On the one hand, I would've been normal and that would've been a relief. That I could fit into society. On the other hand, it's . . ." Iri didn't want to complete the sentence.

Atu did it for her. "It's what makes you, you."

Iri should've known he'd understand. "Yeah. If I'd lost the ability, it would've been like losing a part of myself. And much as I hate that my gift's made me an outcast, it's who I am."

Atu crooked a finger at her. "Come here."

Iri cocked her head. He was up to something. She wasn't sure what.

"Iri, come here!"

The way Atu was looking at her, Iri knew if she didn't go to him, he would get out of that bed and come to her. She had no choice. If she didn't want him overdoing things, she'd better comply. Slowly, Iri paced the few steps to the side of his bed. She stopped a foot away.

"Closer."

Iri's eyes were on anything except Atu. She noticed the water jug next to his bed. "Want some water?" Not quite how she had wanted that to come out, her voice husky and somewhat breathless.

"Yes."

Iri eyed Atu suspiciously. Had that "yes" sounded more like he was answering a different question?

Atu sighed. "Iri, are you going to get me that drink of water, or do I have to call the nurse?"

The words galvanized Iri into action. She splashed water into the glass, noticing her hands were trembling as she stepped closer.

When his hand shot out and grabbed hers, trapping it, Iri jumped back, but his grip was surprisingly strong. Never taking his eyes from her, Atu eased the glass from her hand, leaned sideways, and set it on his side table.

"Hey, you could've poured your own water!"

Atu's smile touched every part of his face. "But then I wouldn't have gotten you this close. I wouldn't have been able to do this." He gave a quick jerk on her arms so Iri tumbled onto the bed next to him. Before she could slide away, Atu wrapped his arms around her, his face close to hers.

Caged there, Iri's heart thundered. She tried thinking of something to say. But she could only focus on how close Atu was. How those soft brown eyes were looking at her. How amazing those hands felt on her back.

Atu moved a hand to caress her eyebrows, her cheeks, her lips. Iri groaned. She wanted him to kiss her. She opened eyes she hadn't realized she'd closed.

"Iri, never forget, I love you just the way you are. With or without your gift."

Iri was still stumbling over his words, the way he said them with such adoration, when Atu dipped his head and kissed her. For a nanosecond, Iri froze. She had never dared believe anyone could love her. Yet here was a man who loved her as she was. Iri melted into his arms. Savored the tender kiss. Ran her arms around his neck and then down those powerful muscles in his back.

Iri lost herself in the kiss. Lost herself in Atu. This incredible, kind man who could see *her*. Iri. Not the odd person most of the rest of the world saw. The person most of the rest of the world shunned.

When they drew apart some time later, Atu's grin was brilliant enough to challenge the sun rising outside. "I plan on doing that again. However, I would prefer if I could do it when I didn't stink. It wasn't particularly romantic of me to kiss you smelling like this!"

Iri laughed. "You think I care?"

She pulled him into another kiss.

CHAPTER SIXTY-ONE

Jaden woke with a start, then groaned. *What possessed me to stay up so late last night?* It had been a chaotic few days. The hospital discharged Markov, Atu, and Vicken the day after they'd arrived. Then it had been the tedious trip back home, lightened considerably by the companionship of friends and family and the terraporter's comfort.

Arriving back in Daxsos had been a rude awakening for Jaden. He had forgotten he would have to say goodbye to Kayla again as she left for her own home with her parents. When their 'pod took her away, his heart wrenched. Kayla wouldn't be with him twenty-four-seven anymore. Or so he'd thought. Somehow, despite living in their own homes, they'd created a routine that allowed them to spend every day together and a large part of most evenings.

Last night had been no exception. He, Kayla, Iri, Atu, and his childhood friends sat around the fire, toasting s'mores and talking into the wee hours. Iri and Atu had stayed on with Kayla and Jaden's families, respectively, when they'd returned. Atu's parents were happy to let them spend time with their newfound friends without the pressure of saving the world handing over their heads.

While Jaden had wondered whether the end of their quest would herald the end of his new friendships, it had done the opposite. His old friends had accepted Kayla, Iri, and Atu like they'd always been a part of the crew, and the group was tighter than ever.

Jaden grinned and shook his head. *How am I so blessed to have such wonderful friends? Friends who stand by me, no matter what crazy things I do or how crazy I sound.* He recalled telling Markov about the Gaptors and their threat to the world. How Markov had believed him, even though he couldn't see the monsters. How his friends had supported him through all this. How they had joined in this fight. How one of them had died for it. Not because Bree was doing something for Jaden, but because she believed in the cause. Because she had wanted to do her part to preserve what they had.

Jaden sighed. Today, they would honor her. They would say good-bye. It was time to get dressed. An hour later, he sat in the church, Kayla on one side of him, Stovan on the other. Kayla had a death grip on his hand. Grateful for the comfort her touch always brought, Jaden squeezed her hand. Kayla glanced at him, her face drawn.

No sign of her lovely smile today, and those amazing sage green eyes were shaded pools of sorrow, threatening to overflow. Jaden released her hand and put an arm around her shoulder, tucking her into him. When she burrowed in, he took as much solace as he gave.

Jaden held her there, wishing he could ease her grief. Not only hers, but Stovan's. That of their friends. Bree's little sister. Bree's parents. His own. But death was a foe they couldn't defeat. This scar would mark their hearts as long as they lived.

Avoiding looking at Bree's coffin, Jaden's eyes skittered across the platform and landed on her picture, her spiky hair tipped pink in the image. The same color it had been when he'd last seen her. Jaden closed his eyes against the sight of her falling off her glider. *If only I could've . . . what?* Jaden grasped for the words Stovan had given him at Sven's. *"It wasn't your fault."*

Initially, Jaden hadn't accepted the words. But as their mission had worn on, he realized Stovan was right. There was nothing he could've done. Bree alone had made her choice to join this battle. She had known the risks. And she would trounce him soundly if he did Bree the disservice of not acknowledging her sacrifice. Of bring narcissistic enough to make this all about him.

Well, maybe not trounce me, but certainly withhold her delectable edible creations. The thought finally brought a smile to his frozen face. He'd found his tribute for her when it was his turn to speak.

It was a moving service. The pastor's words were exactly what Jaden had needed to hear. After her parents' eulogy, Stovan said his piece. Then Jaden, followed by every single member of their group. From start to end, there wasn't a dry eye in the church.

When Jaden knelt next to Stovan to lift Bree and carry her to her final resting place, he wasn't sure he could stand the grief ripping him apart. But for Stovan, he kept it together. As did Markov, Shianna, Atu, Iri, and Kayla. Jaden made a point of not looking at Kayla. Her grief would've been his breaking point.

After that, Jaden didn't remember much. How he got to the cemetery, he didn't know. By then, he was too numb to think. He didn't even hear if they spoke any words. Beyond tears, Jaden could only stare as Bree's coffin was lowered into the ground. Could only walk on wooden legs when his turn came to drop in daisies. His offering fell, adding to the countless others already covering Bree, forming a beautiful white and yellow blanket of the happy little flowers she'd loved so dearly. Then he was moving on so the next person could take his place.

Jaden stood to the side, not sure what to do. At a loss, he scanned the surrounding area. Perhaps he could find somewhere to sit.

A tiny movement in the distance caught his attention. His eyes focused on the area. Nothing. About to turn away, it twitched again. Wanting something, anything to think about other than Bree, Jaden honed his attention on the area.

That was when Jaden saw her, trying to stay hidden behind a tree. He wasn't sure what he felt at that moment, but Jaden knew what he had to do. It was the one thing he could remedy, and he would seize the opportunity.

Jaden sprinted across the lawns between them. She saw him coming, turned, and began running herself. Away from him. "No, Tarise, wait!" She didn't slow down. "Tarise! Wait. Please!" No effect. Never mind. Jaden knew he was faster. Dimly, he heard the commotion behind him, but he paid it no heed.

Ducking his head, he hoofed it. With no other way to stop her headlong flight, Jaden tackled her, bringing her to the ground so she landed on top of him. He lay on his back, breathing hard as Tarise squirmed in his arms.

"Let me go! I just wanted to say goodbye. Let go of me!"

"Tarise, stop. I don't want to hurt you. I just want to talk to you."

"You're lying! You hate me more than all the rest of them combined." She struggled more violently.

"Tarise, I—" Jaden sighed. He tightened his grip so she couldn't slip free. "True, you're not my favorite person, but I don't hate you."

Tarise stopped wriggling. "If that's true, then let me go!"

"Only if you promise not to run away."

Tarise was quiet for a moment. "You won't try and hurt me?"

"No, I promise. I just want to talk."

"Okay, I won't run. But I will stand far enough away that I feel safe."

"Fair enough."

Jaden released her, and Tarise scrambled away, her eyes impossibly wide. She scurried to a spot a few feet away. "So talk!"

Jaden sighed. She would not make this easy. "Could you maybe come a little closer so I don't have to shout?"

"No, I'm fine where I am."

Biting back irritation, Jaden took several deep breaths. Speaking to her without calming himself wouldn't help. It would only carry over in his tone, which wouldn't allow her to hear what he wanted her to understand.

"Are you going to say something, or are you just thinking of how you can catch me again?"

Jaden didn't allow the barb to penetrate. "Tarise, I've wanted to take the blame for so many things that haven't been my fault. It's been humbling to realize I can't control everything or everyone. I can only be responsible for the things I do. What others do is up to them and their conscience."

"You're saying I don't have a conscience?"

Jaden had forgotten how difficult Tarise was to reason with. "I'm not saying that at all." A small huff from Tarise. He'd better cut to the chase. "The way I treated you after the battle was unfair. I was distraught, but that didn't give me the right to judge you. It didn't give me the right to speak to you the way I did. For that, I am truly sorry."

Tarise stared at him, her gray eyes dubious. "Fine. Can I go now?"

"Not yet." Jaden took a deep breath. He wasn't sure he could do this. But he'd promised himself that if he ever got the chance, he would. Without stopping to rationalize further, Jaden said, "I forgive you."

Tarise eyed him shrewdly. "Does that mean you'll give me a second chance?"

There had been too many years and too much water under the bridge for Jaden to not see the trap she was trying to set. Genius she might be, but she wasn't very smart with people.

"Let's be clear: I'm giving you a second chance at proving yourself to the group. Not a second chance at anything other than friendship with me. My heart belongs to Kayla and always will. There's nothing you could ever say or do to change that." Tarise's face grew stormy. "In fact, nothing anyone can do to change that, in case you think I'm singling you out. I'm not."

"There's no way this is your forever person. You're too young. We'll get our chance."

The contempt in her voice infuriated Jaden. He was about to reply when someone beat him to it.

"No, you won't. Never." Kayla slipped her hand into his, gifting him with one of her glorious smiles.

It gave Jaden the air he needed. He looked squarely into Tarise's steely eyes. He'd always thought her eyes were a soft gray, but now he saw them for what they were. Cold. Unrelenting. Heartless. "I've spoken as plainly as possible. I haven't given you false hope. What you do with information is up to you."

Tarise's lip curled in a sneer. "Trying to convince yourself you won't be responsible if something happens to me?"

Kayla growled. It almost made Jaden laugh. He'd never heard that sound from her. But one look at her face told him not to mess with her. "Tarise, why can't you accept Jaden is willing to be your friend? That's he's found it in his heart to forgive you for what you did? Do you even care that Bree's dead?"

Tarise jerked back like Kayla had burned her. "Of course I care," she hissed. "It's you who doesn't. Coming in where you don't belong and taking things that aren't yours."

Kayla shook her head and sighed, then glanced at Jaden. "I tried. There's no reasoning with her. I'm done here."

Jaden cast a last glance at Tarise. "As am I." Turning, he paused, then faced Tarise again. "If you ever come to your senses and decide you want to accept the friendship I'm offering, I will honor what I said and give you that opportunity. But," he took a few menacing steps toward Tarise, satisfied when she backed away, "if you ever try and harm Kayla again, know your actions will have consequences."

Turning his back on Tarise, he took Kayla's hand and led her away. Jaden was debating the wisdom of the action when he heard the sobs. *Is this just a ploy to get me to relent?* Everything in him wanted to keep on walking. To leave Tarise in her misery. *But I'll have to live with my actions.* He sent Kayla an apologetic glance.

She smiled and took his face in her hands. "It's fine. Go."

"No need," another voice chipped in, one Jaden knew well. Markov stepped from behind the tree that had kept him out of sight.

"You too? Who else is here?" Jaden gaped as the rest of the gang appeared from assorted hiding places. "You were all here?"

Stovan passed Jaden on his way to join Markov. He whispered, "We didn't want you or Kayla alone with her."

"Thanks for having our backs," Jaden whispered back.

The others crowded around Tarise. He wasn't sure what they were saying to her, but her tears seemed genuine enough. Either way, he was done for the day. If he stuck around, he might say something else he would regret. "Ready to get out of here?"

Kayla's face was sober. "Am I ever!"

CHAPTER SIXTY-TWO

Jaden flopped onto the blanket, stretched out on his back, and dragged in a lungful of air. It was cool up here, high in the Shadow Mountains. The silence was another blessing, as was the sight of all his friends lounging in the wildflower-sprinkled meadow bordering a crystalline mountain lake.

Not the same lake they'd visited this time last year. One at a lower altitude and where the snow had already vanished under the warmth of the spring sunshine. *How is it spring again?*

"What's on your mind?"

Jaden glanced at Kayla, lying on the blanket next to him. He took her hand. "Can you believe it's been a year since Zareh turned our lives upside down?"

"No. I still wonder where the time went."

Jaden stared at the clear cerulean sky overhead. "Do you think we'll ever be able to look at the sky again without worrying about Gaptors appearing?"

"Nope. I'll always be looking for them. You?"

"Yeah, same."

They allowed the silence to wash over them again, hearing the occasional chatter as their friends set up their own blankets and rested after the strenuous climb.

"Why the sad face?" Kayla asked.

Jaden realized she'd been looking at him. "We could only do this hike because Bree isn't with us. She never joined us when we came here. Said she didn't fancy the climb. Perhaps we should've chosen a different spot."

Kayla's hand went to his chest, and she rolled onto her stomach, lifting herself onto her elbows so she was right in Jaden's face. He stared into those incredible green eyes, so close to his own now. He could get lost in them, in the love that shone there.

Aware she had his attention, Kayla said, "Perhaps it's better this place has no memories of Bree."

"Why do you say that?"

Kayla's eyes shifted sideways, and she nodded her head toward another couple. "Do you think it will help Stovan move on if he's constantly reminded of Bree today?"

Half-smiling, Jaden tucked a lock of Kayla's golden hair behind an ear. "No, you're right. He's had a rough time. I'm happy he's found someone who can help him heal."

"Not just someone," Kayla said, waggling her eyebrows.

Jaden chuckled. "Yeah, how could I think your best friend from your last complex was just anyone?"

Kayla's laughter splashed over him. "It still makes me laugh every time I think about Grailynn and her family moving here. Who would've thought we would only have had to spend the summer apart?"

"She would've been a useful ally had she been here."

"True, but I am glad she didn't have to be a part of it."

"You don't think she would've coped?"

Kayla smacked his chest. "No, silly! I wouldn't have made friends with you or Iri or Atu or any of the others if Grailynn had been here."

Jaden grinned. "She's just that all-consuming?"

"Ah, I don't know. Perhaps you should ask Stovan."

Chuckling, Jaden pulled her down so he could kiss her. He would never get enough of the taste of her. Of her sweet fragrance. Of the heady sensation she still invoked in him.

"Now, now, enough of that."

Atu's voice cut in, and Jaden could've punched him. Releasing Kayla so she could sink back onto her elbows, Jaden said, "I suppose you and Iri weren't similarly engaged a few minutes ago?"

Atu's face flooded with color. "That's not the point."

"Oh, it so totally is." Jaden laughed. "I saw you kissing her in the shadows under the trees near the lake."

Kayla began laughing too. "Are you denying it?"

"No, but that should be something private."

This only made Jaden and Kayla laugh more.

"What's going on?" Iri looked between them as she ambled over.

"Just teasing your boyfriend about kissing you," Jaden answered.

Iri smiled and linked her fingers with Atu's. "Yeah, he's quite the shy one. I'm trying to break him out of his shell. But old habits . . ." She broke off giggling when Atu's dark eyes flashed. She leaned over and kissed him chastely. His instant appeasement had Jaden and Kayla laughing again and Atu's ears turning pink.

"Alright, alright, you four can't have all the fun. How about joining us for a gridpost game before lunch? I'm thinking all this chatter means everyone's had enough of a breather." Markov was smiling at them, his face hopeful.

"Only as long as I get to be on your team," Kayla said.

"Done!"

"Traitor! What about my team?" Jaden complained.

Kayla stood in one lithe movement and held her hand out to him. "I'll be on your team any day on the arrowball court. But for gridpost, it's Markov's team all the way, baby."

Jaden laughed. "If you say so. But don't cry when our team clobbers yours."

"We'll see about that." Her green eyes were alight with mischief.

"And what do you have up your sleeve?" Jaden murmured, leaning forward and kissing her gently before stepping back again.

"You'll just have to wait and see," she murmured back, too softly for the others to hear.

"Are we picking teams or standing around?" Atu asked, fidgeting next to Iri.

Jaden grinned at his discomfort. "Want to be on my team?"

"Yes!" The vehement response sounded like it was Atu's way out of hell. It had them all rolling again.

They picked teams, drew lines, and the game began. Jaden forgot about Kayla's threat because she waited until the end to deploy her mischief. He was running the ball in for the winning point when Kayla blocked his path and raised her arm. Jaden blinked, not sure what she was doing.

One moment, he was running. The next, he was in the air, his legs still pumping but taking him nowhere. He glanced down. "Sven! Put me down! This isn't how the game is played."

Sven's laughter boomed across the lake. "Ah, but this is the way the game ends now."

Before Jaden could object, Sven dumped him in the lake. Jaden almost choked, inhaling sharply at the water's icy touch. Sputtering, he rose to the surface still clutching the ball. Sven stood there, meaty hand on his hips, grinning down at him. Along the bank, the others had lined up, their faces sweaty from the game and laughing their heads off. Jaden couldn't let that laughter stand.

Racing out of the lake, he swept Kayla into his arms and sprinted back into the water, dropping her like a stone. She came up gasping and laughing, pulling him back down with her. A free-for-all followed, Sven the only person not fully immersed. That was until all the guys ganged up on him and dumped him in.

Minutes later, they were on the bank again, teeth chattering. They hastily built a fire to warm themselves. The girls hived off to one part of the nearby forest and the boys to the other, exchanging wet clothes for dry behind temporary screens made from blankets. Then they gathered around the fire, spreading out their blankets and the food they had brought in their packs.

Chatter filled the air as they shared their food. Jaden snuggled closer to Kayla to warm her when he noticed she was still shivering. She smiled her thanks and offered him a plate of food.

Jaden took it, noting Sven had chosen a spot next to them. "It's wonderful to have you here with us."

The bear of a man smiled. "Only possible because of what you did, no? Closing that gate and the threat it posed. My government could hardly ignore that you saved our planet."

Jaden shook his head. "Not me, us. All of us. Together. We wouldn't have succeeded without your tech."

"Nonetheless, I am grateful to you. Without you acknowledging me, without you leaking the information to the world about why I was in hiding, I would never have been a free man. They would have hunted me for the rest of my life. Now I am absolved, and I may visit with you any time. It is good then that I do that, no?"

Jaden laughed. "Absolutely. But what makes you think it was me who cleared your name?"

Sven's eyes glinted suspiciously. "If not you, then who? You are one of the few people who knows my story. And the only one of that group with the skills to leak the information without being caught."

"If you say so."

Sven boomed a laugh. "It remains our secret then. Now, could you pass me more of that chicken?"

Jaden handed it over, spotting Markov and Shianna off to the side of the fire. Their heads were bent and their lips were moving, but Jaden couldn't hear what they were saying.

"What are you two whispering about?"

His question quieted the rest of the group. Shianna looked guilty, but Markov shrugged. "We were talking about Tarise."

Jaden regretted asking. The levity went out of the group, and he could've cut the tension with a blunt plastic knife. But Jaden had worked through his issues with Tarise. Calmly, so the others didn't think it was a taboo subject for him, he asked, "How's she doing?"

Not the response anyone had been expecting. Shianna stared at him. Markov blinked a few times before getting it together and answering Jaden's question. "Much better. Her doctors say she's found an effective way to cope with her . . . issues."

A mental institution had been Tarise's home for most of the last year. The dismal brick. The gray walls. The cheerless visiting room. He felt sorry for her. Once her doctors had explained her fascination with him was a mental health issue, he had wanted to help in whatever way he could. But they had banned him from visiting her, claiming it only set her back, so Jaden had kept his distance. "I'm glad she's receiving the care she needs and is making progress. Will you keep us posted?"

Markov nodded, too surprised to verbalize a reply. Jaden pretended not to notice. He turned to Iri, finding a gentle, knowing smile on her face. He really wished she was as blind to his emotions and motivations as she was to Atu's. "So you and Atu are joining us here in the compound soon?"

"We are. Atu's mom has a cousin who lives here. She has two spare rooms with her kids grown and out of the house. Just think, I'll be able to plague all of you a lot more now that we'll be closer. Hmm, all those secrets I can spill."

Jaden wasn't the only one laughing. They all knew the lengths Iri went to so she wouldn't shove her gift in their faces, so she would respect their privacy. In the time since their quest had ended, the rest of their close-knit group had learned the full extent of Iri's gifts.

When they had accepted her as readily as Kayla, Jaden, and Atu, Iri had told them about having no parents. Then it had almost been a war to see who Iri stayed with after that, all the parents insisting she couldn't live out in the forest on her own.

The easy, quiet lifestyle Atu and his parents offered had won out, but Jaden and Kayla still secretly agreed she had chosen them and not Kayla's family so she could be close to Atu.

Just as well though, because Iri might've felt isolated with Grailynn's return. Jaden glanced Grailynn's way and found her resting her back against Stovan's chest.

So much had changed, and so much was the same.

"You've got your thinking cap on again," Kayla whispered.

Jaden smiled. "Yeah. I was thinking same annual hike. Different place. Different group configuration. But the same love and friendship I've always known."

"You think it will always be this way?"

"I believe it's something we should treasure while we have it. If the last year has taught me anything, it's that there's truth in something I once heard."

"Which was?"

"'The dogs of doom guard the doors of destiny.' I don't know who said it, but there's a very real truth there. When Zareh sent us on that mission, if we'd let our fear get to us, we would never have succeeded. If we'd believed all the negative things people said about our chances of success, we would never have fulfilled our destiny and saved our world."

Kayla nodded. "Profound words about the past. What about the future?"

"Nope, no words of wisdom. As long as you're by my side, I can do anything." Kayla's glorious smile lit his world, reminding him of something he'd thought of on the hike up. "Let's promise each other we'll always try something once. That we won't be afraid of failure. Fear of failure is failure in itself. Let's live and love and hope like there's no tomorrow."

"I can get behind that." Kayla leaned into him then, drawing him into a kiss that made Jaden forget anyone else existed.

Loud, obnoxious, pointed throat-clearing from where Atu sat had Jaden smiling into the kiss. Reluctantly, he drew back, leaving Kayla with a whispered promise. "You'll get my undivided attention later."

Kayla's throaty chuckle had his toes curling. She whispered back, "I look forward to it."

Jaden dragged his eyes away from her mesmerizing gaze. He glared at Atu. "Okay, I got the message. Will s'mores please you?"

Kayla's squeal of delight made Jaden grin. "Did you think I'd forgotten your new favorite camping snack?"

"Have I told you I love you?"

"Just this morning, but you can tell me again."

"I love you."

"I love you too." Sending Atu a wicked smile, Jaden planted a short, sweet kiss on Kayla's cheek. She batted her eyelids at him.

Atu simply rolled his eyes. "We get it already. Where are the marshmallows?"

Jaden found the bag in his pack and tossed them over before retrieving the rest of the s'mores makings. As Jaden put his own marshmallow on a stick, he noticed individual conversations had started up again. The fire cackled and danced, eagerly licking at the sugar they offered it. Leaning back, stick in hand, Jaden tucked Kayla against his shoulder and surveyed their group.

His heart overflowing, Jaden absorbed the sights and scents around him. His friends chattering around the fire. Wildflowers weaving their sweet fragrance into the smoke. Birdsong filling the air. It was spring and new life abounded everywhere.

This spring certainly heralded new beginnings. For all of them. College beckoned. New romances were blooming. Old restrictions had been lifted. And though it all, they had been, and would remain, together. Working as a team, helping one another and providing support as they reached for their dreams. Life was what you made of it. And for him, it was sweet indeed.

THE END

Looking for more of Bronwyn's writing? Pick up *Forecast of Shadows* for something completely new!

ALSO BY BRONWYN LEROUX

Forecaster has the ability to see the future. Question is, can it keep her safe from the monster who haunts her dreams? Pick up *Forecast of Shadows* for a short, gritty afternoon read.

Need a change of pace? Curious about how this all this began? Pick up *Breach*, the *Destiny* companion novella, FOR FREE!

Other books by Bronwyn Leroux:

Breach (A *Destiny* companion novella)

Dawn of Dreams (*Destiny*, Book 1)

Dogs of Doom (*Destiny*, Book 2)

Doors of Destiny (*Destiny*, Book 3)

Duel of Death (*Destiny*, Book 4 - this book)

Forecast of Shadows

IF YOU ENJOYED THIS BOOK . . .

I would love it if you would please share it!

Reviews are the fairy dust that keep my wheels turning, thinking up fresh and exciting books for you - and they help other readers just like you discover new books to enjoy.

You can leave a review at https://bronwynleroux.com/DoorsReview

GET THE FIRST BOOK IN THIS SERIES FOR FREE

I love interacting with my readers and getting to know them as people. I also understand my readers hate spam as much as I do. For this reason, I only send the occasional newsletter with details on new releases, special offers and other bits of news you may find noteworthy. If you are interested in writing your own book, you can opt in for the additional bonus of weekly writing tips.

Enjoy these wonderful benefits, including your above-mentioned welcome gift, by signing up at https:// bronwynleroux.com/FreeBreach

For my husband who has been my most vocal supporter

ABOUT THE AUTHOR

Born near the famed gold mines of South Africa (where dwarves are sure to prowl), it was the perfect place for Bronwyn to begin her adventures. They took her to another province, her Prince Charming and finally, half a world away to the dark palace of San Francisco. While the majestic Golden Gate Bridge and its Bay views were spectacular, the magical pull of the Colorado Rockies was irresistible. Bronwyn's family set off to explore yet again. Finding a sanctuary at last, this is Bronwyn's perfect place to create alternative universes. Here, her mind can roam and explore and she can conjure up fantastical books for young adults.

f facebook.com/AuthorBronwynLeroux
y twitter.com/bronwyn_leroux
O instagram.com/bronwyn.leroux